THE
OF GLORIETA

A Fr. Jake Mystery

Albert Noyer

Plain View Press
P.O. 42255
Austin, TX 78704

plainviewpress.net
pk@plainviewpress.net
512-441-2452

Copyright © 2011 Albert Noyer. All rights reserved under International and Pan-American Copyright Conventions. No part of this book may be reproduced or distributed in any form or by any means, or stored in a data base or retrieval system, without written permission from the author. All rights, including electronic, are reserved by the author and publisher.

ISBN: 978-1-935514-03-9
Library of Congress Control Number: 2011925847

This is a work of fiction. Names, characters, places, and incidents either are the product of the author's imagination or are used fictitiously. Any resemblance to events, locales, or actual persons — living or dead — is entirely coincidental.

Cover art: Painting by Albert Noyer
            Fictional village of Providencia and the Church of San Isidro
Cover design by Pam Knight

*With sincere gratitude to the published writing group
Jennifer, Carolyn, Roy and
Mary Lynn, who helped start it all*

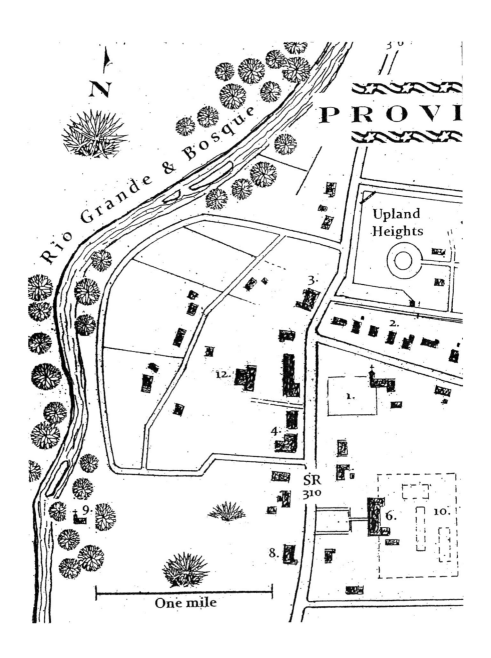

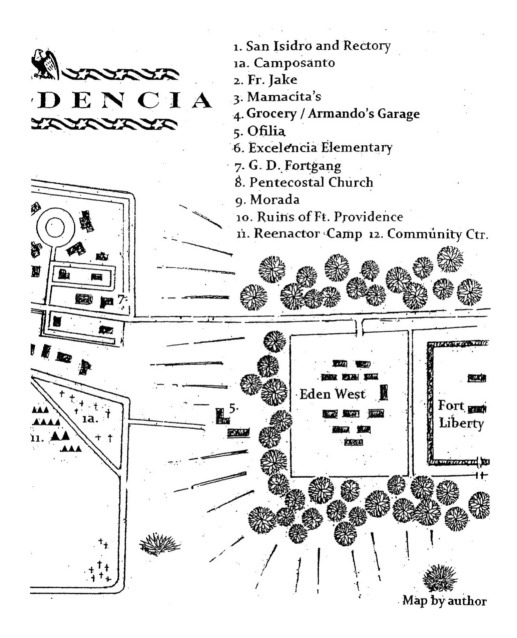

1. San Isidro and Rectory
1a. Camposanto
2. Fr. Jake
3. Mamacita's
4. Grocery / Armando's Garage
5. Ofilia
6. Excelencia Elementary
7. G. D. Fortgang
8. Pentecostal Church
9. Morada
10. Ruins of Ft. Providence
11. Reenactor Camp 12. Community Ctr.

Map by author

The Ghosts of Glorieta

PROLOGUE new mexico/may 15

On the morning of the San Isidro fiesta, May sunlight glinted off colorful miter crowns and fringed masks that concealed the faces of twelve *Matachine* dancers. Multi-hued ribbons and silk capes, printed or embroidered with the image of the *Virgen de Guadalupe*, swirled at their backs. Dressed in dark suits, the men practiced the graceful processional steps they would perform to enter the church. They waved three-pronged wands across their bodies with one hand, and rattled gourds in the other to keep time with the melody of violin and guitar music.

Church members and a few curious visitors stood on the dancers' flanks, watching the *Matachines*. A Socorro County deputy sheriff had parked his patrol car at a far end of the plaza, while he directed fiesta traffic onto the church grounds. Spicy aromas wafted from booths lined up along one side of the open space. Parish women had prepared chile-laced fiesta foods—*enchiladas*, *burritos*, *tamales*, pork stew, and fruit *empañadas*—to sell after the church service. *Curandera* Ofilia Herrera stood at one booth, hawking packets of her medicinal herbs and bottles of curative oils before Mass.

Fr. Jake, dressed in an alb that was too short and a white chasuble that Deacon Maldonado had borrowed from another church, waited to concelebrate the fiesta Mass with the pastor, Fr. Mora. He watched the exotic masked dancers with interest.

Armando Herrera noticed and walked over to the priest. "You ever seen *Los Matachines*, Father?"

7

"No, tell me something more about the fiesta custom. There's nothing like them in Michigan."

Armando brushed a cotton-like tuft of white from his sleeve, then glanced up at a sky as blue as the *Virgen's* mantle. The soft flocks swirled down in the light breeze and formed mini-drifts at the corners of the church. "Almost looks like *Natividad*, don't it Father? This early spring made the cottonwoods in the *bosque* lose cotton a coupla weeks early …" He looked back at the dancers. "Well, Father, the *Matachines* are at all our fiestas, but nobody really knows why that is. Those wands they carry represent *Santo Trinidad*, the Holy Trinity. That little girl dressed in white is *La Malinche*. *El Monarcha* will lead her into the church for the fiesta Mass. People pin dollar bills on her clothes."

"She's beautiful in her First Communion dress," Fr. Jake remarked.

"Yeah, Father. After Mass, the *bulto*, that wood statue you seen of San Isidro, our patron saint, is carried in procession to the home of a sick person. Last year it was Rosita, but she died. I don't know to who it is this year that Father Mora will give a blessing. After the fiesta lunch, we'll see a fake battle on the plaza between good and bad. *El Toro* is the evil guy—."

"Where is Father Mora?" Deacon Maldonado interrupted, tapping his watch with a stubby finger. "The procession shoulda started twen'y minutes ago. You seen him, Father Hakub?"

"No, we didn't vest together." Fr. Jake noted that the deacon's green stole still bore wine stains; Maldonado had promised to dry-clean the sash for the fiesta.

"He's not at the rectory," he complained. "I looked there."

"Maybe still in the *sagrario?*" Armando suggested. "He spends a lotta time there with Jesus."

"It's worth checking," Fr. Jake said. "Let's go around and find out."

The *sagrario* was a small chapel that Fr. Mora had built onto the southeast end of his church to display the Blessed Sacrament host in a monstrance. Such a separate building was part of many Mexican churches.

Cynthia Plow noticed the three men threading their way around bystanders. The schoolteacher and Armando had been the only church members to befriend Fr. Jake since he arrived from Michigan in mid-April. Armando had warned him that acceptance by the closely-knit parishioners would be difficult. They resented an Anglo *Norteño* with the unpronounceable name of "Jakub-owski." Most had shortened it to Hakub, with a Spanish-sounding J. Rumors still circulated that he had come to replace their saintly, if reclusive, pastor, Fr. Jesús Mora, who suffered a long, mysterious illness.

"Father, aren't we ready to start?" Cynthia called to the priest.

"We can't find Father Mora," Armando answered for him. "We're gonna look in the *sagrario*."

Cynthia joined the men in walking around to the right side of the adobe church. They found the chapel door closed.

Fr. Jake rapped on the wooden panel. "Father Mora, are you inside? Father Mora?"

Maldonado placed an ear against the door. "Padre, you all right? It's time for you to start th' fiesta."

After no one answered, Armando said, "Maybe he fell asleep prayin' in there."

"Only one way to find out…" Fr. Jake pushed on a warped door that was unlocked, but sticking at the bottom. As the panel scraped open, a rush of warm, smoke-filled air escaped. He coughed and put a hand up to cover his nose and mouth. "Father must have fifty votive candles burning on the rack—"

The inside of the chapel was thick with choking blue smoke. All candles were alight, flickering wildly in the rush of air from outside. The haze smelled of burning plant leaves, not the familiar paraffin scent from votives. The odor was not as distinctive as marijuana, yet faintly sweet in an unidentifiable way.

Fr. Mora lay sprawled on the tile floor, next to an unpadded wooden kneeler.

In the smoky interior, the candles cast a dancing light that seemed to animate the priest's frail body.

"Good God!" Fr. Jake gasped. "Deacon, help me pull Father outside. Leave the door open to clear out that smoke."

Coughing from the fumes despite holding a hand over their mouths, the two men dragged the priest's body through the door by the arms, to the backside of the chapel and out of sight of those attending the fiesta. Fr. Mora's body was stiff, as if paralyzed, yet not enough time had elapsed for rigor to set in.

White cottonwood tufts settled on his chasuble as Fr. Jake knelt to check for a throat pulse. He looked up and shook his head in a grim gesture. "He… he's dead. Father apparently was asphyxiated by all that smoke."

Albert Noyer

"What, from candles?" Maldonado protested. "That ain't possible."

Cynthia held a headscarf over her nose and went into the small room. Moments later, she came out with one hand in a closed fist. "The smoke cleared a bit," she said, opening her fingers. "I found a few of these red seeds next to the candles. Others are imbedded in melted wax."

"They look like little red jelly beans," Armando said. "What are they?"

"Zamia seeds. I have a biology unit where I warn my students about poisonous plants. Despite being toxic in all its parts, *zamia furfuracaea* is a popular garden and houseplant. The seeds taste sweet, so dogs will eat them. Most vomit up the residue, yet many pets die."

Fr. Jake stood up for a closer look at the deadly seeds. "You're saying, Cynthia, that someone poisoned Father Mora?"

She shrugged an uncertain opinion. "Burned, and their smoke inhaled, zamia seeds probably can be as toxic as if actually eaten."

Deacon Maldonado glanced into the chapel's interior. "*Madre de Dios!*" he exclaimed. "The *Sacramento* is gone missing from the monstrance!"

"What?" Fr. Jake saw the rayed, golden reliquary atop a small altar. At the center of the rays, a large, white host was missing from the compartment of an open glass door. "Why would someone want to steal the Blessed Sacrament and not take the gold monstrance? Makes no sense—"

Maldonado scowled and placed his squat body in front of the priest, to poke his chest with a fleshy finger. "You proba'ly was the last person to see Father Mora. If we got a murder here, Father Hakub, you got a lotta explainin' for the sheriff. I know y' never liked our priest an' didn't get along with him."

"True, we disagreed on some outdated liturgical practices, but that… that's ridiculous. Deacon, are you accusing me of killing Father Mora?"

Maldonado took his hand away, shuffled both feet, and glanced down at the sandy ground. "Aw, I only said y' got explain' to do."

Oh fine. I'm assigned from Michigan to New Mexico, where I didn't ask to come. I've been here less than a month and find myself practically accused of murdering a fellow priest!

1 michigan / april 1

The Reverend Casimir "Jake" Jakubowski scratched a blob of toothpaste off the glass of his bathroom mirror, wiped away opaque steam with a hand towel, and squinted at his moisture-streaked reflection. "Not *too* bad for someone seventy years old today," he told the lean, Slavic face staring back at him. "So, Father Jake, it's both Happy Birthday and April Fool's day! Be glad they didn't celebrate this date that way in Poland, when you were born." He gave his reflection a skeptical grin at an aging joke about aging, "'Seventy' *is* the new 'Fifty,' right, Father?"

The priest rubbed overnight beard stubble that matched the steel-gray of his hair. "Skip that hair dye in the TV ad that says youth trumps experience. Those forehead creases and furrows alongside your nose are all about 'Character!' Okay, the ears are a bit on the large side. Not quite Dumbo-sized, but...."

Fr. Jake touched at a rash that had abruptly appeared on his left arm a few months earlier. *Good, doesn't itch just now.* He pulled up a sink knob that closed a worn drain plug rimmed by rust, where enamel had long chipped away, ran his usual three fingers' depth of hot water into the bowl, then a splash onto shaving soap in a made-in-China mug. St. Mary's College was stenciled in red on one side. After swishing the splayed bristles of a twenty-year-old shaving brush over the soap, he lathered his cheeks, picked up the handle of his safety razor, and scowled at the twin whisker-clogged blades.

"I understand they make razors with five blades now,' he muttered and looked down for a fresh cartridge in the plastic holder. "Empty. Maybe go buy yourself a birthday present of a newer one?"

Fr. Jake winced as two dull blades scraped down a lathered cheek. The effect reminded him of the church custodian's plow clearing his driveway.

O

His Excellency, Archbishop Stanley Sredzinski, of the Detroit Diocese, had summoned the priest to his Chancery office for a 10:00 A.M. meeting on his 70th birthday—the mandated retirement age for diocesan clergy. In January, Fr. Jake had submitted a letter requesting to continue his ministry; given the serious shortage of priests, he was sure the archbishop would accept. He asked to retain his present assignment, St. Barnabas-on-the-Lake Parish at Lake Sirius in northern Oakland County, and felt confident the archbishop would confirm that assignment at the meeting.

St. Barnabas was, in a sense, a "vacation parish." For nine months of the year, the church served a few hundred permanent residents in the town of Sirius. In late spring, hordes of summer visitors arrived at the lakes area, along with varying numbers of seasonal Mexican farm workers. Each June-to-Labor Day, the cut-off jeans of women seemed to get tighter and shorter. Too many male beer-bellies sucked beltlines into white flaps of gut. Boys' sagging, "one-size-fits-none" cargo shorts, and girls' bare-midriffs or tight retro-Capri pants were beyond a priest's reprimands—they would go unheeded in today's permissive atmosphere.

Hunting season brought different Sunday worshippers. Two miles north of Lake Sirius, Oakland County merged with Lapeer County in a steppe-like flatland of endless dry, rustling cornfields. October's pheasant hunting season found city and suburban dwellers at the 7:30 A.M. Mass—men huddled in $300 camouflage parkas, hung-over and bleary-eyed from playing poker and guzzling Heineken or Jack Daniels late into the night at the Idle-a-Wile Motel. On those fall weekends, the distant, staccato pop-pop of shotguns reverberated all morning. After the season ended, there was blessed quiet once again.

The Ghosts of Glorieta

O

Fr. Jake dressed and went into his small kitchen for a breakfast of coffee and half a banana cut into raisin bran. It was Holy Thursday as well as his birthday and near the end of the Lenten season. He would have to leave the archbishop's office in time to return for the 7:00 P.M. Evening Mass of the Lord's Supper and Washing of Feet.

Originally built as a summer weekend and retirement cottage by a Ford Motor Company worker, the two-bedroom-one bath, white clapboard rectory was five years older than the priest. It faced Lake View Lane, with twin windows in back framing pines and elms now grown dense enough to block any view of the water. St. Barnabas-on-the- Lake Roman Catholic Church, also a white clapboard building, was not directly on the lake, but stood on the Lane, across from the rectory. The narrow, asphalted road meandered around the shores and joined Lapeer Road, US 24, at two entrances.

In the decade that Fr. Jake had lived in the rectory, the rooms never lost their mildew-and-kerosene-lamp smell. On the wall of the cramped living room, a dusty, stuffed walleye pike hung above a sofa bed covered in a large flower pattern. He never replaced it. A chrome kitchen table with four chairs was set against a wall near the back door. Green-painted, steel-frame windows swung open with a crank, but creeping rust made that more difficult—and risky—each year. With an income still assured, perhaps the windows he opened the most could be replaced, a couple per year.

Fr. Jake's bedroom, paneled in faux cherry-wood fiberboard, was large enough for his single bed, a computer desk, two chairs, and a 19" TV that picked up Pontiac or Flint PBS channels 56 and 28. An upper "second bedroom" held a single twin-mattress-size bed, a scarred pine colonial-style desk, and a garage-sale dresser, all crammed into the narrow dormer above the front entrance. His few overnight guests invariably bruised their foreheads on the 60°-sloped ceiling.

O

At their first summer weekend Mass, retirees who opened their cottages, invariably joked, "How's 'St. Barney on the Take' Father? Aw, jus' kiddin'. How ya been?" or "You 'sirius,' about that, Father?" Each year the same vacationer asked the same question about an old cartoon character: "Comin'

Albert Noyer

from Poland like ya did, Father, ya wouldn't remember Barney Google wouldja?"

A young Casimir Jakubowski had never found such familiarity toward clergymen in Poland. Yet he observed that even in America a kind of "Cassock Curtain" separated clergy from laity. Most parishioners ventured a shy "Mornin', Father," yet kept a personal distance, which almost suggested that clergymen might be leprous. Mexican workers never jested with a *padre*: most treated priests as if they possessed supernatural powers of intercession with Jesus Christ, the Virgin Mary, Saints, and God in that order. With their hair covered in lace shawls, the women lighted candles to Barnabas without knowing about him. After all, he *was a santo*, a Catholic saint.

Certainly, Barnabas was neither the most popular nor well known saint in the Church's hagiography. *The Catholic Encyclopedia* listed his feast day as June 11th. Fr. Jake always summarized the apostle's life for that months' vacation arrivals: a Levite; born on the island of Cyprus; settled in Jerusalem; a later companion of St. Paul on his travels among the Gentiles. "Them Gentiles, they wasn't Jewish. Right, Father?" According to *Acts* 13: 4-12, the two proselytizers converted a pagan governor of Cyprus to Christianity.

○

Fr. Jake had selected tan slacks and a blue dress shirt for his interview with the Archbishop. It was overcast and cool outside, threatening enough rain to warrant wearing his navy-blue nylon windbreaker. He was reluctant to put on a clerical collar while in Detroit. The Chancery Building, where the archbishop maintained an office, was located downtown on Washington Boulevard, next to St. Aloysius Church. Whether parking on the street or finding space in a parking garage, the white symbol of priesthood at his throat elicited curious stares at best; at worse, homeless vagrants materialized and stumbled alongside him, clutching his sleeve until they received a two-dollar hand-out. "The poor you have always with you," Christ had warned, yet President Reagan's order limiting admission to mental facilities had far exceeded the Savior's misunderstood "prediction." Catholic Charities and other relief organizations could only do so much, and the continuing recession exacerbated the homeless problem and thus, crime.

He brushed a few mouse droppings from the sink counter into a wastebasket, and poured a carafe of tap water into his 4-cup coffee maker; the small capacity kept him from ingesting too much caffeine. Quintana

The Ghosts of Glorieta

Ruiz, his once-a-week housekeeper came today, so he doubled his usual two-cup measure of coffee to offer her some.

After pouring raisin bran into a chipped bowl, Fr. Jake sniffed milk remaining in an over-dated carton, then poured the dregs on his cereal. The first spoonful tasted this side of sour, yet a sip of black coffee after each bite would take care of that. While eating breakfast, he used a wooden napkin holder to prop open a used 2005 reprint of James J. O'Donnell's biography of St. Augustine. The *New Republic*'s blurb on the back cover had piqued his interest: "O'Donnell's vibrant new study brings this imperfect saint to life, both in his wrenching smallness and in his exhilarating grandeur." The author's other book on the fall of the Roman Empire made a convincing case for blaming the emperor Justinian, so the author's take on the revered saint should be interesting.

Fr. Jake had finished eating and begun reading in Chapter VII, when a timid rap sounded on the wooden front door.

He glanced at his watch. "That will be *señora* Ruiz," he muttered to the empty bowl and stood up. "*Entrade, por favor, señora.*"

"*Gracias Padre,*" came her musical response.

A short stout woman in early middle age entered, carrying a bucket heavy with cleaning supplies. Except for her darker Indio-Mexican features, she was a physical prototype for many of the same-age Polish women Fr. Jake had known. Rosa, her 18-year-old daughter, followed with a sullen expression, chewing gum and holding a broom and mop. In contrast to her mother's cotton frock and apron, the teenager wore fashionably torn jeans and a turquoise Junior Tee. The screen-printed design in pink and chartreuse on the front brazenly proclaimed, "HOT MESS." Rosa was bra-less—and visibly pregnant.

The girl must have gotten married in Mexico since last year, Fr. Jake noted.

Quintana Ruiz greeted the priest in Spanish. "*Buenos dias, Padre* Hakay. *¿Como esta usted?*"

"*Muy bien, señora Ruiz.* You should speak in English," he gently admonished and smiled at Rosa. "*Usted tambien, señora…señora….*"

Mrs. Ruiz glowered at her daughter. "*Rosa no tiene un esposo.*"

No husband. That may help explain why she was not at Mass last Sunday. I'll talk to her about contacting the Vicariate's Catholic Social Services. "Yes, well, as I said, I'm the one who must practice Spanish. Please speak in English, both of you."

Albert Noyer

"*Si*. I…I mean 'yes,' Fadder Hakay."

He smiled at Ruiz's pronunciation of 'Jake.' "*Señora*, I've told you that my name is not pronounced as softly as it would be in Spanish. Say, 'Father Dj-ache'. J-ake."

Rosa came out of her sulk to demand, "Where you goin', Father Jake? *Porque* you wearin' fancy clothes today? No priest collar?"

Mrs. Ruiz spoke rapid Spanish to her daughter in a tone that reprimanded the girl for being too familiar with a priest. Rosa shrugged, popped her gum, and pretended to examine the broom handle for splinters.

Fr. Jake tried to defuse a mother-daughter argument that was all too common. "Rosa, at ten o'clock, I'm meeting with the archbishop in Detroit…" He made a key-turning motion with his hand to Mrs. Ruiz. "*Señora*, this is the first time you've come this year. Remember, I gave you a rectory key on Sunday, so don't forget to lock up when you finish." He gestured toward the coffee maker on the sink. "I brewed extra coffee this morning. *Por favor*, serve yourselves."

Quintina Ruiz blushed to a darker mahogany tint. "*Ah, gracias, no, Padre.* We… we come to work, not sit, drink *café*."

"And I'm grateful that you came." He went to the sink, rinsed out his cereal bowl, and looked back. "Seriously, ladies, take a midmorning coffee break."

"Break?" Quintina Ruiz frowned and glanced around. "*Madre de Dios*, What has break?"

"Nothing. I meant take a…a kind of mini-siesta. Stop work for a cup of coffee. Oh, and Mrs. Ruiz, I left your pay envelope next to the computer in my room."

"*Si, gracias, Padre.*"

Fr. Jake checked his watch again. *7: 45. Still time to try out a little more Spanish before I leave.* "How is your husband? *¿Como esta su esposo?*" he asked Mrs. Ruiz, who had stooped to pull rags and a spray bottle of all-purpose cleaner from the bucket.

She looked up. "*Gracias* for your help of him."

"Your help to him," he corrected.

"*Si, Padre*, 'Your help to him'."

"You will learn, *señora*. I also was a stranger in a strange land."

"What that mean, *Padre*?"

"*Señora*, you know I was born in Poland and still have a bit of trouble pronouncing the English "th" sound correctly."

The Ghosts of Glorieta

"*Si. Raul dice—*"

"English, please. Raul says?"

"Raul is good. Now see if *manzano* tree be okay after winter."

"Yes, heavy snow may have damaged the apple trees. *Señora*, Raul said?"

"*Gracias* for you to find house in village for us."

"Well, the Pontiac Vicariate helped with that. After all, your husband is the farm workers' supervisor. He's contracted with whom this year?"

"Again, *Señor* Maxwell. Only Raul, two other men, here now."

"*Bueno.*"

"*Si.*" She reached over to shake her daughter's broom handle. "Now, Rosa, we work."

Fr. Jake checked his watch again. *Going on 8:30. I have about a half hour to read the day's office in my breviary.* He went to the bedroom for his daily missal, car key ring, and wallet, then called back from the front door, "*Señora*, I'm going to the church, and then heading for Detroit."

"*Si, Padre*," she replied, prodding Rosa as they came from the kitchen. "*Vaya con Dios.*"

"*Gracias.*" Fr. Jake glanced at the overcast sky as he walked along the gravel driveway to cross Lake View Lane. When an approaching car's horn beeped, he waited to wave at Aloysius "Al" Franzek, a parishioner heading to work in his Pontiac law office, then crossed the street toward the church's entrance. A sign "St. Barnabas Roman Catholic Church" listed the Mass schedule. Spray paint had not marred it, as happened to vacant cottages and even church property of all denominations in the lake area. The previous spring, For Sale signs sprouted as thick as crocus blossoms on the lawns of many cottages. The recession had cut into retiree pensions; their children had done well—businesspersons, attorneys, doctors—but now grandchildren attended summer soccer or science camps. Kids vacationed with their parents at Cabo San Lucas or on dazzling white Caribbean beaches, not at weedy suburban lakes.

Inside, the church nave smelled of fresh paint that tempered an encroaching mold odor that predominated in damp weather. Al Franzek said he would round up a volunteer crew to paint the inside walls before the summer visitors arrived and had kept his word.

Pews of Michigan white pine, stained a colonial tan, seated a hundred worshipers. The barn-wood mosaic wall behind a freestanding altar of Michigan limestone was a contribution by parishioners. Each one brought a piece of weathered wood to form a back wall that was tangible participation by church members. Centered on this grayish mosaic and backed by cloth hangings, whose changing colors—green, white, purple, red—symbolized the seasons and feasts of the liturgical year, hung a wooden image of the crucified Christ. Raul Ruiz had brought the handcrafted figure from Mexico. Terracotta Stations of the Cross were a student project from a nearby art academy. The only commercial plaster statuary remaining was of St. Joseph holding the baby Jesus, and Our Lady of Grace. Both were sentimental leftovers bought in 1935 by the founding pastor. The overall effect was simple and pleasing, a kind of *feng* arrangement without the *shui*. Fr. Jake was glad to have taken an art history class taught by a part-time lay instructor at the college.

He bowed his head to the bronze tabernacle set on one side of the altar, then knelt in the foremost pew to open his breviary at a purple ribbon marker.

Holy Thursday is when I renew a commitment to priestly service. Fr. Jake re-read what he had repeated for forty-three years about accepting the responsibilities of priesthood, then went on to the Introductory Rites of the Mass and the liturgy of the Word. He read the Mass service that would be celebrated that evening, then glanced at his watch. 8:58. *A trip into Detroit takes about an hour. The morning rush will be over on I-75. Barring slow-ups from accidents, I'll be early for meeting with the archbishop.*

The priest stood up, bowed to the tabernacle, and relocked the front door. Outside, he pulled the collar of his windbreaker tight against a freshening breeze that smelled strongly of rain. He felt confident as he walked to a carport next to the rectory, which sheltered his 1997 Ford Aspire. Archbishop Stanley Sredzinksi, a classmate, would be pleased to renew his tenure at St. Barnabas. He could continue his ministry to the Mexican workers and the spiritual journey of residents and summer vacationers. July would mark the 75th anniversary of St. Barnabas on the Lake. A committee of parishioners had agreed to his proposal for a Hispanic, fiesta-type weekend of activities that might make migrant workers feel more comfortable. Invited pastors of non-Catholic denominations in Ortonville, Oxford, and Lake Orion would add a timely ecumenical dimension to the occasion. Most, if not all, of the ministers would be married. One was a woman rabbi. His congregation would see, in the flesh, results of advocacy for optional celibacy for priests and an increased role for women in the Church.

It's an overused cliché, Fr. Jake thought, *but "Life is good."* Yet, as he reached down to unlock his car door, a sudden spasm of apprehension wracked the

The Ghosts of Glorieta

pit of his stomach. The sick feeling was rare, yet persuasive, and always surfaced when he faced serious difficulties or a crisis. *Perhaps I've been too optimistic. Given the shortage of priests, the archbishop might tell me that he must close little St. Barnabas. And I'm admittedly a nuisance for mouthing my liberal stances on Church reform. Despite being classmates, he just might send me to some God-knows-where Michigan Upper Peninsula parish!*

2 detroit / april 1

The hollow ache in Fr. Jake's stomach gradually lessened as he turned the Aspire onto U.S. 24 and drove through a declining Lake Sirius business district that stretched on either side of the highway. Bracketed by a motel and food market at either end, handsome, tree shaded, wood or brick homes, mostly built in the 1930's to 1950's, backed up a half dozen undistinguished commercial buildings.

The northernmost bracket, Idle-a-Wile Motel, proudly proclaimed itself American-Owned!!! Fr. Jake knew the proprietor, Amir Fakhouri. Whenever poor winter weather made driving unsafe, the Fakhouris attended the St. Barnabas eleven o'clock Mass. They sat in the back pew. Normally, the family drove thirty miles to attend a Chaldean Catholic Church in West Bloomfield. Their Sunday day of rest turned into a jovial outing among fellow Chaldeans. They were Roman Catholics, but the war in Iraq and Afghanistan had heightened suspicion of anyone who looked Middle Eastern. The Fakhouri family did not mingle much with Lake Sirius residents.

Despite unsuccessful local opposition, the single gas station's Amigo! Convenience Store sold package liquor, a department heavily patronized on weekends by residents, vacationers, and hesitant Mexican men from the camp, who spoke enough English to buy liquor.

A few locals lined up for coffee at a Joe's Java Joint take-out window. An Oakland Country sheriff's patrol SUV idled in the parking lot. Aside from light lunches served at Joe's, Mum's Diner—est. 1948—was the

Albert Noyer

only restaurant in Sirius. Now, the twin children of the eighty-one-year-old British war bride ran it. Even though her WW II Air Force husband had drowned in Lake Orion, Mum had remained in the area to raise her children.

Christian Boggs, a mechanic who owned Christian's Auto Fix Up and Bait Emporium, tuned in each day—*all day*—to Victory 600 AM, Flint's Christian Radio station. His alcoholic wife, Jodie, bore a skinny resemblance to a young Jodie Foster. She kept the books and sold bait in summer. In the off-season, Jodie made daily rounds of bars in Pontiac. Despite their addiction to Christian broadcasts, neither former Kentuckian attended any church, evangelical or otherwise, that Fr. Jake knew about.

The Sirius SuperMarkette was the southern bracket, desperately trying to keep afloat by offering specials that competed with national food chains in Lake Orion and Pontiac. Next-door was the boarded-up Oakland Prime Realty, a victim of declining sales in the area. The plywood still hosted peeling OBAMA-BIDEN and McCAIN-PALIN campaign posters. Alongside, a former antique shop owner, Bill Deutsch, now advertised estate sales, and his wife, Renate, sold inexpensive thrift store items culled from the doomed collections.

A mile down the highway, at the entrance to Oxford Township Stony Lake Park, Fr. Jake checked his speed.

45. *Last year I tried an evening outdoor youth Mass and campfire potluck in there. As soon as it was dark, kids slipped away to skinny dip on the far side of the lake or make-out in the woods. How can the Church catch the interest of young people? It's a problem that concerns the Vicariate. Youth Ministries meet once a month to help parishes collaborate on dances, events, trips and service projects, yet only eight or nine parishes are active participants.*

He slowed to 35 m.p.h. on approaching the Village of Oxford. Its two-block-long business center was a pleasing mix of well-maintained shops, restaurants, and taverns located in restored historical buildings. The North Oakland Historical Museum explained the region's history and displayed artifacts dating from as early as 1834. Stately homes graced the one-square mile of what the Chamber of Commerce boasted was "a small town look." Oxford had the nearest post office and high school for Lake Sirius residents.

A mile on, Fr. Jake further slowed his speed to pass through the Village of Lake Orion, a slightly larger, less tidy replica of Oxford. Michigan towns reminded Fr. Jake of Kraków, his birthplace in Poland, and his arrival in America. In 1949, the recently ordained Karl Joseph Wojtyla, was assigned

The Ghosts of Glorieta

to a church in Kraków. The future Pope John Paul II eventually began a study group in the historic city, the *Rodzinka* or "Little family." Members met for prayer and philosophical discussions. In 1955, although only fifteen, Kasimierz Jakubowski became the youngest member. Impressed with the youth's maturity, after Wojtyla became auxiliary bishop of Kraków, the prelate sponsored him as a student at the Orchard Lake Schools in Michigan. Kasimierz breezed through college and seminary and was ordained.

Seven miles on, Fr. Jake reached the entrance ramp to I-75, the freeway that snaked in a backward S-curve, until it straightened out at its intersection with the east-west I-696. From there it ran due south, about forty-five minutes to Detroit.

When he sighted the hazy outline of downtown Detroit on the horizon, he thought of the city. A TIME special report, "The Tragedy of Detroit," had documented how a great city fell and how it could rise again. *I was newly ordained, assigned to St Hedwig's in Hamtramck when the 1967 race riots erupted. They reminded me of the 1956 Poznań Protests, Poznański Czerwiec. Between 57 and 68 people were killed there in a political, not racial protest. At Hedwig's we took in frightened residents, black or white.*

An 18-wheeler semi bearing muddy plates abruptly swung into the right lane without signaling. Fr. Jake reacted quickly enough to brake in time. *I better concentrate on traffic.*

As the Detroit skyline grew larger and the priest thought of his meeting with the archbishop, the hollow feeling in his stomach returned. *Perhaps I have been foolish in thinking I would stay at St. Barnabas. The archbishop may well have decided to close my church, and yet we're seminary classmates. Surely, that should count for something.*

The moment passed quickly; of immediate concern was navigating the intricate maze of Detroit streets involved in arriving at the Chancery Building on Washington Boulevard. Fr. Jake exited the Chrysler Freeway at Madison, took a left on John R, and left again onto Washington, a short four-block boulevard with a median.

A half block north of the Chancery building, the back-up lights of a parked Lincoln Continental flashed on. *What luck. Someone is leaving.* Fr. Jake pulled aft of the left rear bumper, while the driver maneuvered his luxury car into the street. The smaller Aspire would easily fit into the space. *Parking on the street in midmorning is probably safer than leaving cars in a dark parking garage.*

A gentle rain started to fall as Fr. Jake key-locked the car and walked around to check the parking meter. *Forty minutes are unused. Another two*

23

quarters ought to be enough. He checked the passenger door of his hatchback. A parishioner, the husband of a woman who owned the Aspire and suddenly died, had given him the car nine years ago. It had 23,000 miles on it then; now, at about 110,000 miles, it ran like new.

The Chancery was a narrow, Tuscan Revival, eight-story limestone building set next to the kindred design of St. Aloysius Church. He turned up the collar of his wind-breaker against the drizzle and ducked under store awnings for shelter until he reached the Chancery. The lobby directory listed the archbishop's office on the third floor.

The stress rash on his left arm again began to itch.

A middle-aged secretary in the reception area wore a wedding band. She smiled and greeted him in Polish. "*Dzień dobry, Ojciec Jakubowski.*"

"*Dzień dobry, Panny…?*"

"Mrs. Belinski, Father." She reverted to English in telling her name. "I'll announce you to Archbishop Sredzinski." She punched a button on the interoffice phone.

Fr. Jake was mildly surprised when the prelate himself opened the door. *A good sign that His Excellency hasn't forgotten me.*

"*Dzień dobry, Ojciec Kazimieriz,*" the archbishop beamed, grasping his hand. "*Sto lat. Wszystkiego najlepszego z okaji urodzin!* A most happy birthday to you."

"*Dziękuję, Ekscelenjo.* Your Excellency, thank you." He bent to kiss the prelate's ring, but Sredzinski pulled his hand back.

"*Nie*…not necessary, Father. After all, we were classmates. Come, please, into my office." The archbishop gave the receptionist a quick hand signal, closed the door, and motioned Fr. Jake to an upholstered armchair a few feet from his massive, dark-stained mahogany desk. An oriental rug lay in front, perhaps a subtle buffer against overeager visitors.

The room's decor was a warm gray. Oak bookshelves stained tan held a compendium of Catholic orthodoxy and surrounded a marble faux-fireplace—a common embellishment in offices that dated from the 1920's. A Tiffany lamp on the side table gave out a soft glow through its stained glass shade. The archbishop's modern desk light was harsher.

Rain sounded a soft drumbeat as it streaked in hesitant rivulets down a window that overlooked a wet and gloomy Washington Boulevard.

Archbishop Sredzinski's black polyester suit revealed a Roman collar at the neck. Under his suit jacket, the chain of a pectoral cross gleamed a

The Ghosts of Glorieta

soft gold as it hung suspended across his shirt, the cross itself tucked inside a left pocket over his heart.

The prelate seated himself behind his desk, where a back wall displayed his framed theological degrees and photographs with notables, including President Obama and Pope Benedict XVI. Honorary membership in the Committee to Save Detroit was a recent testimonial. Above them was the same official photograph of the pope that parishes displayed. The pontiff's dark-shadowed, slightly mismatched eyes looked off to his right. A thin horizontal smile seemed to say, "I did it! This Bavarian lad became Pope!"

Archbishop Sredzinski adjusted his glasses, looked up, and augmented his smile. "And Father, there will be no more 'Your Excellency' nonsense. *Nie*...no. After all, we are ...were...classmates."

Dobrze." Fr. Jake shrugged acceptance and laughed. "Very well, 'Shreds'."

The prelate's smile evaporated. "*Przepraszam*. Excuse me, Father?" The archbishop's question was cold as a marble paperweight on one side of his desktop.

Fr. Jake felt the itch in his arm increase intensity. "Ah, don't you recall? 'Shreds' was a college nickname from your surname, Sredzinski. I was "Jake" Jakubowski. The...the yearbook photos..." His voice trailed off as he clawed the itching in his arm through the windbreaker. *So much for informality and being classmates.*

The archbishop cleared his throat, a new stiffness in his manner. "So, how have you been, Father? I notice you scratching an arm."

"A rash came on about three months ago. Come to think of it, just after I received your invitation to come here."

"Some sort of allergy?"

"There is mold in the rectory and I think—"

"Father," Sredzinski interrupted as he opened a side desk drawer to pull out a manila file envelope. "Father Kasimierz," he continued without looking up, "I am delighted that you have not considered retirement."

"*Dziękuję*...thank you, Excellency. I'm quite happy at St. Barnabas."

"I am sure you are," he agreed absently, while thumbing through documents in the folder.

Fr. Jake scrutinized his college and seminary classmate, forty-some years after ordination. *'Shreds' has hardly changed since then. Same smooth, round*

25

face. Cropped, dark hair still, maybe touched up a bit now. Similar glasses, horn-rimmed then, stronger now. His nervous habit of continually adjusting them.

"Ah, here." The archbishop held up a sheet of paper "You conduct a ministry with migrant Mexicans through the Pontiac Vicariate CCRT."

"I do work with them."

As Sdrezinski glanced up, a flash of light reflected on his glasses from the table lamp. "Do you speak Spanish, Father?"

"*Mas o menos*, Excellency. 'More or less'." The itch flared up and it took all Fr. Jake's resolve to keep from rolling up his left sleeve to soothe the bare arm. "*Mas poquito*," he added, "but I'm learning more in a night class at Oxford High School that I attend once a week."

"Your parish youth ministry, Father?"

"Minimal, I'm afraid. Most St. Barnabas parishioners are elders. Kids who come in summer with parents are there to vacation, not attend Faith Formation classes."

The archbishop adjusted his glasses to peer at the priest. "Father, may one ever vacation from a deeper knowledge of Christ's Church?" He sifted through more pages and slipped one out. "You attended the Call to Action conference in Milwaukee last year."

"Is that a question?"

"*Nie*. No…no."

"Of course, you have the information right there." Fr. Jake perspired now. "Excellency, may…may I take off my jacket? It's quite warm in here."

"Please do, Father."

He folded the jacket on his lap, still damp from rain. Without quite knowing why he needed to justify his actions, he explained, "Call to Action and FutureChurch are organizations that try to continue the stalled reforms of the Second Vatican Council and re-instill liturgical practices of the early church—"

"You are not lecturing me, are you, Father?" the archbishop interrupted. His voice softened and returned to a sympathetic tone, "Father…Father Kasimierz. Among other, shall we say, 'controversial issues,' you send letters to our Catholic paper advocating optional celibacy for priests and a greater role for women in the ministry. One letter *demands*…your word… full communion for gay parishioners."

"*Tak*, and for our divorced laity, Your Excellency." Fr. Jake noticed that his former classmate had no longer objected to the use of his ecclesiastical

The Ghosts of Glorieta

title. "I have the apostle Paul as my guide. He mentions married bishops, presumes women Eucharistic celebrants—"

"I suppose," Sredzinski interposed, "that you'll include women at the Washing of Feet ritual during your evening Mass today?"

"The rubrics call for 'the *full* participation of the whole community...' Unquote."

"I've *read* the rubrics!" the prelate snapped, then held up a sheaf of stationery in both hands. "Look at these letters from loyal Catholics who are offended by your views. And here. Our Catholic newspaper's editor refuses to publish any more of your submissions..." He waved a page at him. "Here's your latest one, returned to me. 'Rome tries to jam its priests into a one-size-fits-all clerical collar, when there are as many personalities as there are men who become ordained. This might work with religious orders like Benedictines, but not seminarians. Religious novices have a trial period that allows them to decide if they actually want to be monks or brothers. With the priesthood, you are ordained, then, poof! You find yourself in a parish, ready to sink or swim'." The stern look over the glasses again. "Really, Father, such diatribes—"

"*Diatribes*, Excellency?"

"Perhaps I use an unfortunate term. My point is—"

Fr. Jake took a sarcastic guess. "Your point is that I must recant?"

"*Nie*, no, Father. This is not an...an—"

"Inquisition?" Fr. Jake was surprised at his irreverence, but his patience was wearing thin. "Excellency, the 'sermon police' have already come by St. Barnabas a number of times to make sure that I preach orthodoxy."

"A zealous laity." Archbishop Sredzinski jammed the letters back into the folder and took off his glasses with a hand that shook a little. "Jan Benisek, the Archbishop of the Santa Fe, New Mexico, Diocese, is a friend of mine."

"Benisek? Does *he* speak Spanish?"

Ignoring or unaware of the sarcasm, Sredzinski continued, "We met at last year's bishop's conference, shared similar views. Archbishop Benisek is concerned about a priest of his who is assigned to a Rio Grande community and quite ill."

"In New Mexico?"

"Well, yes. *Tak*. I believe, Father, that an assignment which might help the ailing priest back to health also would be of great benefit you."

27

"By my going to New Mexico? I've never been west of St. Louis University in Missouri."

"That conference on anti-Semitism in Poland between the wars."

"I did attend that." *Good heavens, the bishop knows everything about me!* "So, Excellency, you're sending me to a kind of gulag out in the far west?"

Sredzinski's eyes widened in puzzlement. "Gulag, Father?"

"I forgot that you didn't live in Poland under the Communists. I did, for nineteen years. Those who disagreed with the regime found themselves in 're-education camps,' basically, Soviet-style gulags. There were over forty of them when I left—"

An ornate clock on the fireplace mantle chimed the quarter hour, sparing the archbishop a response. Fr. Jake glanced at the hands. *Going on eleven o' clock. Do I still have time on the parking meter?* In an awkward silence that followed, only the small pendulum's click-clack and the muffled cadence of rain buffeting the window glass were audible. The table lamp flickered momentarily, but stayed alight.

As Archbishop Sredzinski leaned forward, his leather chair creaked and broke the silence. "*Ojciec* Kasimierz," he said, resuming a persuasive tone and a half-smile, "I'm talking about perhaps a year. Consider it a sabbatical at full pay. I understand that half the population of New Mexico speaks Spanish. Just think of what that would do to expand your vocabulary."

"A year? Would I then resume my work at St. Barnabas?"

The prelate shrugged and spread his hands in a gesture of helplessness. "What can I promise about a year from now? Churches and schools are consolidating to remain open, while others are forced to close."

Silence again before Fr. Jake asked, "May I ask the name of this Rio Grande community?"

The archbishop replaced his glasses and slipped a letter from under the paper-weight. He read a sentence, mispronouncing, "Providencia de San Isidro."

Fr. Jake said, "San Isidro…Isidore…is a Spanish saint, the patron of farmers."

The prelate's laugh was slightly nervous. "See, Father, you're at home already."

"This ill priest's name?"

Sredzinski ran a manicured forefinger down the letter. "Ah…here. Father Jesus Mora."

The Ghosts of Glorieta

"Excellency, his name would be pronounced 'Haysous' and not with a hard 'J' as we say 'Jesus'.

"Indeed." He glanced at the clock, then pressed a button on his intercom. In a moment, the receptionist knocked softly, then entered and placed a small, open cardboard box on an edge of the desk.

"*Dziękuję, Panny Belinski.*"

She said, "*Eksclenjo*, your next appointment is waiting."

"*Tak*. I…I just want to give this memento to Father Kasimierz." He searched through shredded newspaper in the box, pulled out his gift, and set it in front of the priest.

Fr. Jake stared in disbelief at what surely ranked high in the category of religious kitsch sold at pilgrimage sites: a full-color cardboard image of the Virgin of Guadalupe was set inside an upright abalone shell. Various smaller seashells, a dried sea horse, and colored pebbles surrounded the base and crept halfway up both sides of the shell. An electric cord connected to the shrine was unwrapped; Mrs. Belinski and the archbishop had tested the nightlight bulb behind the cardboard image of the *Virgen*.

The archbishop explained, "As you undoubtedly know, Father, the Virgin of Guadalupe is the patroness of the United States."

"Also of Mexico and South America, Excellency."

"Yes. I'm told this shrine was crafted in Mexico with shells collected from both the Atlantic and Pacific shores of the country, thus emphasizing Mary's universal role as Benefactress. A lamp lights up behind the Virgin." The archbishop glanced at the clock again while asking, "What do you think of it?"

"Your Excellency, I'm overwhelmed at your generosity."

"Nonsense, it's an appropriate souvenir in light of your forthcoming assignment."

Fait accompli, then. "When am I to leave?" Fr. Jake asked.

"This is April first. Within two weeks, I should think. Archbishop Benisek is very concerned about Father Mora's rapidly declining health."

"I'll have to close the rectory. St. Barnabas church—"

"*Nie, nie.* A deacon at St. Joseph's will conduct a Eucharistic service each week at what was your eleven o'clock Mass…" Archbishop Sredzinski stood up as his mantle clock concurrently chimed the eleven o' clock hour. "Mrs. Belinski will give you a travel voucher for the flight to Albuquerque. I wish you a fruitful ministry over the next year, Father…" He placed both hands on the priest's head in a blessing. *Udają się z Bogiem.* Go with God." From

Albert Noyer

habit, the archbishop held out his ring hand, then pulled it back, pushed forward the box, and smiled. "Don't forget the Virgin."

"No." As Fr. Jake picked up the shrine to repack it, he glanced at the plywood bottom: *Panny* Belinski had forgotten to peel off an oval "Made in China" sticker.

3 albuquerque / april 16

Just after dark, the left wing of a Boeing-300, on a Southwest Airlines flight, dipped in a wide turn on an approach to land at the Albuquerque International Sunport. Directly below, a broad expanse of lighted residential streets, playing fields, and parking lots shimmered in a sparkling panorama of almost surreal luminescence.

A flight attendant had seated herself next to Fr. Jake in readiness for landing. She leaned across him to point out the window. "There's the Duke City, Father. Real beautiful, isn't it?"

"Yes, Vicki," he agreed. "Almost celestial, one could say."

Vicki, a pert blond woman, maybe 24, had spotted the priest's Roman collar at Detroit Metro and smiled at him while checking seat belts before take-off. Later, when serving him a Sprite and an extra package of snacks, she volunteered that she was Catholic. That was when Fr. Jake told her his name. Vicki said she graduated from Pius X High School in Albuquerque.

At Cincinnati, the only stop the flight made, Vicki upgraded the priest to the window seat of a passenger who lived in the city and had left the plane. It was at a front emergency exit with more legroom. The young flight attendant with the fashionable, bright-red lipstick smiled at him whenever she passed.

Vicki did not wear a wedding band. Fr. Jake guessed that she had a kindred-Catholic interest in him, or he was a reminder of her father. She was not one of the women he occasionally encountered who seemed attracted to priests. Was it that clergy were "safe" because of their vow of

31

Albert Noyer

celibacy? No commitment possible from either side? Yet human contact was crucial to a person's physical and psychological wellbeing: did not God, in Genesis, form male and female out of clay with his own hands? Humankind had been created in the spiritual image of God, yet the Hebrew writer understood the significance of this Divine Touch. *No wonder that many Catholics espouse optional celibacy for priests.* "Espouse," a pun bandied about at clergy get-togethers.

Despite parishioners who could number from a hundred into thousands, the priesthood was an occupation stalked by loneliness. Too often, alcohol lessened the pain. A recent book, **Alcoholism** / *A Sourcebook for the Priest*, gave advice, both practical and spiritual, by men and women religious who had been alcoholics. It combined the 12-Step program of AA with "the mysterious working of divine grace." He had clergy friends at Guest House in Lake Orion. Their program was similar and had a high recovery rate.

The plane's intercom crackled: the captain announced their imminent landing, thanked passengers for flying Southwest, bid them a pleasant evening in Albuquerque, and hoped they would choose to fly with the airline again. Fr. Jake was mildly surprised not to hear the announcement repeated in Spanish. *Perhaps Spanish is not as prevalent here as Archbishop Sredzinski thinks.* He pulled up a jacket sleeve to glance at his watch. 8:55. *Ten minutes early. Good. Glad Vicki told me to set my watch back two hours.*

Fr. Jake's travel voucher was for a $99, one-way "Wanna get away" fare. The flight made a single stop where passengers did not change planes. It had the shortest travel time—4 hours, 55 minutes. A flight arriving around 4:00 P.M. cost more, but took over eight hours to get to Albuquerque. It was late now, yet he could choose to stay at a nearby hotel or find out when a bus might go toward Providencia.

He pulled down his carry-on case to be one of the first off the aircraft. It held his Mass travel kit—chalice, pyx, burse holder for hosts, and small wine and water cruets. Once, the outline of the chalice shape had puzzled a TSA inspector scanning baggage X-ray images. The man had detained the priest and asked him to open the case.

A side pocket held a sketchbook, pencils, and Millennium ink pens. His favorite subjects were Michigan barns and lighthouses, an aptitude in drawing that the art history instructor at the college had encouraged him to continue.

At the door, Vicki smiled again and extended a hand. "Nice to meet you, Father. I hope you like New Mexico."

The Ghosts of Glorieta

"I'm quite sure I shall, Vicki. *Vaya con Dios.*"

"Pardon, Father?" She cocked her head at him. "I didn't take Spanish."

"It means, 'Go with God.' You know, God be with you'."

"Oh. Thanks, Father. You too."

Other passengers, impatient to leave, strained forward. He gave her a goodbye wave and walked down the corridor to enter the airport concourse.

Signs at the end of two arrival-departure gate areas directed passengers to Baggage Claim. Fr. Jake passed the arrivals waiting lounge and entered a main concourse that was deserted at this hour. Shops, a restaurant and coffee bar had closed. *Albuquerque Sunport is a compact airport compared to Detroit Metro.* Down an escalator, the main concourse hall displayed a fine collection of southwestern paintings, folk art, and Native American works. *So much for the archbishop's kitschy Virgin of Guadalupe.*

Fr. Jake found Southwest's baggage retrieval area at the bottom of another escalator and waited for his one battered suitcase to shunt around on the conveyor. A nearby visitor's welcome booth was dark. *Can't ask anyone there about a hotel or bus station. I should have done more homework about what to expect on arriving.* Above a set of doors, signage marked "Transportation" led to outdoor covered platforms, where arriving passengers were picked up. Shuttle buses drove to nearby parking lots and airport hotels.

While Fr. Jake waited with other tired passengers for the conveyor belt to start clacking its hesitant way around the sign for his Southwest flight, he thought of the farewell party that resident parishioners had organized for him at Mum's Diner the night before. The restaurant served no liquor, so several men had brought bottles of wine. Al Franzek made an uncharacteristically emotional toast, which summarized how the parish would miss him and hoped he would soon return. The gathering was a rare occasion for the "Cassock Curtain" to be timidly pierced and fraternal love expressed. The usual superficial jesting was absent, and, at the end, a few men even embraced him in bidding good luck. Some women brushed away tears when they grasped his hand to wish him a safe trip. It was as the Church should be—something more than a liturgical round of formal rites and pain-of-sin obligations. At Lake Orion, in a joint ecumenical service with the vicar of an Episcopal Church, the congregation certainly had let out all stops in warmly embracing each other at The Peace ritual.

33

Albert Noyer

The conveyor began its noisy, chattering circuit. Fr. Jake spotted his suitcase, deftly pulled it off, then went outside to decide what he would do next.

Several automobiles and shuttle vans idled at the curb, their drivers alongside, waiting for friends or clients. A taxi stand headed the still procession.

The April evening was cool, but nauseous-smelling with exhaust fumes from waiting vehicles. After the priest put down his suitcase and carry-on to look for bus information, a voice behind him drawled, "Where y'all goin' Pod-ray? Need a taxi?"

Fr. Jake turned to see a short, unshaven, shaggy-haired man wearing cowboy boots and a western straw hat. The taxi driver pronounced 'Padre' as if it rhymed with 'X-Ray.'

"Taxi, Pod-ray?" the man repeated, tossing away a cigarette butt and grinning. "I saw yer white collar. Where to?"

"I...I was hoping to find either a bus or hotel."

The cabbie shook his head. "Bus station's in town, but they ain't runnin' this late. I *could* take y'all to a Merry-rot..." He chuckled at his spin on the Marriott hotel's name and extended a hand. "Name's Vernon."

He grasped the cabbie's rough palm. "Father Jake."

"Where d'ja say y'all were goin'?"

"Providencia..." He took a folded map from his inside windbreaker pocket and angled it toward an overhead light. "Here, I've circled the location in red."

"Lemme see that..." Vernon studied at the map a moment, then thrust it back. "Shi... I mean shucks, Pod-ray, I *know* the place. I can drive y'all down there for less than stayin' in a hotel, an' then takin' a bus tomorra."

"Vernon, how much is less than staying at the Marriott?"

The taxi driver mentally calculated a moment. "Well, that village is way past Belén. 'Bout a hun'ert, hun'ert-twen'y bucks should do it."

True, a hotel would cost more. A taxi to get to it...breakfast...finding the bus station. "How long a trip is it, Vernon? I figured Providencia as being forty-five miles from the airport. Is that about right?"

"'Bout right, Pod-ray. Give 'r take an hour to get there..." Vernon pointed to his cab, a white, four-door Chevy Cavalier with ABQuik Cab • 505 883-QUIK stenciled in green on the side. He bent down to grasp the handle of the scuffed suitcase. "We got us a deal, Pod-ray?"

He grinned. "Deal, Vernon."

The Ghosts of Glorieta

"Good. Boy, this baby's been around, ain't it?" he mocked, hoisting the suitcase to walk toward his cab.

Fr. Jake laughed agreement. "It's not the latest Swiss Army luggage on the market, but I don't travel that much anymore."

Vernon stashed the suitcase in the Cavalier's trunk. "Throw the carry-on in back, Pod-ray. Y'all can sit up front with me."

The cab reeked of stale cigarette smoke. Pebbles, stalks of grass, and torn paper scraps littered the floor mat. Fr. Jake cranked the passenger side window open a few inches. Vernon gunned the engine and swung out in front of an approaching shuttle bus. The driver braked and beeped his horn.

"Shove it!" the cabbie muttered to headlight reflections in his side-view mirror. "Pod-ray, we'll start on the freeway, I-25, an' get off at Belén. Lotsa cabbies woulda taken y' on SR 47, through them Mexican communities. Takes longer, cost y' more…" He pushed his straw hat back and eased a Marlboro out of the pack in his shirt pocket. "Mind if I smoke?"

"Actually, I do, Vernon."

"Suit yerself." He shoved the cigarette back with a finger.

Fr. Jake asked, "Vernon, what do you mean by 'Mexican communities'?"

"You know, the people what live there. Most of 'em talk Spanish."

"Isn't 'Hispanic' or 'Latino" the proper term?"

"Whatever…"

The lights of buildings in downtown Albuquerque sparkled on the right as Vernon accelerated down the freeway on-ramp and headed south on I-25. Fr. Jake checked his watch. *Going on 10 P.M. Maybe I should have taken that earlier flight, gotten there in daylight. I'll have to find the church and rectory in Providencia and wake up Fr. Mora. Guess I'm lucky that Vernon said he knew the village.*

Blue and yellow halide yard lights alternated with black, unlighted patches of ground skimming past on the highway's right side. The glare of grouped-together lights marked the hoppers of several gravel-hauling sites. Weaker halides barely revealed the darkened ghosts of junked automobiles in a number of reclamation yards. Farther on, a pale brightness reflected off white oil storage tanks that clumped together like giant, grounded drums. *Looks like we're passing through an industrial zone.*

The left side seemed to be an unlighted, barren, hilly wasteland.

Albert Noyer

Rio Bravo had the first brightly lit green exit sign. *Spanish. Perhaps the archbishop was correct in assuming I could improve my knowledge of the language.*

A Repo Mobile Homes placard flashed by. Another reflective exit sign for Bosque Farms and Peralta slid past. An overpass leading to the State Route 47 that Vernon had mentioned followed it.

The slim crescent of a new April moon had set at about the time Fr. Jake arrived. Now the sky was a dense canopy of brilliant stars that were visible in brief intervals of darkness, between the glare of automobile and yard-lights. A dim glow on the horizon revealed a chain of low mountains on the far left, but landscape details were murky. Vernon gunned his Cavalier to the 75 mile-per-hour speed limit.

Shortly after passing under the SR 47 overpass, the cabbie nudged Fr. Jake with an elbow. "Where d'ja hail from Pod-ray?"

"Detroit." The priest braced himself for the inevitable, "Yeah, 'Niggertown'," that was the usual reaction of those who spouted racial clichés. The cab driver's response surprised him.

"Things pretty bad up there?" Vernon asked. "Y' know, the car companies crashin' an' all."

"Yes, but they're working to improve things. Ford isn't doing too badly and—"

"Me," Vernon interrupted to talk about himself, "Me, I'm from Amarilla." He pronounced the city's name to rhyme with vanilla. "That's up in west Texas."

"I know." *Amarillo. 'Yellow' in Spanish and pronounced 'Ama-reeyo'.*

"Y'all ever bin there?"

"Nope."

"Wasn't nothin' much t' do," he complained. "I almost got me a GED, a edu-cation, 'so ranchin' or meat packin' wasn't to my way of thinkin'. And I ain't guttin' no chickens fer Tyson all my life. Y'all know what I mean?"

"I think so."

This time Fr. Jake did not object when Vernon deftly plucked a Marlboro from his pack and flicked a lighter to it with one hand. He exhaled blue smoke at the sun visor and continued, "Then, *Olay, Hosay!* 'Bout twenty years ago Mexicans started movin' in, got all the good jobs."

"I doubt that's true," Fr. Jake disagreed. "Migrant workers and even Green Card holders mostly take jobs that Americans don't want."

"That ain't what Russ Limbog sez."

The Ghosts of Glorieta

"Rush is hardly an unbiased source, Vernon."

"Don't know what y' mean Pod-ray. Them knee-jerk liberal gays want t' shut him up. Good man, Russ…"

A white cross set up beyond the road's shoulder reflected the headlight's glare. *That makes three I've seen, decorated with artificial flowers.* "Vernon, what are those crosses set up along the highway?"

"Well, that's where a Mexican or two was kilt in a accident. They bury 'em right where they croaked."

"Vernon, that's hard to believe. Most Hispanics here would be Catholic. The Church, and surely the highway department, wouldn't allow it."

"Believe what y' want, Pod-ray. I'm tellin' it like it is." He flicked a stream of red ash off his cigarette in the wind-stream outside his window. "Them mountains y' can hardly see on the left is the Manzanos. Means 'watermelon' in Mexican."

"The word means 'apples,' Vernon. *Sandia* is 'watermelon'."

The cabbie's fingers tightened on the steering wheel. "Seems like y' know it all, Pod-ray," he said, staring at the dark highway ahead.

A tense silence followed, broken only by the sound of the speeding car's engine.

Barren hills flattened out into farmland. Fr. Jake barely read a bridge and sign that identified the Rio Grande River. He decided to ask the cabbie about the village where was going. "Vernon, tell me about Providencia. I'll be working there."

"Well…" He hesitated and held the cigarette out the window again to flick away ash. "First off, I think mostly Mexicans live down there."

"You mean Hispanic-Americans?"

"Whatever. All I know is give 'em their beer, tortillas, an' salsa, let 'em get boracho, an' they're happy as clams."

Fr. Jake felt his blood pressure shoot up a few points. *Hold your tongue, Father. Just ask about the village.* "Vernon, where is the church and rectory in Providencia? I'm afraid I'll have to wake up the priest."

"There's gotta be a gas station," the cabbie hedged. "Prob'ly a little market stays open late. Maybe even a McDonald's. Go ask them about findin' the church."

Vernon fell silent. As I-25 curved south, Fr. Jake felt an uneasy sense of what he called "approaching doom"—usually as a joke. Yet, this situation was far from humorous. The Cavalier's headlights illuminated another reflective green highway sign that identified the Isleta Indian Reservation.

37

Albert Noyer

The yellow-orange pinpoint lights of homes along the highway were gone now; only the dark silhouettes of rolling hills and barren scrubland loomed on either side.

The Cavalier brightened another reflective sign. *Belén is twenty miles away*, Fr. Jake noted. He mustered up courage and hoped there would not be an ugly confrontation with the cabbie. "Vernon, you've never really been to Providencia, have you?"

Instead of replying, he tossed the butt of a second Marlboro out the window. A stream of red sparks trailed the car and bounced off the asphalt. Vernon muttered "Shee-it," gripped the steering wheel with both hands, and increased the Cavalier's speed above the 75 mile per hour limit.

Clusters of lights and low buildings broke the darkness below a massive outcropping of roundish stone. A UNM Valencia Campus sign flashed by with barely enough time to read it.

The high beams picked out what looked like the carcass of a dead coyote lying on the shoulder.

Farther on, the headlights illuminated the foremost of a row of orange barrels that imperceptibly moved to the left and blocked the right lane for repairs. Vernon misjudged the distance, clipped the first barrel, and sent it spinning into the shoulder. He regained control of the cab, but not a slowly simmering rage at being contradicted by his passenger.

Vernon swore again as he veered the car around the crimson tail-lights of a semi-truck doing the speed limit. Another set of semi lights appeared in the distance.

The priest ventured, "Maybe...maybe you should slow down a bit, Vernon?"

"Who's drivin', Pod-ray?" he snarled.

Ten miles from Belén, the brightness of businesses and a housing development at Los Lunas did little to ease the priest's apprehension: the cocoon of warm light was gone in under three minutes and darkness engulfed the slate-colored landscape again.

In eight minutes, highway signs indicated that there were three exits leading into Belén. Vernon screeched the car into middle Exit 191. He braked violently at the red light on a road that crossed the bottom of the ramp, Camino de Campo. On the right, the lights of a 4-story motel glowed an invitation. Vernon ignored waiting at the traffic signal and gunned the Cavalier to the left. He drove east along the Campo, through a residential neighborhood—well above the posted 30 m.p.h. limit.

The Ghosts of Glorieta

Vernon is still ticked off at being discovered lying to me. I guess I can stand a few more miles of his silent resentment, until we reach Providencia.

The Cavalier stopped at a traffic light on South Center Street. Instead of turning right, Vernon made a wide swing to the left and onto the right hand lane.

"Where are you going, Vernon? Isn't Providencia in the opposite direction?"

The cabbie took out another Marlboro and flicked his lighter to it.

"Vernon?"

His face was rigid as blew smoke at the front window and turned onto a street to the right. A sign read Train Station.

"Where are you going, Vernon?"

Without looking at the priest, he said in a dead voice, "Pod-ray, my shift's over. I'm takin' y'all to the Rail Runner station. If yer lucky, y' might find a bus there. Maybe even a cab."

"Vernon, the deal was that you would take me to Providencia for a hundred and twenty dollars."

"Gimme me a hun'ert an' we'll call it even…"

"What if there's no bus or cab?"

"Tough shee-it…" The Cavalier climbed an overpass above railroad tracks, then squealed left twice and into the station's parking lot. The front tires scraped against the curb in coming to a jarring stop in front of the station—a pair of covered waiting platforms. Vernon popped the Chevy's trunk lid with an inside lever, heaved himself out, and hoisted the battered suitcase to the pavement. "Pod-ray, get yer carry-on and my hun'ert dollars out…" Vernon's tone and eyes had an edge of menace to them.

Fr. Jake noticed "Vietnam Veteran" stitched onto the cloth band of Vernon's cowboy hat. That probably was not true, but he pulled twin fifty dollar bills from his wallet.

Vernon snatched them and stormed back into his cab. He raced the engine and made a screeching U-turn back toward Center Street. When the Cavalier's front wheels bumped up over the opposite curb and down again, sparks flew from the steel under-carriage.

Fr. Jake watched the cab's rear lights fade away, then turned to scan the two dimly lit platforms. A few cast iron benches were ranged along the outside. Only halogen lights threw pools of scattered brightness over the parking lot asphalt. Across the way, a dim light illuminated a sign on the Placitas Café, but the restaurant had closed. Its darkened windows were less

39

than reassuring. The area was ominously deserted; a few distant lights on Center Street shown beyond a line of freight cars on the tracks. No cabs waited in a taxi stand in front of the platforms.

A lone car had parked under the furthest light at the south end of the lot.

The stark scene reminded Fr. Jake of an Edward Hopper work, "Nighthawks," yet in that painting the restaurant was open and aglow with warm light. He shivered and eyed the iron benches around the station. *If I must, I could sleep on one of those—*

Abruptly, the driver's door of the parked car—a black Chevy Camaro—opened. A young man wearing dark clothing stepped out. As he walked rapidly toward the priest, parking lot lights cast his pitch-black shadow on sickly gray asphalt paving.

Fr. Jake saw him. Reacting to a fear that he occasionally felt in Detroit, he fished in his pocket for the whistle on his key ring. His fingers sifted only loose change.

Blessed Jesus, I left my keys at the rectory! If…if ever I needed a guardian angel, now is the time.

The Ghosts of Glorieta

4 providencia / april 16

As the man strode closer to the priest, his voice called out, "Father Hakub? Haku-b-owski?"

"Jakubowski. Who?"

"Relax, Father, it's okay," he said to reassure him. "I'm from Providencia."

"Providencia? But how? How did you know I would be here?"

"The archbishop, he sent us a letter that you were comin'."

"Yes, but I mean...*here?*"

"In Belén? Father, let's go stand over on that platform."

The yellow light waxed the handsome, light-brown face of a man in his mid-twenties. *Longish black hair parted in the middle, straight brows, a light mustache and half-beard,* Fr. Jake observed.

The young man grinned and looked the priest in the eyes to extend a hand. "Armando Herrera. Father, you pronounce your name with an Anglo 'J.'"

He laughed, not the least from nervous relief. "Yes, Armando, with a hard, not soft Spanish sound like you did."

"*Bueno.* You speak Spanish, Father?"

"*Poquito.* I use a little with the Mexican workers in my outreach ministry."

41

Albert Noyer

Armando frowned and shook his head. "Mexicans, they don't speak good Spanish. And, Father, you won't have to use it much in Providencia. Mostly *viejos* talk it when they don't want you to understand."

"I'm surprised to hear that."

"Kids," he shrugged, "they don't want to learn it now. *Mi madre* spoke Spanish *en la casa*, so I learned all of mine there." White teeth shone in the light as Armando laughed while adding, "And I forgot most of it."

"I see." Fr. Jake glanced around again at his desolate surroundings and sighed in relief. "Armando, I still can't believe that you found me."

"Almost didn't," he admitted. "I was dozin' off, so if the cab hadn't made that noise when it took off, I wouldn't realize you were here. Cynthia musta missed you at the airport."

"Cynthia?"

"Cynthia Plow. She teaches at the elementary school. I didn't want her waitin' here alone in the dark, so she went to find you at the airport while I was here." Armando thought a moment, then pointed at the sky. "Belén is short for Bethlehem, Father. We don't have a big star tonight, but somethin' told me you'd be here. You know, like the Wise Men found baby Jesus."

Fr. Jake said, "That you found me, Armando, is nothing short of a miracle."

"Or maybe it was San Isidro. A *santo* can perform miracles." He reached down for the priest's suitcase. "You ready to go? I'll bring your stuff to the car, Father… Father H̲akub-owski."

"Armando, please call me Father Jake."

"Oh, no, I don't think so. Father Mora, he don't let us call him with his first name."

"Well, 'Father Jesús' *might* be a little awkward."

"No, he could be a Juan and still didn't want it." Armando carried the suitcase to his Camaro, opened the passenger door, and heaved the case into the back seat. "Buckle up, Father."

"Thanks." In reaching around for the seat belt, the priest noticed a rosary dangling from the rear view mirror. The Camaro's interior and gray cloth seats were spotless. "Nice car, Armando. What year?"

"'87 IROC-Z, Father. 305ci V8 engine." Armando started the car and maneuvered out of the parking lot in a wide circle. "We'll take a shortcut I know, cross to the Rio Grande east side, then just a few miles to Providencia." Armando spoke English with a soft, lyrical accent that was absent in the migrant workers.

The Ghosts of Glorieta

"How big is your village?" Fr. Jake asked.

"Now?" Armando shrugged a guess. "Some people left. Maybe five hun'ert…seven-fifty…up to a thousand. There's a new part where some Anglos come to retire."

"'Anglo.' That's the second time you've used that term, Armando."

"It doesn't mean disrespect, Father. If you're not Hispano or Indio, that's what you're called here."

"I see. Tell me about Father Mora. I understand he isn't well."

"Oh, he's a very holy man." Armando gestured toward his rosary with a hand to emphasize. "Vigils, rosaries, novenas…you name it. I personally think all that penance is makin' him sick. Man, he even built a *segrario*—"

"Segrario?"

"Like in Mexican churches they have a special chapel to show off the *Santo Sacramento*. Father Mora spends a lotta time there just bein' with Jesús."

"Just what is his illness? Why is he sick?"

"Who knows, Father? He doesn't go to the clinic an' just becomes thinner and thinner. The *viejos* say that someday he's just gonna float up to heaven on smoke from his votive candles."

Fr. Jake eased himself against the seat back, feeling relief now, yet still drained by Vernon's insane cab ride. The cool April air smelled of moist earth where beans, corn, and alfalfa sprouted, of wood smoke, and faintly of the nearby Rio Grande River. Black shapes of cottonwood trees and a few scattered homesteads materialized on a dun landscape. At this hour only a few house windows glowed with a pale light.

After the Camaro's wheels thumped over the tracks of a railroad crossing, Fr. Jake asked, "What do you do for a living, Armando?"

The young man grinned and caressed the Camaro's dashboard with one hand. "Wouldn't ya know, Father. I fix cars."

"Good. In this recession, I imagine people are repairing their old automobiles, instead of buying new ones."

"*Bueno*, you got that right."

Armando drove on in silence. Several miles after he turned south onto SR 310, a wider highway, the Camaro's headlights flashed off a green and white highway sign identifying Providencia.

43

Albert Noyer

"Upland Heights Estates'," Fr. Jake read aloud from a subdivision's illuminated sign mounted on a sandstone base. "Isn't 'Upland Heights' redundant?"

Armando shrugged. "Like I said, that's pretty new, Father. Some developer thought rich retirees might wanna live here."

"Anglos?"

"Mostly…" He half turned toward the priest and laughed. "'Anglos.' You're catchin' on, Father. We got you a little adobe right across from the church. It belonged to Rosita Salazar, a *viuda*, a widow, who herself died. She left her *casita* to the parish."

Armando slowed to a stop, waiting for an approaching car to pass before making a left turn onto Calle San Isidro. On the right side of the highway, a dim light burned at the doorway of a darkened restaurant named Mamacita's. "Great food," he praised, swinging the Camaro onto the side street, then pointing to the dark outlines of a building on the priest's side of the car. "That's our church, San Isidro."

"No light over the entrance?"

"Our *mayordomo* ain't always on the ball."

"Mayor…?"

"*Mayordomo*. Dionisio Maldonado is like, volunteer janitor at the church. His wife helps. He's a holy deacon, too…" Armando turned into the gravel driveway alongside a small flat-roofed house across from the church. "Here's your *casita*, Father. I'll bring the suitcase."

The door was unlocked. In the dark, Armando found a wall switch on a rough- plastered, adobe wall and clicked on an overhead light bulb. He apologized for the furnishings. "Rosita's kids came an' took everything, Father. When we heard you were comin,' so soon, we only had time to get some stuff from a resale shop in Belén."

Fr. Jake touched his arm. "Armando, this will be fine. *Gracias*. Thank you."

"Nooo, look around, Father. See if you need anything. They say this adobe is a hun'ert years old, maybe old as Rosita was. Said she was born here. Oh, that thermostat over there runs a propane furnace, but you won't need it for a while. No, really, look around."

Fr. Jake put down his carry-on and went to the rear of the farthest room. In a galley-size kitchen, dead flies speckled a faux-wood Formica counter. *Evidently, the bug season is earlier here in New Mexico.* A wall cupboard held mismatched dishes and glassware. The stainless steel sink had one basin.

The Ghosts of Glorieta

Aside from the scarred refrigerator, an under-cabinet coffee maker, and microwave oven were the only other appliances.

Armando explained, "We disconnected the propane from the stove. "Rosita, she was pretty feeble. We didn't want her burnin' herself up."

"Understandable."

The cramped bathroom next to the kitchen housed a stained toilet and immense, deep-sided bathtub set on claw feet. *No shower.* When the priest switched on the light, a live mouse scurried around the inside of the tub's curved enamel bottom, frantically trying to hide in the drain hole.

Armando deftly caught the rodent in a bath towel, grinned, and went to shake it out at the front door. "Vamoose, *Miguelito.*"

The bed was without a headboard, but the mattress pad looked new. Blankets lay folded at the foot with two pillows on top. A small, scarred bedside table held a lamp and garish girlie ashtray advertising a distant Casino/Hotel.

Armando went to a corner and pulled aside a curtain suspended on a rod where two end walls met. Wire coat hangers dangled from another rod inside. "You can hang clothes here, Father. These old adobes didn't have no closets."

"Thanks, Armando. That will do very nicely for what I brought."

In what was a small living room, a gold shag rug still bore a few stains, yet looked to have been hand washed. *Rosita probably owned cats and wasn't capable of emptying their litter box often enough.*

Overall, the *casita* smelled of mild disinfectant that could not cover the residue remaining from an old woman's careless housekeeping. The used chrome kitchen set, unmatched bed, dresser, living room couch, and single armchair all betrayed their resale shop origins.

"Truly, Armando, this is fine," Fr. Jake assured him once again. "Please thank the parishioners who were responsible."

"*Bueno.* I gotta work tomorrow, but the deacon will come by in the mornin'." He extended a calloused hand with grease-blackened fingernails.

Fr. Jake warmly shook his palm. "I am grateful, Armando. I certainly look forward to my ministry here…getting to know you, Father Mora, the other parishioners. Bettering my Spanish."

Armando nodded without answering. At the door, he paused a moment to look back. "Father Hakub," he warned, "I gotta be honest. Most people here are not gonna like you."

45

5 providencia

Morning sunlight streamed through a shade-less window in the eastern wall of the adobe and illuminated a religious calendar on the opposite wall. A funeral home advertised Immaculate Conception Parish in La Fonda. A calendar page turned to March pictured the Church of St. Francis of Rome; Rosita's kids had left it open on the month in which their mother died.

A familiar sound of roosters crowing outside to announce a new day roused Fr. Jake. For a moment, he thought he was in his rectory at St. Barnabas, then rubbed his eyes and glanced at the hands of his Wenger wristwatch. "6:28. Rise and shine, I guess." The small house felt damp, chilly. He lay in bed a moment longer, thinking of a fitful sleep in which his airline journey from Detroit Metro, the wild cab ride, abandonment by Vernon, then being miraculously found by Armando in the middle of the night, had raced through his mind. *What did he say about people not liking me?* After sliding out of bed and performing morning ablutions, but without shaving, he unlocked his suitcase to hang up wrinkled clothing.

He had swaddled the souvenir shrine of the *Virgen of Guadalupe* that the archbishop had given him in bubble-wrap and clean undershirts, yet three of the shells became unglued. After reluctantly setting the tasteless object on the dresser top, he hung up the clothes he had brought along—black clerical trousers and suit coat, a corduroy sport jacket, shirts, and jeans. He dusted the bottom of the dresser drawers with a handkerchief and arranged his clerical and white shirts, underwear, and socks inside. Later, UPS would send on his few other belongings. *It's Saturday. I'll wear something casual to go out and look around. Maybe that restaurant will be open.*

After dressing, Fr. Jake opened the refrigerator door. The inside was warm. A half-empty jar of salsa sat on a door shelf, the sauce coated by gray mold. He plugged in the appliance, relieved to hear its motor purr back to life. Deciding to deal with breakfast later on, he opened the front door and stepped onto a narrow, roofed-over entrance deck added to the adobe's front.

The sky was of a blueness rarely seen in Michigan, yet rather than the familiar greenery surrounding Lake Sirius, dry scrub bushes spotted the sandy soil around his adobe and other homes along the street. To the far right, a stretch of greening cottonwood trees marked the *bosque*, a strip of lush vegetation and trees bordering the Rio Grande. On the rise of land to the left, a dense wood of juniper, piñon pine, and cottonwoods began about a mile off. A low range of bluish mountains broke the distant horizon. All else in between seemed desolate scrubland, parched by a relentless winter sun that quickly had melted away any snowfall, and dried up meager rainfalls.

The church of San Isidro stood across the way, the side facing him pink with a low morning sunlight that cast the adobe building's dark, elongated shadow along the ground. Chipped stucco marred the adobe walls, and sienna-colored rust streaked down the metal panels of a corrugated iron roof. A cross atop a bell tower above the entrance leaned askew. One smaller cross was missing from two miniature towers set on each side at the roof's edge.

Ideal subject for a picturesque drawing. Fr. Jake went back inside to find his sketchbook and pen, then carried a kitchen chair out onto the porch. He had half completed his sketch of the church's front when a stocky, bearded man, with the wild hair-style of a Medusa, came out of an adobe three houses away. A blonde-haired woman in spike heels, a short denim skirt, and yellow V-neck tee under an unbuttoned crimson sweater, trailed him. She held both arms folded across her front, each hand grasping an elbow. Even at a distance, it was obvious that she had taxed the limits of breast enlargement surgery. The man wore faded jeans, sandals, and a short-sleeved black Tee with an image of the *Virgen de Guadalupe* screened on front. A green deacon's stole that angled across his chest from the left shoulder partly hid Our Lady. A silver-plated crucifix pendant dangled on a nylon cord around his thick neck.

He came up to Fr. Jake, unsmiling, eyes narrowed in suspicion under bushy brows. "You gotta be the *Norteño* priest the bishop said was comin' here."

"Yes, I'm Father Jakubowski." He smiled and stood up.

The Hispano extended a coarse hand. "Dionisio Maldonado, deacon here at San Isidro."

"I see that," Fr. Jake said, wondering why the man wore his stole of office outside of church. The raveled edges were dirty and wine stains spotted the polyester material. "My pleasure, Deacon…" He returned the man's handshake, a grip that was threatening in its implication of brute force.

Maldonado waved a hand to indicate the woman standing behind him. "This here is Raylene, *mi esposa*. Bein' Anglo, I don't suppose y' know what that means."

"Well, I studied Hebrew in seminary. If I recall correctly, Raylene is a form of Rachel, the daughter of Laban and one of Jacob's wives. It means something like 'small lamb.' *Mi esposa* is, of course, 'my wife' in Spanish."

Maldonado scowled at a perceived, yet unintended, reprimand and turned to his blond *esposa*. "Raylene," he ordered, pulling a twenty dollar bill from his wallet, "why don't you get in the car an' go buy somethin' for dinner in Belén. I'm takin' Father to Mamacita's for breakfast."

"Why can't I come too?" she pouted, stamping a foot. "I'd enjoy talking to somebody intelligent for a change."

Maldonado ignored a criticism he undoubtedly had fended off many times. "We're gonna talk church, Raylene. You wou'n't be interested." He took his wife's arm and turned her toward the porch steps. "Now scat and bring me back change." She flounced off toward the house, bare legs wobbling on high heels. 'Good lookin' woman, but not too much savvy," the deacon snickered. "She'd buy pricey steaks here, 'stead of findin' a manager's special at the meat counter in Belén."

"Yes, well…*How many times have I heard the same husbands' complaints in the confessional?* "I don't have any food here, deacon, so I'll accept your kind breakfast invitation and be happy to 'talk church.' I wanted to do that anyway." Fr. Jake waved a hand over his new pair of jeans, plaid shirt, and brown loafers. "Am I dressed all right?"

"Where's your priest collar?"

"I usually don't wear one when I'm not on a ministerial call."

"Father Mora wou'n't be caught dead without his."

"I'll keep that in mind, deacon. Do you normally wear your stole when not assisting at Mass?"

Maldonado ran a nervous hand through his hair. "Jus' wanted to show you. Let's go."

Albert Noyer

"Let me put away this sketch pad and lock my front door."

"Nobody in Providencia locks doors," he scoffed.

"I'm from Detroit and it's hard to break a good habit. I'm quite sure that many people in Albuquerque feel the same way."

Maldonado took off his stole, folded the band, and stuffed it into a back pocket. The two men walked in awkward silence along the Calle de San Isidro. At the highway, the words LA RAZA were spray painted in black on a stop sign.

"Crazy Chicanos," the deacon complained. "They want us to secede an' join Arizona an' California in some new country they call 'Atlas.'"

"I see…" The name was Aztlan, but Fr. Jake did not correct the man.

It was Saturday and Mamacita's was crowded. The restaurant's warm air smelled of spicy foods. The room's retro-1950's chrome tables and chairs did not all match, and some possibly were originals. Walls displayed faded reproductions of old Mexican bull fighting posters.

Fr. Jake paused at display shelves near the cash register that held a collection of carved wooden figures of various saints. A sign above them read, "Santos made in Mexico."

"Deacon, is there a San Isidro there? I'd like to have one for my *casita*."

Maldonado glanced back. "Proba'ly. You can take a look when we leave."

He chose a small table with two chairs. When a high-school-age server brought glasses of ice water, the deacon pushed aside a menu she handed him. "Gimme two coffees, black, and two orders of *huevos rancheros*, extra tortillas, green chile on the side with one. That okay with you, Father?"

"Deacon, I trust your judgment."

Maldonado sipped from his water glass, then asked, "So, Father Hakub… Hakub…?"

"Jakubowski."

"That a Greek name?"

"Polish, actually. I was born there."

He thought a moment. "Yeah…your people make sausage. I see Polish sausage at the market." He pronounced "Polish" as if it were an automobile wax.

Fr. Jake smiled at the server and leaned aside when she brought his coffee. "Deacon," he asked, popping open a small cream container, "may I ask what your day job is?"

50

The Ghosts of Glorieta

"I was in construction, but hurt my back. Raylene is a secr'tary at the element'ry school. She used to work in Socorro."

"I see. You know, calling you 'deacon' all the time is a bit formal. Is it Dio... Dionisio?"

"Make it 'Donny.' That's what Raylene and guys call me because of my last name."

"Fine, Donny. You wanted to talk about San Isidro church?"

Maldonado bent to blow on his coffee, slurped a mouthful, then said, "Father Mora is pretty sick."

"That's why I was sent here, to help your pastor."

"*Si*, so we don't want y' doin' nothin' to upset Father."

"Such as?"

"Well, you know. We're pretty conservative Cath'lics here, an' you comin' from up north an' all."

Is this what Armando was talking about? My being an outsider? "What do you think we...I...do up there, deacon?"

"I'm just sayin' we don't wanna change things from how we do 'em now."

"What would I possibly change at, say, your five o'clock Mass this evening?"

"We don't have Mass then, just on Sunday at eight and eleven. I was gonna say, y' can introduce yourself tomorra at the eight o'clock."

"Fine, deacon, I'll do that."

The server brought their breakfasts, immense platters of fried eggs in a folded tortilla. The deacon's had been smothered in green chile, but Fr. Jake's portion was in a small plastic cup. Both had Spanish rice and refried beans on the side, with a shredded lettuce garnish.

"Careful," the girl warned. "Those plates are hot."

Fr. Jake asked for her name.

"Julia," she replied. "I go to the local high school."

"Thanks, Julia. This looks wonderful."

Fr. Jake had tasted his rice and beans and was about to cut into the tortilla, when a young woman, somewhere under thirty years of age, interrupted—correctly pronouncing his name. "Father Jakubowski?"

He looked up at her. "Yes, but how—"

"Did I know?" She laughed while brushing long strands of reddish hair back under a floppy Boonie hat. "We were expecting you, Father, and you're

51

Albert Noyer

with Deacon Maldonado. A no-brainer." She extended a hand. "I'm Cynthia Plow. I teach at the elementary school, and hope you'll start a children's Faith Formation class at San Isidro. I'd like to teach it."

Maldonado scowled at her. "We don't want nothin' changed here, Miss."

Fr. Jake ignored him and stood to shake her hand. "Then, Cynthia, I'm doubly pleased to meet you. I have boundless admiration for teachers." When he noticed her cheeks redden, he said, "With the work boots and coveralls you're wearing, you look like you might teach, well, agriculture?"

She took off black-rimmed glasses and tucked them into a leather case in an upper pocket. "Fifth grade, Father, but I'm also a budding archaeologist. We recently found out that my school, and maybe even our church is built over old Civil War Fort Providence. There's another one, Fort Craig, south of Socorro, but no one knew much about this place. I've gotten permission from the BLM Field Office in Socorro to dig at one corner. This is Saturday, and—"

"—And you've told me all that in practically a single breath!" Fr. Jake smiled. "I applaud your enthusiasm, Cynthia."

"Thanks, Father. Will you be introduced by Father Mora tomorrow?"

"Miss, I told him t' introduce himself," Maldonado growled. "You know our *padre* ain't too well."

She nodded acceptance of a poor explanation. "Must go, Father, but I hope you like it here. I wish you *Bueno suerte*."

"*Gracias*, Cynthia. I'll need all the luck I can round up."

The priest watched her leave, then sat down to finish eating. "Nice young woman."

"She could ditch th' glasses," Maldonado criticized, "an' do somethin' nice with that stringy red hair, but she'd never turn into a beauty and catch her a man, like at the end of some movies I seen."

What do they say about beauty being skin-deep? Fr. Jake resumed eating cold *huevos*, rice, and frijoles.

At the far end of the room, a longhaired, bearded man, sitting at a table with a younger version of himself—undoubtedly a son—had been watching the two men. He stood up with one of the printed tracts he distributed among patrons and limped toward Fr. Jake's table.

"Elder Jeremiah," he said by way introducing himself. "Art thou the new presbyter from the north come to the House of Idolatry?"

The Ghosts of Glorieta

Art thou? House of Idolatry? After swallowing a piece of tortilla, Fr. Jake asked, "House of Idolatry? Elder, if you mean San Isidro church, I haven't seen the inside yet."

Jeremiah waved his tract. "Thou shall not bow down to idols.' Exodus 20: 2-3. Leviticus 29: 1."

"Elder, I hoped to see some hand-carved *santos* like those on sale here, yet I certainly won't bow down to worship them."

Quoting scripture, the old man went on, "'Their priests, who say to a graven piece of wood, Thou art my father, and to a stone idol, thou hast brought me forth...'" Jeremiah placed a tract on the table titled, The Living Tabernacle of Divine Truth. "Thou wouldst be welcome to witness the charismatic joy of those 'baptized in the Spirit.' Acts 1: 5. 'I baptize thee with water, but Jesus will baptize thee with the Holy Spirit'. Matthew 3:11. Mark 1—"

Maldonado stood up, his narrowed eyes angry, his mouth half-full. "Don't be botherin' our new priest or you'll answer to me!" he snarled, then swept the offending tract off the table with a pudgy hand.

Patrons stopped eating to stare at a potential brawl, but Jeremiah replied softly, "As thou wish, but the end times foretold in Revelation are upon us. Revelation 15—"

"Shove it," the deacon mumbled, sitting down again. He breathed hard from the confrontation.

The younger man got up and came over to speak softly with Jeremiah. The Elder scowled at him, but left the restaurant.

The youth picked the religious tract off the floor and apologized. "Sorry, my dad sometimes is over zealous in doing the Lord's work. I'm Brother Caleb. May I pull a chair over?"

"Of course, Brother Caleb. I'm Father Jake."

"I guessed as much."

Maldonado had not swallowed fast enough and his intended protest faltered.

The young man slid a third chair from an adjacent table and laughed. "Actually, my name is Caleb Parker. We're from Springfield, Illinois."

"And now you're here?" Fr. Jake knew an interesting story was coming.

Maldonado frowned, looked for Julia, and tapped his coffee cup on the table for a refill.

53

Albert Noyer

Caleb explained, "I guess that back in the 'Eighties my dad was a classic hippie. He and my mom set out in…believe it or not…in a VW van to explore the west."

While Julia refilled the deacon's cup, Caleb paused to run fingers through his long hair. Fr. Jake asked her to bring a cup for the young man.

"We're supposed to abstain from coffee, but…" Caleb's grin of protest was innocent.

"But father doesn't always know best?" Fr. Jake teased, instinctively liking the youth.

"Something like that." After Julia poured his coffee, Caleb took a sip, then clutched both hands around the cup as if she might try to take it back.

Fr. Jake asked him, "Of all places, how did your parents end up in New Mexico?"

"Wouldn't you know, the VW broke down for the last time outside Providencia. They had about run out of money, but dad knew how to build straw-and-tire earth lodges and found work. Then mom died of I-don't-know-what. I was pretty little…four, I think…and dad took over a struggling Pentecostal church here."

"He 'got religion'?"

The youth's gray eyes narrowed in a frown. "Are you mocking us, Father?"

"Sorry, Caleb, that was uncalled for."

"Accepted." The grin returned. "I guess you could call us 'free-range Pentecostals.' We don't belong to UPCI."

"United Pentecostal Church International."

"You know about the group?"

"We had a few ecumenical encounters in Michigan," Fr. Jake told him. "None took deep root."

Caleb sipped his coffee, then went on, "I like to think of our commune members as 'squeaky green' Christian environmentalists. Did you see the highway sign saying that we pick litter up off the road?"

"No, I came in late last night."

"We sell the scrap metal and have an orchard, market the fruit. 'Ye have been given stewardship over the earth, and of every tree of the Garden ye shall freely eat.' Genesis 3:15—more or less."

King James Version, more or less. "Caleb, does Elder Jeremiah really speak like that all the time?"

The Ghosts of Glorieta

"He actually does, Father, blessed with the gift of tongues by the Spirit." Fr. Jake wasn't sure if Caleb was serious, but the young man continued, "Elder J., my dad, that is, started building 'Earthships.' Like I said, they're lodges made of used tires and rammed earth, or straw bales. Off the grid energy-efficient. Well, you should come and see. We don't just sit around spouting Revelation." His grin faded as Caleb saw an old woman approach a nearby table of diners. "Uh, oh, here comes *La Bruja,* hawking her plant remedies."

"*Bruja?*" Fr. Jake looked her way. "She's a witch?"

"That's what some call Ofilia ..." Caleb stood up to leave. "The old gal's a *curandera,* a folk healer. Armando Herrera's aunt." He stretched out a hand to the priest. "Take care, and thanks for the caffeine jolt."

"God Bless."

"Deacon."

Maldonado ignored the man's acknowledgement and stood to beckon Ofilia toward his table. The herbalist was a petite, wiry woman, wearing a flowered cotton housedress and blue knitted sweater. Her gray hair was cropped short. Relatively free of wrinkles, Ofilia admitted to being "*en las setentas*"—somewhere in her seventies.

"*Curandera,*" Maladonado told her, "this is th' Anglo *padre,* come to help Father Mora."

"*Padre?*" She peered at the priest, then rummaged among the herb packets in a wooden tray suspended by a leather strap around her neck. "*Yerba del Cristo,* Padre," she said, pushing a food storage bag toward him. "Good for you have headache."

"*Gracias, señora,* but, fortunately, I don't suffer from them."

"Bad skin, maybe?" she insisted. "Impetigo?"

He admitted, "I...I do have a nasty rash on my left arm..." *Come to think, it hasn't bothered me much since Armando found me.*

While Fr. Jake rolled up his sleeve, Ofilia unscrewed the top from a small green bottle. "*Fresno...limon...yerba del pajaro,*" she boasted and held the bottle to his nose. "Smell, *Padre.*"

The oily concoction had a pleasant lemon scent, similar to furniture polish, yet stronger. Fr. Jake glanced down at his arm to apply some with a paper napkin, but the red blotch was almost gone. He looked up at her and the deacon. "I...I don't believe it. I've had a rash on this arm for...for about three months. How can it disappear so suddenly?"

55

Albert Noyer

Ofilia shrugged with a malicious grin. "Maybe a welcome, *Padre*, to you from Providencia. You keep medicine, rash may come back." She held out a gnarled palm, stared at him, and murmured impassively, "Ten dollar."

"A bargain I'm sure, Ofilia." He handed the old woman two five-dollar bills from his wallet. *Maybe her lemon remedy is also good for polishing furniture.*

Ofilia crammed the bills into a coffee can on her tray and moved to the next table.

Maldonado nervously fingered the cross at his chest. "Father, if you're finished, I gotta go do some work 'round my adobe."

"Yes, thank you, deacon. Where can I buy bread and milk? A few food staples like that?"

"I'll point out the Providencia Grocery down the highway. I try to get Raylene not to shop there much. They got gas, too, but I see you don't have a car."

"No. Will I need one?"

"*Padre*," he scoffed, "in New Mexico everybody's gotta have a set of wheels."

"I see. Well, thank you again for breakfast. I've met some interesting people, but you didn't tell me anything about meeting Father Mora before Mass tomorrow. When can I do that?"

"Like I said, he's pretty sick, so proba'ly not much before seven-thirty, just before the eight o'clock. That's when I get to church an' vest up."

Fr. Jake slipped another dollar under the one the deacon left as a tip, then followed him outside.

Maldonado pointed south along Highway 310. "Down there, 'bout a half-mile."

"*Gracias*, again."

Fr. Jake walked in the direction of the grocery. Along the way, behind Western Savings, a bank in a doublewide manufactured home that shared space with the post office, a new-looking white building was unoccupied. A name over the doorway was too far away to read. Two windows flanked each side of an entrance tower. The roof was terra cotta tiles. *Wonder what that building is for and why is it isn't being used?*

The grocery was larger and better stocked with provisions than the deacon had implied. Cluttered might be a more appropriate word, yet everyone in the village undoubtedly knew where to find everything. One

The Ghosts of Glorieta

wall had a cooler with fresh sandwiches, milk, assorted cheeses, soft drinks, beer, and basic frozen foods. Three center aisles were crammed with bread, packaged cereal, canned goods, and toiletries. Fifty-pound sacks of pinto beans lay stacked on a wooden palette. The smell of brewed coffee came from an alcove on the left. A microwave oven stood next to the coffeemaker.

A handsome, middle-aged woman behind the counter, wearing a white apron over a flowered dress, greeted him in Spanish with *buenas dias.*

"*Buenas dias, señora,*" he responded, but continued in English. "I'm Father Jake, here from Michigan to help minister along with Father Mora."

"Ah, you're a priest. Father, I live down the highway, so I go to a different Catholic mission." She extended a hand. "Carlotta Ulibarri. Anyway, welcome…*bienvenido.*"

"*Gracias.* You have a very nice store, Mrs. Ul…Uli…."

She gently laughed at his confusion over pronunciation. "Father, just call me Carlotta." She indicated her premises with the wave of a hand. "Small, but maybe you saw my sign outside, 'The small store with the big heart'."

He grinned. "I like that, Carlotta."

A small bell hanging on the door tinkled. An old Hispanic man, whose dark, weathered face reflected a lifetime of outdoor fieldwork, shuffled in. He wore a mangled cowboy hat, soiled white shirt, worn jeans, and rubber boots. The *viejo* muttered a *buenas* to Carlotta and headed toward the coffee.

"*Buenas dias,* Eulalio." Carlotta walked around from behind the counter and sighed. "'S'cuse me Father, look around. I have to pour his coffee and heat up a *desayuno burrito* every morning at this same time."

"I just need a few staples until I get more settled in."

"So look around." She took out a wrapped burrito from the cooler and disappeared around the corner, chattering in Spanish with her customer while she microwaved his breakfast.

Fr. Jake picked up a hand basket and found 2% milk, whole wheat bread, raisin bran, and ground coffee. He found a frozen lasagna he could cook in his microwave for supper. Bananas were expensive and over-ripe. Returning to the counter, he noticed that a wall near the doorway had shelves with an identical collection of hand-carved *santo* statues as at Mamacita's. *Must be a lot of tourists coming through here that buy these.*

He waited with his purchases for Carlotta to return.

A young woman came in with a child and nodded to him. "Carlotta, *aqui,*" she called out to the storekeeper.

57

Albert Noyer

"*Si, momentito.*" Carlotta returned wiping her hands on her apron. "You're all set, Father?"

"For the moment, but I wanted to ask you about those *santos.*"

"Mister Fortgang brings them to sell to visitors, although you know, this highway dead-ends at La Fonda. Not too many come." As she rang up his purchases, Carlotta explained further, "Mister Fortgang is one of yours and lives in one of those fancy houses at the new subdivision."

"Upland Heights Estates?"

"*Si.* Funny name, don't you think?"

"I do." Fr. Jake paid and slid the plastic bag off the counter. "Well, thank you, Carlotta. I'll be here again and perhaps buy a San Isidro *santo.*"

"Good luck in Providencia, Father."

"God Bless." As he went out the door, Armando Herrera came around the corner from his auto repair shop.

"Hey, Father Hakub," he greeted. "How did you sleep?"

"Not too well, but that should change. And I've just met some interesting people."

"Oh, yeah? Who?"

"Deacon Maldonado took me to breakfast at Mamacita's."

"Donny. Who else you see there?"

"Cynthia. A teacher at the elementary school."

"She's cool. I told you about her waitin' at the airport."

"Yes. Also your aunt, the *curandera.*"

"*Tia* Ofila?" Armando laughed. "She got ya to buy somethin' from her, right?"

"Oh, she's a great salesperson. And the Elder Pentecostal and his son, Caleb, spoke to me."

'Them…" Armando pointed to distant woods on a rise of land across the highway. "They pretty much keep to themselves in a kind of commune up there. They name it Eden West, but also got a storefront kinda church down the road. So, you're makin' friends already, eh, Father Hakub?"

"I met Carlotta just now."

"She's cool. I'm gettin' a couple burritos from her for lunch."

"As to friends…" The priest tilted his head and shrugged uncertainty. "The restaurant was crowded and I'm sure many of the other patrons were San Isidro parishioners. They saw me with the deacon, but none of them came over to…to, well, to even say *buenas dias.*"

The Ghosts of Glorieta

Armando nodded sympathy. "I know, but don't say I didn't warn you last night."

"You did."

The mechanic touched the priest's arm. "Aw, cheer up, Father Hakub. It'll proba'ly get better."

"Thanks, Armando." *That's exactly what I would have said if our situations were reversed.*

The Ghosts of Glorieta

6

Fr. Jake spent the balance of Saturday tidying up his *casita* with a few cleaning supplies he found under the sink, took a short walk around the neighborhood, ate his lasagna supper and went to bed early. In the two-hour time difference, 9:00 P.M. was eleven o'clock at night.

O

The next morning he smiled at the sound of roosters again announcing his second day in Providencia. "You're like priests," he jested to them. "Never have a day off."

He put on a black clerical shirt and trousers to go into San Isidro for his first concelebrated Mass with Fr. Mora. Outside the church, tilted to one side, a green and white sign in Spanish announced the worldwide Year of the Priest— *Año Sacerdotal / 2009-2010*. Spray-painted on one side was a black LA RAZA, presumably by the same persons who had defaced the stop sign. *Do they also plan to revive the Aztec custom of human sacrifice?*

He pushed open the church's unlocked wooden door, leached gray by afternoon sun, and entered a narrow entrance foyer. A curtained vesting alcove was on the right side. A rack of faded pamphlets stood on the opposite end. There were no Sunday bulletins on a table in front of a wall-mounted corkboard, hung with a jumble of out-of-date announcements and faded pictures of saints cut from calendars and religious magazines.

61

Albert Noyer

It was chilly inside the nave of whitewashed walls. *Evidently, adobe holds seasonal temperatures for a long period.* Dark-stained cottonwood beams supported the ceiling, the cobwebbed space between them filled with small branches arranged in a slanted chevron pattern. Telltale water stains ran down one side of the wall from a leaking roof. Framed color lithographs of the Stations of the Cross ranged around from one sidewall to the other. A waist-high adobe shelf along the right side was crowded with as many plaster statues of Christ, Mary, and various saints as it could hold. *That closed door at the far end must lead to the* segrario *that Armando mentioned.*

Warped, wood-grain fiberboard paneled the adobe wall behind the altar A plaster statue of the Sacred Heart and a wooden carving of San Isidro flanked the central life-size Mexican crucifix that depicted Christ's raw knees, bloody elbows, pierced side, and thorn-spiked head. *It's similar to the one that Raul Ruiz gave me for St. Barnabas. Dare I consider this a good omen?* Isidore, the Spanish farmer-saint, knelt in prayer. At his feet, a miniature angel directed two oxen plowing a field.

Two rows of scarred pews needing fresh varnish took up space on a floor of weathered planks. Two missing pews gave access to a confessional, half-set into the left wall. Colorful Zapotec blankets covered the entrance. The air in the church smelled of both damp mustiness and countless ritual incensing.

As Fr. Jake inspected the statues, the door of the *sagrario* slowly opened. Fr. Mora limped out. A slight man, the priest's sallow face was emaciated and unshaven. Thinning hair added at least ten years to his age of fifty-five. He wore a white alb, over which he would put a white chasuble to celebrate the Mass. After bowing to the altar, he turned and glanced up, startled to see someone in the church this early.

Fr. Jake came forward to extend a hand. "Father Mora, it's my pleasure to meet you. I'm Father Casimir Jakubowski."

Mora's red-rimmed eyes squinted at him under untrimmed eyebrows. "You…you are the one come to take over my church?" he demanded in a weak, suspicious voice.

"Take over? Of course, not, Father. Your archbishop knows that you aren't well and requested that I come help you regain your health."

He looked toward the crucified Christ and shook his head. "That, you cannot do."

"Surely, I can ease your ministry and help with visits to the sick. Whatever you ask of me—"

The Ghosts of Glorieta

"Only God can forgive me and heal my soul."

"Forgive you for what, Father?"

"My great transgression—" Light flooding in as the front door opened interrupted the priest. Mora shaded his eyes with a thin hand without finishing an explanation.

Deacon Maldonado entered with Raylene, who held wine and water cruets. "*Padre* Mora," he said, "I come to light the altar candles."

"*Si*." Mora ignored Fr. Jake and limped to the entrance alcove to finish vesting.

"I'm callin' you Father Hakub," Maldonado said, "like Armando. We don't got a extra chasuble for you."

"No problem, deacon, I've brought my stole with me. I'll go back to the house for it."

When Fr. Jake returned, a few parishioners were inside the church, kneeling to pray their rosaries or quietly sitting in pews. Most of the women wore cotton house-dresses, but the men were in jeans and short-sleeved sport or Tee shirts. Raylene stood at a side table near the altar, arranging the cruets and priest's chalice. She came down the platform stairs and bowed to the altar. After nodded slightly to Fr. Jake without smiling, she took her place in a front pew as *mayordoma*.

By eight o'clock, the small church almost had filled with worshipers. Armando was three pews from the front, with his *curandera* aunt. Cynthia Plow sat behind them. Fr. Jake had not met an Anglo man—balding, eyeglasses, fiftyish—who sat alone in a rear pew. He wore a dark suit, flowered tie, and cowboy boots. A western-style Stetson hat lay on the seat next to him.

The congregation stood up when Deacon Maldonado rang a small bell. He processed down the center aisle ahead of the two priests. *No music?* Fr. Jake wondered as he walked alongside Mora. *No sung entrance antiphon?* The three men bowed at the bottom stair of the altar platform. Fr. Jake started up the stairs to stand at the left side of the altar, but Fr. Mora remained where he was and crossed himself.

"*In nomine Patris, et Filii, et Spiritus sancti…*"

"He's beginning a Latin Mass," Fr. Jake mouthed silently to himself as the pastor continued the antiphon, also repeating the deacon's response.

"*Introibo ad Altar Dei. Ad Deum qui laetificat juventutem meum.*"

Mora did not continue with the Latin verses of Psalm 42, but climbed the altar stairs to recite a barely audible Penitential Rite in English.

63

Albert Noyer

"I confess to almighty God, and to you my brothers and sisters, that I have sinned through my own fault…"

A few in the congregation leafed through tattered pamphlets, but most knew the words and joined in repeating them with him. Afterward, they recited the *Kyrie Eleison* in Spanish.

"*Señor, ten piedad. Cristo, ten piedad.*"

"*Oremus.*" Mora went to the center of the altar to read the Opening Prayer from the missal in English.

Afterward, Maldonado strode to a scarred wooden lectern for the first readings on the Third Sunday of Easter. The deacon omitted the Responsorial Psalm and went on to the second reading. When he immediately began reading the gospel, the congregation stood to sign their forehead, lips and heart.

No lector from the congregation for the readings, Fr. Jake observed, *and Father Mora didn't bless the deacon before the gospel reading.*

After Maldonado ended the gospel, the congregation mumbled, "Praise to you, Lord Jesus Christ," and sat down for the homily.

The deacon remained at the lectern, frowning. "This priest here today, Father Hakub, says he was sent by Archbishop Benisek to help our Father Mora. I'm gonna let him tell you 'bout that."

As Fr. Jake went to the lectern, church members sat in silent suspicion: rumors had already passed around that the Anglo *Norteño* had come to replace their pastor. He looked over faces that generally were less swarthy than his Mexican workers, yet unmistakably Hispanic. "Thank you, Deacon Maldonado. *Buenas dias*…good morning. I'm Father Casimir Jakubowski, which I know is a mouthful, so 'Father Hakub' will do nicely." He waited for a few chuckles, yet no one even smiled. "I'm pastor at a church of about this size in Michigan. I'm pleased to be in New Mexico, a state I've never visited." Except for an occasional cough, the congregation remained respectful, yet silent. "As your deacon said, I am here to help your pastor, but hope to be of service to all of you. I work with Mexican farm workers in my parish and see this as an opportunity to improve my Spanish, which is, admittedly, *non muy bueno.*"

Armando half-turned to Cynthia and smiled at the priest's gentle criticism of himself. She also did, but no one else among those listening reacted in a friendly way.

Fr. Jake, aware of the suppressed hostility, also sensed a suspicious indifference to anything he still might say. He turned toward Fr. Mora, who

The Ghosts of Glorieta

sat hunched in his chair, eyes down, staring at the floorboards. "And so, I thank your pastor for allowing me this opportunity to serve you."

Mora did not acknowledge his thanks, but roused himself and stood to recite The Profession of Faith, the *Credo*, in Latin. There were no Prayers of the Faithful, nor lay persons to bring up the Offertory communion wafers and wine cruet. While Deacon Maldonado brought the chalice, paten, host, wine and water cruets from the side table to the altar, the well-dressed Anglo man collected paper bills and coins in a wicker basket. No one had Sunday offering envelopes.

Fr. Mora ignored his concelebrant and began the Liturgy of the Eucharist by reciting the Preface in English. When he arrived at the consecration of the bread and wine into Christ's body and blood, he again reverted to Latin.

"*Hoc est enim corpus meum*," he recited over the wafer, then elevated the sacred white disc for the people to see.

After an obviously painful genuflection, he held the chalice of wine in hands that trembled. "*Hic est enim calix Satanus meum ad altare Domini inferni—*"

Fr. Jake immediately realized the words of Transubstantiation were wrong…in fact, blasphemous. *What—?*

Fr. Mora paused a moment. His pasty complexion paled further, then he collapsed onto the floorboards. Close to him, Fr. Jake was able to catch the sick priest under the arms, but the chalice slipped from his hands. Red wine spilled onto the altar cloth. An old woman in a front pew, black lace covering her hair, hurried forward to dip a handkerchief in the Sacred Species.

"*No, abuela*, that wine is not consecrated!" Fr. Jake called to her. "Deacon, help me with Father Mora."

As the priest lay on the floor, trembling in a kind of epileptic fit, those in the congregation who saw what happened stood up. Fr. Jake held Mora's head up off the floor.

Maldonado knelt beside him, stammering, "Wh…what happened… there?"

Fr. Jake shook his head. "I don't know exactly, but call 911. Father suffered some kind of seizure after misusing the Latin words of the consecration. Has this happened before?"

"Coupla times."

"Still, call 911, deacon."

65

Albert Noyer

"No!" he objected, his fists clenched, glowering defiance. "I'll carry Father to his rectory."

Armando was at the altar now, stooping to support Mora's shoulders. "*Si*, deacon, I'll help you. Father Hakub, you just finish Mass."

The priest hesitated. "I'm not sure. This is unusual. It sounds formalistic, yet the people here have fulfilled their Sunday obligation."

"Obligation?" Armando looked at him, puzzled. "Father, they haven't had no communion yet. The *Sacramento*."

"I should stay with Fr. Mora."

"Oh, I don't think so. He…he wouldn't want you inside his rectory."

"Why not?"

At that moment, the man who had collected the offerings came onto the altar platform. "Father Jakubowski, we haven't had a chance to meet. What all went on here?"

"I'm not sure, but this seems to have happened to Father Mora before—"

"Father Hakub," Armando interrupted, "you got consecrated hosts sittin' in the tabernacle. Give people their communion, and talk to Mister Fortgang after that."

"Very well. It's irregular, but ask them to come up after I recite the Lamb of God that precedes communion."

After Mora was carried to his rectory and communion distributed, Fr. Jake gave the traditional final blessing. The congregation left, gathering outside to discuss in anxious voices what had happened to their priest. Raylene Maldonado stripped the wine-soaked cloth off the altar and folded it for washing.

Only the offertory collector waited for the new priest at the front entrance.

"Mister Fortgang, was it?" Fr. Jake asked him.

"G. Duane Fortgang." He extended a hand. "G.D. for short, Father. Welcome."

"Thanks. I saw your *santos* at the restaurant and general store."

"That's a small side-business of mine. Tourists like them."

"I started to ask you if this had happened to Father Mora before."

"Yes, but not this seriously," Fortgang recalled. "I reckon his illness has something to do with it, don't y'all?"

Reckon …Y'all. Fr. Jake asked, "Where are you from, G.D.?"

"Amarillo." He pronounced the English double "ll" and "o" sounds. "I've been here 'bout twenty years."

"You collected the offerings."

"Parish finance officer, and also an attorney and CPA."

"No offense, G.D., perhaps you do things differently here, but this church is… is…well, charitably put, it's in bad shape. There is no Sunday bulletin. The missalettes are two months out of date. No music, English or Spanish. As celebrated now, your Sunday Mass isn't the joyous occasion it's meant to be."

"Admittedly, Maldonado could do a better job," Fortgang agreed. "His wife keeps hounding him about that. As *mayordoma*, poor Raylene does most of the janitorial work around here by herself."

"Then why doesn't Father Mora reprimand or replace him?" After the accountant shrugged uncertainty, Fr. Jake asked, "Again, no offense, but why does the congregation seem to…to almost worship their priest? He is far too ill, physically and, I believe, mentally, to be an effective pastor. Did you understand what he said in Latin at the consecration of the wine?"

"Can't say I did, Father. I was Southern Baptist before converting to Catholicism, the only True Faith."

Just as well that you didn't understand. "Again, may I ask why Father Mora is so well thought of? Armando believes the congregation would canonize him while he's still breathing, no questions asked."

"Father Jake, y'all haven't been here long…" Fortgang shielded his eyes against morning sun with his Stetson, then pointed with it. "Let's go sit on that bench in the shade of the cottonwood."

As he sat, Fr. Jake noticed a framed, wrinkled lithograph of San Isidro hanging on the tree's lower branches. "G.D., why is a picture of the saint up there?"

Fortgang chuckled. "Well, Father, the folks here want Isidro to see how dry it is so that he'll pity them and make it rain. Usually works, too."

"Eventually."

"Sure, eventually. Now, about Father Mora," the accountant continued. "The Mora family did very well here in Providencia. Farming, ranching, obtaining Santa Fe Railroad shipping contracts. I'm saying they made a lot…I mean *a lot* of money." He swept a hand toward the homes around the church. "All this land and all those houses over there, now belong to Father Mora."

"He owns everything?"

"Yep, and the good *padre* allows people to live there free. Pays all their county taxes and even water bills, since the family also put in our community well. 'Course, that doesn't include me. I live in that new Upland Heights community, but most of the villagers here pay nothing."

"That's incredible. I…I've never heard anything like that anywhere, aside from company towns."

"The coal mines up at Mad-rid were run like that."

"I see."

Fortgang thought a moment before asking, "What was it Father Mora said in Latin at the consecration? He's been using that ancient language a lot lately."

"It was a reference to Satan. He substituted the word '*satanus*' for '*sanguinis*'… blood…and made mention of the lord of infernal regions."

The accountant didn't seem surprised. "Surely, Father, as a priest you're aware of Satan's work in trying to subvert the faithful."

"That doesn't bother me as much as why Father Mora could substitute a reference to Satan in a sacred phrase he repeats hundreds of times a year."

"Father just wants to be authentic, what with all's that going on today in parishes today. And y'all know that Latin *was* the language of the apostolic church at Rome."

"Actually," Fr. Jake corrected, "the liturgy was in Greek until the fourth century."

"Oh…" Fortgang flushed and bent down to pretend brushing dust off his boots.

Fr. Jake did not push to find out his spin on what was going on today in parishes. *He and this conservative congregation undoubtedly oppose optional celibacy for priests. Do they even realize that bishops are discussing it, or that over sixty percent of the Catholic laity is in favor?* "Fr. Mora should make an appointment with a doctor at the clinic I saw here."

Fortgang countered, "I think our pastor sees his illness in the same light as Saint Paul did. A tribulation visited upon him by Almighty God."

"Yes, well, don't you think an M.D. should verify your diagnosis?"

"God works—"

"—in mysterious ways," Fr. Jake quickly added, to block the man's cliché. "I suspect He does, yet are we to second-guess God's purposes? I'll advise

The Ghosts of Glorieta

Father to see a doctor tomorrow and I'd appreciate your help in convincing him to do that."

The Texan stood up and gave his Stetson a tug. "Father, I have to go count the collection and get a bank deposit slip ready for tomorrow."

"Of course. Thanks, G.D., for filling me in on some local history."

"Father, Y'all take care," he replied without smiling.

○

Fr. Mora refused to visit a doctor at the Providencia Clinic. He continued to spend his spare time in the sagrario, and asked Fr. Jake to celebrate the 11:00 A.M. Mass, while he took the eight o'clock alone. Most parishioners attended Fr. Mora's service.

On the first Sunday of May, Armando Herrera came to the later Mass and told the Fr. Jake about an upcoming San Isidro festival on May 15. Church members would celebrate their patron saint's day with a fiesta Mass, food booths, *Matachine* dancers, and a morality play whose ancient origins went back beyond anyone's memory. The fiesta was public, but not generally advertised outside of San Isidro itself.

In the coming days, Fr. Jake sketched the church or village houses and jotted down his ideas for improving lay participation in the liturgy. He would recruit a music director and choir, obtain up-to-date missalettes with both English and Spanish responses.

He would try to organize the Faith Formation class that Cynthia requested, and publish a Sunday parish bulletin. The delicate part would be exactly when to present these ideas to Fr. Mora and the congregation: there was no parish council.

Fr. Jake gradually decided that the pastor's slip of the tongue at the Consecration was just that, or that he himself had misunderstood a Latin he had not heard for a long time.

7 san isidro church / may 15

On the morning of the San Isidro fiesta, May sunlight glinted off colorful miter crowns and fringed masks that concealed the faces of twelve *Matachine* dancers. Multi-hued ribbons and silk capes, printed or embroidered with the image of the *Virgen de Guadalupe*, swirled at their backs. Dressed in dark suits, the men practiced the graceful processional steps they would perform to enter the church. The dancers waved three-pronged wands across their bodies with one hand, and rattled gourds in the other to keep time with the melody of nearby violin and guitar music.

Church members and curious visitors, who were not praying inside the church, stood on the dancers' flanks, watching them or socializing among themselves. A Socorro County deputy sheriff had parked his patrol car at one end of the plaza, while he directed traffic onto the church grounds. A spicy aroma wafted from booths lined up along one side of the open space. Parish women had prepared chile-laced fiesta foods—*enchiladas, burritos, tamales,* pork stew, and fruit *empañadas* to sell after the church service *Curandera* Ofilia Herrera stood at one booth, hawking packets of her medicinal herbs and bottles of curative oils before Mass.

Fr. Jake, wearing an alb that was too short and a white chasuble that Deacon Maldonado borrowed from another church, waited to concelebrate the fiesta Mass with Fr. Mora. He watched the exotic masked dancers with interest.

Armando Herrera came up to the priest. "You ever seen *Los Matachines*, Father?"

Albert Noyer

"No, tell me something more about the fiesta custom. There's nothing like them in Michigan."

Armando brushed a cotton-like tuft of white from his sleeve, then glanced up at a sky that was as blue as the *Virgen's* mantle. The soft flocks floated down in a light breeze and formed mini-snow drifts at the corners of the church. "Almost looks like *Natividad* don't it, Father? This early spring made the cottonwoods in the *bosque* lose cotton a coupla weeks early." He looked back at the masked dancers. "Well, Father, the *matachines* are at all our fiestas, but nobody really knows why that is. Those wands they carry represent *Santo Trinidad*, the Holy Trinity. That little girl over there dressed in white is *La Malinche. El Monarcha* will lead her into the church for the fiesta Mass. People pin dollar bills on her clothes"

"She's beautiful in her First Communion dress," Fr. Jake remarked.

"Yeah, Father. After Mass, the *bulto*, that wood statue you seen of San Isidro, our patron, is carried in procession to the home of a sick person. Last year it was Rosita, but she died. I don't know to who it is this year that Father Mora will give a blessing. After a fiesta lunch, we'll see a fake battle on the plaza between good and bad. *El Toro* is the evil guy—"

"Where's Father Mora?" Deacon Maldonado interrupted, tapping his watch with a stubby finger. "The procession shoulda started twenty minutes ago. You seen him, Father Hakub?"

"No, we didn't vest together." Fr. Jake noted that the deacon's green stole still bore wine stains; Maldonado had promised to dry-clean the sash for the fiesta.

"He's not at the rectory," he complained. "I looked there."

"Maybe still in the *sagrario?*" Armando suggested. "He spends a lotta time there with Jesús."

"It's worth checking," Fr. Jake said. "Let's go around and find out."

The *Sagrario* was a small chapel that Fr. Mora had built onto the southeast end of his church to display the Blessed Sacrament. Such a separate building was part of many Mexican churches.

Cynthia Plow noticed the three men threading their way around bystanders. "Father Jake, aren't we ready to start?" she called out to the priest.

"We can't find Father Mora," Armando answered for him. "We're gonna look in the *sagrario.*"

Cynthia joined the men in walking around to the right side of the adobe church. They found the chapel door closed.

The Ghosts of Glorieta

Fr. Jake knocked on the wooden panel. "Father Mora, are you inside? Father Mora?"

Maldonado placed an ear against the door. "*Padre*, you all right? It's time for you to start th' fiesta."

After no one answered, Armando said, "Maybe he fell asleep prayin' in there."

"Only one way to find out..." Fr. Jake pushed on a warped door that was un-locked, but sticking at the bottom. As the panel scraped open, a rush of warm, smoke-filled air escaped. He coughed and put up a hand to cover his nose and mouth. "Father must have fifty votive candles burning on the rack—"

The inside of the *sagrario* was thick with choking blue smoke. All candles were alight, flickering wildly in the rush of air from outside. The haze smelled of burning plant leaves, not the familiar paraffin scent from votives. The odor was not as distinctive as marijuana, yet faintly sweet in an unidentifiable way.

Fr. Mora lay sprawled on the tile floor next to an unpadded wooden kneeler. In the smoky interior, the candles cast a dancing light that seemed to animate the priest's frail body.

"Good God!" Fr. Jake gasped. "Deacon, help me pull Father outside. Leave the door open to clear out that smoke."

Coughing from the fumes despite holding handkerchiefs over their faces, the two men dragged the priest's body out through the door by the arms, to the backside of the chapel. It would be out of sight of those attending the fiesta. Fr. Mora's body was stiff, as if paralyzed, yet not enough time had elapsed for rigor to set in.

White cottonwood tufts settled on Fr. Jake's chasuble as he knelt to check for a throat pulse. He looked up, shaking his head. "He...he's dead. Father apparently was asphyxiated by all that smoke."

"What, from candles?" Maldonado protested. "That...that ain't possible."

Cynthia put a headscarf over her nose and went into the small room, then came out with one hand in a closed fist. "The smoke has cleared a little," she said, opening her fingers. "I found a few of these red seeds next to the candles. Others were imbedded in melted wax."

"They look like little red jelly beans," Armando said. "What are they?"

73

Albert Noyer

"Zamia seeds. I have a biology unit where I warn my students about poisonous plants. Despite being extremely toxic in all its parts, this is a popular garden and houseplant. The seeds taste sweet, so dogs will eat them. Most vomit up the residue, yet many of the pets will die."

Fr. Jake stood up for a closer look at the deadly seeds. "You're saying, Cynthia. that someone poisoned Father Mora?"

She shrugged a guess. "Burned, and the smoke inhaled long enough, Zamia seeds probably can be toxic as if somebody ate them."

Deacon Maldonado glanced in at the *sagrario*'s interior. "*Madre de Dios!*" he gasped. "Th' *Sacramento* is gone missing from the monstrance!"

"What?" Fr. Jake saw a rayed, golden reliquary atop the small altar. At the center of the rays, the large, white host was not inside the round compartment of an open glass door. "Why would someone want to steal the Blessed Sacrament and not take a gold monstrance where it's displayed? Makes no sense—"

Maldonado looked from his dead pastor to the *Norteño* priest who had arrived a month earlier. He scowled and placed his squat body in front of Fr. Jake, to poke his chest with a fleshy finger. "You proba'ly was th' last person to see Father Mora. If we got a murder here, Father Hakub, you got a lotta explainin' for the sheriff. I know y' never liked our pastor."

"True, we disagreed on a few outdated liturgical practices, but that… that's ridiculous. Deacon, are you accusing me of killing Father Mora?"

Maldonado took his hand away, shuffled both feet, and glanced down at the sandy ground. "Aw, I only said y' got explainin' to do."

"Father"—Armando's voice interrupted the two men—"I'll get that deputy to quit directin' cars an' come over here. Hilario Griego is on duty."

"We should get EMT paramedics here, too," Fr. Jake said. "Where's the closest station?"

"Half way between here and Belén." Cynthia took a phone from her purse. "I'll call them from my cell."

Maldonado demanded, "Father Hakub, what y' gonna do about the fiesta?"

"Go ask the parishioners, deacon, but Father Mora would have wanted it to go on."

"I'm gonna put out those votives first…" Maldonado stepped around Fr. Mora's body and went inside the chapel to begin extinguishing candles with a bell snuffer.

The Ghosts of Glorieta

He had finished when Armando came back with the deputy sheriff. Griego looked about forty years old and well built. A drooping moustache followed the curve of his upper lip, and his fresh haircut perhaps honored the fiesta.

Armando introduced him to Fr. Jake. "Hilario, this is Father Hakub, the new priest that came from up north."

"Father…" The deputy removed his right glove to shake hands. "Armando told me some of what happened here. The victim's…Father Mora's…body still inside?"

"No, we moved it…him…outside, away from the fumes. I checked his pulse—"

Griego frowned and wagged an index finger. "Father, that wasn't smart. We wouldn't want nothin' here disturbed."

Cynthia put away her cell phone and picked seeds out of her coin purse to show Griego. "Deputy, Father Mora was poisoned by smoke from these Zamia seeds. I found them in the wax and others were around the votive candles."

"That a fact? You go in that room, Miss?"

"Yes. I…I mean that's where we found Father lying on the floor. The deacon put out the candles and propped the door open—"

"Jesus, Miss!" Griego interrupted impatiently. "Don't none of you watch CSI shows on TV? First thing you don't do is compromise a possible crime scene by messin' around with it."

Fr. Jake said nothing, but Cynthia defended herself, "I…I wanted to see if I could find a reason for why Father Mora died."

"Well, now Miss, that weren't too bright of you, since you probably also left fingerprints in the candle wax. Aren't you a teacher at Excelencia Elementary?"

"Yes, fifth grade. I…I called EMT right away. They should be here any minute."

Griego turned from her to squint at Fr. Jake. "You did mess with the body, right Father?"

"I checked Father Mora's throat pulse to ascertain if he was dead."

"You didn't turn him over or nothin'?"

"No, the deacon and I just pulled him outside."

"Jesus, Father…"Griego scratched his head, frustrated by all the ineptitude. "And he was face down in the chapel?"

75

Albert Noyer

"Pretty much sprawled on the floor."

A siren from an approaching ambulance sounded in the distance. Deputy Griego went to inspect the priest's body. He looked at the ground in front of the *sagrario* door, then went inside the chapel.

Deacon Maldonado came in after him. "Sheriff, the host's been stolen from the monstrance."

Still annoyed, Griego ordered brusquely, "Sir, step back outside."

Maldonado took a step toward the altar. "See, the monstrance door is open."

"Sir, I said step outside. I'm treatin' this as a crime scene."

"That's what I'm tellin' *you*, a blasphemous crime. The sacred host—"

The EMT vehicle screeched to a halt alongside the church, drowning out the deacon's protest. By now, curious parishioners and several fiesta dancers came to watch; people had noticed the deputy leave his post on the highway and hurry toward the church.

Griego escorted Maldonado outside and came to talk to a man and woman EMT paramedics about the death scene.

Maldonado asked again, "Father Hakub, what ya goin' to do about the fiesta Mass? Food? Our afternoon *Ensaye*, the morality play?"

"What would you suggest, deacon?"

"People saw the EMT truck come, so I'll just go tell 'em Father got sicker an' we'll go on with Mass. Good idea?"

"I'd tell them that Father Mora died suddenly, but that the fiesta should continue. Your pastor would want it that way and can watch from heaven. Good idea?"

Maldonado glowered at being contradicted, but stalked off to tell the onlookers.

Deputy Griego left the paramedic attendants to their work and called Fr. Jake aside. "I'll have to take prelim statements from everyone, Father, but this is a first degree felony crime, so a medical examiner and detective will come out to investigate. Mind if I start with you?"

"Please."

"*Bueno*. You got a sheet you can put over the victim? I'll radio in for the M.E. and detective, then bring barricade tape an' my report forms. You go sit on that bench by the cottonwood."

When he returned, Raylene Maldonado had put a spare altar cloth over Fr. Mora's body. The deputy fastened yellow crime scene tape around the *sagrario*, then came to sit next to the priest. He filled in his own name on the report, mumbling, "Hilario Griego."

"Deputy, the name 'Hilario' had to come from a relative," Fr. Jake remarked.

"*Mi abuelo*...grandfather," he answered without looking up. "I get razzed about it."

"There's a Hilarion and Hilary of Arles," the priest recalled, "but neither saint is that well known. Hilary's feast is October twenty-first."

"Yeah, my birthday too..." Griego paused with his pen above the next entry line. "Look, Father, no offense, I was raised Cath'lic but don't go to church. The wife does, but I tell her, 'Miranda, every day I see crime...perps' doin' robberies, rapes. *Viejos* gettin' assaulted.' There were...I dunno... umpteen murders in the county last year. I ask her, 'Miranda where is God in all this? Sittin' on his throne twiddlin' his holy thumbs?'"

"A colorful metaphor," Fr. Jake conceded, "if not quite from the Book of Revelation. Should you want to, we could talk about that sometime."

"To reconvert me?" Griego scoffed. He pointed his pen toward the *matachines*. "Hell, Father, any one of those Cath'lic masked hombres over there could be responsible for this murder."

"We don't know for sure that Fr. Mora *was* murdered, do we? He may have thought he was sprinkling incense on those candle flames."

"If he did, then somebody musta put poison seeds in the incense can, no?"

"*Bueno*," Fr. Jake conceded. "Excellent point, Deputy."

Griego continued, "If you're going on with the fiesta, I'll take your statement first and that deacon's next."

"I appreciate that."

"Don't mention it, Father..." The deputy's pen hovered above the next line. "Uh, spell your first and last names real slow."

○

The fiesta Mass necessarily was subdued, the congregation in shock at the news of their pastor's death. A few oldsters denied the truth of it. That an unfamiliar Anglo priest they barely knew conducted the familiar service added to their distress. There was no procession of the Saint Isidro statue to an ill person's home. Church members bought and ate their fiesta food in silence.

Albert Noyer

The *Ensaye*, an ancient morality play symbolizing the struggle of good and evil, was performed without the usual good-natured horseplay. While *El Toro*, the personification of evil, tried to subvert little *Malinche*'s purity and goodness, a Socorro assistant medical examiner crouched a hundred yards away, taking photographs, and finishing paperwork for the transfer of Fr. Mora's body to the morgue for an autopsy.

After the fiesta participants left, Fr. Jake was untying the cord of his alb in the vesting room, when he heard his name called.

"Father Casimir Jakubowski?"

"Yes…" He turned to see a slim Hispanic woman with lustrous, green eyes and a clear olive complexion at the curtain. She had dressed in dark slacks and a leather jacket. Her jet-black hair was neatly tucked under an oversized cap.

She held up a leather case with police identification. "Detective Sonia Mora. I need to question you about the murder of my uncle, Father Jesús Mora."

8

"Father Jakubowski, I've read deputy Griego's report," Sonia Mora told him. "Could we go into the *sagrario* chapel, where he presumes the alleged crime took place?"

"Presumes? We...we found Father Mora lying dead on the floor inside."

"Shall we go there?" she repeated. No hint of emotion clouded her professional voice.

"Of course." *Does she think her uncle might have been killed elsewhere?*

From a distance, the bright-yellow police tape that surrounded the chapel might have been mistaken for fiesta day decorations. The M.E. had ordered Fr. Mora's body removed; only four blue plastic flags on a wire stuck in the dirt marked the position where it had lain.

"Those are my markers," Sonia explained. "The M.E. took photographs of the body's actual position." She looked toward the chapel entrance. "You and"—she flipped a page of the report—"you and Deacon Maldonado pulled the victim's body outside?"

"That's correct. Miss...is it?"

"'Detective' will do. We'll go inside in a moment, but don't touch anything. Deputy Griego writes that the female teacher took away plant seeds. The deacon used a snuffer to extinguish the votives."

"They were trying to help."

Albert Noyer

"Father Jakubowski, that excuse did not convince the deputy, nor does it hold much water with me."

"You think they both were trying to cover up a crime? Detective."

"I think I should draw my own conclusions and your answers to my questions may help. Where were you before finding my uncle's"—Sonia caught herself—"finding the victim's body?"

Fr. Jake pointed to the papers in her hand. "Isn't that in the deputy's report?"

"Father…."

He flushed at her tone of reprimand. "Sorry. Of course, you want *me* to answer. I came to the church early, but didn't see Father Mora. There was only the borrowed chasuble hanging in the vesting area, so I figured he had already put his on for Mass."

"And after you vested?"

"I looked inside the church for Father. It was beautiful. In fact, I was pleasantly surprised at just how nice it looked. Flower arrangements in front of the altar…. blossoms and paper decorations around the statue of San Isidro."

Sonia remarked dryly, "Father Jakubowski, I thought you realized that Latinos take their saints seriously. Anyone see you in the church?"

"Some ladies and a man or two were saying rosaries or praying to San Isidro. Oh, Duane Fortgang, a parishioner, knelt in a rear pew. I've noticed that he usually prays there before Mass."

"He was in place before you entered?"

"Yes."

"Alone?"

"By himself. Duane is the parish finance officer."

"Would you happen to know the names of those ladies and men?"

"No, they probably attend their pastor's early Masses, not mine. People here haven't quite opened up to me yet."

Sonia finished jotting down what the priest had said in a spiral note pad, then tucked it into a jacket pocket. "Father Jakubowski, follow me into the *sagrario*, but don't touch anything."

"Detective, I'm called Father Jake in Michigan and Father Hakub, here. Either is less of a tongue twister."

Sonia nodded acknowledgement without smiling. "My crime investigation kit is in the car, so we'll just look around a bit, then come

The Ghosts of Glorieta

back here and bag evidence. I need more of those poison seeds the teacher mentioned."

The chapel still smelled faintly of toxic fumes. Sonia glanced around, then went over to examine the votive stand. "Seeds are imbedded in the wax. There's the metal candle snuffer, probably contaminated with the deacon's fingerprints and useless as evidence. The glass on that open monstrance *might* have latent prints…" She pointed to another entrance. "That far door leads to the church, correct?"

"Yes, Father Mora came from there when I first met him almost a month ago."

"So anyone could enter the chapel from inside the church."

"Correct."

Sonia took out her pad again and wrote down the information. "I'll come back. Let's go to the rectory now, see what we can find there."

"Won't you need a warrant to get in?"

"Warrant?" she scoffed. "Father, you've been watching too much CSI. Besides, I'm family and now the last member of the Socorro Moras."

"You did say that you were the priest's niece."

"That's right. We weren't close…nobody was to my uncle…but I asked to be assigned this case." She pulled her car keys from a jacket pocket. "Let me get my C. I. kit."

Sonia opened the trunk of a red, mud-spattered, 2005 Plymouth Neon and lifted out an executive-size briefcase. "I have a monster Universal 101 kit, but it's got shit in it that you'd only need for another 9/11. That sucker weighs twenty pounds, so I made up this smaller case."

Sonia just lapsed into macho male detective talk. It must be a hard job for a woman detective—

"Father…" Her voice jarred him out of thought. "Father, I'd like you to go in the rectory with me and explain any priest stuff I might find and not understand. Put on these latex gloves."

"Priest stuff? Of course, detective."

The rectory, an adobe house somewhat larger than Fr. Jake's, was about seventy-five feet from the south side of the church.

Sonia snapped on her gloves and tried the worn knob of a blue-painted front door; it was unlocked. The living room was dim, with shades drawn over the only two windows. Yellowed bed sheets covered minimal furniture: a couch, armchair, and coffee table. A floor lamp, with its shade askew, stood next to the chair. Outdated copies of *Our Sunday Messenger* were

81

Albert Noyer

haphazardly stuffed into an old-fashioned magazine floor rack. On one wall, faint light reflected off glass that covered a wrinkled litho print of Christ praying in Gethsemane. The opposite wall had a reproduction of that trick head of Christ, where an accusatory look in his eyes followed you around the room.

Sonia lifted the corner of a bed sheet. "Jeez, this is the same couch, same furnishings his parents…my *abuelos*…had before they died. Ten years ago, I was fifteen, when we came here for my uncle's ordination anniversary. The place already smelled this bad back then." She straightened up and reverted to a professional tone. "Let's take a look in the victim's bedroom."

The room had a scarred ponderosa pine dresser that surely had belonged to the priest's parents. Above it, a tinwork-framed mirror reflected an armchair, floor lamp, and antique oak roll-top desk. A yellowed shade on the single window was drawn down.

"Get some light in here…" Sonia laid her investigation case on the unmade bed and snapped on a wall switch. A 40 watt, three-lamp ceiling chandelier brightened the room enough on the far side of the bed to reveal a wooden kneeler. Evidently, the priest continued his penitential devotions there, in front of a wall crucifix.

The curved front of the roll-top was locked. In rapid succession, Sonia pulled open the center desk drawer and four side drawers. "Anything of value would be secured in top compartments." She went to her kit and selected a lock pick on a five-set jack-knife.

CSI notwithstanding, Fr. Jake wondered about her possible illegal "breaking and entering." *Sonia is family, yet is she doing this by the book?* He watched the detective spring the lock and ease open the roll top.

On the upper right, four vertical compartments had letters inside: a Citibank form letter listing credit card terms; the notice from Santa Fe Archbishop Jan Benisek, informing Mora that a Michigan priest was coming to help him. One compartment held several old religious cards from parishioners congratulating him on past birthdays.

A pale yellow, greeting card-sized envelope stood alone in the last compartment. Sonia slipped a black and white photograph from under a dirty polyester ribbon tied around the envelope's four sides. The dog-eared print showed a young woman wearing a calico dress of the unflattering style favored by splinter-group Mormon wives. She stood in a vegetable garden and smiled as she held up an enormous zucchini. No inscription was on the photo's back, but a girlish scrawl on the envelope read "Father Morea."

"'Father More-a'," Sonia muttered. "Spelled wrong."

The Ghosts of Glorieta

Fr. Jake glanced over her shoulder. "Is that a relative of yours, detective?"

"If so, she can't spell our name correctly. I've never seen the woman."

"Aren't you going to read what's inside the envelope and find out who she is?"

The detective sighed at his naiveté and handed him all the letters. "It's evidence that's tied…sealed, if you will…by a ribbon. Bag these together in a Ziploc…Father Jake. Label them 'Bedroom desk / Rectory', then we'll go back to the *sagrario*. I'll have Griego put crime scene tape up around the adobe."

At the chapel, Fr. Jake looked around while Sonia used tweezers to pick out and bag any remaining zamia seeds. He checked the kneeler from which the priest had evidently fallen. *No knee padding. Fr. Mora probably considered that discomfort as an additional penitential offering to God.* Bending down, he noticed a shard of unpainted wood underneath the kneeling board. "Detective, there's something here we… you've… over-looked."

Sonia came and knelt to retrieve an object she recognized. "Know what this is? It's a quarter-inch-thick piece of wood with a glass jewel in it, broken off a *matachine*'s wand."

"Deputy Griego did mention that any of the masked 'hombres'…his term, detective…could be the murderer."

"Griego watches too many CSI episodes. Still—" Sonia slipped the wood into a plastic bag and patted it with one hand. "This could be an important clue if we could match it to a broken wand. The lab will test it for blood, hair, anything that might suggest Father was struck with one." She glanced around again, while brushing floor dust off her dark slacks. "I'll check the reliquary glass for fingerprints, but first I want to talk to that deacon while his memory is clear."

As they walked to her car, Fr. Jake ventured, "Detective, I know priests in Michigan who avoid greeting parishioners after Mass and seem to want very little contact with their parishioners. You mentioned that your uncle wasn't close, even with relatives. Was he always like that?"

"No…only since about…I dunno, maybe a dozen years," she recalled. "That was when uncle became even more distant, more ascetic-like. He wasn't fun to be around."

"Detective, I've been here four weeks and Father hadn't spoken a dozen words to me that didn't directly deal with Mass. This…this social phobia of his may indicate a serious psychological condition called social anxiety disorder."

83

Albert Noyer

"To late to worry about that, we have to identify the psycho who murdered him."

At the car, Sonia consulted her note pad, then looked across the street at a row of adobe houses. "Maldonado and…Raylene…his wife. They live over there?"

Fr. Jake pointed to his own residence and swung his hand to the right. "The third place on the right from mine."

Sonia took out her ID wallet. "Here's my card, so call me anytime you need to." She tucked away her pad and almost smiled. "Father Jake, you're different from most priests I've met."

"Different? How so?"

"Not stuffy. You don't talk in what my dad called an 'S.G.V.'"

"S.G.V.?"

"'Stained Glass Voice'."

He laughed. "I'll take that as a compliment."

"Do." She adjusted her Baker-Boy cap to leave. "Father Jake, you may call me Sonia, but *only* when those macho-ass deputies aren't around."

9

Detective Mora was able to expedite the medical examiner's autopsy report of her uncle's death. A deep, narrow laceration on the back of his skull led the M.E. to conclude that Fr. Mora had been struck from behind by a vicious blow that rendered the priest unconscious. Toxic zamia fumes quickly suffocated and paralyzed him.

Not to compromise their investigation, the sheriff's department withheld details of the murder, including the shard of wood from a *matachine's* wand, the poisoning itself, and the missing communion host from the monstrance. Reporters from the *Socorro News*, who check the County Sheriff's Blotter each day for articles of interest, found only a brief report.

Providencia, New Mexico – May 15. At 10:20 A.M. the body of Fr. Jesus Mora was discovered in a side chapel at San Isidro Church. Details about the cause of death are being withheld pending autopsy results.

O

With the release of Fr. Mora's body to a Belén funeral home, the priest's burial Mass was scheduled in San Isidro for 10:00 A.M. on Saturday, May 22.

That morning, a little more than an hour before ten o'clock, a white Dodge Durango 4 x 4 Limited pulled up in front of Fr. Jake's adobe. Stenciled on the van's door, one panel of a split coat of arms bore the Franciscan-inspired emblem of the Diocese of Santa Fe; the other panel had the

Albert Noyer

red-checkered, white eagle arms of Archbishop Jan Benisek. A curved banner underneath the crest proclaimed,

Be Steadfast.

Two men wearing black clergy suits and Roman collars stepped out of the Durango. The younger looking, dark-haired priest carried a manila folder. A gold chain glinted under the older man's suit jacket.

At a rap on his front door, Fr. Jake came to open the portal.

The younger priest checked the name on his folder. "Father Casimir Jaku… Jakubowski?"

"Yes, Father—?"

"I'm Father Ramón Gutierrez, secretary to Archbishop Jan Benisek." He turned and nodded to the prelate standing behind him.

Archbishop Benisek came forward, smiling as he extended a hand. "I'm delighted that we finally meet, Father Casimir. Archbishop Stan spoke so highly of you."

"You…Your Excellency." Fr. Jake stammered. "I didn't expect this visit."

"Father, just 'Bishop' is fine. May Father Ramón and I come in?"

"Please…" He stepped aside and gestured toward a corner of the room near a window. "Take that armchair, Bishop. Father Ramón and I can sit on the couch. I could offer you coffee."

"We're good." Benisek settled back in an old armchair that he felt might not be in too antiseptic a condition.

"Fine. I'll just go turn off my coffeemaker."

The archbishop and his secretary looked around the small room and its resale shop furnishings, then glanced at each other without commenting. Fr. Jake returned from the kitchen and sat next to Father Ramón.

The archbishop smiled in remarking, "Charming old adobe, you have here, Father."

"A hundred years old, I'm told," he replied, realizing that tact was one of the unlisted virtues a prelate should have in abundance.

Archbishop Benisek unbuttoned his suit coat jacket and leaned forward. "Father Casimir, we were saddened to learn from Mister Fortgang about Father Mora's tragic death."

"Yes, Duane told me he would inform you." Fr. Jake checked his watch. "Bishop, the funeral is in about an hour."

The Ghosts of Glorieta

"I know. Father, may I officiate? I'm scheduled to celebrate a Four P.M. jubilee Mass with Father Mingh at Immaculate Conception in La Fonda, but thought I would come here early. Well, it...it's the least I can do for Father Mora."

"Of course, the parishioners will be honored." *Clerical rank aside that tanned Slavik face, ready smile, and tousled boyish hair should make him an instant hit.*

Fr. Jake was about to ask if Duane Fortgang had told the prelate about the cause of death, when the archbishop reached for the manila folder that his secretary leaned across to hand him.

"Father Casimir, there's another rather unhappy matter I came to discuss with you personally." Benisek opened the folder and leafed through sheets stapled onto the back cover. "Mister Fortgang gave me this report on San Isidro's finances. Not good at all. I pretty much had decided to close this parish long ago, yet...well...out of deference to Father Mora, I kept it open. Now...." The archbishop's voice trailed off without completing the sentence, but his meaning was clear.

Fr. Jake thought that Benisek had arrived at the near side of admitting that the pastor's death was "providential," and then realized what a horrifying pun that would be on the village's name. "So, Bishop, will you close the church now?"

"Sad, Father Casimir, and yet your congregation could be absorbed by any of two nearby parishes."

"And"—Fr. Jake held back from putting a persuasive hand on Benisek's shoulder —"I can go back to Michigan?"

The archbishop hedged, "I *have* received anonymous letters criticizing you, but, of course, I discount them."

"May I know what they say? I mean, just to correct my failures?"

"People with too much free time..." Benisek closed the folder, kept it on his lap, and deftly changed the subject. "You're from Poland, Father Casimir?"

"Yes, Kráków."

"You Poles soon may have another saint, with JP II's beatification."

"Pope John Paul." *The bishop seems to have relaxed after telling me the bad news, or he's putting off an answer to my question about returning to Michigan.* Fr. Jake probed, "I understand that you met Archbishop Sredzinski at a conference?"

"Yes. My parents were Moravian immigrants so, in a sense, we're fellow Slavs. Well, like you are, Father. In addition, Stan and I shared like philosophies. Of course, we still had some disagreements. I'm in favor of greater collegiality, letting bishop's councils form a more viable direction that the Church should take."

"Rather than from the top down, you mean? The top being the pope."

Benisek nodded agreement and chuckled softly. "Basically, I was a Colorado ski bum before I heard the Holy Spirit's call. That was at St. Joseph's High School in Colorado Springs. They...the Holy Spirit, that is...directed me to a seminary in Denver. Once I realized my vocation, there was no stopping me." He laughed in self-appreciation this time, and pointed to the crest on the Durango. "After all, the Benisek family motto is 'Be Steadfast'."

Fr. Jake barely held in a smile. "And here you are, Bishop of Santa Fe."

"Yes..." He pushed up a suit cuff to check the time on his Patek Philippe watch. "Gift of a parishioner," he murmured defensively. "Where do I vest, Father?"

"You haven't been here before, Bishop?"

"No, I...I'm afraid not."

"Vest behind the curtain on the right, inside the church entrance. I'll have Deacon Maldonado help you."

"Maldonado?" He looked toward Fr. Ramón, who shrugged ignorance of the name. "A deacon here, you say? Strange that Father Mora never mentioned him."

Fr. Jake opened his two hands in puzzlement. "I just presumed he had been deacon here forever."

"Father Ramón, check in the deaconate ordination file." After the secretary wrote a note on a yellow post-it pad, Benisek stood up and added as a kind of afterthought, "Oh, and, Father Casimir. Archbishop Stan asks that you remain at San Isidro for the present time."

○

Fr. Mora's funeral went as planned, except that the archbishop's unexpected presence excited both the parishioners' curiosity and their faith, perhaps in that order. They had no inkling that, like a worn-out Chimayó rug, their church would soon be pulled out from under them.

The Ghosts of Glorieta

As the priest's only surviving relative—his brother's daughter— Sonia Mora sat in a front pew. As usual, Duane Fortgang was alone at the back of the church. Armando, Ofilia, Cynthia, and other parishioners filed into the benches where they usually sat on Sunday.

During Archbishop Benisek's brief eulogy, Fr. Jake decided he would confront Fortgang after the funeral. He was pastor *pro tem* now and needed to find out what the financial officer knew about the parish's finances and future. There had to be a way of keeping San Isidro open.

Six men from the congregation, including Fortgang, carried Fr. Mora's pinewood casket in a procession from the church to the *camposanto*. The weed-overgrown "holy field," was a triangular-shaped burial ground located to the east of the church. The oldest markers from the late 1800's were of cast concrete, with names and dates of birth and death crudely scratched on in Spanish. Even newer gravestones and crosses had tilted at various angles: family members died or moved away, neglecting the upkeep of their ancestors' burial sites. Weathered stakes built to protect graves had gaps where souvenir hunters wrenched off wooden pickets from the fencing. Reddish dust covered most decorations made of faded artificial flowers set in front of marker stones.

Mora family headstones were the most prominent, yet also the most neglected. Surviving relatives normally redecorated graves on Memorial Day and All Saint's Day, but Sonia Mora lived in Socorro and only Father Mora from the Providencia branch of the family had been alive to maintain them.

Cynthia Plow noticed Armando kneel down to place new artificial flowers in front on his parent's joint grave marker. "About two years ago," she whispered to Fr. Jake, "Armand's mother and father were killed by a drunk driver coming the wrong way on I-25, the freeway."

"How tragic. He lives alone, then?"

"Yes, in an apartment above his auto repair shop, behind the trading post." She looked at her watch, then pointed across a road to the far end of an adjoining field. "Father, the bishop isn't quite ready yet, so we still have a little time. I'd like to show you where I'm digging. I marked the place with excavation flags and I'm sure that's where Civil War soldiers are buried."

"What makes you think so?"

"Come on." As they walked to the site, Cynthia explained, "The location of Fort Providence itself was discovered when contractors dug footings for my elementary school. I've followed the adobe wall foundations around to maybe a thousand square feet. The camp wasn't very large, probably only

Albert Noyer

a post for processing volunteers and then closed a few years after the Civil War ended. The dead would be buried outside the camp's perimeter."

"I'd like to learn more about what happened in New Mexico during the War Between the States. I didn't even realize there had been battles here."

"At the end of May school will be out for the summer," she said. "I'll only teach two morning classes, so I'll have time to dig. Come on by, Father. I have books that will enlighten you about the culminating battle at Glorieta Pass and all the events that led up to it."

"Fine, I'd like that, and perhaps dirty my fingernails a bit with a trowel." Fr. Jake held out his hands. "You know, I did have a small garden in Michigan."

Cynthia laughed. "Then you'd be a big help."

At the site of her dig, blue plastic tarpaulins covered a square excavation measuring about ten by ten feet. Glancing around, Fr. Jake noticed a worn trail coming down from the forest. "What is that path leading to your school?"

"Some of the Pentecostal kids attend. They walk down from the commune. Well, everyone calls Eden West a commune." Cynthia thought a moment. "Father, when we first met I said that I'd like to teach a children's Faith Formation class. If you stay here at San Isidro, could you set one up?"

"Why don't you have those classes now?"

"Father Mora didn't want them. Here, let me show you the dig." Cynthia had bent to pull aside a section of tarpaulin, when she noticed a hand signal from Armando at the cemetery. "I guess you'll have to see this later, Father. We need to go back."

At the open grave, Archbishop Benisek borrowed Fr. Jake's Daily Roman Missal and read a prayer from the funeral Mass for a priest.

"'Lord, you gave Jesús Mora, your servant and priest the privilege of a holy ministry in this world. May he rejoice forever in the glory of your kingdom. We ask this through Jesus Christ…'"

Seated at graveside, facing the highway, Detective Mora watched for suspicious mourners—persons standing far in the back or uncomfortably self-conscious at being present. Discovery of the shard of *matachine* wand was kept secret by the sheriff's department; if the murderer *was* one of the masked dancers and noticed his broken trident, he might return to search the chapel for the missing wood.

The Ghosts of Glorieta

Fr. Jake noticed a glint of reflected light up among the forest trees. *The Pentecostals are watching through binoculars. I'm surprised that at the very least Elder Jeremiah didn't send young Caleb to attend the burial of a fellow cleric.*

After the prayer, Archbishop Benisek threw the first clod of earth onto the wooden casket, then glanced at his watch and nodded to Fr. Ramón.

Fr. Jake noticed him. "Archbishop, Armando told me that Duane Fortgang owns Mamacita's restaurant. He had his cook prepare a private lunch for parishioners. We'd be pleased to have you and Father Ramón join us."

"Very kind. Very kind, indeed," Benisek refused with diplomatic courtesy, "but Father Mingh is expecting us in La Fonda. Still a ways to drive, I'm afraid."

"I understand, Bishop. I'll walk you to your car."

As Fr. Ramón held the Durango's passenger door open for the archbishop, Benisek paused. "I meant to mention this, Father. Mr. Fortgang informed me that he had found a buyer for the church property."

"Already? Who...who is it?"

He made a helpless gesture with both hands. "Don't know. The church actually belongs to Father Mora, not the archdiocese. We lease it for a dollar a year. I suppose that like all real estate deals the devil will be in the details."

"We'll find that out, won't we, Bishop?" Fr. Jake felt an unexpected sense of disappointment at news of San Isidro's sale. Despite the parishioners' continuing distance, he felt he would eventually fit in. Sredzinski said he would have a year to do so.

Archbishop Jan Benisek signed a cross over the priest..."God bless you and keep you, Father Casimir."

"Good-bye, Excellency. *Hasta,* Father Ramón."

The Dodge Durango's tires squealed as the archbishop's secretary gunned the SUV toward the highway.

○

At Mamacita's, Sonia sat at a table with Fr. Jake, Armando, and Cynthia. They saved a place for Duane Fortgang, who was making sure all went well in the kitchen. Deacon Maldonado was at the longest table with his wife, talking to his parishioner friends. Raylene looked bored, as if she wished to be elsewhere.

Albert Noyer

Sonia took a sip of ice water, then said, "Now that the funeral is over, I need to talk about Father Mora's death. Reporters from the *Socorro papers*, *Valencia County Herald*, and *Albuquerque Journal* have been hounding me for details. The *News* plans to write a feature story on the history of the Mora family as an expanded obituary."

Armando recalled, "The obit only said that Father died suddenly."

"Right, and I don't want specific information revealed yet. More than one criminal has tripped over details while being interrogated about an alleged crime."

"Detective," Cynthia asked, "have you come up with a motive yet?"

"That's a question I thought you might help answer. Before Father Jake came, you saw my uncle at least once a week. You would know about what's going on in this parish."

"He didn't have enemies," Armando interposed. "Father Mora never hurt nobody."

A server came by with plates of *enchiladas*, *sopaipillas*, and smaller dishes of red and green chile. On this somber occasion, no one brought up the perennial New Mexican joke about which color condiment to choose.

"Father Jake," Cynthia requested, "give us a blessing before we eat."

The priest crossed himself with the others and began quietly, "Bless us O, Lord, and these your gifts…"

Fortgang came up and continued in a loud voice, "…Which we are about to receive from Thy bounty, through Christ, our Lord." After all repeated the Amen, he said, "Hope you didn't mind, Father. Food looks okay?"

"Fine, Duane. It's very generous of you to host this meal."

"Least I can do. Father Mora and I got along very well." He wiped steam from his glasses and turned to Sonia, "I'll miss him, Detective. Is anything new on the investigation?"

"Sir, not that I can reveal."

Armando pulled out the vacant chair. "We saved your place, Mister Fortgang and was just talkin' about motives."

He sat down and signaled to the server. "Yes, motives. Yes. Why would anyone want to murder a…a saint? You have any ideas about that, Father Jake?"

"Well, I could list the seven classic sins in more modern terms. Anger, greediness, being jealous. There's overeating or drinking and I guess 'lust' is still plain lust. Then there's pride and laziness."

The Ghosts of Glorieta

Armando grinned. "I bet you heard 'em all and more in confession, eh, Father Hakub?"

"People don't generally admit to pride, greed, gluttony or sloth, in or out of the confessional."

"People, let's get back on track, shall we?" Sonia suggested in an impatient tone. "In this case, 'anger' is the only motive I would consider. Was anyone you know mad at Father Mora?"

The group members looked at each other, then shook their heads at her question.

After a pause when his food arrived, Fortgang vocalized the consensus. "Anger? Of course not, detective, the man was a living saint."

"Robbery?" Cynthia ventured. "A sacred host *was* stolen from the monstrance."

"And not the gold monstrance?" Sonia sighed and pushed her plate aside. "Get real, everyone. Any Catholic here could get a communion host from any Sunday Mass and take it home."

"It would be a smaller one."

Sonia asked, "Even so, Cynthia, what would anyone want with a communion host that would make them kill Father Mora for it?"

Father Jake recalled the first Mass, where the priest inexplicably had blurted out the name of Satan before collapsing. "I don't really think this is the reason Father Mora was killed," he said, "but at a Black Mass a consecrated host is used in a sacrilegious parody of the Eucharistic ritual. One was missing from the Monstrance."

"Those damned Eden West hippies!" Fortgang exclaimed. "I wouldn't put it past them to be carrying out satanic rites up there in the woods."

"Look folks, our food is gettin' cold," Armando said. "Father Hakub, have you had sopaipillas before?"

He picked up one of the puffy fried breads. "No, can't say I have."

The mechanic demonstrated with a squeeze jar. "You put honey on it like this, an' eat it with your enchilada. It's not dessert, though."

Sonia watched him and then cut back into her *enchilada*. She ate a piece before asking, "Cynthia, where would someone get zamia seeds?"

The teacher finished swallowing a forkful of rice. "Zamia is a houseplant usually bought at garden shops. I don't know of anyone who would grow one from seeds."

"Ofilia might have zamia plants," Armando volunteered.

93

Sonia put down her knife. "Ofilia?"

"*Mi tia.* She's a *curandera* an' has a house-full of herbs."

The detective took out her notepad. "Where does your aunt live?"

"Up this side of the forest. She has an adobe my uncle built for her, an' a big shed for drying herbs."

Sonia wrote a moment, then said, "I need you to take me there, Armando. Father Jake, I'd like you to come with us. Having a priest along can't hurt. Father?" Sonia repeated more loudly.

Her voice startled him out of thought. "Sorry, detective, I was thinking of that missing host. What did you ask?"

"Will you come with Armando and me to his *curandera* aunt's place?"

"Of course." He squeezed honey onto his last torn-off piece of sopaipilla and tried to rationalize what he had been thinking. *Satan and a Black Mass? Father Mora did babble something about "the lord of the infernal regions," when he mangled that Latin. No. It's impossible that he could have been involved in a rite that honors the devil.*

After finishing his meal and again thanking Fortgang, Fr. Jake got up to walk with Sonia and Armando to his aunt's house. Raylene Maldonado had been watching him. Now she left her table and hurried over to the priest.

The woman glanced at the others, then whispered, "Father, come outside with me in private for a minute."

"Certainly, Raylene. Excuse me, detective."

Sonia nodded. "Armando and I will wait for you here."

Outside, Fr. Jake noticed a bruise on Raylene's cheek that she tried to cover with one hand. Her eyes were dark-circled, as if she were not sleeping well.

"Father, I…I need to talk with you," she confided nervously, "but I don't know should I do it in confession or make a rectory appointment?"

"Whatever you're comfortable with, Raylene. I haven't heard any confessions yet."

"It…" She hesitated as if wondering how much to say. "It's about something private."

"Just let me know when you want to meet."

"Thanks, Father." She looked through the restaurant window at her husband. "I…I gotta get back to Donny now."

Sonia and Armando came outside after Raylene went back in the restaurant. The three took a path that led from the end of the Calle San

The Ghosts of Glorieta

Isidro up a fair distance to Ofilia Herrera's house. In front were garden plots, where she grew herbs not found in local pastures or woodlands.

The *curandera* sat bagging dried plants at a table on her front porch, when her nephew came up the path with the priest and a woman. "Armando!" she beamed. "*Que Bueno! Finalmente tu tiene un novia. Buenas tardes, señorita.*"

"*Tia!*" he protested, "this isn't my sweetheart. Sonia Mora is a detective investigatin' Father Mora's death. Speak English to her."

"*Si.*" Ofilia asked in a disappointed tone, "How are you today, detective?"

"*Señora,* I would like to look at your herbs. Whatever you have in packets."

Ofilia eyed her up and down. "Where you hurt? Female thing maybe? I have for that—"

"I'm fine," Sonia interrupted, suppressing a smile. "Where do you keep your curatives?"

"Come inside, detective." Inside a small alcove off her living room, Ofilia had a 3' x 3' masonite pegboard that displayed twenty-four plastic bags containing various herbs. "I have *Alcanfor, Rosa de Castilla, Altamisa.* Here, *Yerbabuena.* You no tell me problem, detective. What you look for?"

"Zamia seeds."

"*Madre de Dios! Porque? Muy mal...muy mal.*"

"Yes, I know they're bad," Sonia agreed with her, "but do you have any? Has anyone come here to buy some from you?"

"*Porque* buy? Anyone can grow *zamia furfuracaea* plant."

Sonia persisted, "So no one has come here to ask you about buying poisonous seeds?"

"Detective, you old-fashion like my *abuela* was. Look..." The *curandera* pointed to a computer on a side desk. "Use Google. Bing. Find out anything about everything. *Todo.*"

Despite herself, Sonia did smile. "*Gracias,* Ofilia. You've been very helpful."

"*De nada.*" Ofilia turned to Fr. Jake. "You, *padre.* You still itch?"

"My arm is fine, *gracias.*"

"I need to get back to work," Armando said. "Father Hakub, we gotta find you a used car."

"That's what the deacon implied."

95

"I might have somethin'. See ya in church tomorra. G' bye detective."

"Armando, thank you. And I like your aunt." Sonia watched the mechanic half run down the path, then turned to the priest. "Father, I must return to Socorro."

"I'll walk you to your car."

At the Plymouth, Fr. Jake held the door open for her. "Oh, I meant to ask, Sonia. Did you read that letter we found at Father Mora's? The one tied with a ribbon?"

"That's evidence, Father," she replied, her voice suddenly cold. "I can't really discuss it with you."

"Fine." He closed the door and watched her click on the seat belt. "God bless. Have a safe trip back."

All of a sudden my help as a priest that Sonia wanted in the rectory is of no use to her. Fr. Jake walked toward his adobe to prepare a sermon for the next day's Mass. He would inform the congregation that Archbishop Jan Benisek told him he would stay on as interim pastor. What would be their reaction? *No one spoke to me at Mamacita's, not even Maldonado. Just Raylene, and she wanted to discuss a problem in private.*

Sonia's abrupt manner was puzzling. *I'm sure she's read the letter and that it has something to do with her uncle's murder. The archbishop said the church had been sold, yet didn't know to whom. That's one of the "devil's details" I'll still have to face.*

○

The devil, as it turned out, would be a brash Texas filmmaker named Jefferson Davis "Tex" Houston, and in more ways than one.

10 san isidro church / may 23

On Sunday morning, Fr. Jake arose even before the roosters announced the new day. He wanted to go over one last time the sermon he would give his congregation. After brewing coffee, he sat at the kitchen table with three hand-written pages of a legal pad. He would comment on the Second Reading from the Book of Revelation's prediction about the New Jerusalem, then tie that into letting the congregation know that he was their new pastor. Although the passage from Revelation ended with the words, "See, I make all things new!" the priest thought it best to wait longer before passing out the list of changes he had in mind to improve the liturgy and his congregation's participation at Mass. Until he knew more details, he hesitated to tell them that the church was sold. If the building would no longer be a Catholic church, there was no point in doing anything to refurbish the interior.

A knock sounded on the door. Fr. Jake glanced at his watch and put down his ballpoint. *Who would come here at 6:55 in the morning?*

When he opened the door, Armando and Cynthia stood on his front porch. She quickly apologized for both of them.

"Father, hope we're not bothering you. We just thought you might need some moral support before Mass today."

Armando added, "You know, with Father Mora not here an' all."

"¡*Entrad!*" Fr. Jake made a sweeping motion with an arm. "Come in. come in. I can put on more coffee."

97

Albert Noyer

"We're good, Father Hakub," Armando said. "*Gracias*, anyway." He held out a sheaf of pungent smelling dried herbs tied with a red cord. "This is a sage smudge bundle I got from *Tia*. Burn it in a dish an' it's gotta make your house smell better."

"Ah, very thoughtful Armando. *Gracias*."

Cynthia seemed worried. "Sure we're not disturbing you too early, Father?"

"Not at all. I was refining what I'll tell the congregation today. Don't tell anyone, but you're the first to know that the archbishop told me San Isidro has been sold."

"What?" Armando exclaimed in disbelief. "Can…can he do that?"

"He can. The Archdiocese of Detroit is closing churches, and that probably has happened here, too. Archbishop Benisek said there were two other parishes the congregation could attend. I'm not yet ready to inform everyone about the sale, so, as I said keep it under your hats."

"So who's buyin' San Isidro, the Pentecostals?"

"Armando, the archbishop didn't say, but I doubt Elder J. would buy 'the house of idolatry.' Benisek also told me I was to stay here as interim pastor for the present."

"That's great, Father!" Cynthia exclaimed

"Thanks. Even though we may eventually lose the church, I still have ideas to talk about with members. One of the first is that Faith Formation class you wanted."

"That would be super!"

"Armando. I'd wager that you play the guitar?"

"Yeah, I do, Father. I usually perform at Mamacita's on Fridays. A few gigs in Belén—"

"Armand is very good, "Cynthia broke in. "I've heard him play."

"Great. Armando, I'd like you to be San Isidro's music director."

"Me?"

Fr. Jake jested, "*Usted… vous… Sie…* you. Pick your language."

"Well…sure… I guess, Father, but I gotta know what to do." He glanced toward Cynthia.

"That's cool, Armand." she agreed. "Tell him more, Father."

"We'll use Spanish and English in the hymns and parts of the Mass. And, oh, I noticed a bell in the tower, but I've never heard it rung."

The Ghosts of Glorieta

"We call it *Fidelidad*," Armando told him. "The yoke pinions are probably rusted solid. That's why it don't ring."

"'Faithful,' I like that," Fr. Jake remarked, then lightly punched the mechanic's arm. "Surely, Armando, someone who can repair a Lexus could put *Fidelidad* to right."

"Yeah, some of the guys and I could climb up, take a look." Armando's surprise at being asked to participate in the church was tempered by news of its sale. "When did the archbishop say sellin' our church would happen?"

"He didn't..." Fr. Jake glanced at his watch again and went to the window. "I see that Deacon Maldonado and his wife are already outside the church. Armando, your aunt is usually one of the first. Where is Ofilia?"

"*Tia* is probably out lookin' for field plants. She says that, to cure good, they gotta be picked with dew still on the leaves."

"Come on, Armand..." Cynthia eased her friend toward the door by the arm. "Father, we'll let you finish working on your sermon. We just wanted to let you know that we're on your side."

"I hope it doesn't come to choosing sides."

"You know what I mean."

"I suppose I do, Cynthia. *Gracias* and God bless you both."

Fr. Jake penned a few more notations, put the pages inside a manila folder, and took a last gulp of cold coffee. "I've *got* to get a computer with a Word program," he told dregs in the cup.

When he walked to the church's front door, Maldonado and Raylene stood near-by, talking with Duane Fortgang. He nodded toward them and tried to pull the door open by its bronze handle. It was locked. Puzzled, Fr. Jake called to Maldonado. "Deacon, why isn't the church open? Did you lose the key?"

"You're locked out, *Padre*," he said, loping toward him. "A bunch of us wrote a letter to the archbishop, askin' him to send us one of ours."

"Ours? Donny, *I'm* a Catholic."

"Y' know what I mean."

"Actually, I don't."

"Donny," Raylene whined, stroking his arm, "why don't you just let Father say Mass?"

"Shut up!" he snarled and pushed her hand away. "San Isidro is stayin' locked up until we hear from the archbishop about a new *padre*."

Albert Noyer

As they usually did, a few other women parishioners had arrived early to pray the rosary. Fortgang spoke to them quietly about the lockout, then came over to the priest.

"Sorry, Father. I guess the deacon is in charge until he hears from Archbishop Benisek."

"Not really, Duane, I am. Before he left, the archbishop told me that I was to stay on here. That makes me pastor."

Maldonado heard and demanded, "Father Hakub, you got that in writin'?"

"Do you doubt my word?"

"Don't matter." The portly man stepped in front of the door, his eyes defying Fr. Jake to resist. "You're not goin' in."

"Fine, Deacon. I'll just go get my portable Mass kit and we'll have the service outside, under that big cottonwood. Armando, would you help me bring my kitchen table out here as an altar? The people can stand and sit on the ground. There's certainly biblical precedent for that. Come to think of it, today is Pentecost Sunday, when the Apostles went outside and preached to a great crowd about the marvels of God."

Fortgang relented and offered to help. "I'll go with Armando. Father, you just bring the Mass kit."

"Thanks, Duane. There's a clean sheet in the bottom drawer of my dresser. We'll bring that to use as an altar cloth."

A few people Cynthia knew from school arrived. After she spoke to them, most stayed for the outdoor service, yet when Fr. Jake returned, only about a dozen women from the congregation remained. Those who left hurried to tell others about the lockout and near confrontation between the *Norteño* priest and Dionisio Maldonado.

Caleb Parker arrived and waited alongside the church for Fr. Jake to come back. A few of his Pentecostal members stood at a distance, watching him.

"Nice to see you, Brother Caleb." Fr. Jake shook the youth's hand while the table was being prepared for the Eucharistic service.

"Just Caleb, Father, and I shouldn't really call you that. Elder J. quotes the warning of Jesus, 'Call no man Father'."

"How is the Elder…your father?"

"He's fine," Caleb said, then rubbed his eyes, and reversed himself. "No, he's not. Dad seems to get weirder every day."

"How so?"

The Ghosts of Glorieta

"Read the book of Jeremiah. Dad is starting to think that he's been called to save America in a time of crisis, like the prophet tried to do with the kingdom of Judah. I planned on coming to the funeral, but dad forbade me. I wanted to tell you."

"That's appreciated, Caleb. You know, that first morning at Mamacita's, your father seemed particularly annoyed with me."

Caleb laughed, then quoted, "'And I see a boiling caldron, and the face thereof is from the north'."

"That's from the Book of Jeremiah," Fr. Jake recalled.

"Right, and you came from Michigan. Up north."

"What? Jeremiah thinks I've come here as a kind of sinister apocalyptic force?"

"I told you dad was acting weird." Caleb nodded his head toward his companions. "We're going to prepare the Tabernacle for our nine o'clock service."

Fr. Jake recalled that Armand had said the Tabernacle was a storefront church. He noticed that two women with the other man wore long dresses, similar to the girl's in the photo that Sonia Mora had found in the rectory. *Could she have been a member of the Elder's church, who died and was buried there?*

"Gotta run," Caleb said. "You might have guessed that today is big for us."

"Sure. Pentecost equals…'Pentecostals'."

Caleb laughed. "Right. Take care, now, Reverend."

"You, also, son, and my regards to Elder Jeremiah."

At the cottonwood tree, Fr. Jake put on his stole, arranged his chalice, paten, the burse containing hosts, and a Mass booklet on the table. After pulling a bench closer to the makeshift altar, he put the wine and water cruets, a bowl, and towel on the seat. Fortgang lighted two candles.

"Armando," the priest called to him, "you'll be the server."

"I never done that before."

"I'll cue you on what to do." Fr. Jake looked toward Maldonado. "Deacon, I'd be pleased if you assisted me."

When her husband hesitated, Raylene pleaded, "Donny, please do it. Help Father."

"I told ya to shut up!" Maldonado snapped and stalked off toward his house. He stopped ten paces away to glance back and threaten his wife. "Raylene, you *better* be comin' with me if y' know what's good for ya."

101

Albert Noyer

In this situation, Fr. Jake could only deplore the man's threat of abuse, but resolved to counsel him about his marriage at the next opportunity. He turned to face the few worshipers and recite the Mass's opening sign of the cross. "In the name of the Father, and of the Son, and of the Holy Spirit."

Without warning, the loud blare of an automobile horn, playing a tune that approximated, "The Yellow Rose of Texas," drowned out the congregation's response of "Amen."

A bright yellow, 1955 Cadillac Biarritz convertible turned onto Calle de San Isidro from Highway 310, then slowly proceeded toward the church. A set of wide steer horns decorated the front grille. With its outrageous tail fins and horned grille, the Cadillac looked like a Terry Gilliam steer-and-fish composite montage for a Monty Python Flying Circus TV episode.

Standing up on the passenger side, a man in an outlandish white suit raised a cowboy hat in greeting and bowed, while shouting, "Howdy!" "Howdy, there!" "How, y'all?" to a few persons watching on the side street. A white semi-truck crawled behind the Cadillac. The automobile horn again shattered the morning calm with a harsh rendition of "Yellow Rose."

Fr. Jake paused in the service to make sense of the interruption. *Where are the elephants? The other clowns? No, a circus coming to town wouldn't do so at eight o'clock on a Sunday morning.*

"What the hell…" Armando muttered.

Cynthia asked, "Who…what…is that, Father?"

"We'll soon know. Whoever it is will want us as an audience."

"I'll have the sheriff after that ass," Duane Fortgang threatened. "How dare the S.O.B. put on this vulgar show near our church."

The Cadillac slowed to a crawl and stopped at the curb in front of San Isidro. After a final jarring claxon chorus of the song, the cowboy stepped out of the car.

After he saw him—and not amused—Fr. Jake remarked to Cynthia, "Surely that outfit would take first prize in a Bad Taste Costume Hall of Fame contest."

At best a show costume, vermilion and chartreuse swirls embroidered on the white jacket and trousers glittered with hundreds of multicolored sewn-on sequins. The heels of his white cowboy boots were fitted with shock absorbing springs that gave the wearer an additional two inches of height, yet also a bouncy awkwardness while walking.

The man's lean face was handsome, tanned, and shaded by his white cowboy hat. A round yellow campaign-size button pinned on front read,

The Ghosts of Glorieta

"Don't Mess with Tex!" "Tex" was maybe in his forties. A young Hispanic man in a chauffeur's uniform followed a few steps behind, carrying a red rope folder under one arm. The congregation watched with a combination of curiosity and sacrilegious horror at having had their Mass interrupted.

While still ten feet from Fr. Jake, the Texan extended a gloved hand and apologized, "*Padre* Mora, I'm sorry for breakin' up whatever it is y'all doin' here. I got every rev'rince there is for the Almighty—"

An angry Fortgang stepped up to confront the man. "Father Mora is dead, and you've interrupted our Mass."

Affronted at the rebuke, Tex drawled, "Well, now, hold on there, pardner, don't get riled up. I told the Rev'rind I was sorry."

"It's okay, Duane." Fr. Jake put a restraining hand on his shoulder. "I'm Father Jakubowski," he said to the Texan. "Mister Fortgang just told you that Father Mora was dead. What did you want with him? Who are you?"

Tex whipped out a business card from a breast pocket of his glitzy cowpuncher's jacket and handed it to the priest. Fr. Jake read, "Jefferson Davis 'Tex' Houston," aloud at the same time the showman spoke his name.

He grinned and added, "But, Rev'rind, jus' call me 'Tex'."

"Tex," Fr. Jake said, "I recognize the pentagram symbol enclosing a Witch's Sabbath goat on your company logo. What exactly is Pentacle Pix Productions?"

He turned and pointed to the white semi, now pulled up behind the Cadillac. Painted on the side was the same pentagram with 'Pentacle Pix Productions' lettered beneath. "*Padre, "*he boasted, "that's mah rig and comp'ny. Y' all may not know that New-ayvo May-hico is real nice to filmmakers like me." Tex grinned and rubbed his thumb and forefinger together. "Tax breaks…loan advances…lotsa moolah. We're here to make a document'ry of yer charmin' little village and that fort datin' from the War Between the States."

"So, Tex, why the satanic name and symbol?"

"Well, Rev'rind, we don't just make document'ries. Bein' a man of the cloth, y'all may not 'a seen many horror flicks. My tortillas an' salsa come from Teenflix like 'Babes in Boyland,' 'Zombie Rave,' and adult horror films. Well, 'Fright Nite at the Morgue'…'Ninja Aliens'…is two of 'em."

Shlock B films, Fr. Jake decided. "Tex, couldn't you have waited until tomorrow, Monday, to put on your show?"

103

Albert Noyer

"Figured folks'd be workin' then. I wanted 'em to be here when they can look inside my semi."

"What *do* you have in the truck?"

Tex leaned in close to whisper, "Rev'rind, you takin' *Padre* Mora's place now?"

"I am pastor. Don't tell me you're the one who bought San Isidro church?"

Tex hedged an answer. "Kin we go to where y'all live? Before we peek inside the semi, Roberto here brought along somethin' of mine I need to show you. Y'all got a lawyer handy?"

"A lawyer?" Fr. Jake looked toward Duane. "Mister Fortgang?"

He nodded. "I did practice law, but not for quite a while. I do CPA work now."

"Shucks," Tex drawled, "y' won't need to be Attorney General to look over what I brought."

Fr. Jake turned to Armando. "I really didn't get far in the Mass. Could you put a sheet over the table and tell those people that I'll have another service at eleven o'clock."

"Sure, Father. Cynthia can help me."

"Thanks…" He pointed to his house. "Tex, my place is over there. Duane, if you don't mind coming with us?"

"Course not," he agreed. "Be happy to help if I can."

Inside the adobe, Tex looked around at the sparse furnishings, frowned, then grunted, "Rev'rind, you got a table we can sit around?"

"Actually, no, it's out there by the church being used as an altar."

The man's Texan charm blossomed. "*No problemo, Hernando.* Roberto, spread them deeds out on the rug."

"Deeds?" Fr. Jake felt the itch in his arm abruptly return as he watched the Texan's assistant loosen an elastic cord around his maroon envelope and spread documents onto the floor.

"Rev'rind," Tex explained, "maybe y'all didn't hear that *Padre* Mora's family owns this town?"

"Yes, I did know that."

"Well, I was told that he was letting everyone live in their *casitas* for free. Paying their taxes, water bills, you name it. Everything."

Fr. Jake shifted uncomfortably to one leg. "So I understand. Isn't that true, Duane? You were the one who told me."

The Ghosts of Glorieta

He nodded. "A saintly priest, Father Mora. In his will, he probably left everything to folks living in his houses."

Tex pushed back his cowboy hat. "He probably woulda done that, too, 'ceptin' he didn't own none of it anymore."

Fortgang's face reddened. "What do you mean, that Father Mora didn't own Providencia? Where's your proof? What are you getting at?"

An ugly set to Tex's mouth replaced his smile. "Now git down off that high horse, Mister CPA man. Your *Padre* ain't paid any county taxes for years and years. I did want to buy the church from that bishop up in Santy Fay, but"—Tex nudged the documents on the floor with the toe of a dusty boot—but all these are quitclaim deeds that I bought up by paying back taxes on the prop'ity. This whole town belongs to me…smock, frock and spitoon!" He bent to pick up several of the deeds and held them out. "Look for yourselves."

"Hold on," Fr. Jake said as Fortgang reached for the documents. "Tex, that's the worse pretend-Texas accent I've ever heard. You picked that lingo up in a drama class, right?"

Tex's tanning salon complexion flushed to an unhealthy mahogany. After a pause, in which he removed his hat and nervously flicked off imaginary lint, he said, "Okay, Father Jay, I admit that it's all showmanship. But, Rev'rind, them quitclaim deeds on the floor are right enough all the genuine, legal thing!"

The Ghosts of Glorieta

11

"What tipped you off abut me, Father?" Tex asked, patting the hat back on his head and settling in the armchair. As he sat down, his bizarre, stiff costume crackled.

"Back in Michigan, I was in a few college plays," Fr. Jake told him. "I noticed that after you became upset with Mister Fortgang and started talking about the deeds, you totally lost your accent…'smock, frock and spittoon'."

The Texan grinned. "Father, I see you thought that was a pretty good spin on the phrase."

Not amused, Fortgang demanded, "So, Tex, who are you, coming here with such a cock and bull story about owning the village?"

He raised a hand as if under oath. "No, sir, it's God's own truth. The good Father hadn't paid taxes on his properties and so the county put them up for sale."

"There would have been letters of non-payment sent to the rectory," the accountant objected. "Delinquency notices in the *Socorro News* and *Valencia Herald*."

"What can I say?" Tex spread his hands in resignation. "Pentacle Pix has legally bought up all the properties."

Fortgang warned, "The village will fight you on this, tooth and nail!"

"Mister CPA man," Tex drawled, "I don't b'lieve this here village has enuff money fer doin' that."

107

Albert Noyer

"Hold on, everyone," Fr. Jake broke in, "let's drop the threats and sarcasm so we can sort this out in a civil manner. Tex, who is your secretary, or is the young man an assistant?"

When the filmmaker nodded toward him, he stood up. "I'm Roberto Rios, Father."

"Roberto, you can put your deeds away until we talk some more."

Tex broke into a smile again. "Father Jay, I'm glad to hear you say that. You see, I'm doing this for the good of the village. I'll explain how that will work—"

Fr. Jake held up a restraining hand. "First, Tex, tell us about yourself. Such as, what is your real name?"

He nodded toward Roberto, a signal to gather the deeds back into his folder. "Okay, Father, ready for this? My actual name is 'Aleksandër Bazhuaishvili.' Naturally, that was shortened to 'Alex Bazhu.'"

"Albanian?"

"Very good, Father! My *baba*…father…was a surgeon in Durrës. That's on the coast of Albania, south of the capital. In 1974, after the Chinese opted out of their support for us, life was a bit more free. The Communist government allowed *baba* a short vacation in Italy, so he took mom and me with him. I was nine. As he tells it, a pen pal at UTA medical school secretly arranged for the American Embassy at Rome to give us refugee status….asylum. *Baba* defected and we ended up in Austin. He went to work at the medical facility."

While Tex explained, Fortgang fidgeted with his tie. He looked at Fr. Jake, and shook his head impatiently. "With respect, Father, knowing all this is well and good. What I want to know is how Tex, or Alex, or whichever investors put him up to it, thinks this news is so good for Providencia."

Fr. Jake cued him. "Alex?"

"I prefer 'Tex.' Can't let my image slip, by folks wonderin' who this Alex feller is."

"Then go ahead, Tex."

"After getting my B.A. degree from UTA, I decided to study filmmaking. Rob Redford was promoting Indies at Sundance I., so I latched on, got a few awards. But they were too serious there. After all, this is America, not Albania, and I realized that vampires, werewolves…were the future for the kind of money-producing pix I wanted to make."

Fr. Jake remarked dryly, "That's not too flattering an assessment of our American movie-going public."

The Ghosts of Glorieta

"The under twenty-five set? You don't get out much to movies, do you?"

"Go on."

Tex stood up, bounced on his spring heels a moment, then sat down again. "I rounded up a flock of investors and we incorporated Pentacle Pix. I guess you have heard that a lot of movies are now being shot in New Mexico?"

"Tex, I'm from Michigan and haven't been here very long."

"Well, they are. There are even a few permanent movie sets here… Eames Ranch, the old Silverado location out near Santa Fe, but they ain't open t' the public."

Fr. Jake noted, "You have a habit of lapsing into your 'Don't Mess with Tex' routine."

"Yes," Fortgang complained. "Just get to the point, man."

The Texan hitched a booted leg onto the other, fiddled a moment with the heel spring, then leaned forward. "Well, now, I'm gonna show y'all what that point is. See, I'm going to let 'most everyone keep their houses. Maybe charge 'em minimal rent. Haven't decided yet, depends on funding. Isn't that right Roberto?"

His assistant nodded agreement, while tightening the elastic cord that secured the folder.

"Now," Tex went on, "I *do* want that church property and maybe up to the school. What I see is a tourist destination, kind of a permanent Amityville Horror kind of movie set, for a series I'd make. Like the 'Addams Family' a ways back. A haunted church, graveyard, and you bet I'd hire a lot of the folks livin' here as extras. Dress 'em up in costumes so that the payin' tourists could take digitals. Stuff like that. And with that Rail Runner train soon going clear down to Truth or Consequences, we don't need to worry about the highway endin' at La Fonda. Besides, there's a bridge over the Rio Grande a ways south of here." Tex took off his hat and swept it around the room as if to encompass all of Providencia. "Y'all see how that would perk up the economy here?"

Neither Fr. Jake nor Fortgang spoke; both had been dazed by the man's obviously well-thought out—yet unacceptable—plan.

"Whatcha think, Reverend? You're the one who people would listen to about this. I'm counting on your cooperation…" Tex rubbed his thumb and forefinger together to silently signal 'moolah.' "Know what I mean?"

"Actually, Tex, I'm shocked by the schlock you propose."

109

Albert Noyer

Unfazed by the priest's criticism, Tex chuckled and continued, "Reverend, you haven't seen the model yet. That's what's in that semi parked outside, a complete miniature representation of what the village set will look like. I mean, I paid a Disney designer plenty to come up with it." He looked toward his assistant. "Roberto?"

"Mister Houston would like you to call a meeting at the church, where he can show his model and explain the financial benefits of this project to the entire community."

That's a memorized speech he prepared to give Father Mora. How many other communities had the filmmaker planned to contact? Fr. Jake asked, "Tex, where are you staying?"

"I got me a nice motor home on property I leased 'bout a mile north of here. See, I'm really excited about y'all finding that old Civil War cemetery. I was planning a documentary of the village, showing it both before and after it's been turned into a movie set. That soldier's buryin' place makes it that much more…more—"

"Gruesome?"

"No, that's not the word. I'm thinking 'box office.' What about that meeting, Father Jay?"

He turned to the CPA. "Duane? What do you think?"

Fortgang held a hand at the side of his mouth. "Come into the kitchen, Father." He took the priest to the farthest corner of the house and whispered, "I think you should do it."

"Call a meeting of the villagers?"

"Yes, stall for time. Tell him you'll need a vote. That will give me an opportunity to check the validity of those quitclaims with the county assessor in Socorro."

"I'm sure they're valid," Fr. Jake said, "and Tex wouldn't start construction without proper permits. You said you're an attorney, as well as a CPA?"

"Right. I went to law school at UTA in Austin and practiced there until I moved to New Mexico. Father," he repeated, "stall for time."

"All right, Duane, but suggest a time for the meeting."

"How about Sunday, a week from today? Three P.M. in the afternoon."

"That sounds good. I'll tell Tex, but I need more information about the church sale."

110

The Ghosts of Glorieta

In the living room, the Texan had gotten up to bounce again on his heels in a kind of nervous callisthenic. When he saw the priest returning, he looked hopeful. "Well, Father Jay?"

"Tex, have you already closed a deal on the church property?"

"Not yet...it's still an option. I guess that bishop has got to get an okay from the Vatican. Some mucky-muck higher up."

That would be the pope... "I see. Tex, Mister Fortgang and I have decided to call your town meeting for next Sunday...that's May thirtieth...on the plaza at three in the afternoon."

The Texan grinned at the news and patted his white hat back on. "Father, that's super. I'll have the semi ready and picture maps of the set to pass out. Free hot dogs and soft drinks at a food stand. Burritos, too. See, the truck's side opens up and everyone can take a good look at the model."

"Do you have a name for this new Providencia."

"I do, Father and it's 'pentacular'!"

"I'm sure, Tex. What is it to be called?"

"'Horridusville.' That's from Latin, gives it a bit of class, don't ya think?"

Fr. Jake suppressed his true opinion of the horrendous name. "Tex. we'll see you on Sunday at three o'clock."

O

On Monday, G. Duane Fortgang went to the Socorro County Assessor's office to research the quitclaim deeds. He planned to stay at a motel in the town until he had found out about their validity.

Fr. Jake obtained a copy of the map Tex had printed up to pass out at the meeting. He had not heard again from Detective Sonia Mora and presumed she was working another case. Had she read the letter found in her uncle's desk?

Armando Herrera sold Fr. Jake a 2004 Nissan 2.5 Altima in excellent condition for $4,900. The mechanic went to Belén on a trial run with the priest, where Fr. Jake registered the car and bought an HP Notebook laptop computer at Walmart.

Still fuming at having been humiliated by Fr. Jake's alternative outdoor Mass, Deacon Maldonado kept out of sight, waiting for a response letter from Archbishop Jan Benisek.

Albert Noyer

Raylene Maldonado was at school the first three days of the week, grateful to be away from her oppressive husband most of the day. She filled out paperwork needed at the end of the Excelencia Elementary school year, and registered students for summer classes. A banner with the school's slogan ¡**Ex—El**! was draped across the main corridor.

School classes ended for Cynthia Plow on Friday, May 28th. Sunday was Memorial Day, yet the holiday would be celebrated on Monday the 31st. She had a week before her fifth grade morning summer school classes would begin.

○

On Saturday afternoon of the Memorial Day weekend, Fr. Jake sat on his porch, his face turned up to absorb the late May sunshine. Cottonwoods and scrub oak were in full leaf now. To the west, beyond the highway, fields of growing alfalfa, pinto beans, and corn gently sloped down toward the Rio Grande and its lush, protective belt of trees and vegetation. The acequia irrigation ditches were open. Now, long, straight trails of life-supporting water glittered in the sun and separated the fields. On the east, the forest greenery was thick, hiding any sign of habitation by the Pentecostals. Fr. Jake thought about how he had not yet been able to take up Caleb's invitation to visit the commune. In fact, the offer had not been repeated. Perhaps Elder Jeremiah had changed his mind about having an idolater come and risk polluting his charismatic followers.

Fr. Jake thought of the next day's meeting with Tex and the villagers. *I'll announce the meeting at Mass, and the reaction is sure to be negative. After people hear that they can be evicted from homes their families have occupied for generations, violence is sure to threaten. The jobs that the Texan promised are demeaning ones, creating Disneyland caricatures of the villagers. I can only hope, pray God, that Duane will find some loophole in the sale, or that Tex can be persuaded to go elsewhere—*

Fr. Jake's thoughts were interrupted by the loud sound of an automobile accelerating rapidly in his direction, from the east end of the Calle San Isidro. He stood up and recognized Cynthia Plow's Hyundai Tucson heading his way.

The teacher screeched her SUV to a stop at the curb in front of the house. She hurried out of the driver's side, leaving the car door open. Cynthia had on the bib overalls and floppy Boonie hat she wore when excavating at her archaeological site. Dirt crusted her knees and heavy work boots.

112

The Ghosts of Glorieta

"Father! Father Jake!" she called out, running toward him. "I've made the most amazing discovery at the dig! Come and see."

"Calm down, Cynthia." He walked down the stairs to meet her. "What *did* you find that rates such excitement?"

She took a couple of deep breaths, before reminding him, "You know I always believed that corner of the field was Fort Providence's military cemetery."

"Yes, and you promised to tell me more of its history."

"Well, I literally *dug up* some of that history. I found the remains of both Union and Confederate dead. Some other men that are buried at a slight distance are probably Buffalo Soldiers."

"Buffalo soldiers?"

"They were Negro troops, well, African-Americans, who served with the U.S. Ninth and Tenth Cavalry Regiments. After the Civil War, the Army stationed many of the soldiers out west. They earned the respect of Native Americans, who gave them that nickname. Last year I was helping at a dig in Fort Craig, when archaeologists discovered some Tenth Cav. bodies. They were reburied in Santa Fe National Cemetery."

Fr. Jake grinned and wagged a finger at her. "Slow down, Cynthia, that's a lot of local history you've given me in one breath. I still only know a little about it"

"You must read Don Albert's book about the battle of Glorieta, or Edrington's account, and there are others," she told him, brushing earth from her overalls. "They're in our school library, so check them out when I start summer school."

"Thanks, Cynthia, I will."

"Father Jake, my most unusual find was a woman's remains. She probably was a camp follower or some officer's pretty lady. It is the Memorial Day weekend, so I left phone messages at the Socorro Historical Society and the Historical Society of New Mexico Also with a couple of state archaeologists that I know. Come and look before authorities close my dig to the public."

Fr. Jake got in the Tucson's passenger side. As Cynthia gunned the Hyundai back around the corner of the Calle and headed toward the excavations, he hung on. "How did you discover the soldiers...the bodies?"

"As I told you, Father, I was convinced that area contained the fort's cemetery. It's far from the main buildings, and I've been digging there over

113

Albert Noyer

a year and a half. Yesterday, I was cleaning away dirt on level four, when I encountered what looked like blue cloth. You know, I'm so careful in clearing that site, yet was such a klutz at the *segrario*. I just barged in and started picking up zamia seeds. No wonder Deputy Griego was upset."

"I wasn't exactly professional myself," he confessed. "Armando and I brought Father Mora's body outside and compromised the crime scene. Go on about your find."

"Okay. This morning, after brushing more dirt away, I found bones and some 21 millimeter-size brass buttons. They were corroded, but I could make out the Union Eagle and 'C' for cavalry on them. A little more exploring uncovered a lozenge–shaped C.S.A. belt buckle and leather scraps."

"Where was this female corpse?"

"Off to the left of that path the Pentecostal kids take to school. I know the woman was from the same period because she was buried in an old fashioned, ankle-length gown."

"Cynthia, how long have you worked on archaeological digs?"

"About eight years. It's what I volunteer to do in summer. You can apply to the state and they'll steer you to dozens of sites. I like the Civil War period." Cynthia braked the SUV ten yards from the excavations and pulled off the road outside an area she had roped off with blue tape. Plastic tarps of the same color covered the excavated burial sites. "Here we are. The archaeology pros will take over and put a canvas roof up over everything, but I thought you'd be interested, Father. You know, bless the corpses or something."

"Cynthia, let me take a look first," he said as they climbed out of the car.

"Sure, Father."

At the largest dig, she pulled back a tarpaulin. A square of ground, ten feet by ten feet, had been neatly excavated in seven-inch steps that went down to a depth of about four feet. The skeletal bones so far exposed at the bottom were aligned side by side, in a way that suggested a formal military burial. Union blue woolen cloth predominated over Confederate gray or patterned calico shirts and farmer trousers: some Texas volunteers in the invading regiments had supplied their own civilian version of uniforms.

Fr. Jake blessed himself and knelt in silent prayer. Cynthia bowed her head, then crossed herself with him when he stood up again.

"Father," she explained, "that poor woman might have died of cholera. Her remains are over there. She isn't buried quite as deeply as the others. I don't know why."

114

The Ghosts of Glorieta

Cynthia led the way across the path to a smaller excavation. She had brushed away more of the soil and exposed most of a full skeleton, lying on its back. Woman's hair that might once have been blond surrounded a yellowed skull. Rotted remnants of a long cotton dress starkly outlined the underlying bones. Father Jake knelt to examine the remains more closely, then abruptly stood up. He breathed in short gasps while staring down at the burial pit.

Alarmed, Cynthia grasped his sleeve. "What is it Father? Are you all right?"

He nodded and knelt down once more to inspect what remained identifiable of the dead woman's gown. *That flower pattern design is something like the one on a long dress the woman wore in the photograph that Sonia found in Father Mora's desk....*

Concerned, Cynthia repeated, "Father! Are you ill?"

"No. I...I just believe that woman's body might have something to do with the murder of Father Mora."

"What do you mean?"

He straightened up and looked at her. "I'm sorry, Cynthia, I can't tell you. Do you have photographs of this grave site?"

"Sure, several views are on my digital."

"Good..." Fr. Jake slipped Sonia Mora's card from his wallet and gave it to Cynthia. "Could you e-mail them to this detective's Internet address? Say that they're from me, and that I'll contact her first thing Monday morning."

115

The Ghosts of Glorieta

12 eden west / may 23

Elder Jeremiah peered a moment longer through the lenses on his binoculars, then slowly let the instrument down and turned to the youth next to him. "Brother Caleb, today the idolater-priest came with the woman."

"Dad, I'm your son," he protested once again. "Can't you just call me Caleb or even Cal, like I keep asking? That's what you and mom named me, isn't it?"

The Elder ignored his complaint. "Sister Rebekah told me thou visited the idolalter on Sabbath last. That is against mine instructions."

"Sister Rebekah is a busy-body snitch."

"Nay, Brother," Jeremiah disagreed, his voice stern. "She be a comely woman, strongly possessed of the Holy Spirit. A fit match for thy manhood—"

"Dad..." Caleb reached over to put a hand on his father's shoulder. "Dad," he pleaded, "let's not argue again. I'll tell you when I'm ready to marry."

Jeremiah shrugged his son's hand away and maintained a stiff silence by staring at the village below. To temper the awkward moment, Caleb ventured another question. "I don't remember, but before mom died, did you talk in biblical language like you do now?"

Taken aback, the Elder mumbled, "Surely, Satan hath posed that question in Thee. Thy...thy mother was...was—" He avoided a complete answer by painfully standing from his crouched position among a grove of scrub oak. "I must return to Eden West and prepare for this night's ritual."

117

Caleb stood up alongside him. "So you'll hold a Black Mass again this year?"

"Satan has not defiled Eden West since my last ritual."

"But that has nothing to do with being a Pentecostal and receiving the Holy Spirit." Jeremiah turned away without replying, but Caleb persisted, "You and mom were kind of hippies, weren't you? Is that when somebody said that you could appease Satan with a Black Mass once a year? You're losing followers by doing that—"

"Silence!" the old man shouted, his bearded face crimson with rage. Jeremiah had raised a trembling hand to strike the youth, but slowly regained composure. "Persevere in thy disobedience," he warned hoarsely, "and thou shalt be no son of mine. 'If thou withdraw from me to go after empty idols, thou shalt become empty thyself'."

Caleb recognized a quote about infidelity by the Hebrew prophet Jeremiah, but merely said, "Dad, I'll be there tonight. May...may I walk back with you?"

He took the Elder's grunt as one of assent.

The half-buried tire-and-earth Earthship houses of Eden West were arranged in a north-south axis around a central plaza, as in Indian pueblo villages. Each building was fitted with large slanted windows on the south to catch winter sun. The households' subsistence gardens were on that side. Except for a few goat pens in the back yards of homes, the commune's cows and mules were corralled near the southeastern end, away from northern and westerly winds.

Inside Eden West, Caleb saw a new friend, Rodrigo Jirón, pulling weeds in his garden plot. Rod worked at a bank in Belén, contributing a tenth of his salary to the church. A few other Pentecostals also held jobs outside the compound: collecting cans along the road and selling the extra vegetables they grew did not bring in enough income to cover expenses.

"See you later, dad," he said to Jeremiah. "I'll stay here and help Rod for a while."

The preacher limped on without acknowledging his son's parting words.

Rodrigo had heard the two and straightened up. "Hey, Caleb, is your father all right? Elder Jeremiah, I should say."

"Oh, he's miffed because I won't marry Rebekah. Dad's also setting up the ritual for tonight."

"Ritual?"

The Ghosts of Glorieta

"I forgot that you're new here. Elder J. is fully convinced that Satan is up to no good in this world."

"Caleb, remember that the devil even tried to tempt Christ. Matthew 4: 10."

"I know the passage, Rod, but Elder J. has latched onto Revelation 20, where John predicts that Satan will be released from the angel's imprisonment—"

"After a thousand years."

"Correct, to 'go out and deceive the nations.' I don't know how he figures out these things, but he's convinced that we're now in year nine hundred ninety-nine or so. Way back he decided that performing a kind of Black Mass once a year in the spring is a way of appeasing Satan."

"A Black Mass?" Rodrigo whistled in surprise. "I've read a little bit about the ritual."

"That way Satan will leave our commune of Eden West alone. Some members refuse to come to a non-Christian service." Caleb laughed and gave his friend a playful punch on the arm. "Relax, Rod, by attending you won't lose your job at the bank. We won't impale a naked virgin on the altar or drink children's blood out of a skull. In his ritual, Elder J. recites some Latin mumbo-jumbo, then burns a consecrated host if he can get one. You know, what Catholics at San Isidro church eat every Sunday."

Rodrigo nodded and looked away. "Yes, I used to belong."

"Right. Dad normally would roast a thin slice of turnip, but I think he somehow got hold of a real host for this year. That *really* should scare Satan away!"

"Brother Caleb, Thou soundeth a bit irreverent." Rodrigo's mocking smile quickly turned grim. "About losing my job. Rumor is that Western Savings may cut back my hours in this recession."

"Sorry to hear it, Rod. Don't we have a bank branch here in Providencia?"

"A small one," he confirmed, "but they may close that. I know the commune needs money. Does the Elder lease that land out in back?"

"To Billy Ray Scurry and his survivalist followers? No, Scurry's a real nut case, but he owns the property."

"Even so, their warning signs frighten *me* away, and I've heard a lot of target shooting over there. What's with the guy?"

Caleb replied, "He and whoever else is with him keep to themselves by trying to be totally self-sufficient. They have gardens and raise goats,

119

sheep…cows. Maybe mules to do the plowing. We really don't know." He knelt to pull weeds that encroached on leafy cabbage plants. "Old Billy Ray is in his fifties. Have you seen the guy, Rod?"

"Not yet."

"Balding dude…really mean eyes. He wears a drooping walrus mustache that matches his bushy eyebrows. Scurry looks like he's sucking a lemon all the time and would like to spit the seeds right out at you."

"In other words," Rodrigo jested, "a charming feller."

"Yeah, Billy Ray is anti-government, probably packs a .45 in a shoulder holster. The survivalists holed up there don't pay income taxes and supposedly cut up their Social Security cards and mailed them back to the government. They consider themselves to be 'sovereign citizens'. The place is called Fort Liberty."

Rod asked, "Where do they get cash money?"

Caleb made a smoking gesture with his right thumb and forefinger. "Probably by growing pot to sell in Albuquerque."

"You're joking."

"Hardly. Ofilia Herrera, the old *curandera* woman, grows marijuana. She'll tell anyone around that she uses it in her medications." Caleb glanced around the garden. "What else did you plant?"

"At the March commune meeting, Elder Jeremiah assigned me cabbage, green beans, and tomatoes."

"As in Acts 2:44." Caleb quoted, "'All who believed were together and had all things in common.' Rod, we share with each other after the harvest. It's God's plan."

"Still, at times, I don't understand the Elder," the young man admitted. "He went ballistic when I said I wanted to plant zucchini."

"He doesn't let anyone grow that gourd. Why? Who knows? He gets stranger and stranger about certain things." Caleb picked up a hoe and sifted through weeds that Rod had piled up. "Good you took out the Goatheads. The leaves and yellow flowers look pretty, but I found out the painful way that the stickers are murder on your fingers."

"I found that out too." He stripped off his green gardening gloves and stood up. "I'm done weeding for now, Caleb, but thanks for offering to help me."

"*No problemo, amigo,*" he said, slapping his friend on the back. "You'll find out about the Black Mass ritual after supper."

The Ghosts of Glorieta

As Caleb walked to his Earthship lodge at the far end of the plaza, he passed Rebekah, milking a ewe. She paused to look up and smile at him.

"Hi, Sister Becky..." he called out, with a cursory wave. *No point in shunning the poor lovesick girl, but those long gowns Elder J. makes the women wear don't help their figures. I'd refuse if I was one of them.*

O

Sunset on that day of Saturn came shortly after 8:00 P.M. Leaves on the forest trees filtered a brilliant, orange-red mosaic of western sky that according to ancient mariners foretold clear weather for the Lord's Day. A bright full moon would rise about two hours later.

Elder Jeremiah, having noticed villagers light bonfires on their saints' feast days, ordered commune members to build seven, two-foot-high stacks of pinewood around the perimeter of the plaza's open space. *Luminarias*, the Hispanos called the brightly burning bonfires. *Farolitos* were small candles set in half-sand-filled paper bags and placed along walkways or on the flat parapets of adobe buildings.

At the center of the plaza, a picnic table draped with black cloth that had a white pentagram star embroidered in the center served as an altar. Seven black candles half- surrounded a glowing charcoal brazier set on the satanic symbol. In front of it, a black ceramic dish held the white host used in a Christian Eucharist. Tongs lay alongside. To the left, dried herbs filled a bisque-ware bowl. An inverted crucifix at the front of the altar faced the area where Eden West commune members would assemble.

The bonfires were alight, pine pitch crackling and throwing up swirls of red sparks into an indigo sky, when Caleb saw Rodrigo standing alone at the far edge of members who arrived. "Edenites" the Elder had dubbed them. Caleb walked over to stand with his friend.

"Rod, I said that you didn't have to be part of this," he reminded him.

"Curiosity and the cat, I guess. I don't think being here will kill me, but I do know that Satan is an active force for evil in this world. We need to control him by any means possible."

"You think the old guy worries about Eden West?"

Rodrigo's reprimand was swift. "Caleb! When you talk like that I wonder if you're really the Elder's son."

"You mean a preacher's boy shouldn't blaspheme? Uh oh, speak of the.... Here comes Elder J."

121

Albert Noyer

The heavily bearded patriarch had put on a long, black gown with a white pentagram over the heart side. A hood barely concealed his wild salt-and-pepper hair. Rebekah and Sister Charity, another white-clad "virgin priestess," walked a step behind Jeremiah, holding a bottle and small bowl. The filmy Greek tunics the two women had put on and belted beneath their breasts were provocatively sensual in comparison to the shapeless cotton dresses normally worn.

With the priestesses to his left, the Elder stood behind the altar, facing the dying sunset. Firelight cast his flickering shadow as he raised his hands to begin by quoting from the Book of Revelation.

"'And when the thousand years are finished, Satan shall be loosed out of his prison and shall come forth to deceive the nations which are in the four corners of the earth.' Revelation 20:7.

"Edenites," he continued, "these days are nigh upon thee. In Matthew 6:24 and Luke 16:9, the Lord Jesus advised thee to befriend Evil. Thus, on one day of the year we honor Satan, the Lord of Darkness, that he may not seduce thee as followers but bypass thee to subvert others."

Jeremiah held up the Eucharistic host. "Edenites, this is the abomination that the priest-idolaters worship. In II Corinthians 11:14, Paul warns of them. 'For even Satan fashioneth himself into an angel of light. It is no great thing therefore if his ministers also fashion themselves as ministers of righteousness.' I shall blacken this on the Fire of Purification and ye shall partake of its pieces. After inhaling the Smoke of Purification, ye individually may have Sister Rebekah and Sister Charity tattoo a cross on the soles of thy feet with soot from the black candles."

He put down the host, bowed, and intoned, "*In nomine magni dei nostri Satanus, introibo ad altare Domini Inferni.*"

"*Qui laetificat juventutem nostrum,*" the two women repeated in response.

"*Satanus Domini,*" the Elder prayed.

"*Eleison,*" both women responded in unison.

"*Domini Inferni*"

"*Eleison.*"

Caleb glanced around the fire-lit circle. *Probably less than a third of our members are here. A lot, like Rod, came out of curiosity and several already have left. Why does dad persist in doing this crazy ritual?*

Jeremiah picked up the host with the tongs and held it over the charcoal fire.

The Ghosts of Glorieta

After he stepped aside to let the blackened bread cool and break it into small pieces, the priestesses scattered dried herbs on the glowing charcoal. An herbal-scented bluish smoke wafted into the air, but its predominant smell was that of marijuana.

Once the Elder summoned commune members to come up and eat shards of the bread, and inhale the hallucinatory fumes, Caleb turned away to return to his house. Rodrigo joined him.

"Seen enough?"

"I have, Caleb. This isn't what I thought you did here. Where was the Holy Spirit in all that?"

"Don't worry, Rod. Tomorrow, we'll go to our Living Word Tabernacle of Divine Truth in the village and be our regular Pentecostal selves for the rest of the year."

Rodrigo wondered, "What is that cross tattoo on the feet thing?"

"Treading on a Christian symbol pleases Satan. Sister Charity will use a scalpel to cut a thin cross on the initiate's soles and rub soot into the lines. Rebekah will apply an oily herbal extract to prevent infection and help the wound heal."

"That's...totally sick. Then what happens?"

"Elder J. will conduct a closing ceremony ritual to thank Satan for not bothering us for another year, then...well...you know what Acapulco Gold does to inhibitions."

"That's even sicker, Caleb."

"I agree, Rod. What do you say we go start our own squeaky green community somewhere without all this satanic mumbo-jumbo?"

"Think you're kidding, Caleb? If I lose my job that just could happen..." Rodrigo yawned and shook his head to clear his mind of what he had seen. "I'm beat. Going to bed now."

"Same here. We'll see how many clear-headed Edenites show up for Tabernacle services tomorrow morning."

"Good night, Caleb."

"Rod—"

The young man turned back. "Yes?"

Caleb advised quietly, "Leave this place."

"What do you mean?"

"I'm thinking of doing so, yet it...it's all *I've* ever known. Oh, the women here were kind enough to me as a child, but I've never had a real

123

mother. Dad actually might have impregnated mom at a ritual like this." He thought about the charred Eucharist bread. "Where do you suppose he got that host?"

"No idea," Rod admitted, "but even as an ex-Catholic that part bothered me the most."

"You heard how that priest down at the Catholic church suddenly died, and yet no details about his death were ever released."

"They sent a detective out to investigate. As to leaving Eden West, you said this ritual happens only once a year?"

Caleb nodded. "And the rest of the time I wonder what gifts the Holy Spirit has in reserve for me. Paul speaks of teaching, healing...the expression of wisdom. Interpretation of tongues. Mighty deeds. Jeez, all I've ever done is sort used tires and collect trash like the aluminum cans we sell to recyclers." Caleb looked at his friend with a worried half smile. "I...I've sounded off enough. Good-night, Brother Rodrigo."

Goodnight, Brother Caleb, I'll think about what you said. The peace of Christ be with you."

"And with you, *mi amigo*."

The Ghosts of Glorieta

13

On Sunday morning, Fr. Jake found himself again locked out of San Isidro church. Deacon Maldonado guarded the door, but without his wife being with him. Armando and Cynthia waited for the priest farther away from the building entrance. A larger than usual number of congregation members waited to see what would happen.

"We called around, Father," Cynthia explained, "and told people about the meeting this afternoon. You'll talk about it at Mass, right?"

"That's correct, Cynthia."

"Y' know, Father Hakub," Armando added, "The Gonzalezes woulda called the Garcias, who called the Chavezes, who called the Lopezes, an' on down the line. We got the word around, all right."

"Thanks, Armando." Fr. Jake nodded toward the front door. "It would be better if I could be inside the church to talk. Take a look at what's happening on the plaza."

"Yeah, those film guys got here early," Armando remarked. "Check out all that movie equipment."

The semi-truck had been moved to one side of the open space, where Pentacle Pix workers were setting up a stage, food stands, Klieg lights, and sound equipment: It was clear that Tex Houston was going to film the villagers' meeting and use it as an introduction to his docudrama about how Providencia had been converted to Horridusville.

Two sheriff's patrol cars idled at the plaza's far side.

125

Albert Noyer

Armando volunteered, "I'll go over an' talk to the deacon about gettin' inside the church."

Cynthia watched him walk toward Maldonado. "Father, the deacon's in a foul mood. He told us that Raylene left a couple days ago with his car. She's probably visiting her parents in La Fonda."

"Probably? Didn't he call them to find out?"

"They won't talk to him, Father, and he's too macho-proud to try. Raylene's done that before…" Cynthia held her arms around her body and shivered to make a point. "With her husband's temper, I wouldn't want to be her when she comes back."

"Yes, it's obvious their marriage needs serious counseling…" Fr. Jake noticed Fortgang coming toward him across the field from the plaza. "Ah, here's Duane back from Socorro."

Striding rapidly from the parking area, the man looked grim. He reached the priest and glanced at the young woman. "Father, I must talk to you in private."

Cynthia understood. "Sure, I'll go help Armand convince the deacon to open up the church."

Fortgang led the priest back to the street curb. "I got in late last night, Father, and my news isn't good."

Fr. Jake's stress rash itch surfaced again. "What do you mean, Duane?"

"Father, all week I combed through public tax assessment records for the past five years. Sure enough, Father Mora had not paid the taxes. Delinquency notices were sent to him, but either they were never acknowledged or somehow he didn't receive them."

"What about legal notices in the Socorro newspaper?"

"I'd have to look through back issues in their archives."

"Can you appeal?"

He shook his head. "I never practiced law in New Mexico and don't have a license. Stayed in Austin where I got my degree. That was the state capital, with plenty of lucrative cases to spread around."

"So we would have to hire a local attorney?"

"I'll personally pay to do that, but probably should save my money. I can already tell you that he or she would say the quitclaim deeds are legit. Tex owns everything that Father Mora did." Fortgang glanced around and pulled the priest by the sleeve into the street. "I did some more inquiring," he confided in a low voice. "Raylene Maldonado worked in the assessor's office before getting that secretary's job at the school last September."

126

The Ghosts of Glorieta

"Her husband has back trouble," Fr. Jake recalled. "Donny probably forced her to work closer to home in order to take better care of him."

"Perhaps, but it's suspicious." Fortgang whispered again, "Father, I wouldn't tell these people about the quitclaims at the meeting. You know how they are."

"No, 'how are they'?"

"Well, you know...." The CPA's voice trailed off.

"Duane, I do know that in 1956 Poznan there were riots, when 'those people' protested the Communist government's attempt to...I believe the term still is 'screw'... to screw them into accepting something patently unacceptable."

If Fortgang was shocked at Fr. Jake's use of a vulgar verb, he did not react. "What I'm saying, Father, is just be careful about how you let the villagers know about losing their homes. There could be violence and—"

"Duane, shall we start Mass now?"

Cynthia and Armando, plus more *Providenceños* arriving for the service than Deacon Maldonado had ever seen before, persuaded him to unlock the church.

Inside, waiting in front of the altar, Fr. Jake found San Isidro packed with villagers. Some stood just inside the entrance; others leaned against the inside walls. Most came because they had heard about the meeting. A few were curious about seeing the Anglo priest. Others knew there would be a kind of afternoon fiesta with free food and drink. A few *viejos* believed they would be told that Fr. Mora was not truly dead.

A still-belligerent Maldonado put on his soiled deacon's sash to assist at Mass.

Fr. Jake decided that before starting the service he would brief those attending about the arrival of the film production company and Tex's plan for the village.

"*Bienvenidos*," he began, "Welcome to San Isidro Church. For those new here, I'm Father Casimir Jakubowski, but simply 'Father Jake' will do. I truly am pleased to see all of you here this morning. First, I want briefly to lay out the reason for this afternoon's meeting and tell you what will happen there.

"Pentacle Pix, a Texas movie-making company, has taken an interest in your... our...village. They plan to make a documentary of a New Mexican community and the recently discovered Civil War fort and cemetery." He paused to look around at the congregation. "I...I wish that were the limit of what they want to do."

127

Albert Noyer

Murmuring rippled through the congregation as people glanced at each other, wondering what the priest would tell them next. Some were pleased; perhaps they would be actors in a movie. Others worried about bad news. Why else would an Anglo priest bother to help a Texan filmmaker?

"Mister Tex Houston, the owner of the company," Fr. Jake went on, "will explain his plans more fully at the meeting this afternoon. He has a model to show you of the way he wishes to transform Providencia into a kind of movie set. He promises jobs for many of you."

The babble of voices was louder and happier now. Smiles broke out on both smooth and weathered *Providenceño* faces. Who had not heard of their state's new fame as a popular place to make movies? Some knew friends elsewhere who were hired as extras; why not right here in their village? A few recalled that twenty-three years ago Robert Redford had energized the economy of the north with *The Milagro Beanfield War* movie. Actors like Redford, Tommy Lee Jones, Ed Harris, and John Travolta were glimpsed in various locations around New Mexico.

Fr. Jake raised a hand to quiet down the babble. "To learn more about this project, about any jobs you might be offered, attend the meeting in the plaza at three o'clock this afternoon. Now, please stand for the sign of the cross.

"In the name of the Father, and of the Son, and of the Holy Spirit.

"The grace of our Lord Jesus Christ and the love of God and the fellowship of the Holy Spirit be with you all."

Most responded, "And also with you."

"I confess to almighty God…"

○

Close to 2:30 P.M., that afternoon, elegantly costumed members of a Mariachi band mounted the stairs of a platform built in front of the semi-truck. The five musicians stood tuning their instruments, wearing heavily embroidered jackets, silver discs decorating the trouser legs, red sashes, and over-size sombreros. A glassed-in section of the trailer was open, the metal side hinged up to act as a stage canopy. Covering the window, a purple curtain with Tex's pentagram logo stenciled on the front concealed what was inside the semi's bed.

The leader of the Mariachi group stepped over to a microphone and welcomed the crowd in English and Spanish. He announced their first

128

The Ghosts of Glorieta

number, George Baker's *Una Paloma Blanca*. A few children and adults who had spotted the hot dog and burrito stand hurried over to get free food and soft drinks.

As the Mariachi group of two violins, two guitars and a trumpet performed the music, couples chose partners to dance in front of the stage.

Fr. Jake, preoccupied about what Fortgang had told him, arrived near the end of the song.

When Tex noticed him, he beamed the priest a grin and hurried to greet him. "Mighty glad y' could make it Father Jay," he said slapping the priest's back as if they were colleagues. "What do y'all think of this shindig of mine?"

"Let's skip the 'Don't Mess with Tex' routine shall we? Plain English will do."

"Sure, Father Jay," he replied amiably—very few things took the Texan aback, including getting people's names wrong. "You know, I'm going to talk jobs to these people. Off the top of my head, I can think of thirty good paying positions connected with making a movie, and they don't even include security, prop masters, script continuity, specials effects. And I *do* use Hispanics. In fact..." Tex beckoned to two people standing next to one side of the platform. "Hey, Ramirez...Mendoza...c'mon over here. He's a crackerjack stuntman. She's a budding actress..." He winked at the young woman, adding, "And buxom, too." When the couple walked forward, smiling professionally, Tex introduced them. "Father Jay, meet José Ramirez and Marissa Mendoza, a coupla my finest." After handshakes and "my pleasures" had passed all around, Tex explained to the two, "I'm tellin' Father that I'll hire village people. José and Marissa, you're gonna give a little talk about how good it is workin' for me. That right?"

José nodded. "Sure thing, Tex."

Marissa popped her gum and threw away the wad. "Delighted to."

At five minutes to three, the band of *Mariachis Mejores* finished the last rousing notes of *El Gusto*, bowed to applause, and went down to circulate among the bystanders and pass out business cards. At the same time, Pentacle workers handed around brochures to the spectators about what Tex Houston would show them.

Two of Pentacles' cinematographers used shoulder HDV/DV Camcorders to film this part of the documentary. One woman with a heavier ENG video camera mounted on a tripod panned the musicians and on through the crowd from onstage. The other two men roamed the plaza, recording close-up images of photogenic villagers.

Albert Noyer

Ofilia Herrera was there, working the crowd to buy her herb packets and lotions.

At precisely three o'clock, Tex, wearing a white Western-style suit, his cowboy hat, and the spring-heel boots, went onstage to the microphone and called to the crowd for attention.

"Folks…. Folks, weren't they great?" Tex's amplified voice boomed into the crowd. "Let's give another hand to"—he glanced at their card—"Mariacheese Medjorays."

The applause was scattered; most bystanders held food plates or read the brochures they had been given.

"Now, folks," he went on, "your good *Padre* has told y'all something about what's goin' on here today. Sure, we got some legal ownership things to talk about, but not right now. Y'all who are livin' where the movie set will be are gonna get letters explainin' everything." Tex looked back at his two Hispanic actors. "Now, Marissa and José are gonna pull back that curtain and y'all will see what I plan for this fine community."

At the cue, each half of the curtain was swished to its corner. The crowd strained forward to look through the window glass at a model of the proposed movie set.

"Now, y'all been given a map there to help you know what I'm talking about." Tex grinned and tapped the center of the glass with a wooden pointer, then used a light pen to spot red dots on what he described. "Here in the middle is a haunted church and graveyard. That's Number One. See them on your map?" He pointed in the general direction of the adobes where Fr. Jake, Maldonado, and a dozen other villagers lived. "Where those houses are over there, we're gonna build more of a Victorian and western frontier-type of movie set. See Number Two on your map? Oh, we gonna have us a haunted saloon, a bank buildin' and gamblin' establishment. Livery stables, whatever it takes to make us a haunted ghost town. And y'all gonna be hired to build and act in it!"

If Tex thought his loud offer of employment was an unquestioned deal-clincher, he was disappointed. Some men in the crowd had been drinking beer they brought along. One in jeans and an undershirt pointed toward the row of houses with a Coors can.

"I own one of those adobes," he shouted. "Are you going to pay me for it?"

Another bearded villager supported him. "Yeah, me, too, and what if I don't want to move?"

130

The Ghosts of Glorieta

Neither man waited for an answer and began arguing with others around them about what Tex had said. Muttered reactions to the Texan's offer of employment sifted through the crowd.

"We gonna have jobs!"

"I ain't trustin' the guy."

"Just another Texan out to screw us."

"The shit you say! I need the work."

An angry woman demanded, "Is he taking over our elementary school, too?"

"Folks! Now, folks," Tex pleaded from the front of the platform. "Y'all hold on a minute. This is just startin'. 'Course we're gonna listen to any complaints, but this here new town is gonna have tourists flockin' in an' spendin' money. Y'all will get a big slice of the pie!"

"Unacceptable," Duane Fortgang muttered. "Does Tex truly think he'll get away with this?"

"You evidently thought he would," Fr. Jake recalled. "You said not much could be done about the quitclaims."

"We…we've got to fight him somehow."

"Violence begets violence, Duane."

"I'm talking about legal means, Father."

"Of course, but that takes time," he warned. "Will these villagers wait? I told you they didn't at Poznan."

A now worried-looking Tex beckoned to his secretary, Roberto, who stood waiting on one side of the stage. "Get those *Mejicanos* back here to start playing again." He straightened up, forced a smile, and bellowed into the microphone, "Folks! Folks! Calm down. I'm gonna give y'all a chance to come and look at the model up close. We got lotsa food left, and these here fine musicians will start playin' again. Y'all dance an' enjoy yourselves!"

On observing the mild shoving and loud arguments, the two sheriff's deputies had gotten out of their patrol cars and started toward the crowd. One hand rested on their riot batons. Fr. Jake noticed them and hurried around the spectators to intercept the pair.

"Officers, I think it's all right. The crowd just got a little too excited."

"Okay, Father," one said, holding up a restraining hand. "We'll just keep an eye on things, so's they don't get out of hand."

"I'm sure they won't."

131

Albert Noyer

The mariachi band started playing again. People crowded onto the stage to look at the town model. Children went to the food stands. A few couples danced, mothers holding small children swirled them to the music. A fiesta-like atmosphere returned to the crowd—not many such pleasant events had taken place under Fr. Mora.

Relieved that violence was averted, Fr. Jake had started back to his house when he saw Sonia Mora's red Plymouth Neon turn into the Calle San Isidro and stop at the church. The detective got out and leaned against her car to wait for the priest.

"It's okay," Fr. Jake called out to her. "Everything's under control. Did you get a police call?"

"Police call about what? Father, I don't know what you mean."

He pointed back to the plaza festivities. "A while ago things could have gotten a bit…well…a bit unruly."

"That's not why I'm here." Sonia held up a file folder. "Father Jake, the body of Raylene Maldonado was discovered this morning in a Belén motel room. The M.E. figures she was murdered about two days ago."

"Murdered? That…that's terrible news! Poor Raylene. You went to Belén?"

"Didn't have to, Father. As an inter-sheriff courtesy, we started faxing photos of murder victims in neighboring counties to each other. My idea. I recognized the victim from a fax."

"What was Raylene doing in Belén? Her husband thought she left in a snit to visit her parents."

"The victim registered under her maiden name of Garcia. Seems she was pretty well known at the motel, often stayed there a few of evenings a month, usually in mid-week."

"Any leads?" Fr. Jake asked, but added before she could answer, "You know, Sonia, I *have* watched CSI programs in Michigan. You'll go in there with fingerprint lifting tape and those purple fluorescent lights—"

"LED Ultraviolet Flashlights."

"Thanks. You'll identify any blood and semen remains for DNA testing."

"Clever, Father Jake," she interposed dryly, "except that the victim was strangled in a different room and there was no blood or semen detected. That other motel room was cleaned and rented out again, thus pretty much useless for gathering evidence."

The Ghosts of Glorieta

"Sorry…" He slapped his forehead in remorse. "Guess I was trying to show off. You know, be one of the guys."

"Forget it. This is putting us all on edge. I came to inform Mister Maldonado about his wife, but thought he'd like to have his priest there when I told him."

"Very thoughtful, Sonia, let's go." Fr. Jake stopped and held her back by a sleeve. "Come to think of it, I didn't see him at the plaza meeting."

"Still miffed at you being here, Father?"

"Well, he did consent to open the church this morning."

Weeds grew wild on the patch of land in front of the deacon's tin-roofed adobe. In the backyard, a dog barked viciously at the approaching footsteps. After he answered the knock, Dionisio Maldonado scowled at his two visitors from his open door. "Yeah?"

Sonia held up her badge. "Sir, may we come in?"

"I know who y' are detective. Father."

Fr. Jake returned his acknowledgment with a handshake.

Maldonado motioned them in and gestured toward almost a week's worth of newspapers scattered around the living room. "Sorry about the mess…" Through a doorway, unwashed dishes were visible stacked in the kitchen sink. Half-burned waste paper choked a small fireplace. Above the mantle, a rifle was displayed beneath a rack of elk antlers mounted on a wood plaque. Maldonado explained, "Y' know Raylene's down visitin' with her folks an' my back's been actin' up again."

"Sir, please sit down," Sonia told him softly. "I'm sorry, but the Belén sheriff's department has discovered your wife's body in a motel room there."

"Raylene?" Maldondado shook his head. "Naw, she…she's in La Fonda."

"No sir, her body has been identified by the motel owner."

Maldonado's scowl changed to a look of confusion. He ran a hand through uncombed hair. "That…that can't be. Raylene—"

"It's true, Donny," Fr. Jake confirmed. "How can I help you? I can arrange a rosary at the church for tomorrow evening or whenever you want."

"Sir, the medical examiner is conducting an autopsy." Sonia took out her spiral note pad. "In a case like this, I'll have to ask you routine questions."

"Raylene's a good woman," Maldonado mumbled, covering his face with a shaking hand and holding in sobs. "Sure, we had our outs, but what married couple don't? I suppose I coulda been nicer sometimes…" His voice trailed off as he thought of what-might-have-been.

Strange, how differently people react to news of a death. "Detective," Fr. Jake suggested, "perhaps you could hold your questions until tomorrow, Monday?"

After a moment, Sonia agreed. "All right. Monday is Memorial Day."

Fr. Jake reached over to touch the deacon's arm. "Donny, in the morning I'll have a nine o'clock Memorial Day Mass. Will you feel up to participating?"

"Raylene's a good woman," the deacon repeated through suppressed sobs.

Sonia tucked her note pad into a pocket and stood up. "I'll leave Father Jake with you, sir, and come by tomorrow morning."

Maldonado nodded slowly, but said, "You don't need t' stay, Father."

"Can I notify anyone? Children?"

"We didn't have kids. I…I'd like to be left alone now."

"Of course, Donny. If you're not at Mass tomorrow, I'll stop by afterward. Memorial Day is when graves are decorated and you must have relatives buried in the *camposanto*."

"We put flags on the stones," he said to the priest.

"If you want, I can help you do that. Do you have anything to help you sleep?"

"Raylene got some of them sleep pills in th' bathroom."

"Take a couple…" Fr. Jake put his hands on Maldonado's forehead. "God bless you and keep you, deacon, in your hour of need."

Maldonado did not get up when the two left. Outside, Fr. Jake walked Sonia back to her Plymouth. "That was quite a rifle the deacon had under those elk horns," he remarked. "Donny is obviously a hunter."

"It's more than a hunting rifle, a Yugoslavian SKS semi-automatic carbine. Russian design, 1944."

"I'm impressed, detective. How do you know all that?"

"Father, don't you try to learn all you can about the priest business?"

"Point taken. Where would Maldonado get a gun like that?"

"Mail order," Sonia replied, "or a sporting goods store in Albuquerque. They're collector's items."

"The deacon was quite broken up about his wife's death. It's obvious he didn't have anything to do with her murder."

The Ghosts of Glorieta

"The victim had a bruise on her face when she came to talk with you at Mamacita's," Sonia recalled. "Maldonado has a record of being abusive, and it generally takes a man to strangle a woman." She unlocked her car door and looked back. "Obvious? Father Jake, nothing is obvious in many of these murder cases. After my uncle's funeral, what did she talk to you about outside Mamacita's?"

"Raylene wanted to make an appointment and meet with me to discuss something personal."

"Well, did the victim ever get that chance?"

"No, Donny's wife never came to see me."

Sonia slid into the driver's seat. "Point made, Father Jakubowski."

14

Dionisio Maldonado did not respond to Fr. Jake's offer to recite a rosary, nor was he at the 9:00 o'clock Memorial Day Mass.

Before the service ended inside San Isidro, a line of Union and Confederate Civil War reenactors had formed up on the church's plaza. Dressed in uniforms of the period, the men and women parked their cars or campers and fell into formation. On orders from Union cavalry Captain Karl Schiller, the troop began a march onto Calle San Isidro.

Puddles of water left after an early rain wet the asphalt street. Along the route, shimmering curbside pools reflected the blue and gray uniforms, colorful Civil War unit banners, and U.S. and C.S.A. flags. The echoing clip-clop of cavalry horses and tread of booted feet sounded on the roadway as the troop marched east up the Calle. At the southeast corner, the lead column flanked right and headed toward the site near where Cynthia Plow had uncovered the graves of Fort Providence's buried soldiers.

Cynthia and Armando came out the church door last with Father Jake. The three joined congregation members in watching the historical parade pass by.

"There's a Company C banner of the Fourth Texas Mounted Volunteers!" Cynthia exclaimed. As Schiller moved past on a chestnut mare, a grizzled veteran rode beside him, wearing a camouflage-tan Gulf War uniform. "U.S. Regular Army cavalrymen are here, too." Cynthia turned to the priest. "Father, have you seen reenactments before?"

137

Albert Noyer

"A few parishioners once took me to a black powder shoot at Henry Ford's Greenfield Village in Dearborn. But, no, not from the Civil War period."

A four-person carriage and mule-drawn covered wagon, carrying women dressed in mid-nineteenth century costumes, went by. Cynthia pointed to a cannon pulled by two mules that followed. "Looks like a mountain howitzer, maybe a twelve-pounder."

Fr. Jake told her, "You know a lot about this for a woman. I admire that."

Surprised at his unintended condescension, she retorted, "I teach history, Father, so it's my job to know enough to get my students excited. I especially cover the Civil war period because in this part of New Mexico the historical remains are all around."

"Sorry, I misspoke. How did you get interested in archaeology? You said you've been actively involved for eight years."

Cynthia laughed, then explained, "Do they still call us 'Army brats'? My father was career Air Force, came to Kirtland AFB to join a Pave helicopter rescue unit. After serving in Vietnam, Dad said he'd rather save people than kill them."

"A commendable choice."

"Yeah, Father Jake. I was an only child, and after graduating from Highland High in Albuquerque, I went to New Mexico Tech over in Socorro. Thought I'd major in Geology, but met archaeologists on a summer field trip and that got me interested in digs. Then I switched to education and joined AmeriCorps…" Cynthia paused. "Father, there's too much to tell right now, but here I am teaching fifth grade in a Providencia elementary school and going on summer digs."

"Amen," he said, smiling. "We'll talk later about the rest."

"The reenactors must have heard about the fort's graves…" Cynthia glanced at the soggy ground, then at a blue sky and brilliant morning sun that was three hours old. "It'll be muddy, but things should dry up pretty quickly. Let's get over there. Armand, you with me?"

The mechanic gave her a high five. "Sure, Cynthia. I like that kind of historical stuff. You, comin' too, Father?"

"Yes, I'd like to talk with some of the men. Let me hang up these Mass vestments, then I'll meet both of you over there. Oh, by the way, did either of you notice Deacon Maldonado in church?"

138

The Ghosts of Glorieta

The two looked at each other and shook their heads. Cynthia said, "Father, you mentioned in your homily that his wife died. What happened to the poor woman?"

"We won't know until an autopsy is complete. Detective Mora promised to keep me informed."

"Okay, Father, we'll see you at the graves."

Near the cemetery site, the Blue and Gray-clad infantrymen stood at parade rest along the roadway, facing the excavations. Jane Doe's grave was marked off separately with crime scene tape. Except for Schiller and the Gulf War veteran, the other cavalry units had dismounted. The men waited on foot, grasping their horses' halters.

Tex Houston's camera operators were at the ceremony; their ENG tripod video cameras panned the troop from the back of a parked Chevy Silverado pick-up.

Captain Schiller prepared to introduce Colonel Billy Ray Scurry, who claimed to be a relative of Lt. Col. William R. Scurry, a Confederate commander at the Battle of Glorieta. The Union captain was straight out of a Matthew Brady daguerreotype: he sat ramrod straight on his mount, a neatly trimmed black beard hosting flecks of gray, his forage cap set at a rakish angle. Scurry, too, was from central casting, a "scowlin', mean-lookin' as they make 'em, walrus-mustachioed, hulk of a man."

"Men," the captain began, "as you know, this year the Bureau of Land Management gave us permission to practice our Glorieta battle reenactment here in Providence." He swept the immediate area with a gloved hand. "There's a good-sized field between here and that little Catholic church over there. We can pitch tents around the field's perimeter. Those fine ladies with us can do the housekeeping, and battle practice will commence in the center of the open field. It will all be caught on professional movie cameras over there…" He pointed at the Silverado, then continued, "Now, this year we have a guest of honor, Colonel B.R. Scurry"—Schiller motioned to the mounted veteran in camouflage uniform—"Colonel Scurry, please ride out in front a bit." After the man halted his horse a few feet from the soldiers, the captain explained, "Not only is Colonel Scurry a veteran of the First Gulf War, but, as many of you 'Confederates' may have guessed, he is a direct descendant of Lieutenant Colonel William Read "Dirty Shirt" Scurry, who led a rebel force at the Glorieta action—"

A number of gray-clad men interrupted by shouting out the rebel yell.

139

Albert Noyer

"Parade rest!" the captain ordered, displeased at the outburst. "Now, for the first time we'll have someone from Tennessee who is related to a fine officer who fought at Glorieta Pass. Colonel?"

Scurry spat tobacco juice aside, then drawled, "Ah'm tickled t' be paht of y' all's celebrayshun. And may the best side win…that being here, the Gray o' course."

Only sparse applause accompanied his inappropriate boast: reenactments were healing occasions that honored the memory of those who had died in the intra-state conflict. These reenactors were Anglo, Hispano, and Native American. Any other "Hyphenated-American" who wished to join was welcome; Schiller himself was of Swiss descent.

"Thank you, Colonel," he said, equally aware of the former soldier's gaffe. "Men, it's fitting that we be here on the weekend of Memorial Day. As you probably know, the occasion was first observed by the women folk of our Southern brethren, even as that tragic war still raged on.

"This evening the New Mexico Territorial Brass Band will give a free concert." The captain looked toward Fr. Jake. "I see a Reverend standing over there, and I'm hoping the good *padre* will let us use his church as a venue for the concert.

"Men, you're to set up tents north of the cemetery or bring your campers over here to park on the street." He raised his right hand to his cap in a smart salute. "Dismissed!"

While Schiller was speaking, Colonel Scurry had taken furtive swigs from a silver flask. Now the Tennessean trotted his stallion over to the officer.

"Capt'in, ah gotta git back to mah camp now."

"Certainly, Sir, and thank you. You live here in Providence?"

Scurry pointed toward the forest. "Up thar, we got us a 'campment. Real secure, too. Call it Fort Liberty'."

"Well, fine, Sir. If you'll excuse me, I'll speak to that Reverend now about tonight's concert."

Scurry rode off, swigging from his flask, a bit unsteady on the saddle, then galloped his mount up to intercept a road that led to his survivalist compound.

Schiller dismounted and walked over to Fr. Jake, who stood with Armando and Cynthia watching the reenactors return to the plaza.

"'Morning, *Padre*," the officer said, doffing his cap. "Ah… *Habla Ingles?*"

The Ghosts of Glorieta

The priest deadpanned a response, "About as well as they do in Michigan, Captain."

"Sorry, Father." The officer's sunburn turned salmon red. "I'm Karl Schiller. About that brass band concert I mentioned?"

"Father Jake, Captain. Of course. Churches were used that way in the medieval period, why not now? I think the villagers would be appreciative."

"Thank you. The music is all-authentic period melodies. " He hesitated, then pointed to Jane Doe's grave. "I was in police work. What's with the crime tape?"

"We're not sure, Captain, it's an ongoing investigation. This is Cynthia Plow, who discovered the graves."

"He bowed slightly. "I'm pleased, Ma'm. Hopefully, we can bury the soldiers' remains at Santa Fe National Cemetery, like we did the Fort Craig men."

"That would be wonderful!" She instinctively reached over to squeeze Armando's hand.

The captain noticed. "This your husband, Ma 'am?"

"He isn't married," Fr. Jake interjected. "Armando Herrera is a parishioner of mine."

The mechanic extended a hand. "How are ya, Captain?"

"Fine, Mister Herrera." As the two shook hands, Schiller eyed the young man. "You know, you might consider being part of our group. You could join the First New Mexico Territorial Volunteers. I'll give you our contact, he... he's also Hispanic."

"Hispanic. Imagine." Armando exchanged rolled-eye glances with Cynthia. "Thank you, or should I say, *Gracias*, sir."

Schiller turned back to the priest. "Father, you're a nice looking man. Strong face, distinguished graying hair, and we could use a chaplain. What do you say?"

"I say thanks and I'll think about your offer. I live across from the church, so let me know when your band arrives. I'll open it up."

"I will. Our annual Glorieta battle reenactment will be at Las Golandinas historical ranch on the Fourth of July. This encampment is practice for our new recruits."

"Mind if I do a little sketching around the tents?"

The captain saluted him. "Be my guest, Father Jake."

141

Albert Noyer

○

The priest strolled among men and women in authentic Civil War-period costumes, who were setting up tents, unloading field desks and footlockers, kerosene lamps, and iron pots. Children helped stack wood for cook-fires, while other women arranged bedding on folding cots inside their tents. Union and Confederate impersonators stacked muskets in pyramids at separate ends of the tent area. The four-man crew of a Model 1861 3" Ordnance Rifle struggled to ease the cannon and its limber off a flatbed truck. Captain Schiller moved through the camp, directing its construction: it was obvious that the reenactors were experts at setting up an encampment.

Ofilia Herrera circulated among the tents with her tray of curative herbs and lotions.

○

After an hour and a half, Fr. Jake flipped through the pages of his sketchbook as he started back home to fix himself lunch. *I did a few drawings of men and women setting up tents and tending their cooking fires. The wagon and cannon sketches aren't bad, but I really need to improve my figure work.* He stopped at a drawing of Ofilia selling herb packets to a reenactor woman. *The curandera must have radar in that tray she carries. Armando's aunt turns up at every sales opportunity.*

In returning home, the priest passed Dionisio Maldonado's house, but decided not to bother the man. Perhaps he had stayed away from Mass to deal with his grief. Fr. Jake was a house away from his own, when he saw Sonia Mora's red Plymouth turn left onto the Calle. He waited in the driveway, leaning on his Nissan, while the detective U-turned and parked at the curb in front.

Sonia stepped out of the driver's side with a plastic bag holding the yellow envelope she had found in her uncle's desk.

"Detective, you missed the parade," Fr. Jake told her. "It was a fine spectacle."

Sonia was uninterested in small talk. "I got those digitals of Jane Doe's burial from Cynthia. Could we go inside? I've read that woman's letter to Father Mora."

The Ghosts of Glorieta

"Of course." In the living room, the priest waved a hand toward his armchair. "Sonia, take that one. I'll sit on the couch."

"Read this…" Before sitting down, she handed him the envelope and took off her cap.

"Should I read out loud?"

"To yourself."

He read the young woman's scrawled handwriting.

Dear Father Morea,

I am so sory for what happin last nite but you been so kind to me about my problem with my husbind Jim Parker. He is geting so strange that I worry a lot. I didn' t mean for that to happin, but he told me to do it. I think it was nice but I know you are a preest and shoun't do that. Here is a picture for you of me with a big zookini I grew. Hee, Hee. I hope you don't think I am a bad girl.

Love, Aimee

P.S. I don't know what I will do about staying with Jim.

Neither one spoke until Sonia reacted in anger. "So my priest uncle had sex with another man's wife. From her looks, a juvenile, really."

Fr. Jake replied softly, "If that's what Aimée refers to."

"What do you think she refers to?" Sonia shot back, her black eyes accusatory under a frown. "Are you covering up for my uncle because he's a priest like you?"

"Of course not, Sonia."

She snatched the letter back from him. "There's no date on this and the girl doesn't mention a child. Perhaps Caleb hadn't been born yet."

"Aimée disappeared when he was about four years old. If she ran off," Fr. Jake speculated, "wouldn't she have taken the child with her?"

"Not necessarily." Sonia folded the letter, then slipped it and the envelope into the plastic bag and her purse. "A DNA test will determine paternity."

"You have Father Mora's?"

"Don't you watch CSI?" she mocked, using local law enforcement's cynical take on the TV shows. "It's standard procedure with the M.E. now.

143

At the fort's cemetery it was taken from Jane Doe's hair, bone, and sinew, but we'll have to go up and get cheek swabs from Jeremiah and Caleb."

"How soon after that will you know?"

"Testing might take a while. Right now our crime lab is down, awaiting accreditation. The FBI requires that so we can enter DNA results into its Combined DNA Index System."

"Sonia, you vocalized 'we' as if you wanted me to go to the compound with you."

She hesitated a moment before admitting, "Look, Father Jake, I haven't told you everything about the autopsy results. The M.E. found faint crosses tattooed on the bottom of each of my uncle's feet. I could research the symbolism, but thought you might know what they mean."

"Well, treading on a Christian symbol could be a sign of Satanism. That and the pentagram are visual evidences."

"If whatever took place happened at Eden West, it means my uncle went up there, and Jeremiah has the reputation of being somewhat of a religious nut. No offense, Father."

"None taken. You want another 'sane' religious person to interact with Jeremiah?"

"Something like that, I guess."

"Sonia," he decided to ask, "I notice you're now calling the victim 'my uncle' instead of 'Father Mora.' Isn't that rather personal?"

"It *has* become personal, since I'm a Mora family member. Don't worry though, it won't interfere with my objectivity. When can you come with me?"

"With the lab down, are you in a hurry?"

"Why, Father?"

"I feel somewhat isolated, so tomorrow I planned on driving to Belén and buying a cell phone. Something that just makes calls, not the mini-computer *cum* game players I see advertised. Also, I'll open a checking and savings account at Western Savings."

"Wednesday, then?"

"Fine."

Sonia stood, adjusted her Baker-Boy cap back on, and picked the purse off the floor. "Everyone at Eden West should be up by ten o'clock. I'll come by for you by then. We'll drive up to the commune entrance through the Upland Heights subdivision."

The Ghosts of Glorieta

"I'll be waiting."

"You, of course, realize that what you just read and I told you are confidential?"

"Seal of the confessional," he replied, then wondered if she understood what he meant.

"Good enough for me, Father."

"Fine. God bless until Wednesday."

As he made himself a turkey-ham sandwich, Fr. Jake felt a twinge of guilt. *It wasn't a lie. I just didn't tell Detective Mora that tomorrow I also plan on talking to the clerk at that Bellemonte Motel where Raylene Maldonado's body was found.*

The Ghosts of Glorieta

15 belén / june 1

The Bellemonte Motel was neither beautiful nor located on a mountain: a pseudo-Mission-style office and row of shabby, outdated rooms under a portico took up most of a short avenue west of Center Street. Fr. Jake parked his Nissan near the office, away from cars in the gravel lot that faced the front doors on rooms of a few "late sleepers."

On the ground, flies crawled over uneaten pizza left on paper plates. Cork-tipped cigarette butts and plastic vodka mini-bottles lay scattered around the parking lot gravel. *A lot of folks seem to have spent the long Memorial Day weekend celebrating here.* A buzzing red neon sign in the office window flashed VACANCY through scum-streaked glass. Below a blue Bellemonte sign above the entrance, an added-on panel proclaimed, "American Owned. God Bless America."

A bell fastened to the inside jingled as Fr. Jake opened the door to an office anteroom that reeked of stale cigarette smoke and industrial disinfectant. An old-fashioned porch glider with cushions upholstered in a white flower pattern took up the window wall. Facing it, a 1950's-style coffee table held scattered sections of the *Valencia County Herald* and two un-emptied ashtrays. A half-stocked travel brochure rack set against a wall advertised tourist attractions as far west as the Grand Canyon.

A clerk resembling a balding Nicholas Cage clutched a copy of *Playboy* as he parted curtains that covered a doorway behind the desk. He raised his eyebrows on seeing a priest at the counter, yet kept the magazine in one hand.

Albert Noyer

His nicotine-stained, toothy grin was forced. "Looking for one of yer lost sheep, *Padre,* or takin' up a collection?"

"I guess 'lost sheep,' as you put it." He extended a hand. "I'm Father Jake."

"Randall Clark."

"Randall, the woman who was murdered here was a parishioner of mine and—"

"Yeah," he interrupted, "sorry about that. Raylene was one of my regulars."

"Regulars?"

"Look, *Padre...*" Randall smacked a pair of copulating flies on the counter with his magazine, then flicked the bloody corpses toward an ashtray with a fingernail. "*Padre,* it ain't good business to be too nosy about guests here 'long as they pay. Raylene Garcia rented a coupla rooms a coupla days 'most every month for about a year now. You investigatin' on your own?"

"Sort of."

Randall pointed his magazine at the priest. "Lemme give ya a tip, *Padre.* Cops don't much like that."

He ignored the warning. "So, why did Raylene rent *two* rooms?"

"Expecting company, if ya take my meanin'. Like I said—"

"I know, 'it doesn't pay to be nosey.' Let me ask you, Randall. Did you ever see anyone use the second room, male or female?"

"Ask the cops. They'll tell ya what I said." Randall shoved the magazine under the counter and flicked his lighter to a Camel. He blew a blue cloud toward the ceiling, then came around to the counter front. "*Padre,*" he said, his eyes squinting from cigarette smoke. "I gotta supervise my *Mejicanos* working here. Have yerself a nice day."

"You, too, Randall."

Outside, Fr. Jake glanced around. The houses along the street were at least fifty years old, yet well maintained. The Bellemonte was an obvious eyesore on the neighborhood, perhaps grandfathered in when the city limits crept into this area after the Second World War. As he stood by his Nissan, the priest noticed yellow police tape strung in an X over the door of the second from the farthest motel room. *The Sheriff's department is still investigating the crime scene. Poor Raylene didn't have great taste in motel ambience. What was her lover like? A lot tidier than Randall, one would hope. I wish she had come to see me after Father Mora's funeral, but never made an appointment.*

148

The Ghosts of Glorieta

The priest took a slip of paper from his shirt pocket and unfolded it. "Let's see, Cell-Mart is on South Center Street. Western Savings Bank is also in that direction. I could probably walk to them, but leaving the car here...." He opted to drive, swung out of the parking lot, turned left, then checked traffic and made a right onto Center.

A sign at small parking area behind Cell*Mart warned, "Customers Only," but had a single car. A bored clerk inside played a video game with his thumbs. He was young and sported a Goth haircut, yet had mastered more about the working of electronic devices than Fr. Jake ever hoped to know. The priest settled on a pre-paid Broadband that had no long-term contract and charged only by the month, paid for by credit card.

Western Savings Bank was a few doors south. When Fr. Jake suggested that he could leave the car in his Cell*Mart space and walk to the bank, the clerk muttered "Whatever"—without losing a nanosecond of concentration on his game.

The bank entrance was through another Mission style portico; unlike the motel's stucco, this was new and unmarred. Even after the long holiday, no customers were inside. Two tellers were on duty, the nearest one was a handsome Hispanic man with the name "Rodrigo" on a nameplate at his window. He smiled when he saw the priest enter.

"Good morning, Father. How may I help you?"

"Good morning." Fr. Jake showed his Michigan driver's license. "I'd like to open a savings and checking account. I'm Father Jakubowski, assigned to the church in Providencia."

Rodrigo's smile broadened. "Of course, you're the new priest at San Isidro. I live at Eden West, up in the forest. What most people call a commune."

"Yes, I've met the Elder and his son, Caleb."

"Small world..." The teller extended a hand. "Rodrigo Jirón, Father. Our manager, Mr. Ramirez, will have you fill out an information card, then you'll be all set."

"Thank you." Fr. Jake put away his license while probing, "Rodrigo, did you know Father Mora at San Isidro?"

"I used to attend there, Father. No offense, but I got nothing spiritual out of Father Mora's Masses. I'm not that happy at the commune either, but...." Rather than finish his sentence Rodrigo switched to a new subject. "Father, we're having a contest this month to see who can sign up the most customers for renting a safety deposit box. Could I interest you?"

149

Albert Noyer

He chuckled. "I wish I had enough valuables to warrant renting a box."

Rodrigo glanced to either side, then leaned forward to whisper, "Look, Father, I'm not supposed to reveal this, but a lot of people living in Providencia have boxes. You'd be in good company. Duane Fortgang has the biggest one we rent. Cynthia Plow has one and…and people you probably haven't met so far. Let's see, you must know Raylene Maldonado and Carlotta down at the trading post."

"Yes, I've met everyone you mentioned." *He doesn't know about Raylene's murder.* "Rodrigo, does Mister Maldonado have a box?"

"No, it's registered only in her name, but I assume they both use it."

"Has he ever come in with his wife?"

"Not that I recall. Father, what do you say to a deposit box? You'd get peace of mind and I might win a one hundred dollar prize."

Fr. Jake gave a slight shake of his head. "I don't think so, Rodrigo, but I wish you luck."

The teller's smile remained. "That's fine, and this is only the first of June. I'll come around and introduce you to Mister Ramirez."

Fr. Jake couldn't resist a try. "Remember what Jesus said, 'Knock and it shall be opened to you'."

"Come back to San Isidro?" Rodrigo looked down, pretending to check his cash drawer. "I don't know, Father."

"Well, God bless."

In his office, Mr. Ramirez acted as deferential as most laypersons did around priests. He said that he attended a parish in Belén, then suggested a regular savings account that paid interest, and 55 Plus Checking in its simplest form, "since Father may only be here a year."

Before returning to Providencia, Fr. Jake drove to the train station where Vernon had unceremoniously dumped him off in the middle of that April night. He walked to the covered waiting platforms and looked at the iron benches where he might have spent the night. He sat on one to reflect about his almost miraculous escapade. "Jacob," the Polish derivation of the prefix of his surname, suggested a Jewish connection in Poland. The young twin of Esau had tricked his brother out of his inheritance for bread and a bowl of lentil stew. Jacob then fled to Haran to avoid Esau's wrath. *I didn't willingly flee to this place of exile, but then Jacob did return to Canaan. That could happen to me, 'Canaan' being Lake Sirius. On the other hand, perhaps my guardian angel had greater things in mind for me when Armando showed up. He credited*

The Ghosts of Glorieta

San Isidro. Fr. Jake glanced at his watch, then toward a compact building with the sign Placitas Café. *Good, the restaurant is open and the thought of Esau's stew made me hungry.*

At the restaurant, instead of lentil soup, Fr. Jake tried a bowl of green chile stew, which the menu described as, "A savory blend of pork, potatoes, tomatoes, onions and garlic, with just enough green chile to keep your eyes from watering!!! Served with a tortilla."

The stew tasted as good as advertised. Sipping the rest of his iced tea to cool off a biting chile burn on his tongue, Fr. Jake thought of the murdered woman. *Raylene held jobs, but didn't earn near enough money to buy gold and stash it in a bank vault. If she had gotten an inheritance from relatives, the deacon would have made sure that she spent it on him. The woman probably owned jewelry, but driving to Belén each time she needed to wear it? I don't think so. Then what did Raylene keep in the box?*

He paid the bill, left a dollar tip, and headed toward Highway 310.

Driving back, Fr. Jake decided to explore Romero Loop, the side road at Providencia that turned west toward the Rio Grande, then zigzagged back to the highway near Carlotta's grocery.

The river's fertile bottomland was lush with maturing alfalfa and cornfields, as it had been for some two hundred years. Horses grazed near a few territorial-style haciendas. A few immense cottonwoods dotted the flat land like silent, brooding ghosts of the past. The Nissan bumped over the bridge of an *acequia,* one of the many ditches that channeled life-giving water from the river to the fields. At the top of the loop, the road paralleled the *Acequia Madre,* a main channel that was opened each spring to allow Rio Grande water to course in. An *acequia mayordomo* closed the sluice gate in October.

Fr. Jake stopped the car and got out to look at the shimmering channel of water and nearby undulating ribbon of green *bosque* bordering the river beyond. The Rio Grande flowed south on the far side of the cottonwoods, a river that rivaled the Nile in the area's economic importance, yet which generally disappointed those who saw it the first time. "Didn't think it was that shallow or muddy," they complained.

He looked around to the east. The bell tower of San Isidro was visible, then the rise toward the forest where Eden West was located. *Rodrigo had implied that there was trouble in Paradise. Well, Providencia isn't quite Paradiso either. Father Mora murdered. Raylene Maldonado strangled. Tex Houston buying up the town for an Amityville West. Those all are tragic scripts that haven't played out their endings yet.*

151

Albert Noyer

To the far left were the streets and new houses of the redundantly named Upland Heights Estates gated community. *That's where G.D. Fortgang lives, but he's never invited me to his home. I really don't know much about the man. Is he married, with his wife attending a different church in a weekly one-hour "denominational divorce?" Duane must be well off financially to afford such an upscale neighborhood. At any rate, we're lucky to have his legal expertise in dealing with Tex Houston.*

Fr. Jake followed the Loop back to the highway and stopped in at the trading post for milk and another single-serving frozen lasagna he could microwave for supper.

Carlotta greeted him. "Good afternoon, Father. Look what I have for you." She pulled a statue from under the counter. "Mister Fortgang came by with more *santos*. One was San Isidro, so I saved him for you."

"Very kind, Carlotta, thank you."

The saint wore the traditional wide-brimmed hat, green, belted tunic, and tan trousers tucked into field boots. His eyes gazed heavenward, with hands folded in prayer. Fr. Jake turned the figure over to look at the base. A round sticker on the center read Hecho in Mexico and the signature *A. Reynoso* in blue ink. The price was written in pencil. "So he costs forty-five dollars?"

"Plus tax, Father."

"I don't see how Duane can market these so cheaply. You and Mamacita's must sell a lot of them."

"Mostly, some guy has a gift shop in Albuquerque and comes in to buy." Carlotta took the statue from him to wrap in tissue paper.

Fr. Jake asked, "Why doesn't the man deal directly with Fortgang?"

"We get fifteen percent, so I guess Mister Fortgang wants us to have a little extra money. Nice guy." She put the milk and lasagna in a plastic bag. The saint, wrapped with tissue, into a separate one. "Here you are, Father. $53.05 in all."

"Thanks, Carlotta..."He gave her three twenties and pocketed the change. "God bless."

When the priest pulled up in his driveway, late afternoon shadows stretched along the ground. He was mildly surprised to find letters in his mailbox from Detroit's prelate, Stanley Szredzinski, and Archbishop Jan Benisek at Santa Fe. The Detroit address was to Rev. C. Jakubowski / —Fr. Jesus Mora / San Isidro Rectory, but the woman mail carrier, a parishioner,

The Ghosts of Glorieta

knew where the Anglo priest lived and put letters for him in Rosita's old mailbox. Inside, he sat at his kitchen table.

"'Shreds' takes precedence," Fr. Jake muttered, slitting Archbishop Sredzinski's envelope along the top with a table knife. A check was included with the letter, which was from the prelate's secretary on an Archdiocesan letterhead.

Dear Fr. Jakubowksi;

It is my pleasure to include your salary check for this past May.

His Excellency suggests that for the June payment you set up an account in New Mexico, as a means of direct transfer to a bank. This is the safest and quickest way to receive funds. Please notify me of the bank or credit union's name and location, as well as your new account and routing numbers.

Fr. Jake muttered, "Hmm, Father Roggers is correct, but is there a not-too-subtle signal in there that I might stay here longer than the archbishop first implied?"

His Excellency sends you best wishes for success in your New Mexico ministry.

Sincerely in Christ,

Rev. Frederick Roggers / Secretary to the Archbishop

"Well, Father Fred," Fr. Jake whispered to the signature as if the priest were there, "I drove up to Belén today and did just that. Seems that 'Shreds' has no idea of what has happened here. Father Jesús is dead and there's been the murder of a parishioner. A Texas filmmaker bought up the town and wants to make an Amityville Horror West of it." He picked up the other envelope and asked himself, "What could his Moravian Excellency want?"

Alarmed at feeling the stress itch on his arm return, Fr. Jake tore the short edge of the letter and shook out Archbishop Benisek's message. It was from the prelate himself, dictated to Fr. Ramón.

My Dear Father Jake;

It was my distinct pleasure to meet you, and I am most truly grateful to you for allowing me to celebrate the funeral mass for Father Mora. Parishioners

153

Albert Noyer

will sorely miss him, yet I have every confidence that you will most ably fill his "clerical shoes." About the matter of "Deacon" Dionisio Maldonada. Father Ramon has researched the Archdiocesan diaconate ordination files and can find no evidence that the forenamed person ever was consecrated to the Diaconate. It is therefore my wish that you inform Mr. Maldonada that he must immediately cease the ecclesiastical privileges associated with this office. Should Mr. Maldonada offer proof of his ordination, please forward such documentation to Fr. Ramon.

Fraternally yours in Christ,

Rt. Rev. Jan Benisek

Archbishop of Santa Fe

RR

Fr. Jake set the letter aside. *'Maldonado' is misspelled and the man's diaconate status challenged, yet with his wife murdered, that's the least of Donny's concerns at the moment. Still, I will have to confront him as soon as it's feasible.*

○

It was just after 2:00 A.M. that night when Fr. Jake awakened to the wail of fire engine sirens.

The harsh sound dopplered closer and closer, and finally slowed down to a whine near San Isidro. He glanced out the front window: bright flames and thick black smoke billowed from the direction of the plaza, lighting the church and field between in an eerie orange glare.

"*Jesu Christe, eleison!*" he gasped. "That looks like Tex's semi-trailer on fire!"

The priest tugged on jeans and slipped into sandals. He ran through the field and saw other residents coming out of nearby homes and from the direction of the highway. The volunteer fire fighters found a hydrant and attached hoses, but it was clear that the trailer and its Horridusville model would be reduced to cinders before enough water could be directed at the inferno to extinguish it.

Shielding his face from the heat along with the other horrified spectators, the priest noticed Armando Herrera running from the apartment he lived in above his shop, A****Auto Repair.

When he saw Fr. Jake, the young man could only mumble, "Jeez, Father..."

154

The Ghosts of Glorieta

"Tex's dream. Our nightmare," Fr. Jake remarked, in a spontaneous metaphor.

"No. I mean, I'm not surprised that it happened so late."

"What do you mean, Armando?"

"You didn't hear about the village of Tierra Amarilla? Reis Tijerina?"

"N…no. Should I have?"

"Guess not, *Padre*, you're a *Norteño* from up in Michigan." Armando's criticism held a distain in his voice that the priest had not heard before. "Tijerina got tired of our land grants bein' taken over by Forest Service guys. Same crap as what the Texan is tryin' to pull with his friggin' quit deeds. Look at that sign over there."

To the left of the truck's cab, flickering orange light bathed an unpainted plywood panel supported by two stakes hammered in the ground.

"'*Lo Mismo Providencia o Muerte*'," he read aloud. "The Same Providencia or Death."

"Friggin'-A right, Father. Up in Tierra Amarilla it was *Tierra o Muerte*. And 'bout forty years ago people died when Tijerina and a few of his *Alianza* members took over the courthouse. Staties brought in the Army, then it seemed every jerk that owned a gun showed up. Happened at Golden twen'y years later with quit deeds. That's only sixty miles from here…" Breathing hard, Armando stopped and touched the priest's arm. "Sorry, Father, for getting' my gander up, but this Texas cow-shit guy is tryin' to screw all us Hispanos."

"Mister Fortgang is hiring an attorney to battle him in court."

"Maybe these flames talk louder than any piss-ass lawyers?" Armando glanced at the priest. "Aw, I gotta watch my language. Cynthia would kill me if she heard. It's just that—"

"—That violence begets violence, Armando. I saw it in Poland and also in Detroit." When the mechanic did not reply, Fr. Jake asked, "What happened to… Tijerino…was it?"

"Reis Tijerina. He got three years in the pen at Santa Fe, but he's still around, older an' quieter. Now we got these La Raza guys stirrin' up trouble." Armando watched the dying flames a moment longer, then slapped his forehead. "I just had an idea. Let *them* take care of ol' Cowboy Tex!"

Fr. Jake winced as a section of the semi's roof tumbled onto the floor of the burned trailer. *If they haven't started already.*

155

The Ghosts of Glorieta

16 eden west / june 2

In the morning, Fr. Jake read the day's entry of his breviary at the kitchen table, while sipping a second cup of coffee. He had been neutral about the First Reading in the Book of Tobit, but the Responsorial Verses of Psalm 111 struck a chord.

"I need to know more about Tobit, but the Psalm is hopeful. 'The heart of a just man is secure, trusting in the Lord,' and 'He has no fear of evil news…with a steadfast heart he will not fear; he will see the downfall of his foes'."

He set the book aside to think once again about the night's event. *Tex will be furious when he learns about the fire and his destroyed model. No telling what he'll do.*

As if on cue, the blaring notes of "Yellow Rose of Texas" sounding on the horn of the filmmaker's Cadillac, reinforced the priest's thought. He went to the front window: Tex Houston and his secretary, Roberto, were getting out of the garish, yellow-finned convertible. Tex wore the same white outfit he had on at Sunday's meeting. Roberto Rios, in a dark business suit, carried the red rope folder tight to his body.

Fr. Jake met them at the door, prepared for an angry outburst from the Texan. "Come in, gentlemen. I'll put on more coffee."

"Father, don't trouble yourself." Tex held up a silver thermo cup with UTA and the University of Texas Austin logo engraved on the side. "I only drink this optimal energy herbal substitute. No caffeine, high potassium, alkaline, rich in inulin…" He took a sip, then laughed. "Shucks, I sound

157

like a testimonial, but it's a mighty healthy drink. How are you Father Jakubowski?" He pronounced the name as "Yakubofski," with the correct Slavic J and w letter sounds. Today, Jefferson Davis Houston was very much Alex Bardu, the Albanian-American business mogul, with only a hint of the old Tex.

"I'm well, Alex, or should I keep it 'Tex'?"

He glanced at Roberto. "Alex is fine when we're out of the hearing of my fans, but keep it Tex." He gestured toward the couch with his silver cup. "May we sit down?"

"Please."

The filmmaker left his hat on and slumped on the couch next to his secretary. Fr. Jake settled in the armchair.

Tex looked around the small room. "Smells nice in here."

"I finally burned enough of a sage smudge bundle to make a difference. Look Tex, I want to express regrets for what happened to your truck."

"Father, don't give it a thought. These things happen."

"But…but your model."

He laughed at the priest's concern. "All insured, 'smock, frock and spittoon.' Besides, it wasn't an actual model, and I've got another semi equipped just like it."

"What do you mean, not an actual model?"

"VR…Virtual Immersion Reality. THVIR, actually, a revolutionary kind of hologram. Roberto, y'all explain to Father."

Rios shifted the folder from his knees to a side of the couch. "Mister Houston has developed Tex Houston Virtual Immersion Reality, THVIR, an immersive, highly visual, three-dimensional virtual environment that does not need multimodal devices such as a wired glove, Polhemus boom arm, or omnidirectional treadmill to be activated."

Fr. Jake shrugged and scratched his gray whisker stubble in a helpless gesture. "You've lost me, Roberto."

Tex boasted, "Got me patents on it, too. What Roberto is saying is that THVIR will replace CAD software and any technical limitations in projecting holograms now in use. Have you seen a hologram, Father Jay?"

"Yes, at Detroit auto shows."

"Well, my technique allows full sized, VIR 3-D images to be projected in front of most any backing surface with perfect clarity. The trailer was empty and that model was all an illusion, a kind of hologram that I could make

The Ghosts of Glorieta

any size I wanted. Now, I do have only one production camera operational and that's guarded like gold at Fort Knox."

"Tex, that's all quite amazing, yet you didn't come over just to tell me, did you?"

"No, as a matter of fact, no. Roberto."

The young man held up his red rope folder. "Mister Houston is ready to implement the acquisition of his property through these quitclaim deeds."

"What Roberto is saying is that I'm about to start construction, but this village isn't incorporated and has no mayor. From what I recall in Albania, the local priest was the arbiter, the go-between, of just about anything. I mean, old ladies would touch his robes so that their holy magic, or whatever, would rub off on them."

"That was the Orthodox Church," Fr. Jake told him. "I saw some of what you describe in Greece, but we Roman Rite priests aren't held on quite the same magical level."

Tex missed the sarcasm. "Just the same, Father, people here look up to you."

"That would have been Father Mora. I came as an outsider from Michigan. While I'm not exactly shunned in the Amish sense, I've yet to gain most parishioners' confidence. I mean, even to get them to attend my services."

"Just the same…" Tex glanced out the window, then stood up. "You've got company, Father. A red car just pulled up behind my Caddy." He slipped into his "Don't Mess with Tex" mode. "Well, now, *Padre*, that's a mighty pretty young lady comin' up to your door."

Fr. Jake got up and recognized the Plymouth Neon outside. "Tex, that 'pretty young lady' would be Detective Sonia Mora. She's investigating her uncle's murder."

"Detective, you say." Tex pushed his cowboy hat back from his forehead. "Hmmph, Roberto. Imagine that pretty lady bein' a detective."

After Sonia came inside, Fr. Jake introduced the two men. "Detective, this is Tex Houston. His aide, Roberto Rios. You already know about his documentary project."

She shook their hands, "Mister Houston. Mister Rios," then turned to the filmmaker. "Mister Houston, I—"

"Ma'am," he drawled, "jus' call me Tex."

159

Albert Noyer

"Mister Houston," Sonia continued, "I have Deputy Griego putting up crime scene tape around your vandalized property. An arson team will investigate, so do not let any of your employees tamper with the site before they can go over it."

Tex winked and handed her his card. "Well, now, detective, I sure would have a nice actin' part for you in my documentary."

"Did you understand my instructions, Mister Houston?" she repeated in a tone bordering on disgust, just short of anger.

Tex looked down and scuffed his cowboy boots one over the other. "Yes I did, Ma'am."

She turned to the priest. "Father Jake, I'm sorry to interrupt what's going on here, but we need to take those DNA cheek swabs up at the commune."

The filmmaker recovered enough pride to ask, "This about that dead *padre*, detective?"

She ignored his question. "Ready, Father Jakubowski?"

"Yes, of course. Tex, we'll have to discuss your business with me sometime later."

"Why sure, Father. I'll get my camera guys to film over by the river. You know, get a feel for the land around here." He tipped his cowboy hat to Sonia. "My pleasure, Ma'am. Y'all have my card, if y' ever—"

"Shall we go Father?" Outside, Sonia walked rapidly to her Plymouth and opened the passenger door. "Get in and belt up." With deft turns of the steering wheel, she headed the car away from Tex's Cadillac and back toward the highway. "The entrance into Eden West is on Camino Alto, through the subdivision."

"Upland Heights Estates."

"Correct."

"Ah, need I ask what you thought of Tex?"

"Man's a prick."

"A rich one, though. He now owns a good part of Providencia."

"So a jerk-off owns your town. I live in Socorro." Sonia made a hard right onto Camina Alto, then braked the car so abruptly that her priest-passenger braced his hands against the dash. "Shit," she muttered under her breath. "I forgot Griego."

"The deputy is coming with us?"

The Ghosts of Glorieta

She made a U-turn back to the highway without answering, barely waited for a gravel truck to rumble past, then looped back to the San Isidro plaza. Yellow crime scene tape surrounded the burned-out semi-trailer. Hilario Griego waited in his patrol car, reading a *Valencia County Herald*.

Sonia pulled alongside his window. "Whadja find?"

"Accelerant started the blaze. Arson felony."

"No-brainer. Follow us up to Eden West and be sure to park on this side of the entrance."

"Got it, Detective." He gave her a "thumbs up" sign as he started the engine.

When Sonia turned up Camino Alto again, Fr. Jake asked, "Why do you need a sheriff's deputy? Aren't Pentecostals peaceful people to deal with?"

She replied, "The acreage back of the old guy belongs to a wacko survivalist militia group. I don't take chances."

"'The old guy' being James Parker, a.k.a. Elder Jeremiah?"

"Sorry, Elder Jeremiah, of course. Sometimes I lapse into talk like some of the deputies I work with."

The Plymouth whined up the rising street and reached a brick gatehouse. The guard station was vacant and a cream-colored steel gate had been propped open. The recession had slowed construction, so a security guard promised in the homeowner's covenant was never hired. Up ahead, three houses still under construction looked abandoned. About a dozen homes were finished, yet buyers had not bought all of them.

The last house on the Camino Alto was near an end wall of adobe-colored cement panels that surrounded the subdivision. Street paving ended there, but a dirt road continued on through an access in the wall. As Sonia slowed the car in front of the last mansion on the left, Fr. Jake read "G.D. Fortgang" and the number 14 on an oversized mailbox in front.

"That's where the accountant lives," he remarked. "Fancy house."

"Yeah…" Sonia's hand-gestured out the driver's window for Griego to follow her onto the ruts of the unpaved road.

The roadway continued as a widened trail beyond the entryway to the Pentecostal commune. Letters cut into the wood of an arch gave its name.

EDEN WEST

The Lamb shall dwell with the Wolf. Is. 11: 6

161

Albert Noyer

Sonia swung her car to a stop on the right of the arch. Deputy Griego arrived seconds later, but parked his patrol car further along the road's shoulder, beyond the commune's entry.

"Jeez, I told him to park on this side." Sonia got out of the driver's door and reached on the back seat of the car for her CSI kit.

Twenty feet past the Eden entrance a barricade of two sawhorses blocked further access to the road. A plywood sign on one read:

FORT LIBERTY

!!!don't TREAD on me!!!

Griego stepped out of his patrol car and went to look at another notice hung on a barbed wire fence opposite the barricade. "Hey, detective," he called back, "This says 'Private Property -Trespassers Die.' Someone drew a skull and crossbones on the—"

An echoing gunshot obliterated the deputy's final word: a rifle bullet had shattered a hole through his patrol car's windshield, leaving a shower of small glass shards glittering on the front seat.

Griego simultaneously unholstered his .38 Colt Police Special and rolled into a weed-overgrown drainage ditch below the fence. Sonia Mora dropped her CSI kit, shoved Fr. Jake behind a cottonwood tree next to the Plymouth, and drew out her Glock G19 Compact revolver.

The loud noise had frightened away birds and chirping insects.

Moments later, everything again was eerily quiet.

Sonia checked her watch. After waiting a full minute, she slowly holstered her gun and called to Griego, "Deputy, that was a warning shot. It's safe to come back."

"Crazy bastards," he growled, still brushing brambles from his tan uniform. "We gotta get them *pendejos* one of these days."

Fr. Jake recovered from alarm at the unexpected action and stood up from a crouch. "Yes, who are they?"

Griego asked, "You never been shot at, Father?"

"Not directly," he said, still trembling a bit.

"That's an armed camp over there," Sonia added. "The Survivalists may well be preparing for some kind of 'sovereign citizen' showdown."

"Why *don't* you arrest them?" he asked.

"Mark, one of Billy Scurry's four sons was caught in the trading post," Sonia told the priest. "A State Trooper who detained him was bitten on the arm, and the kid tried to take his revolver away."

162

The Ghosts of Glorieta

"Bastard bonded out," Griego added, "and never showed up for trial."

Fr. Jake thought he recognized the name. "Did you say 'Billy Scurry'?"

"Yeah, Father. Billy Ray Scurry."

"Sonia, he was a Colonel in the First Gulf War and guest of honor at the re-enactors' opening ceremony."

"What? The Gopher came out of his hole?"

"That's right, detective."

"Aw, we should have known that," she complained. "You have gophers in Michigan, right, Father? You ever tried to catch one nosing out of a burrow?"

"I have. It's virtually impossible."

"The way it is with Billy Scurry. We had an informer at his compound. Before the officer was found dead in Belén, he managed to tell us that different individuals buy any outside supplies the commune needs. Scurry himself rarely leaves the fort."

"Scurry." Griego laughed. "Real good name. The guy *scurries* right back into his gopher hole."

Sonia added, "DEA, FBI, and IRS agents would like to know what goes on in 'Fort Liberty.' Where they get their cash flow, how much, and who keeps it."

"Then why don't the authorities come to interrogate and/or arrest Scurry?"

"Remember Waco, Father? Two sheriffs have thought of doing that, but decided they didn't want the responsibility...or bad publicity...for another massacre. Besides, these guys do live like gophers in underground houses that are each one a fortress." Sonia pointed to the fence. "Look at that dirt berm they've built up past the razor wire. That thick boxwood hedge behind it has to be six feet high. Take a tank to bust though." When she picked her CSI kit up off the ground, her hands shook a bit. "Let's go find the Elder."

As he walked under the arch, Fr. Jake looked up again at the verse from Isaiah. *The Elder has Isaiah 6 somewhat backward, but with Scurry living in his yard, the wolf indeed is threatening the lamb.*

The arrival of the automobiles and proximity of the gunshot had alerted some commune Pentecostals. Curious men in coveralls and a few women dressed in cotton gowns watched the three strangers come through the entrance arch. Caleb Parker, helping sort used tires, dropped from a 1960's Ford stake truck, recognized the priest, and ran forward.

163

"Father Jake! You should have told me you were coming. Is that sheriff's officer here because of the shooting? That goes on all the time…target practice…but never this close."

"Caleb," he explained, "someone from there shot out the front window of the deputy's patrol car—"

"Father, I'll handle this." Sonia held forward her ID. "Detective Mora, Socorro Sheriff's Department, sir. This is Deputy Griego. You already know Father Jakubowski."

"Yes." As Caleb shook the two law officers' hands, the priest told him, "Detective Mora wants to obtain cheek swabs from you and your father for DNA testing."

"DNA? Why?"

Sonia asked, "Sir, is James Parker here?"

"Dad's at our place, but he doesn't like to be disturbed—"

"Sir, could we go to where you and your father live?"

"Sure thing, detective." Caleb pointed to the left. "It's that last Earthship lodge over on this side of the back fencing."

"'Earthship', Caleb?"

He laughed; the name always baffled newcomers. "Father Jake, that's what we call our homes. You'll see why."

The Edenites went back to their tasks at mounds of excavated dirt and the discarded tires that were stacked just beyond the entrance.

Walking back, Fr. Jake commented about the back fence. "So, Caleb, that razor wire separates Fort Liberty from your commune?"

"Correct. At this point, there's twice the space between the wire and boxwood hedge. Teams of two armed guards patrol the whole perimeter, 24/7. They pass by about every twenty minutes."

The entrance wall of the Elder's rammed-earth house faced north. Large solar array windows were on the opposite side. Roof clerestory windows oriented north and east gave light to this side of the house. Two square solar panels on the roof faced south-west. Caleb led the way through the graceful curved facade of an adobe porch that sheltered a doorway. A verse above the portal read, **YE HAVE BEEN GIVEN STEWARDSHIP OF THE EARTH**. The entrance door led into an anteroom of tan, cement-panel walls.

"Dad!" he called out. "Dad, a detective is here to see you."

The foyer's archway led into a large room. Soft light flooded in from six south-facing solar array windows covered with translucent insulated

The Ghosts of Glorieta

blinds. Small windows set in two of the larger ones were opened to admit a cool breeze. In front of the windows, tomato, pepper, and lettuce seedlings flourished inside adobe planters. A galley kitchen was on the right, with sink gray-water piped into the planter.

A fireplace on the north wall was clean of ashes. In this, a living room, light oak paneled the cement walls. The floor was of smooth cement tiles around the fireplace, with oak parquet squares as a floor in the rest of the area. Most of the well-crafted Taos-style furniture was made of ponderosa pine and upholstered in Native American wool fabrics.

Half-facing the windows, Elder Jeremiah sat in an armchair. He looked up when he heard his son, and marked the bible page he was reading with a satin ribbon.

Caleb beckoned the three in. "Dad, this is Detective Mora and Deputy Griego. You know Father Jake."

"Welcome." Jeremiah laid his bible on a side table and stood up. "I don't suppose you're here to join my Pentecostals?"

"No, sir," Sonia told him. "I need to take cheek swabs in order to process you and your son's DNA. If you agree, I have consent forms for you both to sign."

"And if we don't, detective?"

"Subpoenas."

James Parker shrugged and looked away from her to Fr. Jake. "And how are you Reverend? As you notice," he jested, "I still retain my Midwestern accent."

"I noticed. The King James's Version 'thees' and thous' *can* become tiring—"

"Father..." Sonia warned him in a sharp tone of voice to keep quiet.

"Sorry. Detective, please continue."

"Sir, the skeletal remains of a young woman was discovered in the old fort's cemetery. We have reason to believe that she might be one of your Pentecostals."

"And why do you believe that?"

"Sir, that's still privileged information at this time."

Parker sat down again and picked up his Bible. Caleb pulled over a Santa Fe-style chair near his father and said, "Sit down, detective. Father Jake, Deputy Griego, that Taos sofa by the wall is comfortable. I'll take the planter wall."

165

Albert Noyer

Sonia set her CSI case next to the chair. "Mister Parker, I can tell you that I've been going over a cold case for the last few days."

"Aimée Parker."

She seemed surprised. "Yes, your wife. Sir, you have no obligation to answer, but my questions here would be off the record."

Parker glanced toward his son. "Go on."

"The report you filed in 1992 said that your wife had been missing for three days and left …well…left her son behind."

"Caleb was four years old." Parker ran a caressing hand over the bible cover and continued without looking up, "I was starting the commune, building this Earthship, so we lived in a temporary tent structure I had attached to our VW camper. The police officers who came muttered something like, 'Look at this hippie dump. Don't blame the gal for skipping out.' They didn't take Aimée's disappearance seriously. Not one of them came back."

"But you were interrogated."

"'Course they questioned me and decided I had nothing to do with her running off."

"Your marriage was working out?"

At the question, Parker picked up the bible and clutched it to his chest. "Aimée was sixteen when we married in a…guess you'd call it…a 'flower child' wedding. Afterward, we took off in my VW. She thought that was fun, visiting different places, seeing America, yet I knew we eventually had to settle down. Running out of money here, finding a church I could take over, me knowing carpentry like His Son, well, that all seemed like God calling to me." He looked out the window and half smiled at his recollections. "Oh, Aimée was fun-loving all right, but after a while she became sullen, morose. She went down for some kind of counseling with that Catholic priest at San Isidro."

"Father Mora."

"Right, detective." Parker rested his chin on the bible's gold-edge pages. "Once …once Caleb was born, Aimée seemed to settle down a bit, yet everything was seething inside her—"

"Dad!" Caleb interrupted, red-faced. "Dad, you never told me all this. You…you only said that mom died of something or other."

"What would have been the use? Your mother was gone….skipped out."

166

The Ghosts of Glorieta

Caleb slid off the planter wall to stand up. "But you lied to me!"

Parker leaned toward him to extend a consoling hand. "Caleb, I…I just wanted to protect you."

"All right, folks, that's enough." Sonia picked up her CSI kit and stood. "I'll need those cheek swabs. Caleb, if you're willing, I'll start with you."

"Sure" he agreed, still flushed with anger. "I'll sign your damn consent paper. I'd just like to get away from here and all this satanic bullshit."

Sonia clicked open a ballpoint pen. Following his son, James Parker signed with the bible as a support for the sheet. As Sonia handed the consent forms to Fr. Jake, she asked the two, "Have either of you eaten in the last hour?" The men shook their heads. "Good." She selected two swab-taking packets from her case. "Griego, I'll hand you the used swab. Place it directly in a plastic specimen envelope. Label it with the subject's name."

"Got it, detective."

Sonia tossed him a pair of latex gloves, then snapped on hers. She took a good thirty seconds collecting cells from each man, aggressively scraping the inside of the cheek wall, gums, and inside their lips with an up and down motion, while rotating the swab.

Caleb left immediately afterward, without looking at his father.

After she swabbed the elder Parker, Sonia checked the labeling, dated each packet, and secured them in her case. "Sir," she said to him, "thank you for your cooperation. I will be in touch with you about the results."

"Sister Sonia…" James Parker reverted to being Elder Jeremiah. He went to place a hand on the detective's head for a blessing, but she stepped back. Unfazed, he continued, "Sister Sonia, if this be in accordance with God's will, I thank thee for coming here this day."

"Sir, God had nothing to do with it," Sonia countered. "You can thank the Socorro County Sheriff's Department."

Fr. Jake was not so sure: in Spanish, "*socorro*" meant aid, help, assistance. If what Sonia accomplished helped solve the mystery of Aimée's fate, who was to say?

At the entrance to Eden West, Deputy Griego moaned while checking his shattered windshield and cursed Billy Ray Scurry once again. He softened the F-word in deference to the priest.

"Friggin' *pendejos!* Dumbasses! "Why don't our friggin' sheriff just come out here and torch the friggin' place down?"

167

Albert Noyer

"Like at Waco?" Sonia taunted. "Look, Griego, your patrol car's insured and the powers that be aren't gonna do a G-damned thing. Get back to the station and write up your report. I'll confirm it later."

Sonia backed around and headed her Plymouth toward the Camino Alto. "I'm pissed too, Father," she admitted, "but half the NM National Guard is deployed in the Middle East or along our Mexican border." She gripped the steering wheel in frustration.

After the car passed through the opening in the subdivision wall and onto the paved street, Fr. Jake looked to his right.

"Looks like Duane Fortgang is home now. That's a late model Chrysler in his drive-way, so his restaurant and CPA work must be doing well." A panel truck, with "**A. Reynoso / Mexican Woodcrafts**" lettered on the side, was parked alongside the Chrysler. Fr. Jake wondered, "Why would there be smoke from his chimney on a warm day like this?"

"He's burning trash. Those new homes have incinerators." Sonia became quiet, her tense fingers alternately tightening and loosening on the steering wheel.

Fr. Jake noticed. "You're thinking of your uncle."

She nodded, staring straight ahead. "I have proof that he broke the Sixth Commandment with whom, a twenty-year old? Probably fathered Aimée's child."

"Sonia, you don't have proof yet." When she gave him a disgusted side-glance, he shook his head. "No, I'm not defending a fellow priest, but I believe that Parker isn't telling us everything."

"What do you mean?"

"The crosses you said were tattooed on Father Mora's feet, and Caleb's brief reference to Satanism. Detective, there's a sin, if you will, that a priest would consider worse than adultery."

They had reached the gatehouse. Sonia braked her car to a stop, turned off the engine, and looked straight ahead. "Go on. Explain."

Fr. Jake told her, "As a layperson, you might not have put much significance in a Eucharist host being stolen from a monstrance at the *sagrario*. Catholics believe it is the Real Presence of Christ under the appearances of ordinary bread."

"So?"

"A consecrated host is used in a Black Mass. It would be a real coup to obtain one."

168

The Ghosts of Glorieta

She looked over at him. "Wait a minute, Father. You're saying Aimée might have seduced my uncle to obtain a communion host for one of Parker's...Elder Jeremiah's...rituals and he went up there with her?"

"That could have happened. It would help explain Father Mora's remark to me about only God being able to forgive him."

Sonia pushed back her cap to smooth a hand over her hair. "So, if my uncle was murdered to get a host for another Black Mass at the commune, wouldn't it have to be a parishioner? Wait. We found part of a broken *matachine* wand, so the killer could have been masked—"

Fr. Jake patted her hand. "Slow down, detective! Your uncle could have been merely knocked unconscious to get the host, yet he was suffocated by the zamia fumes. There had to be another reason for his death, and therein lies more, perhaps the core of the mystery. "

Sonia turned the ignition key on the Plymouth. "Somethin' poetic for me to chew on, goin' back to Socorro."

As she put the car in Drive, Fr. Jake said, "I meant to ask. Any autopsy report on Raylene Maldonado yet?"

Sonia nodded. "Meant to share, Father. Strangulation, as we figured. Rivotril, the Mexican name for clonazepam, one of the date rape drugs, knocked her out. No semen, blood, or other physical evidence. Her car was clean. The killer knew her and was very careful."

"Motive?"

"An affair gone from bad to worse, or discovered?" she speculated. "Happens all the time. The deacon isn't exactly Prince Charming, and in these cases the husband is always a person of interest. I'll go back and get the man's deposition as to his whereabouts at the time of his wife's death."

"That motel desk clerk was of no help."

She almost braked the car to a stop again. "What? You went to the Bellemonte?"

"I...I was in Belén," he admitted, trying to suppress guilt in his voice. "Had to open a bank account and finish other business."

"You told me that. Father Jake, you've been reading too many novels where amateur detectives solve crimes. I wish we could get our perps in three hundred pages." She gently slapped his hand as a reprimand. "Don't do anything like that again, okay?"

"Okay, sorry. Ah, could you drop me off at Mamacita's? There's a collection of Mexican *santos* for sale inside. If that San Isidro I saw the

169

Albert Noyer

first time I went is still there, I may send it to Archbishop Sredzinski in Detroit."

"Sure, Father…" She checked her rear view mirror; the deputy's car followed about ten feet behind. "Hilario Griego will file a report on the damage to his patrol vehicle, but, like I said, nothing good will happen short of declaring war on Scurry."

"One more thing," he recalled. "At Western Savings I found out that Raylene Maldonado rented a safety deposit box that isn't shared by her husband."

"Now that's interesting, Father. I'll contact a friend at the Belén sheriff's office. We'll get a warrant to open it."

Sonia dropped the priest off at the restaurant, then continued on Highway 310 to reach the shorter route by a bridge across the Rio Grande. The DNA lab in Socorro would have the swabs processed.

Inside Mamacita's, Fr. Jake nodded a greeting to Julia, waiting tables, then looked through the collection of wooden *santos* on display shelves near the cash register.

"I don't see that San Isidro you had," he told Conchita, the middle-aged cashier. "It doesn't matter too much if you sold it, because I found another one at the trading post. I thought I'd send this one to a friend."

"Oh, no, *Padre*, the *santo* was no sold." she replied. "*Señor* Fortgang, he come at the beginning of all months and take some *santos* away. Then he bring new ones."

"So that San Isidro could be at his house?"

"Maybe, *Padre*…"

Fr. Jake picked up a carved figure of St. Francis and turned it over. Like on his *santo*, the white sticker on the wooden base read, *Hecho in Mexico* and **A. Reynoso** in blue ink. The price $45 was written in pencil.

"I like you, Francis," the priest told the saint. "When I save a little more money, I'll buy you next."

○

In the middle of that night, fire engine sirens again wakened Fr. Jake. Alarmed, he padded barefoot to his front room. An ominous yellow-orange color undulated across the white walls from a fire that was close enough to send the shadows of furnishings dancing in the room. He pulled open the door and looked out.

The Ghosts of Glorieta

Across the Calle, flames licked at the front entrance portal of his Church of San Isidro. The priest scratched at itching in his left arm and abruptly felt nauseous at the thought of the venerable church being destroyed. He grasped the doorframe for support. *With or without his permission, Tex's employees have retaliated for the loss of his truck.*

The Ghosts of Glorieta

17

In the reenactors' camp, a bugle sounded the signal to assemble. A sound of shouting came from that direction; within minutes the dark shapes of running figures appeared at the eastern side of the church, carrying leather buckets. Two of the men headed for the fire hydrant a house away from San Isidro. One of them with a wrench expertly opened a gush of water.

"Over here!" the other man called to those arriving. "Start a bucket brigade leading to the fire!"

The unexpected activity revitalized Fr. Jake's hopes. He came down the steps, shoeless, to try and help.

One of the men crouching at the hydrant saw him. "Aren't you the priest here?" he shouted out. "I saw you at the opening ceremonies."

"Yes, I'm Father Jake, pastor of San Isidro."

He stood and waved him off with both hands. "Just stand back, Father. Lenny and me are Duke City firemen. I noticed this hydrant while we paraded by. We practice fire drills all the time."

"This ain't no drill," Lenny chimed in, "but don't worry. We're gonna save your church, *Padre*."

As sinister flames crept from the doorsill up the dry wood of the jambs and onto the church portal itself, a dozen or so men and women formed a chain from the hydrant to the burning entrance. Strong hands passed bucket handles on to other hands. Water sloshed out of the containers and onto the street and grass, yet enough remained to fling onto the flames. Hissing steam billowed from the scorched wood.

173

Up the street, a clip-clop of a horse's hooves came from the camp's direction. Fr. Jake turned to look. As the rider came closer, the fire's glare illuminated Captain Schiller.

The officer halted his mount in front of the priest and saluted. "Evening, Father. You all right?"

"I am, Captain. It's my church that may not be."

Schiller watched the firefighters a moment before commenting, "Seems like there's a blaze going on here 'most every night. Father, why is that?"

"I'm not sure I'm up to discussing it just now. I...I could make coffee for the men, but only a few cups at a time."

"No, sir, that's not necessary. I'd say you were mighty lucky that our pickets saw flames and alerted the Company."

"Pickets?"

The captain sighed and patted his horse's neck. "Sentries, Father. Guards. I can smell the accelerant, the gasoline that started that fire way back here."

The waning moon had risen about two hours earlier. Now its near-full brightness threw black shadows on a gray scene that showed only weak, flickering orange light from the dying flames as a counterpoint.

The two men watched in silence as the church entrance gradually returned to darkness. Vapors of steam rose from the doorway. The acrid smell of old, charred wood was strong on the night air. The men and women gradually broke up their bucket line and moved back to camp. A few rested on the ground nearby to talk about the arson.

Fr. Jake heaved a sigh of relief. "Thanks to your men, San Isidro is saved."

"Hallelujah!" Schiller detached a canteen from his belt and held it forward. "Father, I'll pass on the coffee, but I've never known a clergyman to turn down a wee nip. How about if I came in and you explained what's going on to me."

Fr. Jake replied in the corny Irish accent he used in a college play. "Sure, Cap'n, an' a wee nip would be welcome 'bout now. If yer promisin' no more than that."

"Sure an' I'm promisin' nary a drop more." The officer chuckled as he dismounted and tied his mount's reins to a rear wheel cover of the priest's Nissan. "Steady, Ulysses," he soothed, stroking the horse's muzzle. "I'll be back shortly, girl."

The Ghosts of Glorieta

"We can sit in the kitchen." Fr. Jake noted that the captain's horsey smell was stronger in his house than the lingering scent of the sage bundle. He took two water tumblers from his cabinet to set on the table. Schiller unscrewed his canteen's top and splashed rum into the glasses.

"*Salud*, Father! Health."

"*Na zdrowie*, Captain! Health and, again, I'm grateful to your men."

The rum was pleasantly warm in Fr. Jake's stomach. He took another swallow before putting his glass down. "Captain, did you name your horse 'Ulysses' after the Greek wanderer of the Trojan War?"

He took off his forage cap and put it on one side of the table. "I'm fond of the Classics, so partly 'yes.' That was also General Grant's first name."

"Right, Ulysses S. Grant, and thus the names of two heroes."

The captain took another sip of rum. "I count a third one, Father. Have you read Julius Caesar's *Commentaries on the Gallic Wars?*"

"Afraid that wasn't required seminary reading where I studied."

"Too bad. Caesar's motto, if you will, was *Celeritas Vincit*...'Swiftness Conquers.' I've tried to keep that in mind in everything I do."

"It certainly worked tonight, Captain. Your men arrived here *summa celeritate*.... posthaste."

He half-smiled and raised his glass. "Hail, Caesar!"

"*Ave*, Schiller!" Fr. Jake responded. After both sipped more rum, he recalled, "Captain, you told me you were in police work."

"Right. So...so what's going on around here, Father?"

"That Texas filmmaker who's putting you in his documentary bought up this part of Providencia through quitclaim deeds. He wants to build a schlock movie set that would attract tourists."

"And the villagers don't like it."

"Would you, Captain?"

"Father, make it 'Karl'." He splashed a tad more rum in the priest's glass, then into his own while asking, "What do you know about this Billy Ray Scurry I introduced to the men?"

"Not much, Karl. Evidently, he and his followers run a survivalist camp up in the forest named Fort Liberty. I was near there yesterday with Detective Mora and Deputy Griego. Someone fired a rifle bullet from that direction and shattered the deputy's patrol car windshield."

175

Albert Noyer

"Felony, Article something or other." Schiller stroked his trimmed beard in thought. "Frankly, I'm disappointed in the man. I found him a real boor ...and I'm being polite."

"How did you meet Scurry?"

"He must have read about us coming here. The man contacted me about being a relative of Confederate Colonel William Scurry. We have a man—he isn't here right now—a man impersonating the Colonel at our reenactment of the Glorieta Pass battle. You know about that Civil War action?"

"Cynthia Plow mentioned it, but I'm not really familiar."

Karl settled back, took a sip of rum, and stretched his booted legs out to the side. "That was the definitive Civil War event here in New Mexico. In February 1862, Texan volunteers under General Henry Sibley moved north. Sibley hoped to reach Colorado, take the gold fields, and then head west to secure Arizona Territory and California for the Confederacy. The Rebs managed to capture Albuquerque and Santa Fe. Our army's main territorial supply base was at Fort Union, about sixty miles north of there. Sibley desperately wanted it taken so that his way up to Colorado would be clear sailing."

Fr. Jake admitted, "I heard nothing about this in my Michigan social studies class."

"Maybe not too well known back east..." Karl held up the canteen. "'Nother wee nip, Padre?"

He pushed forward his glass. "Sure an' why not, Cap'n Karl."

Schiller drank, then slurred his words in continuing. "As I was sayin'... Well, Colonel Scurry...*Padre*, y'oughta read Tom Edrington's account. He's got a differ'nt spin on the battle. Anyway, it was March 1862 and 'Dirty Shirt' Scurry was in charge of the Fourth Texas Mounted Volunteers. Reinforcements were comin' from Fort Union, so ol' Scurry went up Galisteo Creek to Johnson's Ranch. Thought he could stop 'em there. Y'see, there was a kind of truce to bury the dead on both sides."

"That was cert'nly humane," Fr. Jake agreed, smacking his lips.

"Yeah, *Padre*. Uh, where was I?"

"Talkin' 'bout Bully Ray Scuffy."

"Yeah, I don't like him."

"Don't blame ya, Karlton."

The captain chucked foolishly at the priest's version of his name. "My folks *coulda* named me Karlton."

The Ghosts of Glorieta

"Coulda," Fr. Jake agreed, grinning at his own cleverness.

The two men sat in silence, until Schiller abruptly sat up straight. He shook his canteen and listened to how much rum splashed inside, then screwed on the top and stood. "Gotta go feed Ulysses. She's a stalwart mare, so I call her that."

The front door had been left open. The officer picked up his forage cap and stepped onto the porch. After taking a deep breath of night air, he seemed completely unaffected by his drinking. Fr. Jake followed him outside.

"Father, you should take me up on my offer to join us as a chaplain."

"Said that I'd think 'bout it."

"Fine. If you need help with anything, just look me up." Captain Schiller put on his cap and walked down to untether his mount. Looking up, he warned, "You'll be hearing a lot of bugle calls for the next week or so. I trust that won't be a problem?"

Fr. Jake saluted him. "Carry on, Cap'n."

The officer swung easily up onto the saddle, saluted crisply back, and rode up the Calle to his camp.

Fr. Jake looked over at the church. Both the firefighters and curious spectators were gone. Since bright 3:00 A.M. moonlight illuminated the burned entrance, he decided to check the extent of damage to the doorway. Weaving slightly, he walked across the street, still barefoot. The wet soil was cold on his feet. The priest gingerly stepped around the remaining puddles and charred rubble on the cement pad in front of the doorway.

He ran a hand over the blackened boards of the scorched jambs and door. They were damp and still warm. The fire had left unburned patches of white-painted wood, particularly on the right doorjamb. *The gasoline Schiller mentioned was splashed on the left side. Whomever did this must have come from the direction of the highway.*

Fr. Jake ran his fingers over odd-looking burn patterns on the right doorpost, rubbed his eyes, and squinted at them again. "Jesus, Mary and Joseph," he mumbled, crossing himself. "It's either the rum or the poor light, but I'll swear that dark burn pattern on the jamb is an image of the Virgin of Guadalupe!"

177

18

Fr. Jake spent most of the rest of the night awake, pondering what he thought he had seen. Was the image an optical illusion or miracle?

He knew that news media had reported on so-called apparitions of Jesus Christ and the Virgin Mary for over thirty years: the face of Jesus in a tortilla and burned toast; Christ on the frosted glass of a bathroom window in Manhattan; a worn linoleum floor with the image of the Blessed Mother. Even the evangelist, Oral Roberts, in a plea for donations, reported a gigantic standing Jesus outside an Oklahoma hospital he was building. Believers sent him millions of dollars.

Sacred images on everything from fish sticks to cheese sandwiches were for sale on eBay. A Web site reported on "All Things Miraculous and More…" T-shirts, bumper stickers, posters, even an infant bodysuit were advertised on !Jesusburnedtoast Merchandise is Here!

The Catholic Church's position was one of cautious investigation. Fr. Jake recalled an article in the *National Catholic Reporter* he once clipped and saved. While admitting the existence of "private" revelations, such reported phenomena must be consistent with Public Revelation as guarded by the Church throughout the ages. "Visions" that proposed to supplant or improve upon Divine Revelation were rejected. Although these contemporary apparitions had nothing to do with Doctrine, the opinions of prudent clergy were sought, to establish credibility. False mystics were only too eager to prey on the gullible at these sites.

Albert Noyer

Beyond that, the faithful, the curious, and the skeptical flocked to the source of supernatural phenomena. Many trashed their surroundings. At San Isidro, wood splinters would be gouged from the doorframe and stucco chiseled out of the church walls as souvenirs. Unscrupulous zealots might even attempt to smuggle statues out of the building. Hoards of visitors, television crews, and news broadcasters would leave the premises littered with the remains of votive candles, food containers, plastic water bottles, beverage cans and more. Portable toilets would have to be leased, since some of the credulous camped out on the site for days, even weeks. In the latter case, they often left behind sleeping bags and used condoms.

Fr. Jake decided to rise at first light and tack a bed sheet over the burned area. That would hide it from villagers, who were sure to arrive and look for damage to their church. He would carefully scrutinize the image and, if necessary, call Archbishop Jan Benisek for advice.

○

On Thursday morning, the sun's rays burst over the distant Manzano Mountains at 5:21 A.M. Twenty minutes before that time, Fr. Jake had looked over the faint image that had shocked him the night before. The blackened area outlined vertical wood grain with a knothole where the Virgin's head would be. The "praying hands" were lightly charred grain. Not a complete figure, just folded hands, face and mantle. His artistic side kicked in. A little touching up with a black pen. "Don't even think of it, Father," he murmured to himself

A middle-aged man in a blue Ford Tractor cap, T-shirt, shorts, knee socks, and sandals came down the Calle, walking a shorthaired brown dog. He crisscrossed the street, and came toward the church. Fr. Jake recognized a parishioner who had never spoken to him. *I'd better get this sheet up.* He used pushpins to attach the covering over the burned area.

The man paused with a look of surprise on his unshaven face. "*¿Que paso?* What happen here, Father?"

"Good morning," Fr. Jake said. "I've noticed you at Mass. Tell me your name."

"Me? Gonzales. Ray Gonzales."

"My pleasure, Ray. Didn't you hear the trumpet signal in the camp last night around two o'clock?"

180

The Ghosts of Glorieta

"Naw, Millie an' me…" He blushed and looked down at his dog. "Father, I musta slept right through." Ray's dog pulled at his leash to sniff ground closer to the door. "*Asente*, Bruno!" he ordered. Instead of sitting, the animal kept straining forward. "Father, why you coverin' up the door?"

"Someone deliberately set a fire last night that damaged the church entrance. I'm protecting evidence for the police."

"*Bueno*, hope they find the bastard who done it." Ray scratched a leg and tugged the dog's leash toward him. "C'mon, Bruno, let's get to Mamacita's for our coffee."

Our coffee? Bruno has his own bowl at the restaurant? "*Hasta*, Ray," Fr. Jake said, and stepped back to check the makeshift covering. "That should do it for now."

After walking a few steps, Ray turned back. "Father, I'm Donny's neighbor. You know, the deacon. You seen him around?"

"No. Do you know where he is?"

He shook his head. "I ain't seen Raylene, either. Donny's pit bull been barking his head off. Didn't have no water, so I went inside his run yesterday to give him. He scooted out, an' made a bee-line for the forest."

"The woods up there? Interesting."

"Yeah. Too bad about the church, Father. Bastards." Ray pulled his dog around. "C'mon, Bruno, coffee time."

O

While Fr. Jake waited for his own coffee to finish brewing, the 6:00 A.M. reveille trumpet sounded at the reenactors' camp. The recruits would begin another day of training. After finishing his morning raisin bran, he settled in his armchair to read more in his breviary about Tobit. He glanced at the San Isidro he had placed on a side table. Still gazing skyward, its hands clasped in prayer, the wooden statue gave no clue, yet had the *santo* protected his namesake church from the fire?

Around nine o'clock, Fr. Jake dialed the phone number on Archbishop Benisek's stationery to reach his office at St. Joseph Place in Albuquerque. His secretary answered.

"Archdiocese of Santa Fe. Father Ramón speaking."

"This is Father Jakubowski at San Isidro in Providencia. Father Ramón, may I please speak to the Archbishop."

"Can I help you, Father?"

181

Albert Noyer

"I...really need to speak with Archbishop Benisek."

After a pause, the secretary replied, "The archbishop is in conference."

"It's vitally important, Father."

Another hesitation on Ramón's part, then an annoyed sigh. "Oh, just a minute."

"Father Jake!" Jan Benisek's voice boomed into the phone. "How good to hear from you! Everything fine at San Isidro? Did you have a talk with that 'deacon'?"

"No, Maldonado's wife was mur.... Raylene died, Bishop. Her husband has disappeared."

"He's probably with family," Benisek suggested. "Now, what is 'vitally important,' Father?"

"A couple of things, Bishop. It seems that a Texas film producer has bought up the town through quitclaim deeds and wants to turn it into a horror movie set. He wants to buy San Isidro. My church."

"A moment, Father..." Benisek held a hand over the phone while he talked to his secretary, then returned. "Father Jake? Yes, that would be Jefferson Davis Houston. Mister Houston made a quite generous offer for the property."

"That's because he wants to make San Isidro the centerpiece of horror films that he plans to make in Providencia."

"Father, is that the 'problem' you're calling about?" The bishop's caustic tone suggested concerns that were far more pressing. "Seems to me like an opportunity for locals to be hired."

"Bishop, there are three problems with perhaps more to come."

"Go on," he sighed.

"First, the people are against having their town turned into a New Mexico Disneyland."

Benisek countered, "Or, as I suggested, an economic bonanza? Mister Houston told me that he will take on many locals as workers."

"But in demeaning jobs, Bishop. Secondly, Tex Houston's property was vandalized. Perhaps in retaliation, the door to my church was set on fire last night—"

"Great God—!"

"Fortunately, the damage was minor."

The Ghosts of Glorieta

"Good, good. Minor damage. And what else?" The archbishop's voice verged on true impatience.

"An image of the Virgin of Guadalupe seems to have appeared in the scorched wood of the church's doorway."

After an awkward pause, Benisek whispered, "Say again, Father."

"Excellency, an apparition of the Virgin Mary is on the church. I need your advice in how to handle this."

"How distinct is the...the holy image?"

"So-so. I've covered it up with a sheet."

"I see. Good." After a pause, Benisek continued, "There have been authentic appearances here in New Mexico, Father. A painting in Ranchos de Taos—"

"Yes," he interrupted, "but if some of the *viejos* here think it's the *Virgen*, they'll gossip word around. Gawkers and hucksters will arrive from all over the state, even the country. Maybe parts of the world."

"And the Faithful will also come, Father Jake."

He ignored the prelate's remark and went on, "All the media paparazzi will invade Providencia. *National Inquirer*...Television. Jokes about San Isidro on Jay Leno, Letterman, all those other late night guys. Bishop, do you recall the publicity fallout after 'Christ of the Tortilla'?"

"Yes, but Mother Church *is* cautious about attributing divine significance to these...these unusual phenomena."

"Exactly. Yet, on the other hand, Bishop, if this really is 'divine,' it could be a sign that the Virgin doesn't want San Isidro sold to a Texan schmuck."

"Schmuck?" Benisek barely held in a chuckle. "Father...you're pulling my leg."

"Perhaps."

The archbishop reverted to being a no-nonsense shepherd of his diocese. Even his suggestions had to be obeyed. "Father Jakubowski, let me just emphasize this. I *don't* want another scandal in my diocese such as the one about clergy pedophiles. Understood?"

"Understood, Excellency."

"God bless your work."

Fr. Jake sat listening to the dial tone on his cell phone a moment, then closed the cover. *So the archbishop wants me to handle it.* He went outside again. Several villagers who heard about the damage, probably from Ray at

183

Albert Noyer

Mamacita's, had clustered together, talking in Spanish and gesturing about the vandalized doorway.

"*Que paso aqui, Padre?*" asked a man in a battered straw hat and overalls. "What's goin' on?"

"A fire last night almost destroyed the church's doorway."

"So, *Padre*, why you coverin' it up?" a whiskered, toothless *viejo* chimed in.

"It probably was arson and the police will want to investigate. I'm protecting the damage."

His companion made a fist and complained, "That *Tejano* what got his truck torched. He done it! He burned our church."

Fr. Jake shook his head. "We can't accuse Mister Houston or anyone just now. It will take time to—"

The roar of heavy equipment sounding from the direction of the highway drowned out the rest of the priest's reply. A hydraulic excavator and two dump trucks followed a clanking, yellow bulldozer. The machinery turned into the plaza and shuddered to a stop. Tex Houston, wearing an Australian bush jacket, leather Kakadu hat, flared cavalry pants, and knee-high boots, jumped down from a side of the bulldozer cab and strode over to the church. "'Mornin', folks." He looked at the muddy ground, ash rubble, and a sheet billowing away from the door in a light breeze. "Father Jay, what's goin' on here?"

"Someone tried to burn down my church during the night."

Tex sucked in a breath, removed his hat, and ran a hand through blond-dyed hair. "Father, I know what you're thinkin', but I swear on my daddy's grave that I had nothin' to do with this. Nothin' at all."

"No one's accusing you, Tex."

The six men in the gathering murmured among themselves, then began to surround the filmmaker with clenched fists.

Tex held two hands up. "Folks, I swear—"

"Gentlemen..." Fr. Jake stepped up to restrain the angry villagers. "Mister Houston and I are going inside my *casita* to find out what that demolition equipment is all about. You men surely have things to do. God bless you, and don't touch that sheet before the police arrive."

There were more mumbled threats in Spanish, but the group broke up and headed toward the highway and the reassuring comfort of their morning table at Mamacita's.

The Ghosts of Glorieta

Inside, the priest indicated his armchair with a hand. "Tex, I've got coffee left, so how about a mug?"

"Father Jay, I usually have my energy drink, but okay. Black." He took an oversized kerchief from his pocket, mopped his brow, then flicked dust off his boots.

After Fr. Jake handed the Texan a mug, he went back for a kitchen chair and sat close in front of him. "Tex, what do you plan on tearing down?"

He swallowed a gulp of coffee and protested again, "I swear I had nothing to do with a fire."

"Forget that. It's not what I asked you."

"Okay, Father. Well, today these folks are getting a registered letter in the mail, telling which ones will need to move. I plan to start demolishing homes on Monday."

"And today's Thursday."

Tex shifted position and took another gulp of coffee. "Father Jay, some of those adobes are empty, so I'll start with them. Show folks that real progress is being made toward getting them jobs. Why, just this morning I hired three guys sitting around at the grocery."

"And what about the other homes of people who want to stay put and not move? You heard those men at the meeting. The church fire could be a way to threaten them into selling."

"Well, now, I'm still waiting to hear about buying the church from that Bishop. See, I'm going to use that building. Why would I want to burn it down?"

"I understand." *Admittedly, that makes sense. He did say it would be a centerpiece of his movie town.*

Tex took a sip of coffee and glanced out the window. "Say, Father, that pretty detective's red car just went by. A black sheriff's SUV is following her."

"Sonia Mora is probably hoping to talk to Donny, but he isn't there."

"Donny?"

"Maldonado, the former deacon here. Tex, you know that Mister Fortgang is hiring a lawyer to represent the village. He'll appeal your quitclaims."

"Well, now, Father Jay, you can tell him that he'll be getting bad news, but a lotta good news."

Fr. Jake shifted on the chair. "Start with the bad news."

185

Albert Noyer

"Some folks aren't going to get to keep Father Mora's property. It's mine."

"And you say there's good news, Tex?"

He morphed into his "Don't mess with Tex" mode. "Well, sure, Father Jay. Like I said, a lot of them ain't gonna hafta move. I'll charge 'em rent, and they'll have jobs to pay for it and then some—" He noticed the red car return and pull up in front. "Uh, oh. Here comes Miz Mora."

Fr. Jake opened his front door before Sonia reached the porch. She carried a cardboard box. "Good morning, Detective."

"Father…" She turned back to Griego, who had gotten out of the van. "Deputy, go see what happened to the church."

Fr. Jake shouted to him, "Don't touch that bed sheet until I come down to explain."

When Sonia entered the living room, Tex stood and respectfully took off his bush hat. "Howdy, Ma'am."

"Mister Houston." She held the box a little higher. "Well, it's opportune that you're here, sir. What's in this evidence case also concerns you."

Tex grinned. "Ah'm flattered, Ma'am."

After Sonia refused Fr. Jake's offer of coffee, he said to her, "Maldonado wasn't at home, was he? A neighbor just told me."

"I had a search warrant and went in. His SKS carbine is missing." Sonia put the box on the couch and removed its cover. "The Belén sheriff's department opened Raylene Maldonado's safety deposit box at Western Savings. Mister Houston, we found numerous notices from the Socorro County assessor's office in there, informing Father Mora that taxes were delinquent on his property. They go back about four years."

"What?" Fr. Jake asked. "The letters were never mailed?"

"Correct, Father." Sonia pulled out several envelopes to show the un-cancelled postage stamps.

Tex asked, "Why are you telling me, detective? That little lady, Raylene, or whoever, done wrong."

"And you gained from it, sir."

"Pshaw, Ma'am. I merely look up delinquency notices in newspapers and buy the property all legal-like."

"Those legal notices also were never filed. The original typewritten Legals, English and Spanish, are here in this evidence box."

The Ghosts of Glorieta

Confused, Fr. Jake asked, "Yet what could Raylene gain by concealing the notices? I mean, she lost…she and her husband would have lost their home."

Sonia held up some envelopes. "Perhaps more important is why she saved this evidence that implicated her."

Tex slapped on his leather hat to leave. "Well, folks, I have film work to do."

Fr. Jake reminded him, "Tex, you're giving people only three days' notice to tell some of them they might have to move. Can't you extend that by…. by at least a week from Monday?"

"Sorry Father, I got my equipment here now. Doing that would cost me a pile of moolah." He tipped his hat to Sonia. "Nice seein' y'all again, Ma'am."

She stepped over to block the front door. "Sir, you admit that is your equipment parked on the church plaza?"

"Why, yes, Ma'am. It sure is."

"Sir, you're trespassing on church property," she informed him in the bland tone of a law enforcement officer. "Father Jake, do you wish to press charges?"

Her question took both Tex and the priest by surprise. Before Fr. Jake could answer, the filmmaker glowered at Sonia, but evidently reconsidered an objection. He turned to the priest. "Well now, Father Jay, I reckon I can wait a week. Keep the good-will of the fine folks here."

Sonia's raised eyebrows could have sufficed for her question, "How about it, Father?"

"Suits me, detective."

She moved aside. "You're free to go, sir."

Houston paused with one hand on the doorknob, his face red, his mood dark. "Little lady, you're messin' with Tex and he don't like it one bit," he warned, then slammed the door shut.

Fr. Jake exhaled a held-in breath. "Sonia, what was that all about?"

"Man's a prick, as I've said before. Someone at the assessor's office had Raylene withhold the delinquency notices, and Tex somehow has to be involved. My uncle might even have been murdered as part of…of… I don't know. Blackmail? A payoff gone wrong?" Sonia replaced the top on the case, sagged onto the couch, and took of her cap. "I'm stumped right now. You really have coffee, Father?"

"Carlotta's finest grind. It'll only take a minute."

187

Albert Noyer

While the priest was in the kitchen, Sonia noticed his new *santo*. "So you finally got a San Isidro, eh, Father?" she called to him.

"At the grocery, Sonia. It smells good, too…lemon-like." He came in while the coffee brewed and went to hand her the statue.

Sonia ran a hand over the painted wood, sniffed it, then turned the sculpted image over to look at the bottom. "You have a pocket knife, Father?"

"Swiss Army." He took a red-handled knife with a white cross emblem from his pocket and handed her the tool.

She slipped the main blade under the round sticker on the bottom and held it there. "You notice anything wrong about what it says on this label?"

"'*Hecho* in *Mexico*'? No."

"I thought you knew more Spanish than that."

He studied the words a moment longer. "You mean it should be '*Hecho en Mexico*' if the statue was made there."

"Or if the label was printed south of the border." She continued prying off the sticker. Underneath, a cork sealed an inch-and-a half hole in the center of the base. Sonia stood up. "Let's take this outside."

After crouching to pry out the stopper, Sonia poked a finger into the opening, then turned the statue upside down. A stream of gritty sand mounded up on driveway gravel.

"That wood is light-weight," Fr. Jake noted. "The hole is filled with sand to act as ballast that keeps the statue from tipping over too easily."

Sonia sniffed the opening, then held it up to the priest. "Or, Father, for concealing a plastic 'sausage' tube of meth or cocaine? That citrus smell is citronella oil, which has an odor strong enough to repel dogs. Pet shops even sell a No Bark Collar to control nuisance barking."

"So the citronella could confuse drug-sniffing dogs."

"Exactly, Father. Do you know who supplies these to the store?"

"Yes, a parishioner, Duane Fortgang. He owns Mamacita's and also sells *santos* at the grocery. Well, you saw Duane at the restaurant after Father Mora's funeral. Carlotta told me that a gallery owner from Albuquerque comes by regularly to purchase the figures."

Sonia stood up to hand him back the San Isidro and knife. "What do you know about Mister Fortgang?"

"'Pillar of the church' as the saying goes, except he's a bit too conservative for my theological tastes."

The Ghosts of Glorieta

"We'll check him out." The detective brushed sand off her hands and looked toward the church. "What happened over there, Father Jake?"

"Arson, same as at Tex's semi."

"Any proof of that or suspects?"

"No, and Tex swears he had nothing to do with it."

"Why the bed sheet?"

"Come over and look."

"Let me get my cap."

When Sonia returned, tucking her glossy black hair under the oversized cap, Fr. Jake said, "A fetching head-covering, if I might say so, detective."

"Called a Baker-Boy Hat, Father, and roomy enough to hide all this hair. Griego!" she called out. "What didjya find?"

The deputy stood up from squatting on the cement slab and sifting through burned debris with his ballpoint pen. "Father Hakub was lucky. *Padre*, your whole church coulda gone up."

"Amen! If it weren't for firemen camping with those Civil War reenactors, my church would be completely gutted."

"Father, why the sheet?" Sonia repeated.

He wiggled out a pushpin and drew the covering aside. "What do either of you see on the doorjamb?"

Griego squinted at the scorched wood. "Pretty badly burned, but, like I said, you was lucky it wasn't worse."

"Sonia?"

After examining the jamb for a while, she looked back at the priest, her brown eyes serious. "If I were you, Father," she advised quietly, "I'd sandpaper over that odd-looking wood burn and never tell a living soul about ever seeing it."

19

Sonia turned away and toward the deputy. "Okay, Griego, get some crime scene tape up around that doorway."

"Jeez, detective, we're gonna use it all up on this one little place." He went back to the SUV, chuckling at what he considered his private joke.

Sonia took out her spiral pad. "Father Jake, an arson team will be out to investigate your church, just as they did the semi. You say firefighters in the reenactors' camp put out the blaze?"

"I did." He pointed across the street. "They noticed that fire hydrant while marching past on Saturday."

"The team will question them. The arsonist or arsonists of your church and the semi either were on opposite sides, hell bent on revenge, or maybe trying to frame you and the Texan against each other."

"Most villagers don't want their homes destroyed and a schlock movie set built in their places." The priest nodded toward the plaza. "Look at that equipment over there. What can law enforcement do by a week from Monday to stop Tex?"

Sonia watched the deputy tack yellow tape around the church entrance a moment. "If someone sneezed wrong, Father, I suppose I could have the health department slap a quarantine on the entire village for hantavirus infection."

"Really?"

Albert Noyer

"No, not in time." Sonia put her notepad away and started across the street with Fr. Jake to her Plymouth. "I'll get my evidence box and then try to connect some dots. It seems that Raylene Maldonado had an affair with someone in the assessor's office. He…or she…had to be tied in with the Texan, and the delinquency notices hidden long enough for him to buy up my uncle's property."

He said, "Why didn't Raylene just destroy the evidence you found at the bank?"

"She kept the mailings as insurance? Father, the victim was no dumb-blonde. Raylene held onto her job with the county assessor, and the elementary school thought highly of her. Why the woman ever married that jerk…"

"Where do you suppose Maldonado went?"

She shrugged uncertainty. "Don't know, but in my mind he's definitely been upgraded from 'person of interest' to 'suspect, armed and dangerous'."

Fr. Jake told her, "You know, Maldonado wasn't a deacon."

"What?"

"Archbishop Benisek's office checked on him. They have no record of an ordination for anyone with his name."

"Then Maldonado must have bullied my uncle into letting him officiate as one. Jeez," she sighed, selecting her ignition key on the ring, "nobody around here is what he or she seems. The latest is about a phony 'deacon.' Elder Jeremiah is really a hippie carpenter from Illinois. Aimée and Raylene, both proper married women, yet screwing around with other guys." Sonia nodded her head toward the reenactor's camp. "And look at all those civvies over there pretending they're Civil War soldiers." She paused with the hint of a smile. "Father Jakubowski, you came here claiming to be a priest. Who are you really?"

It took him a moment to realize she was joking. "I'm actually a priest, detective, and be glad you don't have to hear the outlandish stories I get in the confessional. I'll bring that box out to your car."

"Thanks, Father." When he returned, Sonia was in the driver's side, leaning over to hold the passenger door open. "Put it on the seat. On the way back, I'm going to swing by Mister Fortgang's with a few questions about those hollow statues he sells."

"Duane is probably in Socorro. I told you he's contesting Tex's claim through an attorney he hired out of his own pocket."

192

The Ghosts of Glorieta

"Generous of him. Oh, by the way, Father, I didn't have a chance to follow up on that broken *matachine* wand. Could you ask Armando if there's a *morada* near here? Do you know what that is?"

"I don't, Sonia."

"It's a small, church-like building where *Penitentes* store the equipment they use during Holy Week."

"*Penitentes?*"

"Look, Father, I can't explain now. Just ask him about a *morada*."

"Fine, I will."

Sonia started the Plymouth's engine. "*Vaya con Dios*, Father, if that's not redundant, you *probably* being a priest and all."

"Priests can use all the help they can get. *Vaya*..." He smiled and slammed the door shut, watching her drive off. *Sonia the Detective has a sense of humor somewhere behind that hard shell of hers. I'll have to ask her why she went into police work.*

Inside the living room, Fr. Jake noticed that Sonia had forgotten to drink her coffee. As he brought her mug to his sink, a trumpet in the camp signaled "Assemble for Drill." He looked at his watch. "Ten A.M. Better go over and see what that bugle call means."

While the womenfolk watched, men in full Union or Confederate uniforms held a variety of muskets, as they formed two lines on the grassy area in front of their tents. Captain Schiller surveyed the ranks from atop Ulysses. Mounted subaltern officers had lined up behind him.

"Atten-tion!"

At a Sergeant Major's shouted command, the men straightened and a wave of sunlight rippled off the bright steel of slim bayonets mounted on musket barrels.

Across the field from them, Tex Houston sat on a director's chair in the bed of a Silverado pickup. Next to him, a camera operator with his THVIR equipment prepared to film the scene in virtual reality. Several set assistants hovered around the truck. When Tex stood up to make sure that unit flags, cannon props, and secondary cameras were in place on the field, he spotted the priest and waved him over.

"Father Jay, come and watch this. Stand by the truck, a little over to the side..." He held up a hand. "Right there is good."

"Thanks." The priest guessed that the Texan's outlandish costume came from watching old Hollywood films in Albania and deciding that was what movie directors wore.

193

Albert Noyer

Tex adjusted his headset microphone and relayed instructions to Schiller. "Captain, like we rehearsed, your Union and Confederate soldiers will go to opposite sides of the field. When I shout 'Action!' that howitzer fires. The two sides run at each other, cavalry in front, everyone yellin' and hollerin', shootin' blanks and mixin' it up, as they reach one another. I got cameras shooting from two, three angles, but the main THVIR is here on the truck. Got that, Captain?"

Schiller saluted back that he understood. Tex sat in a canvas chair to watch the men jog to opposite ends of the battlefield. They formed blue and gray lines, their colorful unit flags billowing in a light breeze. Fr. Jake felt the tension, as if an actual battle engagement was about to commence, then—

"Action!"

The mountain howitzer belched flame and a cloud of blue smoke. The opposing Blue and Gray lines began their run, shouting and pausing to fire muskets in a haze of black powder smoke. Men fell on both sides. Cavalrymen reached the rebel line, slashed through with sabers, then turned and raced their mounts back. As Union and Confederate infantrymen merged in a deadly mêlée of muskets and bayonets, Tex hunched forward, caught up in the confusion and horror of hand-to-hand combat, however simulated.

Without looking way from the battle scene, hazy with blue gunpowder smoke, he explained, "We're recording the sound of gunfire, that smell of gunpowder, even horse sweat, and the way the guys are yelling and screaming. Everything will be tied in with the battle scenes, like you were really there!"

Fr. Jake thought again of the Poznan uprising he had witnessed in Poland, and the devastation caused by the 1967 Detroit riot. This was play-acting, yet the edited holographic images would convey the sights, sounds, and smells of an actual battlefield. After a few more minutes of action, a bugle sounded "Recall from Drill." Tex shouted, "Cut," into his microphone. The men stopped. Blue-clad infantrymen helped up the Gray who had fallen. Medics assisted both sides. Cavalrymen cantered their mounts back to the assembly area.

Tex leaned over the truck's side and spoke to an assistant below him. The man adjusted his headphone and ordered, "Okay, everyone. Break for lunch."

"Father Jay, that was a good take," Tex beamed. "I'd like to demonstrate my Tex Houston Virtual Immersion Reality this evening after it starts to

The Ghosts of Glorieta

get dark. We'll project by the north wall of your church, if that's okay. Y'all can invite everyone in the village to watch."

"I'm anxious to see it myself," he agreed. "Just witnessing the action from here was exciting."

Tex grinned. "Wait 'til you catch it in THVIR. We'll splice in some other takes and it's gonna look so authentic y'all will feel like you're trapped inside a real battle!"

O

Fr. Jake called up Armando and Cynthia, asking them to contact parishioners and tell them about the evening presentation. Sunset would be shortly after 8:00 P.M., so people were to arrive by nine o' clock. It would be dark enough then, and moonrise was not until after midnight.

O

After Pentacle Pix workers erected a barricade that closed off the Calle San Isidro, Tex set up his projection equipment on the Silverado. The pickup was parked on the street, facing the church wall. Fifty or so curious villagers dribbled in and sat on the ground to wait. Most brought flashlights, Frito snacks, and drinks. While waiting, children chased each other among the audience, laughing as they shined their parents' flashlights on each other.

Fr. Jake, Armando, and Cynthia stood at the back of the crowd to watch.

"I saw the reenactment this morning," Cynthia said. "I thought it was quite exciting."

"I had to work," Armando complained. "What's gonna happen here?"

Fr. Jake replied, "A projection of this morning's movie shoot. Tex told me that he has a revolutionary virtual immersion reality system that practically puts anyone watching right inside the scene."

"So, Father, is he gonna explain about it first?"

"He didn't say, Armando. It's an enhanced hologram image, so I would think he'll go up there and talk a bit about how it works and what we'll see."

195

Albert Noyer

Tex Houston did not. Abruptly, a bugle sounded. A line of life-size Union soldiers appeared in front of the audience, vibrating slightly, almost as ghost images. The 3-D illusion was not projected onto the church wall, but appeared to be a few feet in front of it. The men primed muskets, then knelt down in a line of blue. A gray-clad Confederate company appeared. The rebels loaded and leveled their muskets directly at villagers seated on the ground.

Gasps sounded from some spectators. A few in front, including men, scrabbled backward on their haunches, away from the perceived danger. Another bugle call sounded, then a command to "Fire and Charge!" Bursts of reddish flame came from gun muzzles as the Confederates rose with a thunderous yell and ran forward, bayonets fixed. Union soldiers returned fire. Men on both sides fell, screaming in agony from bloody wounds. Wielding sabers, cavalry riders plunged their horses through the Gray line and slashed directly at the audience.

The sound of firing and smell of gunpowder engulfed the spectators on all sides; horse's hooves seemed about to trample them. A few children and women shrieked in terror. Some onlookers panicked and scrambled up to run toward the back. They shoved past people standing in the rear and hurried out into the safety of the dark street.

Cynthia clutched Armando's arm as frightened villagers jostled past her.

Fr. Jake felt helpless at preventing what might be a dangerous free-for-all stampede to escape. *I should tell Tex to turn off his projector—* Abruptly, two loud gunshots rang out above the mayhem. An old man stood nearby holding up a pistol and aiming at the illusions. "*Viejo!*" he shouted. "Put down your gun! That isn't real. *No es veridad!*"

"*Si, Padre*, they runnin' right at us," the oldster insisted and let off another round.

Fr. Jake grasped his arm and forced down the gun. Armando came to wrench the pistol from his hand.

The battle scene went black and the vivid hologram images evaporated. A Pentacle worker in the truck directed a spotlight onto the crowd.

"Folks! Folks!" Tex yelled to them. "Keep calm. What y'all saw was my virtual immersion reality, 'S.H.S.' See it. Hear it. Smell it."

"He means it's like a movie, not real," Fr. Jake called out and hurried to the front of the thinned-out crowd. Everyone who remained had crouched down, unsure of what danger would come at them next. Three hollow gouges marred the wall stucco. *Pray God that no one was hit.* "Friends, I agree with

196

The Ghosts of Glorieta

Mister Houston. That was the most realistic presentation I've ever seen, yet he should have warned us ahead of time."

"Shucks, Padre," Tex called to him, "I just wanted y'all to be surprised."

"It all looked so authentic!" Cynthia exclaimed.

"Tex, that's enough surprises for one night," Fr. Jake admonished. "We're lucky no one was hurt."

Angry murmurs of protest at the illusion came from those who recovered from shock.

A man called over to the Texan, "Buddy, you scared the shit out of us."

"Yeah, what the F you trying to do?" another yelled.

Fr. Jake raised his hands for calm. "We all need to go home and think about what we saw. Remember this documentary is about our village."

"Hey," Tex shouted, "I'm puttin' y'all on the map! Givin' y' jobs."

As the grumbling or still-frightened spectators dispersed, Fr. Jake walked over to the Texan. "Mister Houston, warn us next time about what you're showing. Please pack up and leave now."

His persuasive tone convinced the filmmaker. "Hey, sure, *Padre*. C'mon guys, let's wrap it up for tonight."

As the priest watched Pentacle workers stow equipment in the Silverado, the filmmaker came to him. "You know, Father Jay, that wasn't just entertainment," he said in serious tone. "Those folks felt terrified, like they were right in the middle that battle."

"Exactly, Tex. That was the problem."

He raised a hand. "Now hold on. That made them more empathetic to real suffering, to not wanting to ever cause a fight like that. There's real educational value to my invention. In 1989, a conference on Cyberspace at UTA started me thinking."

"Thinking, 'I'm going to make a buck off this'?"

"Well, partly so, Father Jay. Isn't that the American way?"

"Just warn your audience first, Tex. Good night." The priest turned to Armando. "I need to ask you something. Can you come inside a moment? You too, Cynthia."

Both agreed. Inside the living room, he offered, "I can make coffee."

"We're fine, Father," Cynthia said. "Right, Armand?"

"*Si,*" he yawned, and rubbed his eyes.

197

Albert Noyer

"Okay, sit down, please." Fr. Jake looked at the mechanic. "Armando, Sonia asked me if there was a *morada* here. Do you know what she means?"

"Oh, *si*, but it's secret. Only *Penitentes* can use the place."

"Another word I didn't know."

"Father," Cynthia explained, "back when this area belonged to Spain and later on, Mexico, there weren't enough priests to go around. *Los Hermanos*, groups of local men, would conduct their own Holy Week services. They were called *Los Penitentes*. Isn't that correct, Armand?"

"*Si*. The *morada*, Father is where we…I mean they… store crosses, whips, and some of their *Semana Sancta* robes."

"*Los Hermanos*, are The Brothers?"

"'The Brotherhood' they call it. You know, the guys get together to pray, sing *albados*…holy songs. Not eat much. Stuff like that."

"Are *matachines* part of the Brotherhood?"

Armando evaded a direct answer. "Father Hakub, who can tell? I don't know 'em all. I'm not a *matachine*."

The priest persisted, "Would the dancers store their costumes and wands in this *morada*?"

After the mechanic shrugged without answering, Cynthia got up and pushed his shoulder. "Armand, Father is trying to help the detective solve Father Mora's death." She turned to the priest. "Why *does* detective Mora want to know about a *morada*?"

He paused a moment before replying, "She hasn't released this crime scene detail, but we found part of a broken *matachine* wand inside the *sagrario*. Father Mora was struck with it and rendered unconscious."

Armando whistled softly. "*Jesucristo*, she thinks a *matachine* done it?"

"Not necessarily, but if a broken wand is found in there—"

Armando waved his hands in an impatient gesture. "Father Hakub, we don't even know who the guys are. The detective finds a busted wand, nobody's gonna say, 'Hey, sure, that's mine.' Give it here."

Cynthia pleaded with him. "The detective just wants to make sure, Armand."

"Go ask Fortgang," he shrugged. "He knows where the *morada* is."

"Duane is one of the *Hermanos*?"

The Ghosts of Glorieta

"He's a little crazy, Father. Okay," Armando admitted, "I went a coupla times, but they wanted to draw straws to see who would get crucified on Good Friday."

Fr. Jake leaned forward in his chair. "Actually crucified, Armando?"

He stood up and scuffed his shoes on the rug. "Aw, I don't think they really do it, but I quit goin' after that."

"Thanks, you've both been helpful." Fr. Jake stood up. "I'll talk to Fortgang, but please don't tell anyone about the broken wand."

"We won't, Father," Cynthia promised as she got up. "Goodnight."

Armand joined her. "*Buenas noches*, Father Hakub."

The priest placed a hand on each of their heads. "God bless and keep you both. Goodnight. *Buenas noches*."

After the couple left, Fr. Jake checked his watch and decided it was not too late to call Fortgang. The accountant had not been at Tex's disastrous presentation.

After a few rings, he answered, "Fortgang, CPA."

"Duane, this is Father Jake. Hope I'm not bothering you?"

"Not at all. How can I help you?"

"Two ways. First, I forgot to ask, but hoped you would give me a financial statement about San Isidro. Archbishop Benisek is a bit concerned."

After a pause, Fortgang continued in a less than friendly tone. "I can do that. What else, Father?"

"Armando told me what a *morada* is. I'd like to take a look inside the one here, and he said you would know where it was."

"It's located in the *bosque*, near the river. But why would you want to see it?"

Do I tell him about the broken matachine *wand we found in the* segrario? "Ah…it has to do with Father Mora's death. How about sometime in the morning?"

"I suppose so."

"Good. You can bring me up to speed about how your lawyer is doing with the quitclaims."

"I'll pick you up at nine. Goodnight, Father."

"Fine, thanks…." Fortgang hung up. Fr. Jake flipped shut the cover on his cell phone and looked at the *santo* of San Isidro. "Well, that was a little curt," he told the farmer-saint, "but Duane probably is tired." He walked

Albert Noyer

over to the statue and touched the base. "Ah…Saint Isidore, at the *morada*, I'd like to ask you to help me find a clue to Father Mora's death."

At that moment, a 60-Watt bulb flickered in the floor lamp, but then stayed lit.

"Hopefully we're not in for another power out," he muttered and turned off the light switch.

The Ghosts of Glorieta

20 fort liberty / june 3

That morning Billy Ray Scurry had heard the sound of gunfire coming from the direction of the Civil War encampment. He and three of his four sons, Mark, Luke, and Matt, walked around the south edge of Eden West, along a trail they had made through the woods. They devised it as an escape route in case a government raid tried to force them out of Fort Liberty. Scurry's fourth son, Jon, was in the command room, monitoring two security cameras.

"Who's winnin', Daddy?" Luke asked. "Us or them?"

Scurry put down his binoculars. "Aw, they ain't shootin' for real, Lukey. They's reactors, just pretendin'."

The acrid smell of burned black powder discharged from the muskets drifted up toward the men. Scurry stood up in his Gulf War camouflage to inhale the sulphurous fumes. "Man, now ain't that a sweet perfume! Wish't I was down there with the Rebs, whippin' Yankee ass."

Daddy, I got me a idea," Mark piped up. "S'ppose I went down and sold pot to all those reactors?"

"Idiot!" Scurry smacked his son on the side of the head. "We got customers in the big city. Warn't it you that got caught in that grocery and almost went to jail?"

Mark rubbed his sore temple. "I said I was sorry, Daddy."

"'Sorry' don't cut it, boy, when y' got Feds breathin' up your ass." Scurry watched through his binoculars a moment longer, and then slid the

201

Albert Noyer

instrument into a camouflaged case. "Let's get back to the fort. Markey, Matt, y'all got that batch of colored crystal meth ready?"

Matt said, "Still need to stuff the 'Aztec Candy' in plastic bags for shippin'."

"Aw right, go the fuck an' do it!" Scurry ordered. "That Duke City guy is comin' tomorrow." He adjusted the shoulder holster of his 9mm Luger P08 and started back up the trail.

A razor wire fence surrounded Fort Liberty. Ten feet in from the wire an earthen berm and thick boxwood hedge concealed the fort's five buildings from the road. Access on the south side was through a narrow, guarded opening in the hedge. Barred by an iron gate, a heavily posted main entrance was on the dirt road leading up from the Upland Heights subdivision, a quarter mile beyond the Eden West entry.

A guard in a speckled-green camouflage uniform moved aside a wooden saw-horse barrier blocking the south hedge entrance. Billy Ray nodded to him as he and his sons went through. Yellow crime scene tape—ironically, stolen from a crime scene, marked off a safety corridor through the woods to the survivalists' Earthships.

"Now, y'all remember to walk inside the tape," Scurry warned his sons. "We *might* have mines planted outside."

The Earthship lodges of the compound, built by James Parker, were similar to those of his Eden West: heavy outer walls were made of used tires rammed with earth and cement partitions separated minimal interior rooms. The south-facing windows were smaller, but augmented with a larger number of solar panels that provided electrical power. No propane tanks were in sight; residents used wood stoves and fireplaces for cooking or heating. Capped springs were sources of water. Gardens and livestock supplied most of the food for the handful of men and women living there. Rotating male and female compound members bought anything else needed on monthly shopping trips to Belén.

Trees were felled for a distance of about fifteen feet around each fortress-home, providing a clear field of fire for defenders holed up inside the buildings. The Survivalist compound as Detective Sonia Mora had speculated was a defensible fortress that would be costly to attack and likely to turn out as tragically as had the 1993 ATF raid on the Branch Davidians near Waco, Texas. That fifty-one day siege ended only when fire destroyed the compound. Seventy-six people died. Knowing the circumstances, local law enforcement believed in "Lettin' sleepin' dogs lie without botherin' 'em."

The Ghosts of Glorieta

What exactly Billy Ray Scurry hoped to accomplish, beyond defying state and national governments, was as hard to define as his radical views on just about everything from the "Feds," sovereignty, taxation, illegal immigrants, racial purity, domestic terrorists, the role of civilian militias, conspiracy theories, women, and raising children properly.

At the first house, Scurry greeted a compound member washing reddish dirt from an olive-drab military surplus M998 H1 Hummer. "All quiet, Sergeant Allison?"

"All quiet, Colonel," he replied, then thought a moment and added, "Sir, too quiet. We need some action around here."

"'Action'?" Scurry's gray eyes narrowed under bushy eyebrows. "What y'all mean, Sergeant?"

"Hell, what the F are we doing here?" he complained. "Waiting for what to happen?"

Scurry placed a restraining hand on the young man's arm. "Now simmer down, Allison. I got me a lawyer gettin' a writ of secession in the courts right now."

"What do you mean, 'secession'?"

"Fort Liberty becomin' just plain 'Liberty' or 'Libertaria' or some name like that," Scurry replied in an outburst of pride. "A sover'n nation of her own."

Allison scoffed, "That's just plain crazy, sir."

"Y'all think so? I reckon bein' from the east, y'never heered 'bout Spanish land grants? I bought this here acridge free an' clear from that Rev'rind what died in the village. His family got it from a Spanish king. Not from Mexicans, mind ya, but like from the first con-qeestadors before the U. S. was even thought of. I'm claimin' ownership real legal-like."

"Ownership, maybe. Even Feds recognize that, but calling it another country? You think the government's going to fall for your secession plan?"

"Allison," Scurry digressed, "I got one of the Hispanics from the village joinin' us. Came t'other day after his wife ran out on him. Deacon of some kind. Brought a damn nice rifle with him, too."

The sergeant remained skeptical. "What good is a preacher going to do us?"

The look in Billy Ray Scurry's eyes hardened as his right hand edged up toward the Luger. "Sergeant, if you don't like the way I'm runnin' things

203

here, y'all take that Hummer and skee-daddle back to where y' came from."

Allison backed down and stooped to hide his embarrassment by wringing out a wet rag. "I didn't mean anything, Colonel."

"Aw right, son." Scurry half-smiled and slapped him on the back. "Now you and your girlfriend be the next t' drive down to B'len for groceries. Y' don't tell 'em who y' are or where y' live. *Comprendo?*"

Allison came to attention and saluted. "I understand, *Sir*."

"'Course y' do. Y'all was in Eye-raq like me, so y' know about survivin'."

Allison patted the holstered pistol at his side. "Yes, Colonel, I sure do."

Scurry nodded satisfaction and started to walk away, but then turned back. "Sergeant, y'all seen my Command Post?"

"No, sir, I haven't."

Scurry allowed himself a rare grin that did nothing to improve his normally sour expression. "Well, son, y'all come along with me."

Sandbags reinforced the fronts of the semi-sunken buildings that Parker had built. Protected in the same way, sniper positions on roofs faced the main gate.

Scurry led the way down a few stairs to the sunken entrance of an Earthship nearest the gate. "Jon is mannin' the sur-veyance cameras this shift. He's my elder boy." He buzzed himself through a steel door and into a central room that had no windows. Three security camera screens were alight, but Jon had his combat-booted feet up on a desk as he read a comic book.

"Jon-boy, git yer boots down," his father ordered. "Put that comic away an' stand up. This here is Sergeant Allison. Tell him what you're doin', 'cause after he's been with us a bit longer, he's gonna be takin' one of the sur-veyance shifts."

"Yes, sir, daddy." Jon shoved the book into a drawer and motioned Allison closer to the screens. "Well, Sarge, we got cameras watchin' the main gate from three directions. Main one is coverin' the road down to the highway. 'Nother is straight into the woods opposite the gate, an' a third one watches the back side."

"We got west, north, an' east covered," Scurry added with pride. "At night we got trip wires what activate spotlights. Ain't a possum in hell could get past without bein' seen."

The Ghosts of Glorieta

"An' shot," Jon giggled.

"Impressive, Sir," Allison agreed, "but what about that south entrance?"

"Sergeant, I knew y'd ask that. Y'all want to go around that yellow tape and find out?" He winked at Jon, who chuckled.

"Colonel, I…I don't think so."

"Good fella. Lucky, too." Scurry slapped Allison's back again. "We got booby traps here in places y' wouldn't dream about. I'd just like to see the Feds try somethin' until we gets our sover'nty."

"Sir," he wondered, "what about those Pentecostals beyond your front property?"

"Aw, they ain't nothin' to worry about. Peaceful-like, an' they don't like Feds any more'n we do. Why, they go down and pick shit off roads. Ain't that right, Jon-Boy?"

"It sure is, daddy."

"Jon-Boy, the Sergeant here is getting' antsy about not doin' anythin'. Why'nt you take him out back to the shootin' range tomorra? Would y' like that, Allison?"

"Yes, Colonel, I would."

"Well, that's fine. Now, y'all go back, Allison, an' finish cleanin' up that Hummer. That's gonna be my command vehicle. Remember, lunch in the mess hall is at eleven hundred hours t'day, so be there. I'm givin' a speech that you're gonna like."

○

At a quarter to twelve noon, Colonel Billy Ray Scurry watched the compound women clear away the rest of the lunch dishes, then ordered, "All right, ladies, y'all skee-daddle now. Gen'lemen, stand up for recitin' the Oath."

Sitting at trestle tables, a dozen or so men in a variety of camouflage uniforms pushed back their benches, stood, and raised a right hand.

"I, as a sovereign citizen," they repeated, more or less in unison, "affirm that I will defend the Constitution of the United States, as I understand it, against all enemies domestic and foreign, and that I will bear true faith to the same while defending my full rights as a sovereign citizen."

205

Albert Noyer

"Aw right, thank y' gen'lemen. Y'all sit down now an' listen up." Scurry paced back and forth in front of the men, his right hand resting on his Luger's black holster. "Now, some of y', like Sergeant Allison over there, been wantin' some action around here." A few men applauded amid murmurs of "Yeah, Yeah." "Now, I want y'all to meet Deacon Maldorado, who just come up here because he says his wife run out on him." He winked at the men. "Some of y' might say that's not such a bad thing." Laughter and scattered clapping came from the group. "The deacon's from the village down there and y'all might not know that some Texas movie maker has bought up the place. Fact is, he's gonna start tearin' down houses on next Monday. I want us to be there, formin' a cordon around his equipment, supportin' the village folk as sover'n citizens. This has got t' be a peaceful protest, so' we'll have guns, but no ammo. Won't need it. Hell, ev'ry one of those Hispanic men down there got their own huntin' rifles."

Allison raised a hand. "Question, Sir."

The Colonel scowled, annoyed at the interruption. "What is it, Sergeant?"

He stood up. "Sir, by what authority do we interfere with the Texan's right to do what he wants with his own property?"

"Authority? Why, son, we callin' on the right of *Possum Comatose*."

Allison barely held in a laugh in correcting Scurry. "Sir, I think that's *Posse Comitatus*."

"Whatever. We got us a sheriff here with us, Lieutenant Byers. Now, he can call up help whenever a civil disturbance is brewin'. That's what Byers figures is gonna happen down there. Now, sit back down, Allison, an' let me finish."

Scurry stroked his walrus mustache, then went on. "We got us just one minor problem. That new Rev'rind in the church is from up north. Michigan. Name's Jacob. That's Jewish. Anyhow, he'll try to keep the villagers from taking violent action, so we got to get him out of the way 'afore that. We gotta make that Texas guy back down, an' that's where the deacon comes in. Maldorado, c'mon over here."

A light round of applause sounded in the mess hall as Donny shuffled over to stand next to Scurry. Looking tired, his hair still wildly unkempt, and embarrassed in the unfamiliar company, Donny Maldonado merely nodded red-faced acknowledgement.

Scurry raised a hand to continue. "Now, my boy, Jon...y'all know him... Jon is gonna go tell the Rev'rind that the deacon here is sick and needs him

The Ghosts of Glorieta

for…I dunno…a blessin'? Hell, he might even tell him the deacon done somethin' nasty to his wife and wants to confess."

While laughter rippled through the men, Maldonado looked away at his pit bull—it had followed him to the fort.

Scurry went on, "Now, Jon 'll go down and bring the Rev'rind up here on Sunday evenin', just afore it gets dark. We ain't gonna hurt a man of the cloth, jus' keep him nice an' comfy in the brig until Tuesday."

Calls of approval came from most of the men. A few stood up to applaud the action. Scurry smirked, patting his holster and pacing in front of the tables until the demonstration subsided. "Now, that ain't everythin'," he said, facing the men. "Y'all seen that some of the new houses in that subdivision ain't been sold? Under common law we can seize one or two of those places an' declare 'em to be a sover'n republic. I got us posters printed up what say, 'Private property in possession of the occupyin' individuals', an' 'Right to repel force by force.' I got deeds that claim ownership to put in the front windows."

"Colonel," a bearded man shouted, "what did you hafta pay for those deeds?"

"Whatever the printer asked for!" Scurry waited for renewed laughter to melt away. "All right men, we'll be fine tunin' these plans durin' the week. 'Ten-Hut!' Scurry came to attention, as did his audience in a rattle of military equipment. "Dis-missed!"

As the men dispersed, Scurry put an arm around Maldonado. "Son, y'll be a big help. A mighty big help. Why, you'll get credit for takin' your village back from that Texan. You're gonna be a hero!"

207

21

Whether it was due to San Isidro, Luck, or Fate, G. Duane Fortgang and Detective Sonia Mora pulled their automobiles up in front of Father Jake's adobe at exactly the same time. A moment later, a 4-door, black Ford Fusion stopped behind Fortgang's Chrysler.

The petite woman detective had substituted a light jacket of navy-blue nylon for her leather one, but still wore dark slacks and work shoes. She had tucked her lustrous black hair under a baseball cap. A light shade of lipstick was her only cosmetic.

Sonia met Fortgang as he opened his car door. "Sir, I've been trying to reach you."

"Sorry, detective," he apologized, tipping his Stetson. "I've been in Socorro."

"Nice automobile. What model Chrysler is that?"

"Crossfire. Not brand new, I'm afraid."

"Spiffy, though." Sonia turned to meet a tall, distinguished-looking man in a dark business suit who had gotten out of the Ford. Rather than a realtor, even less so a salesperson, his demeanor suggested "U.S. Government." She introduced the accountant to him. "Agent Herrero, this is Duane Fortgang. We're here to see if Father Jakubowski is in this morning."

"He is," Fortgang told her. "I'm to take him to a *morada* near the Rio Grande."

Albert Noyer

"Great!" Sonia exclaimed. "I asked him to find out where one might be located."

Fr. Jake had watched the automobiles arrive and waited at his open door. Inside the room, they refused the priest's offer of coffee.

Sonia introduced the agent. "Father Jake, this is Drug Enforcement Agent Juan Herrero of the Albuquerque District office." After the two shook hands, she asked, "May we sit down?"

"Of course." *Juan Herrero is 'John Smith' in Spanish. Who is Sonia kidding?*

She explained, "The DEA has been monitoring a drug corridor they believe is operating out of Fort Liberty, that survivalist camp up near the Pentecostals. Agent Herrero, will you explain?"

"Thanks, Detective Mora…" He glanced toward Fortgang, then back at her.

"He's okay," she told him. "You can talk."

Herrero nodded, adjusted his tie, and continued, "In a nutshell, Father, law enforcement has been trying to penetrate the survivalist compound for two years. A few months ago, an under-cover agent we had in place was murdered in Belén. We suspect there's major drug trafficking going on up there, with money laundering, et cetera, that is usually part of such an operation."

"Really?" Fortgang interjected. "That helps explain car noises I hear at night going up that way. They aren't by any of the Pentecostals. However much in doctrinal error, they are not prone to leave their commune at night."

"Thank you, Mister Fortgang." Herrero jotted down his remarks in a notebook. "Now then, Governor Montoya wants this operation broken up A.S.A.P. It's an election year and she plans on running again." The agent barely held in an innocent smirk. "Need I explain that connection?"

Sonia added, "Charges against the survivalists would run from failure to register for the draft, to drug trafficking, illegal firearms, and even sedition. Agent Herrero mentioned money laundering. These multiple felonies would involve the DEA, FBI, ATF and Secret Service. Obviously, we can't have officers from four or five agencies running all over the place, so the governor wants only the Socorro Sheriff's Department and DEA officers to take part in a counteraction."

Fr. Jake wondered aloud, "Detective, Agent Herrero, you came here just to tell me all this? Why?"

The Ghosts of Glorieta

Sonia replied, "I told Mister Herrero of your connection with the Pentecostals. Father, tell him what you observed of Fort Liberty from Eden West."

"Razor wire fencing," the priest recalled. "Low earth berms and six-foot hedgerow barriers. Armed guards patrol the perimeter, 24/7."

"What of buildings inside the compound?"

"They can't be seen very well from the road or the Pentecostal side."

Herrero nodded toward Sonia. "Detective, that pretty much confirms what we knew. We have aerial shots of bunker-like housing and a steel gate barring the entrance. Scurry was in the First Gulf War, and probably has RPGs trained on the gate. He could have IEDs sown along the camp perimeter. A direct attack to breach the compound gate would be suicidal."

"For both sides," Sonia emphasized. "Agent, I've told you that at least two sheriffs have opted out of any kind of police action."

Herrero exhaled and ran a hand through his dark hair in frustration. "There would have to be a massive diversion to distract Scurry and allow the gate to be secured."

"How about a parachute assault?" Fortgang suggested. "82nd Airborne."

Sonia threw the DEA agent her 'What-the-hell-is-he-talking-about' look, then said to the accountant, "Sir, I want to question you about the Mexican *santo* figures you sell."

Fortgang mistook her interest and nodded. "Yes, there is a patron saint of police officers and detectives. Saint Michael the Archangel."

"So," she half-quipped, "it would be his sword against steel-jacket bullets?"

"Detective, it helps to have faith."

"As much as wearing Kevlar® body armor, Mister Fortgang?"

Herrero stood up to defuse obvious hostility between the two. "Thanks, Detective Mora, and you, Father Jake. You've both confirmed our intelligence about the survivalists. There would be multiple casualties on both sides and enough bad publicity generated for Governor Montoya to lose the election."

As Fr. Jake went to open the door, he said, "Agent, this is beyond politics. If drug trafficking is going on, it can't simply be allowed to continue. Our young people deserve better."

Albert Noyer

"Father, law enforcement will plan in the light of what you've told me." Herrero turned to the others. "Good day, Detective Mora. Mister Fortgang."

After the agent left, no one spoke as each pondered the deadly consequences of what they heard. Sonia was first to break the silence by taking the San Isidro *santo* off the table and turning it over. "Mister Fortgang, where do you obtain these?"

"Chihuahua, Mexico. Antonio Reynoso is an excellent craftsman. I've dealt with him for years."

She pointed to the sticker with a short, lacquered fingernail. "What bothers me sir, is this hole drilled through the center."

"Why in heaven's name would it? The wood is pine or cottonwood and very light. It's filled with sand ballast for stability."

"Sand, or perhaps cocaine? Methamphetamine?"

Fortgang's pasty complexion turned livid. "Ridiculous!" he fumed. "Detective, I…I truly take offense at that insinuation."

"Sir, I didn't accuse you of anything." Sonia put back the *santo*. "Ready, Father, to go to the *morada*? Mister Fortgang, I'll drive. Lock your car if you haven't already."

At the highway, the CPA, sitting in the back seat of the two-door Neon, sullenly directed Sonia to turn left, then take a right at the Romero Loop Road near the trading post. At the point where the westbound road abruptly swung around to the north, Fortgang told her to park in a field on the left. Shortly beyond, an indistinct trail led toward a thick *bosque* canopy of tangled grass, thorny branches of hackberry with unripe berries, and spiky graythorn shrubs. Off the trail, larger Mexican elder trees displayed bright green leaves above the ubiquitous reddish-brown stalks of salt cedar shrubs. Cottonwoods towered over the greenery, throwing shade on a steamy mini-jungle that buzzed with insects.

As the three threaded their way through the brush, the gurgle of the Rio Grande became louder and more predominant. Three hundred yards or so further along, the tower of a small chapel appeared above the foliage. No bell was evident. The rectangular building of adobe blocks stood in a modest clearing. To one side a low, field-stone cairn supported a four-foot-high cross of weathered tree trunks.

Fortgang was over his angry snit or had sublimated it. "The *morada* is not very large," he said, leading the way to the building. "The Brotherhood uses it to store religious paraphernalia they use during Holy Week services." He pushed open an unlocked door on the near side. A single window gave

The Ghosts of Glorieta

light to a rough interior that smelled of stale urine and incense. "I suppose a few transients occasionally sleep here, yet Christ did say that we should succor the poor."

Sonia glanced around. An altar of red sandstone stood on a wooden platform at one end. On the opposite side, a man-size cross of squared pinewood rested across two sawhorse trestles. Several leather whips with bone terminals hung from pegs along the wall. A wooden storage cabinet was set against a wall opposite the door. "Is that for clothing?" she asked.

"Yes, a *trastero*, detective." Fortgang walked across the room to open the doors and ruffle through black robes hanging on pegs. "The Brotherhood leaves these here rather than at home in a closet. It's a sacred place."

"Are *matachine* wands kept here?" Fr. Jake asked.

"No." Fortgang went over to the large cross. "If only I had the strength to imitate the Savior like the some of the *Hermanos* do…" He ran a loving hand over the rough wood, then sharply pulled it back "Ahhh. I picked up a splinter!" He looked at the injury and sucked blood from a laceration in the web of skin between his thumb and forefinger.

"Here, sir…" Sonia handed him a tissue from the pack she kept in her purse. "I have a first-aid kit in the car. You can put on a plastic bandage there." She took back Fortgang's bloody tissue and gave him a fresh one. After examining his hand and the cross, she said, "Fortunately, the splinter itself is still in the wood. Sir, just hold that tissue over the wound until it stops bleeding and we return to my car."

"I'm fine, detective. *Gracias*." Fortgang dabbed at the cut with the soft paper, then gestured toward the room's sparse furnishings. "I said you wouldn't find anything here. The *matachines* all keep their dance costumes at home, so you would have to question each of them about having a broken wand. I don't even know who they are."

She nodded agreement, realizing it would be a fruitless exercise. "Sir, I'd like to look around outside."

Fortgang volunteered, "They have a Via Dolorosa in back with the Stations of the Cross."

Beyond the clearing, trampled plants struggled back upright in the two and a half months since Good Friday of Holy Week. The faint trail paralleled the river and led past rough, cast-concrete markers, scratched with Roman numerals I – XIV to mark each Station. At the Twelfth Station, a *Hermano* had incised a crude skull under the XII. Behind the marker, a hole in a three-foot mound of earth was deep enough hold an upright cross.

"This represents Golgotha," Fr. Jake remarked. "Whoever was tied on the cross would be lifted up here."

"An amazing expression of faith," Fortgang marveled. "The *Hermanos* flagellate themselves until they bleed."

"It's still done publicly in areas of Spain."

"That so, Father?" Sonia asked. "Weird." She looked around a moment longer, then turned toward the path they had used. "Thank you, gentleman, I've seen enough. Let's go back."

The three retraced their steps in silence. At her car, Sonia took back Fortgang's last bloody tissue and handed Fr. Jake the medical kit. He unwrapped and applied a sterile plastic bandage to the accountant's hand.

As the car re-approached the highway, Fr. Jake asked, "Sonia, could you drop me off at the elementary school, off to the right? Cynthia asked me to take a look at her classroom."

"Sure, Father. *No problemo.*"

"And, Duane, might I see that financial report after lunch?"

After a brief hesitation, he agreed. "Father, I could bring it by at one o'clock."

"That would be fine."

Sonia stopped in the parking lot at the school entrance. "Will be in touch, Father."

"Thanks. See you in a bit, Duane."

Excelencia Elementary was a bright, cheerful building. Bi-lingual signs on a bulletin board in the main hallway encouraged good student goals and conduct.

RESPETO	RESPECT
Muestro cortesia y honoria prójimo	You've got to give it to get it
CHARACTER COUNTS!	*¡EL CARACTER CUENTA!*
I am a person of good character.	Soy una persona de chárácter.

He stopped at a showcase that displayed art projects by students of several teachers: tempera paintings, clay work, and paper mosaics. A section with life-size, brightly painted papier maché masks from different world cultures bore the name, Ms. Plow's 5th grade class.

A small sign directed visitors to register at the office. The glass-enclosed room was near a banner stretched across the hallway and lettered with the school motto.

The Ghosts of Glorieta

¡Ex—Cel!

Sitting at a desk, a trim, dark-haired woman in her late forties looked up. "May I help you, sir? Summer classes won't start until next week."

"Yes, I know. I'm Father Jake, pastor at San Isidro."

"Oh, yes, Father." She came to the counter and shook his hand. "Helene Zamora. I'm principal here at Excelencia."

"Good morning. Cynthia Plow invited me to see her classroom. Is she here?"

"Yes, preparing for Monday. I can walk you down to her room, Father."

"Mrs. Zamora,"—he noticed her diamond wedding band—"just point the way. I don't wish to inconvenience you."

"I need to stretch my legs a bit." She laughed and indicated a visitor's ledger. "Sign in, please."

For her office work at school, Zamora wore a short-sleeved, flowered blouse, dark slacks, and high-heel pumps. The two walked down a hallway that smelled of industrial disinfectant. A swarthy, gray-haired custodian cleaning classroom windows nodded to them as they passed.

The click-click of her heels and shuffle of Fr. Jake's sandals were the only sounds, until he asked, "Do you live in Providencia, Mrs. Zamora?"

"Yes, but you haven't seen me at San Isidro because my husband and I attend St. Phillip's Episcopal Church in Belén."

"I see. Well, perhaps your pastor and I could organize an ecumenical outreach program, similar to one that I held in Michigan."

Her unexpected reaction was cold and noncommittal. "Perhaps."

Fr. Jake realized his innocent suggestion was a mistake. *Wrong thing to say. She thinks I'm trying to weasel her and her husband into the Catholic Church.*

As they turned a hallway corner, Zamora remarked, "Father, we miss Raylene Maldonado. Do you know anything more about what caused her death? I don't believe there's been a funeral yet?"

"No, Raylene's body is still at the morgue. Her husband has disappeared."

"Donny." She spoke his name with distaste. "During the day, Raylene was happy here as our secretary, but became depressed when it approached time for her to return home. In October, our first teacher assessment meeting ran late. Her husband stormed in and tried to drag her out by the arm. My Phys-Ed teacher had to restrain him."

215

Albert Noyer

"I can't comment on the total marriage, just on what I observed, but he did seem the bullying type."

Zamora nodded accord. "Raylene has…had…only been with us since September, but I noticed that she often tried to cover up facial bruises with makeup."

"Still," Fr. Jake said, "we really can't accuse her husband of anything."

"Accuse?" She stopped to confront him. "Father, what do you mean?"

Another mistake of mine. Details of Raylene's murder haven't been made public. "It's just that…well…her death was suspicious. The police are investigating him."

"I see." Her voice became professional again. "There's Miss Plow's room, 105. Sign out when you leave, Father."

"Thank you, Mrs. Zamora."

When the priest came into her classroom, Cynthia was tacking reference pictures of New Mexican wild flowers on a side bulletin board.

"Father Jake!" she beamed in delight. "What a nice surprise."

He laughed at her enthusiasm. "You did tell me to stop by, Cynthia."

"And I knew you would." She went to her desk and held up three volumes. "See. I've set aside these books about the Civil War in New Mexico for you."

"Young lady, I really appreciate that. The nearest library is probably in Belén."

"Exactly, Father."

"Your room looks beautiful." He walked around to look at student work. "I especially liked the masks in that hall showcase."

"That was a combined geography and art project, but they didn't finish all the masks. Look over here." Cynthia went to a windowsill where she had set painted masks to dry, and handed him an unpainted sample. "Papier maché is an old technique and inexpensive. The kids take newspaper strips soaked in wheat paste and mold them into a mask. After it's coated with white gesso and dry, like the one you have, they apply colored designs."

"Interesting."

"I've seen you sketching, Father. May I look at your drawings sometime?"

"Of course." He put the mask over his face a moment, then back down with the others. "Cynthia, I just came from the *morada* that Armando mentioned. There were no wands stored there or anything belonging

The Ghosts of Glorieta

to fiesta dancers. We found only some *Penitente* items used during Holy Week."

"So Father Mora's death isn't any closer to being solved?"

"Sometimes police will sideline cases, yet with his niece conducting the investigation, I'm confident we'll find the person responsible."

'I really hope so."

"As do I. Oh, Duane Fortgang is bringing me a parish financial statement this afternoon. I'll probably be able to order the Faith Formation books you'll need in the fall."

"That's wonderful, Father. I'm about finished with the dig, so I can prepare for the religion classes."

He laughed. "Yes, I see you're not wearing your archaeologist's coveralls."

Cynthia frowned while indicating her clothes with a hand gesture. "Look at me…old jeans and my painting shirt with the tails hanging out. Worn-out Nikes." She twirled a strand of long reddish hair. "I'm getting this cut short next week, and buying contact lenses. I keep misplacing my regular glasses."

"You'll be a brand new woman," he jested. "How about Armando? Is he practicing any church music? I've ordered more current missalettes, but those outdated ones have music he can use."

"He and some guys are working on it, Father, yet don't be too hopeful."

"Okay, but hope is one of the three things that Saint Paul says abides." Fr Jake picked up the three books. "I'll let you finish preparing your classroom."

She walked him to the door. "Wasn't that virtual reality show that Mister Houston put on exciting? I'd love for my students to see it."

"I'm sure that's the future of movie entertainment." He paused before going back to the office. "Cynthia, I think your mask project may have given me an idea, but I'd need you and your students' assistance."

"Anything to be of help, Father," she agreed. "What is the idea?"

"I still have to work it out. May I come by on Monday?

"Of course you can. I'll be here until noon."

"Thanks, God bless. Thanks for lending me the books."

217

Albert Noyer

Fr. Jake had finished a lunch of canned chunky beef vegetable soup and a turkey- ham sandwich, when Duane Fortgang came at precisely 1:00 P.M. The accountant drove up in the delivery van that he used on his purchasing trips to Mexico.

Fortgang refused an offer of coffee and sat on the couch. He removed his Stetson and mopped sweat from his baldhead with a bandana. After polishing his glasses, he pulled a manila folder from a brief case and handed the priest a single computer sheet.

"Father Mora never bothered much about these. He trusted me."

"Duane, it's not so much a matter of trust as efficiency." He skimmed over the entries, "Offerings…Altar Worship…Utilities." He paused at Office Staff and Administrative Expense entries. "I notice 'Janitor' under these. I thought *mayordomos* donated their services."

"Maldonado gets only a deacon's stipend. With him claiming to be incapacitated and poor Raylene doing most of the work, I …Father Mora that is…gave her an allowance."

"I see. Well, thanks, Duane, I'll look this over later. Have you heard any more about Tex Houston's bid to purchase the church?"

"No, why would I?" he asked, tucking his glasses into their case

"I thought the archbishop might be in touch with you as parish financial officer."

"Benisek hasn't." Fortgang stood up to end the meeting. 'Father, come out and look inside my van. I'm driving to Chihuahua to pick up more *santos* and some handmade furniture from *Señor* Reynoso." He glanced around the sparsely furnished rooms. "You certainly could use a few more items."

"Well, maybe a larger bedside table and lamp? I have three books that Cynthia Plow lent me to read."

"Reynoso will have just the thing. Come on outside." At the van, Fortgang put his hat back on, opened wide twin doors at the rear, and pointed to the interior. "That rack up front holds the statues and the center is left free for large furniture. Pretty neat, huh?"

"Indeed, Duane. Where do you enter into Mexico?"

"The Santa Teresa Port of Entry. Highway 45 goes straight down to Chihuahua."

"Well, God bless, and have a safe trip."

The Ghosts of Glorieta

"Thanks, Father." Fortgang slammed the back doors shut, slid into the drivers' seat, and put on sunglasses.

Standing at the van's window, Fr. Jake noticed a silver thermo-cup with the UTA logo in a console cup holder. *Same as the one Tex Houston brought to the house.* "Nice cup, Duane."

"U. of Texas, Austin." Fortgang reached over to hold it up. "UTA, my Alma Mammy."

"So you once told me."

"Father," he joked, "you've gotten quite a reputation for offering every visitor some coffee, but I figured if you had any left over from breakfast, it would be stale. I'll fill this up at Mamacita's." He replaced the cup, and then voiced an afterthought, "Oh, anything new on poor Raylene Maldonado's death?"

"If there is, Duane, I haven't been told."

"That poor lady." He started the engine and grinned. "Father, I'll find a nice table for you."

"Thanks"—Fr. Jake hopped out of the way—"*Vaya con Dios...* Again, safe trip. God bless."

Fortgang waved to him with one hand as he U-turned back toward the highway.

Back inside, Fr. Jake had started to read the accountant's report when his cell tone rang. "Father Jake at San Isidro," he answered.

"Sonia Mora. You know, Father, I am terribly, terribly disappointed in you." Her voice barely controlled an underlying anger.

"Detective, what have I done?"

"Done? You agreed to not tell anyone about that broken tip off a *matachine* wand that we found in the *segrario*."

"And, Sonia, I haven't."

"Then how does it happen that Duane Fortgang said I wouldn't find a broken wand in the *morada*?"

"I don't recall...Wait a moment! He *did* say that after the splinter accident. We were about to leave."

"Exactly. A slip of his tongue and yet—"

"Sonia, I swear that I never told Duane."

After a long pause, her voice returned to normal. "Okay, Father. Has Donny Maldonado come back yet?"

"No."

Albert Noyer

"We put out an APB on him. As far as we know Maldonado doesn't have a car, but a neighbor or friend might have driven him somewhere."

"Speaking of neighbors," he recalled, "one happened by and told me that Maldonado's dog got loose while he was filling its water bowl. It headed up toward the forest."

"The forest? Maybe the 'deacon' has a cozy little Hernando's Hideaway up there."

Fr. Jake chuckled and repeated the word play, "Clever. Hernando's Hideaway."

"What, you don't think Latinos have a sense of humor?" Sonia's sarcasm was unconcealed as she asked, "Haven't you ever watched Debi Gutierrez, or George Lopez and Pablo Francisco on Comedy Central?"

"No. That's just an American song I first heard in Poland."

"Father Jake, I wasn't going to share what I'll say to you, but I do believe you about the broken wand. I'll just have to dig up more dirt on Duane Fortgang."

"Fine, detective. What is it you were not going to tell me?"

"I have DNA results on Jane Doe, Father Mora, Caleb, and the Pentecostal Elder."

He sucked in a cautious breath. "Go ahead."

"The victim *is* Caleb's mother, but my uncle is not his father."

"That's wonderful news, Sonia, congratulations! You must be very relieved."

"Yeah, thanks. I am, but…neither is James Parker, a.k.a. Elder Jeremiah, the father of Caleb Parker."

The Ghosts of Glorieta

22

Sonia waited for the priest's reaction, which was more subdued than she expected.

"I don't know what to say, detective. What will you do?"

"We'll have to go tell them in the morning, and I'll keep seeing what I can find on Fortgang."

"I'm not sure how he could be involved here. Sonia, you sound absolutely exhausted, yet you must be relieved knowing that your uncle wasn't intimate with Aimée Parker."

"Oh, but he was, Father," she disagreed. "What you said about obtaining the communion host for a Black Mass got me to thinking about uncle's behavior. And don't forget about those crosses tattooed on his feet. Jesús Mora always was a fragile person, but as I first told you, he became more and more reclusive. I believe there was a sexual favor exacted in getting that host to Aimée for Elder J."

"Or," Fr. Jake proposed, "perhaps it was freely offered to a lonely, lovesick priest, who had little experience with women?" When she failed to react at his question, he asked another. "So you don't know who Caleb's father was?"

"Or *is?*" she suggested.

"True, the man might still be alive."

Sonia speculated, "Aimée obviously slept around. The father could be a commune member who joined early on, and yet James Parker is now the main suspect."

221

Albert Noyer

"You've have to start over by taking DNA from everyone else up there. Seventeen years later you're not apt to find out who he was, *or is.*"

"That's what police work is all about, Father. Haven't you had parishioners who joined AA, then backslid and had to begin over again?"

"I've even known priests to whom that happened."

Fr. Jake heard Sonia swallow a drink of something he hoped was stronger than tap water. "Father, aren't cold case miracles in your sphere of influence?" she asked.

"I'm not exactly sure how miracles come about, Sonia, but never thought I'd hear you wonder about that."

"Maybe I'm just really tired. I'll pick you up at Ten. Pleasant dreams, Father Jake."

"Goodnight, Sonia. God bless…"

He snapped shut his cell phone and slowly put it down. The DNA results had not solved, but only complicated the mystery. *If a socially immature Fr. Mora had been responsible for an irresponsible girl's pregnancy, however regrettable, that aspect of the mystery would be solved, but both are dead. What had Aimée come to discuss with the priest?*

Fr. Jake took his sketchbook off a table, sat in his armchair, and flipped to a back page. *I could try to doodle some possibilities.*

FR. MORA — AIMEE PARKER — BLACK MASS? — SACRED HOST????

She probably didn't come to discuss a divorce…there was no church wedding. What to do about her life in a hardscrabble commune dominated by a religious fanatic to whom she was married? For advice on how to escape an existence she had come to detest, or the unexpected hardship of raising a growing child under commune conditions? Even for the calculated exploitation of a lonely, lovesick, man—the one person over whom Aimée might feel she had a degree of power?

"Yet Mora was murdered many years later," he muttered to himself. "Who alive now had been close to him? Certainly these two knew him better than any parishioner."

FR. MORA — MALDONADO — FORTGANG — ???

"Where does Jefferson Davis Houston come into it, if at all?"

FR MORA — TEX — PENTACLE PIX — ???

"Tex wants the church for his movie set. The archbishop is willing to sell, but it's not the property of his diocese. No one has mentioned Fr. Mora's will, and there's still the unsolved murder of Raylene Maldonado."

The Ghosts of Glorieta

RAYLENE — DONNY — UNKNOWN LOVER — REASON(S)???

"At Mamacita's she was upset about something. Perhaps Raylene wanted my advice about breaking off an affair? Or confessing to having hidden the tax delinquency notices?

"Houston and Fortgang are at odds. The brash Texan is trying to destroy the church and village where the Catholic accountant…a former Texan… lives. *Duane is from Amarillo, but has been in New Mexico for years. Dead end for a connection there.*

"Or is there?" he asked himself aloud and closed the sketchbook. "After I come back from Eden West with Sonia Mora, I'll go see Tex. He said he was living in a motor home a short distance north of Providencia."

O

When Sonia arrived, Fr. Jake was outside on his porch. He waited for her on a kitchen chair, pondering what he had written in his sketchbook the evening before. She wore the same jacket and baseball cap she had on a day earlier. He glanced at his watch. Exactly ten o'clock. *Sonia is a truly beautiful woman, and yet no wedding band. Has she ever been married?* At the thought, he held in a smile. *She might be a little tough for some men. I'll try to find out a bit more about her on the ride up to Eden West.*

He stood to greet her. "Good Morning, detective."

"Morning, Father."

"You're right on time. Did you drive all the way around from Socorro to Belén, or on that bridge across the river?"

"It depends on how much I have to think about," she replied. "Haven't you driven south of here yet?"

"Afraid not."

"Highway 310 ends at La Fonda, where Raylene's parents live. The place was a staging point on the old Spanish Camino Real. Even Albuquerque merchants brought their trade goods down there for transport to Chihuahua and Mexico City. The railroad still pretty much follows the same route."

"I learn more about New Mexico history every day," he said, walking with her to the car. "Cynthia Plow lent me books about the Glorieta battle. Captain Schiller spoke a bit about it." *Over a canteen of rum.*

"Good…" She held the passenger door open for him. "You ready, Father? I see you picked up a bit of a tan."

223

Albert Noyer

"Doesn't everyone here?"

"Looks good on you. Nice short-sleeved shirt you're wearing, too, and I see a bit of priest collar showing."

"Makes me 'official'," he jested, belting up. "No telling how the Elder will react to those DNA results."

They drove in silence until Sonia turned the Plymouth up the road to Upland Heights Estates and Fr. Jake ventured, "What brought you into police work, Detective?"

"That's a quite personal question," she hedged. "Why did you become a priest?"

"No, ladies first."

"Ladies first?" She threw him a sidewise smirk. "Father, what century are you from?"

He laughed. "Fair enough. I suspect we both went into our respective lines of work because we wanted to serve others. I saw the terrible things that happened to people under Communism and the role of the Church in opposing the government where ever it could."

"You wanted to serve God and not the State?"

"Maybe 'serve' is an outdated word. I guess as a priest I wanted to help people find some purpose at being on earth, and along the way try to discover the nature of God for my own curiosity. Our Catechism says it's 'to know Him, love Him and serve Him, etc.'."

"There's that word 'serve' again."

"The first 'catechism' dates from the sixteenth century, but our English translation is 1839. The terms 'serve' and 'servants' were in vogue then."

"We police are considered as 'public servants'."

"That's about right for me. I'm not the monkish type."

It was Sonia's turn to laugh. "That's for sure, Father."

When the Plymouth reached the gatehouse, Sonia parked a short way beyond and took off her baseball cap. She fiddled with the visor a moment, as if pondering what personal details of her life she should share with a priest. "My…my dad was a cop for over twenty years," she finally began in a low voice. "He was gone a lot of nights. Just mom and I were there to worry about him until morning."

"That's understandable."

"Right, Father," she agreed without looking at him. "After he retired, Dad became depressed. It came on gradually, and he hid it pretty well from us. One afternoon, Mom and I came home from shopping for my senior

The Ghosts of Glorieta

prom dress. The door to the den was closed, but…but that wasn't unusual. My father sat in there most of the time. Mom put on a kettle and brought him his afternoon cup of tea. Dad was slumped in an armchair, his service revolver still in his hand. Shot through the mouth. He…the dear idiot… had put a bath towel over the upholstery so as not to…" Sobs broke the end of her sentence.

"I am so sorry." Fr. Jake touched Sonia's arm in sympathy.

She wiped her eyes with the back of a finger. "You see, crime was still rampant when dad retired, so he maybe thought he'd wasted his life. Made mom look older than she was by worrying so much. Hadn't been around for me when he thought he should." Sonia put her cap back on and started the engine. "Six months later mom died. I was attending the Albuquerque Police Academy."

"You decided to 'avenge' his memory, if that's the right word?"

She sniffled and fumbled for a tissue to wipe her nose. "Crazy, eh, Father?"

He asked, "Do you believe that your dad wasted his life?"

She revved the engine and jerked the Plymouth into Drive. "Father, I, in all fucking honesty, don't know how to answer that."

They drove the rest of the way in the silence of their thoughts. Remembering the rifle shot that had smashed the windshield of Griego's police cruiser, Sonia parked well before the entrance to Eden West.

A work detail of Edenites sorted used tires and recyclable trash near the entrance, but Caleb was not among them. Sonia went directly to James Parker's Earthship lodge with her folder of DNA reports. He was outside, patching the winter cracks that marred his entrance porch stucco.

"Sir—"

After Sonia called to him, Parker turned and touched his painter's cap in a salute. "Detective. Reverend."

She held up the folder. "Sir, I have the DNA test results. May we go inside?"

Parker laid his trowel across a plastic tub of wet stucco. "You can tell me right here, detective. And do it quickly…this material sets fast."

"Is your son on the premises?" she asked.

"No. I haven't seen him since you last came."

"Sir, we compared the DNA of Caleb Parker with that of Father Jesús Mora. There was no match."

225

Albert Noyer

Parker's eyebrows tilted at the absurdity of her report. "Why should there be?"

Sonia continued, "Then we compared your DNA with that of Caleb Parker. Sir, you are not his father."

Parker stared at her, turning crimson, his hands beginning to tremble. "That… that's bullshit, Detective! Pure, unadulterated bullshit!"

"Elder, it isn't," Fr. Jake told him gently. "The margin of error in DNA paternity tests is negligible."

Still seething, Parker bent down to stir the stucco with his trowel. Without looking up he demanded, "So, who's the son of a bitch?"

Sonia closed the folder. "Sir, we don't know. Are you sure you don't want to go inside?"

"I'm sure. I've got to finish this patching."

"Then I must ask you out here. If your wife allegedly was promiscuous, do you suspect anyone in your commune?"

He stood up, trowel in hand, and glared at her. "Detective, we're not into adultery or fornication here."

"Except on 'Devils' Night'?" Sonia asked.

"What? Why you…you…" Parker raised his trowel against her in righteous anger.

Fr. Jake stepped between the two. "Calm down, Elder. The detective is just trying to determine who might have killed Aimée."

Unfazed by Parker's threat, Sonia continued, "Sir, we know about your Black Mass rituals."

"A religious expression protected by Article One in the Amendments," he retorted, lowering the trowel.

"Mister Parker, I'm familiar with the Constitution. Even if you won't help me with the names of possible perpetrators, you're still a prime suspect."

Indignant, he demanded, "How so?"

"Circumstantially, a prosecutor would argue that you discovered your wife's infidelity and put a permanent stop to it."

"Ridiculous," he scoffed, and went back to spreading stucco on a section of wall.

Sonia looked around. "Sir, where is Caleb Parker?"

Parker's shoulders slumped and the trowel slipped from his hand. "I told you that haven't seen my son…him…since you were here to take those DNA samples."

The Ghosts of Glorieta

"I see." Sonia took out her ID case and handed him a card. "Sir, if you won't be the one to inform Caleb about his paternity, please ask him to call me."

He took off his painter's cap in a gesture of conciliation. "I…I apologize, detective. You must understand…"

"Accepted, but don't lose my card." Parker tucked it into a shirt pocket and resumed patching the stucco. "Father Jakubowski, are you ready to go back?"

"Right, Sonia." They had started walking toward the gate when Fr. Jake stopped. "Wait. I need to check something behind Parker's lodge." He went to the razor-wire fence that separated the survivalist compound from the Pentecostals, then came back a few minutes later. "We can go now."

They continued toward the Plymouth in silence, but as Sonia swung the car back toward the highway she asked, "So, Father, what did you want to see behind Parker's lodge?"

"I'll tell you that after I figure it all out."

While passing Fortgang's house, Sonia Mora commented that his delivery van was not in the driveway. Fr. Jake told her that he was in Chihuahua, purchasing more Mexican-made furniture and *santos*.

O

On Sunday morning, a few more people attended Fr. Jake's two Masses. At both he told them that Tex Houston had agreed to postpone the demolition of their homes for a week. The congregation absorbed the information in silence; they would wait to see what actually happened that Monday. After Mass, the priest reminded Cynthia Plow that he wanted to visit her classroom on Monday, when the students were present. She agreed.

While fixing himself a sandwich for lunch, Fr. Jake decided that he would visit Tex Houston in his camper early on Monday morning, before going to see Cynthia at Excelensia Elementary.

O

Tex had leased space on the extensive site of a schoolhouse that had been abandoned when the new elementary school was built. His "camper" was a studio rental, 40 ft., three-level, Mega-star with a 14 ft. curbside slide-out parlor/sleeping niche. The semi-truck with the second display model,

227

Albert Noyer

three other Pentacle Pix trucks, and two smaller crew trailers were parked at a distance from his rental.

After the arson on his semi, the filmmaker ordered a temporary chain-link fence erected around the campsite. At the entrance gate, a black-uniformed security guard with a Pentacle logo on his sleeve phoned the filmmaker about his visitor.

"You're kind of early, Father," he said, while waiting for a response. "Mister Houston don't like being disturbed too early."

"Early?" Fr. Jake read his nameplate. "Bill, it's nine o'clock."

"Mister Houston is taking the day off, if you know what I mean." The guard winked, then held up a hand for quiet. "Mister Houston, this is Bill at the gate. A Father Jake is here to see you."

"Fine, sir, I'll do that. Thank you."

"Guess you can go in, Father. Hope no one died."

"Beg pardon?"

"A joke, Father."

Still tying the waist-cord of his silk dressing gown, Tex met the priest at a door next to the slide-out, three steps up from the ground. "Guard got your name wrong, Father Jay. He called you Jake. Come in. What can I do ya for?"

Inside, the rental's spacious parlor had a 50" satellite TV, VCR, DVD and stereo surround sound entertainment center. A kitchenette featured a microwave oven, refrigerator, and dining table with two chairs. Tex lifted aside a sheet and blanket on the sofa bed inside the slide-out. "Roberto sleeps here. That's his steno desk over there. He's out getting' us…me…a take-out breakfast at McDonald's."

"Nice rig." As Fr. Jake walked around the room, he caught a glimpse of… Melissa…was it? …passing an open door on the third level. She was barefoot and had on a filmy black negligée.

Tex noticed, flushed and blurted, "It ain't like I'm married, *Padre!*"

"I'm not here to discuss your sex life."

"What then? Must be pretty serious to come here this early." After a nervous laugh, Tex asked, "Do I need a lawyer?"

"Not just yet."

"Then what are you here for?"

"Can we sit down?"

228

The Ghosts of Glorieta

"Sure, Father Jay." Tex picked up his cell phone from a coffee table in front of the sofa. "I'll have Roberto order us an extra breakfast."

"Thanks, no," he declined. "Just sit down, please." The filmmaker moved more bedding aside and slumped against the far end. "Tex, don't underestimate Detective Mora's resolve in solving the murders of her uncle and Raylene Maldonado. Who and what might be behind them."

"I don't, Father Jay. Why say that?"

"You've mostly treated her like some eager bimbo hoping to catch a role in one of your B movies." When Tex flushed, yet failed to protest, the priest continued, "We know that someone in the assessor's office had to be working with Raylene in suppressing those tax notices to Father Mora. But she hung on to the evidence. Perhaps she had second thoughts about you buying up her village, or she wanted to extort enough hush money from her accomplice to be able to leave an abusive husband."

The Texan ran his fingers along a satin edge on the blanket. "So, *Padre*, y'all know who she was workin' with?"

"No, Tex, but Sonia isn't just going to put everything she's discovered so far in a cardboard box labeled 'Cold Case'."

"So, what's all that got to do with me?"

"Only that you're the ultimate benefactor of those fraudulent quitclaim deeds."

"Fraudulent?" Tex straightened up as his manner turned hostile. "Now just hold on, *Padre*. You can't come in here making that kind of accusation."

"Oh, but I can." Fr. Jake was silent, letting the man's indignation simmer down, before adding, "Mister Houston, I need a big favor from you."

○

As he signed in at the elementary school office, Fr. Jake waved to Mrs. Zamora, the principal, and mimed that he knew the way to classroom 105.

Cynthia Plow had a summer school class of fifteen 5th grade students. She was in the midst of a remedial reading circle with half the class. Her other students read more or less silently at a table. When she saw the priest outside her door, she stood up and motioned him in.

Curious about the interruption, students looked toward the visitor.

"Class," she said, "I want to introduce Father Jake. Please read silently for a moment." Cynthia went to show him a textbook. "Father, we're using

229

Albert Noyer

the 'Treasures' series that emphasize Southwest authors and themes." She turned back to her students. "Class, say 'Good morning' to Father. Some of you may already know him. He's the priest at San Isidro church."

The students repeated their greeting more or less in sing-song unison.

"Good morning," Fr. Jake said to them. "I really admired your artwork, which I saw on Friday, especially masks in the hall showcase. In fact, I'm here to ask Miss Plow and all of you for a little artistic help."

○

As Fr. Jake parked in the driveway of his adobe, sounds of gunfire came from the reenactors' camp. Their two-week training session would be over in a week and Tex Houston would have finished his documentary. The men and women were scheduled to leave and reassemble later at what Captain Schiller had called Rancho de Las Golandrinas, near Santa Fe, for their Fourth of July reenactment of the Battle of Glorieta Pass.

The priest needed to call Sonia Mora, but first went over to his church; the arson team had completed an investigation and filed its report. Armando promised to recruit volunteers that week and begin replacing the burned doorway jambs. Rather than discard the original door, Fr. Jake decided to put a protective coat of matte varnish over the ancient, leached wood, including the scorched section. It would be a reminder to parishioners that evil did not always triumph.

He noticed that the La Raza graffiti on the outside *Año Sacerdotal* sign had been cleaned off. *Duane Fortgang thought the Aztlan radicals were responsible for torching Tex's semi, yet there hasn't been any more vandalism.*

The cool nave interior of the church smelled faintly of smoke that had seeped in from the fire. He crossed himself with holy water and walked down the center aisle to the altar platform. He knelt on the top stair, in front of the San Isidro *santo* that flanked the right side of the central Mexican crucifix. Praying to saints was a venerable custom in the Church, a logical outgrowth of the petitions to Greek and Roman gods that everyone practiced when Christianity was a struggling sect among many others. But this was now, and the many statues in the church gave rise to the accusations by Elder Jeremiah and others of idolatry—however misplaced.

"I'll keep it short, Isidore," Fr. Jake said half-aloud. "I asked you for help once before, and will truly need it if my plan is to succeed. Please, help your people."

The Ghosts of Glorieta

As the priest stood up, his cell tone chimed. Sonia Mora had dialed his number.

"Detective, you're psychic," Fr. Jake chuckled. "I was just about to contact you."

"That can wait, Father. I checked Billy Ray Scurry's military service at The National Personnel Records Center. He *was* in Operation Desert Storm, 24th Infantry Division, enlisted rank of Private. He received a special courts martial BCD, bad conduct discharge, in 1991 for insubordination."

"Not a colonel at all?"

"Not even close. And his offshoot branch of the Scurries doesn't include the Confederate Civil War hero."

"That should disillusion his followers."

He heard her smother a laugh. "Don't be naïve, Father. The BCD would be a badge of honor among survivalists. Scurry mouthed off to a federal entity and survived to brag about it. Now, what was it you wanted to talk about?"

"I have an idea I want to run past you and agent Herrero."

"Go ahead."

"Not on the phone, Sonia. Where can the three of us meet?"

"About what?"

"My idea."

"Father," she wailed in mock exasperation. "You'll have to be more specific about maybe wasting my time and Juan's."

"Detective, I just complimented you on being psychic. You called me about Billy Ray Scurry and this has to do with capturing our erstwhile 'colonel' and his followers, with probably no casualties on either side. Would that be a waste your time?"

"Maybe," she scoffed. "Don't tell me that you've enlisted Saint Michael and the Hosts of Heaven?"

"Be sarcastic if you want, Sonia, but please meet with me anyway."

The urgency in the priest's voice convinced the detective. She said, "Be at the El Dorado Restaurant on Center Street in Belén, at two P.M. tomorrow."

The Ghosts of Glorieta

23 fort liberty / june 13

At the meeting, Detective Mora and DEA agent Herrero had listened to Fr. Jake's plan about mounting a bloodless raid on the survivalist compound. They were noncommittal and only said that they would talk with the persons whom the priest mentioned.

Fr. Jake had one final element in finalizing his plan. Early on Wednesday, the priest went to Eden West to talk with Elder Jeremiah and received reluctant agreement to use a part of his commine for the action.

○

It was now Sunday evening, June 13, about 8:30 P.M. The sun would set in fifteen minutes, the commencement of a long twilight. Fr. Jake put on jeans, a flannel shirt, and his blue nylon jacket to drive up to Eden West: warm June days cooled off at night much more quickly than in Michigan. After checking to see that his appliances were turned off, the priest stepped onto his porch. Abruptly, an older model, mud-spattered Ford truck careened into the driveway, blocking his Nissan. A young man in military camouflage got out, leaving the driver's door ajar. He looked around in furtive glances, then came to the porch steps.

"Y'all Rev'rind Jacob?"

"Close enough. Who are you, young man?"

"Jon Scurry from Fort Liberty. Colonel Scurry is mah daddy."

233

Albert Noyer

A wave of apprehension chilled the priest. "Wh…why did you come, Jon?"

"Rev'rind, we got one of the Hispanics from your church up at the fort, feelin' real poorly. Name's Maldorado."

Not entirely surprised that the 'deacon' had gone there, Fr. Jake nevertheless was startled. "Donny Maldonado is at your compound?"

"Yeah…" Jon laughed. "Says his wife ran out on him."

"Jon, Raylene Maldonado was found murdered in a Belén motel room."

"Well doggone!" Young Scurry pushed back a fatigue hat to scratch his head. "Mean lookin' hombray, but real quiet. Mostly keeps to hisself with that mutt. Never woulda suspected Maldorado kilt anyone—"

"I didn't say he did. What's wrong with Donny?"

"Don't rightly know, Rev'rind, but he's callin' for ya. I was jus' sent to fetch y'all up there."

Fr. Jake controlled a tremble in his voice at the youth's disastrously timed request. "I…I can't go with you, Jon, but tell you what. I was just leaving to visit the Pentecostals. Why don't you bring Mister Maldonado to the Eden West entrance and—"

"Cain't do that," Jon interrupted, his friendly tone now low and threatening. "Y'all got to come to the fort." He pulled a military M1911A1 semiautomatic .45 pistol from his waistband and looked around to see if anyone noticed. "Rev'rind, I took me a awful risk comin' here, so y'all got to come now. Un'erstand me?"

"All right, Jon, everything's cool." Fr. Jake lowered arms he had instinctively half-raised to calm the youth. "Just put the gun away."

"Get in mah truck, Rev'rind," he ordered, waving him in with the semiautomatic.

Early twilight brooded in the evening sky when Jon shifted into reverse, then screeched the tires toward the highway. He turned right without stopping, then right again at the Upland Heights subdivision entrance.

'Where's a sheriff when you need one'? But how could Scurry have found out about the raid? Fr. Jake grasped the truck's dashboard for support as Jon raced the Ford up past the unmanned guard post, almost clipped the edge of the opening in the cement wall with a side view mirror, then jolted the pickup over deep road ruts before reaching Fort Liberty's steel-gated main entrance. Under a glaring halogen light, two guards in hunter's camouflage stood armed with AK 47s. Their faces, except for eyeholes, were concealed

234

The Ghosts of Glorieta

by webbing. They opened the barrier just wide enough for the Ford to pass through. Jon lurched the pickup to a halt in a cloud of dust next to the half-underground command post building. The sound of a generator hummed behind the lodge.

As Jon came around to open the passenger door, Billy Ray Scurry and Dave Allison stood outside under a light pole, waving aside dust and grinning.

Billy Ray stepped forward without extending a hand. "Welcome to Fort Liberty, Rev'rind. Ah'm Colonel Scurry an' this here is Sergeant Allison."

Fr. Jake felt his legs go limp, still unsure whether that a carefully timed plan to capture the survivalist compound through a diversion had been compromised. "Colonel," he managed to ask, "is Donny Maldonado inside? Your son told me he was ill."

Scurry spit tobacco juice aside, then drawled, "Aw, Maldorado ain't ailin', Rev'rind. I jus' wanted to get y' all up here. Ah knew that sayin' one of yours was sick would do the trick."

Is Scurry toying with me? As his apprehension increased, Fr. Jake felt his palms sweating. "Then why bring me here?"

"Jon, Allison, let's escort Rev'rind Jacob down inside the command post," the colonel ordered.

The three men led the priest down a flight of stairs and into the windowless monitoring room. The three wall-mounted monitor screens barely revealed the darkened road and forest beyond. After Scurry clicked on a wall switch, another generator hummed to life. Outdoor floodlights instantly reflected a white glare on the monitors.

Scurry pointed to them and boasted, "Now, y'see Rev'rind,' we got both sides of that access road lit up, an' even off into the woods. Like I say, ain't a possum alive what could sneak up to our gate."

"An' if he did, mister possum wouldn't live to tell of it," Jon added with a vicious chortle devoid of mirth. "Rev'rind, y'all must recall my shot through that deputy's windshield? He musta been madder than a hornet caught in a barn fire."

Is he still baiting me? Mouth dry, Fr. Jake managed to ask, "Then if it's not to see Donny Maldonado, why did you bring me up here?"

"Sit down over there on that bench," Scurry ordered. "Y'all hungry? We're servin' supper in the mess and Jon 'll bring ya somethin'."

235

Albert Noyer

"Thanks, I've eaten." He sat down on wooden seating set against the wall, sweating even though the room was cool. "Colonel, I asked why you brought me here."

Scurry went into pacing mode, scowling as he strutted back and forth in front of the priest, one hand absently caressing his German Luger. "Well, now, Rev'rind, you're sorta our guest here. We're plannin' a sover'n citizen action tomorra' against that Texas guy what bought up the village."

"Sovereign citizen?"

"Right. We gonna blockade that Texan's demo-equipment an' show the Hispanics down there how to defy him an' the gov'ment. This here Fort Liberty is soon gonna be a sover'n nation."

Fr. Jake felt mildly relieved. Evidently, the plot to breach the survivalist camp was not compromised, yet he—literally—was on the wrong side of the fence. "So, where do I come in all this, Colonel?"

Scurry nodded toward the sergeant. "Allison."

He stepped forward to explain, "Reverend, we figured that you'd try to avoid violence down there. You know, counsel the villagers to take legal action in the courts instead of joining our boycott against their homes being demolished."

"Sergeant," Fr. Jake told him, "we're already taking legal action against Tex Houston's quitclaim deeds. Do you truly expect to accomplish anything tomorrow, other than getting yourselves arrested?"

Allison's tone changed from conciliatory to belligerent. "A lot of patriots feel like we do, Reverend."

"And you're foolish to think that the villagers will join you in this." Fr. Jake looked over at Scurry. "Colonel, get real. Your men up here are living in a societal vacuum."

Scurry's complexion above the walrus mustache turned florid. "Now, Rev'rind, I don't cotton up much to that kinda criticism. Y'see—"

Before he could begin another tirade, the command door was flung opened by a camouflage-wearing survivalist member bursting into the room. "Colonel!" he yelled. "Sounds like a lot of firing going on over by the Pentecostals! Come outside, quick!"

"Son of bitch!" Scurry un-holstered his Luger and checked the monitor screens. "Nothin' happenin' out there."

"Daddy," Jon recalled, "Rev'rind Jacob here told me he was going up to the Edenite compound t'night."

The Ghosts of Glorieta

"That so?" Scurry turned to point his gun at the priest. "This got somethin' to do with you?" he growled. "Come outside with us. Allison, get the men out of the mess hall, armed, and over there, on the double!"

The sound of nearby gunfire had alerted a few men who were dining. They left supper early and got their weapons. In pitch darkness, they followed the colonel in scrambling around the south hedgerow, toward a forty-foot-wide field that separated the Survivalists from the Pentecostals. Billy Ray Scurry, herding Fr. Jake ahead of him at gunpoint, was first to turn the corner of the hedge and run into the vacant space.

He looked around: in front of the two men, seeming to emerge from the dense foliage of the hedgerow, life-size images of blue-clad Union infantry and cavalry soldiers appeared before them. Scurry froze in his tracks to stare at the images in disbelief— ghostly white skulls replaced the human or animal flesh on the face of each soldier and horse. Gunfire and explosions sounded inside the compound. An acrid smell of gunpowder polluted the cool night air. At a shouted order, Union cavalry moved forward, their mounts gaining speed as they began their charge, closing the distance between them and the survivalists. The sound of galloping hooves and a smell of horse sweat increased as they came closer and closer.

Scurry regained his wits and fired his Luger at the nearest cavalryman. The image swept past him without harm. Behind the cavalry, a line of skeletal-faced infantrymen advanced, deadly steel bayonets fixed on leveled muskets. Scurry, his sons, and the men who came with them, fired point-blank at the blue-clad Yankees.

None of the ghost-soldiers fell as their line continued its deadly advance.

Allison and the survivalists he had roused from the mess hall arrived amidst the noisy confusion. After their initial shock, most recovered enough to empty pistol or AK 47 magazines at a phantom enemy that would not be killed. After minutes of useless firing, Scurry's men stood incapacitated by an irrational fear of the ghostly images they saw, shot at, and could not stop. Amid the battlefield noise and smell, none thought to realize that they had not been hit by return fire. Weapons lay on the ground or hung uselessly from hands at the survivalists' sides.

The ghastly spectacle ended in less than ten minutes: the filmed hologram images abruptly stopped. Blinding spotlights flashed on the survivalists from the Pentecostal compound.

Agent Juan Hererro's voice boomed through an amplified bullhorn. "Billy Ray Scurry. Order your men to lay down their weapons. DEA officers and

237

sheriff's deputies have secured your camp and are evacuating women and children. No one need be harmed. Lay down your weapons. Do it now!"

"Son of a bitch!" Beyond the bright glare of the lights, Scurry could see nothing but a black emptiness inside Eden West. He squinted toward Fr. Jake, standing alone, then walked up to the priest, and aimed the Luger at his head. "Rev'rind, this is *your* doin'!" he ranted, eyes bulging in an insane stare. "Y'all tricked me, but ya sure as hell won't live t' brag about it."

The echoing sound of a shot shattered the brilliant, surrealistic, white glare.

The Ghosts of Glorieta

24

Billy Ray Scurry's gun hand fell limply to one side as his lifeless fingers dropped the Luger. The survivalist leader's eyes stared ahead in shock. With his temporal bone smashed by a 9 mm bullet, the left side of his skull dripped blood and brains. His gross body swayed drunkenly a moment, and then toppled forward onto the dry weeds that had been trampled flat by panicked survivalists in his breached compound.

Five yards behind him, Dionisio Maldonado lowered his SKS carbine. "I cou'dn't let him do that, Father," he mumbled and raised the gun barrel to his chin.

"Donny, no!" Fr. Jake yelled. "You can't—" The copper bullet tore away the left side of Maldonado's jaw and his ear in a gush of blood and bone. The priest pulled off his jacket as he ran toward the man to cradle his bloody head in the material. "Donny... Donny!"

Maldonado's eyelids fluttered open. He gazed straight up, unblinking at the harsh lights. Blood frothed around his lips. The words he gasped were thick, almost unintelligible. "Didn't kill... Ray...lene."

"No..." In the blinding artificial glare, a black shadow fell over the two men. Fr. Jake glanced up at Sonia Mora, standing above them. The priest signed a cross over Maldonado and recited a prayer from the Mass for the Dying. "'Lord, keep your servant, Donny, safe in your love. Do not let evil conquer him at the hour of death, but let him go in the company of your angels to the joy of eternal life'."

239

Albert Noyer

Dionisio Maldonado managed an almost imperceptible nod of his head and licked blood from his lips to gasp, "Fort…Fort…."

"Fort Liberty," Fr. Jake finished for him. "Yes, Donny, I understand why you came here. You bolted because you feared being accused of Raylene's murder."

Staring up at night stars that perhaps sparkled on the threshold of a heaven, the dying man exhaled a chilling death rattle. Had his now-lifeless eyes fixed on angels in the joyous eternity that his priest had just hoped for him?

Sonia knelt beside Fr. Jake. "Maldonado wasn't talking about this survivalist camp."

"No? What, then?"

"He was trying to tell you the name of Duane Fortgang."

"Fortgang?" Fr. Jake gently closed the dead man's eyelids and stood up, dazed at what had happened in the past hour. Numb, he shaded his eyes against the spotlights and repeated the accountant's name. "Duane Fortgang?"

"Right." Sonia turned away to wipe away tears of relief with the back of a hand, before giving the priest a tongue-lashing. "Jesus Christ, Jakubowski, what in hell were you doing on the survivalist side? You were supposed to be in Eden West. Wasn't that your plan?"

"Scurry had a plan of his own," he mumbled. "When he sent one of his sons to bring me up there at gunpoint, I really thought the Colonel had discovered our diversion tactic."

"*Your* diversion tactic," she sniffled. "Let's go talk about that." Sonia looked over at DEA and sheriff's officers, who rounded up survivalist members and handcuffed them. With their irascible faux-colonel dead, and his four sons' drug smuggling corridor breached, the ineptly named "survivalist" camp had collapsed like a house of playing cards, all showing the bad luck Ace of Spades. An ambulance had been among the raid vehicles. Sonia stood up and signaled for a medic to take charge of Scurry's and Maldonado's bodies. "Agent Herrero made James Parker's lodge our command headquarters, Father. Let's go there now."

Fr. Jake followed her through a gap cut in the razor wire. In Eden West, Tex Houston's film technicians were disassembling their virtual immersion reality hologram equipment, but left spotlights on to illuminate the compound. The Texan filmmaker was not with them.

The Ghosts of Glorieta

Inside the lodge, DEA agent Herrero spoke on a cell phone, finishing a report to Governor Jane Montoya. "Thank you. Yes...yes...*gracias*, Governor. I'll pass on your congratulations to law enforcement officers involved. Yes, *hasta*." He put down the phone and came to the priest. "Close, Father Jake."

Yes," he agreed, "I'm still shaking. Scurry had me in his pistol's sight."

"I...I didn't mean that, Father...ah...congratulations, but I didn't mean that."

"Didn't mean that I'm still alive? Agent, what *did* you mean?"

"Let's all sit on the couch," Sonia-the-diplomat suggested. "Somebody make Father Jake a cup of herbal tea."

Herrero gestured to an aide, who heard and went to the kitchen. The agent sat between Sonia and the priest. "What I meant, Father, was that the operation was a close call. Our greatest concern was that the survivalists would be shooting toward their lodges and we figured the women would come out with some children to see what was happening. We surveyed the foreground, which had a slight rise, and told Mister Houston's technicians to keep the images somewhat high."

"So any return firing would be well over anyone's head."

"Correct, Father. We were able to evacuate persons outside the lodges or still in them within minutes."

Sonia nodded admiration at his success. "It was a precision commando operation."

Herrero continued, "We had rehearsed 'Operation Vigilance' for weeks with a mock-up of the compound gate, yet, as you recall, we discussed the politics of trying and failing an attack. Governor Montoya is a Lieutenant Colonel in the New Mexico Guard. She threatened to pull guardsmen off border duty and take charge of an assault herself."

"I doubt she would have," Sonia disagreed. "It was a ploy to get you to act."

Herrero turned back to the priest. "Father, after you met with us at the restaurant, Detective Mora and I discussed Tex Houston."

Sonia explained, "I called Mister Houston to say that I wanted to question him about Raylene Maldonado's unknown accomplice at the assessor's office. He flew his company lawyer out here from Austin for the deposition. What you once told me, Father, about Houston and Fortgang owning identical University of Texas silver cups rang a bell. I checked with the Austin Bar Association. Fortgang did legal work for Pentacle Pix before

241

Albert Noyer

moving to Providencia. Their mutual involvement in the fraud was easy to conclude from that information."

"Of course, his accomplice was Raylene!" Fr. Jake exclaimed. "The person had to be someone whom Fortgang knew…" He paused to thank Hererro's aide for easing a steaming mug on the table in front of the couch. The tea bag label read *Pomegranate Pizzazz*. He took a welcome sip before asking, "So, why did Raylene do this for Duane?"

"Father, they were lovers," Sonia concluded. "Are you surprised?"

Fr. Jake shook his head. "Detective Mora, in forty-some years as a priest, I've heard hundreds of parishioners confess to adultery and fornication. Almost all had colorful excuses. Hers was to escape an abusive husband. Duane's was monetary and he used her to get it."

"It's likely, yet I have no proof that Fortgang murdered Raylene. I do have DNA evidence that he's the father of Caleb Parker."

"What? How in heaven's name did you get DNA from… Wait! Of course, Sonia. You saved the bloody tissues from the *morada*."

"Yes, and thank God that he picked up a splinter from that cross."

"Thank God or San Isidro?"

"What, Father?"

"Nothing. Duane is in Mexico right now. If he suspects anything…."

Sonia continued, "He's surely smuggling narcotics across the border in those hollowed-out statues and laundering drug money through his restaurant. I'm just not sure how he by-passes Border Authority checkpoints."

"Duane told me that he comes through at…Santa Teresa…is it?"

"Yes, a relatively new port of entry twenty miles west of El Paso."

Herrero suggested, "Detective, I'd put out an APB on him."

She shook her head. "An All Points Bulletin would alert the guy. Fortgang doesn't know about the raid yet, and I need to apprehend him here with narcotics smuggling evidence…" She absently took a sip of the priest's tea. "Fr. Jake, you actually got Cynthia Plow's kids to make those skeleton masks?"

"They sculpted them with her help. I got the idea from papier maché masks I saw in a student showcase. I threatened Tex with serious quitclaim fraud, when I talked him into using his digital technology to superimpose those skeleton masks on the faces of Civil War soldiers in his documentary. I got that idea after Tex first showed us his Virtual Immersion battle segments outside the church. An oldster shot his pistol at the images."

242

The Ghosts of Glorieta

Sonia remarked, "Then you might say that 'the ghosts of Glorieta' came back to do in our phony colonel and his misguided followers."

"Misguided, Detective," Herrero countered, "and yet I wouldn't dismiss a very real threat posed by the anti-government movements."

"No," she agreed, "yet here's at least one victory the good guys can claim"

Fr. Jake said, "Except for poor Donny."

"Father, he contributed to it." Sonia stood up to remove her Kevlar® bullet resistant vest. "I'll see if we can release Raylene's body now."

"Thanks Sonia. A double funeral would be appropriate."

"Father, I'll drive you home and come back to do paperwork on the guys we arrested."

"Thanks. I am a bit beat…."

They drove back to Fr. Jake's in silence, still stunned at the success of the operation and the deaths of Scurry and Maldonado. When Sonia pulled up in front of the adobe, the hardly discernable dark form of a person was on the porch.

"Father, someone's waiting in your chair."

"Jon Scurry got me out of it in quite a hurry. Has one of those 'sovereign citizens' survived to come after me?"

"Duck down," Sonia whispered, easing her revolver out of its shoulder holster.

A new moon had risen around ten o'clock. The crescent gave meager light, but the person's face became visible by candlelight flickering in a glass votive jar, stenciled with the Sacred Heart. Fr. Jake squinted at a woman whose wrinkled face reflected the candle's orange flame.

"It looks like Ofilia, Armando's *curandera* aunt."

"Good." Sonia exhaled and re-holstered her gun. "You're keyed up, Father. She'll give you something to help you sleep."

He laughed. "Sonia, you mean *sell* me something." Before getting out, the priest turned to her. "I appreciate that you confided in me about your dad and mom. I know the pain still lingers."

"It happened six years ago, but you're correct." She thought a moment, while tapping the steering wheel with a hand. "Dad went to church every Sunday that he wasn't on duty. Mom practically lived there, helped clean both the church and rectory. How…how could God let this happen to them?"

"Sonia, if I could answer that to your satisfaction, I'd have a show on Catholic television that rivaled any televangelist's." He reached over to stop her hand on the steering wheel. "Sorry, I don't mean to be disrespectful."

"That's okay, Father." She eased the car into Drive and held her foot on the brake. "You'll be hearing more from us about the raid. It might already be reported in tomorrow's *Valencia County Herald*, but I'd be wary about what I tell reporters."

"How about 'no comment,' and I refer them to you?" Fr. Jake worked the door handle open. "Good night, Detective."

"'Night, Father Jake. And thanks—"

"Hey, that you, Padre Hakub?" Ofilia called to him from the chair. "*Que paso? Porque* you no come see me again?"

"I better go, Sonia. God bless."

He stepped back and watched her car's tail lights disappear toward the highway, then came up the steps. "Ofilia," he jested, "isn't it way past your bedtime?"

She wagged an accusatory finger at him. "You got *querida*, a girl friend, *Padre?*"

"That was Detective Mora. Remember, we came to your *casita* with Armando. Didn't you hear all the noise coming from the forest a while ago?"

"Oh, *si*. What happen up there?"

"A good thing happened. *Señora*, may I ask why you are here?"

"I come see how is your *comezón*…the itch."

He rubbed his sleeve. "It hasn't bothered me for a while. Stress was the cause, and whatever you gave me helped cure the…the *comezón*."

"So where else you hurt, Padre Hakub?"

Fr. Jake laughed as he opened the door. "Come inside. I'll make you a cup of tea."

Ofilia put down her candle. Her grin of amusement showed gaps in her teeth. "What tea you got? *Yerbabuena?*

"*Si*, I have peppermint."

'Ah…" Ofilia opened a briefcase and took out three packets of herbs to show him. "See, I bring you other kind. Go boil *agua*."

Inside the kitchen, Fr. Jake put fresh water in his kettle and lighted the propane burner. The old *curandera* spread her herb packets on the table to name them. "Look. *Cota*…we call Navajo Tea. *Limonsillo*…good for

The Ghosts of Glorieta

estómago. Orégano de la Sierra. Use for cough, too." She opened the first packet. "*Padre*, I make *Cota*."

Fr. Jake sniffed the fragrances of the other herbs. In a few minutes, the two went back to the living room holding steaming mugs of reddish brown drink. Father Jake took a sip, nodded his appreciation, then asked, "*Señora*, you know Duane Fortgang, don't you?"

Her face wrinkled into a frown. "For'gang, he think he better than other *gente*. No like him much."

"Ofilia, I need to find the man. As a *curandera* do you have any…well… I'm not sure how to say it. Any spells that might help us catch him?"

"*Que es* 'spell'?"

What am I thinking? A petition to a saint may be one thing, but—

"Ah, to do bad thing." The old woman understood and her face brightened. "*Padre*, you want *Hechizo!*"

That sounds like hex. "Ofilia, it's very important that Detective Mora finds Mister Fortgang before he can escape."

"*Padre*, I am *curandera*, no do bad thing. I cure person who suffer from *hechizo*, not give them one."

"I understand. I guess I was feeling desperate and helpless—"

"*Padre*,"—Ofilia stood up to point—"you got San Isidro there." She went to the *santo*, then turned and wagged a bony finger at the priest. "*Muy mal. Muy mal.*"

He was puzzled. "What do you mean, 'very bad'?"

"Look at the saint, *Padre*. He just stand there. No even a votive light."

"And?"

Ofilia muttered a low "*ignorante*," then raised her voice to explain. "San Isidro is *labrador*, a farmer. You need make *altarcito*…little altar…for him. Candle, field thing he like." The woman shook her head at the insensitivity of men and went into the kitchen to bring back an empty water glass from the sink board. "*Padre* Hakub," she ordered, putting the tumbler in his hands, "you go outside, fill with nice dirt. Okay?"

Amused, he took the glass from her. "*Bueno, señora.*"

"You got apple, maybe?

"Look in the refrigerator."

"*Si…*" Ofilia made a shooing motion with a hand. "Go. Go bring dirt now."

245

Albert Noyer

When the priest returned, she had taken a small votive light from her briefcase and set it in front of the *santo*. The sliced apple was next to it. She sniffed the dirt, nodded approval, and placed the glass alongside the fruit. "*Padre*, you light candle now, then *en la mañana* go early to find flower with still *roscio*."

"Still dew on them?"

"*Si*. Maybe forsythia, maybe only *diente de león*. Anyway, you make nice wreath, put around San Isidro neck. Talk nice to him. Tell him about For'gang, what you want."

Worth a try, even if only to make the old woman happy. "Ofilia, *gracias*. Thank, you."

"Oh," she remembered. "You maybe got thing belong to For'gang?"

"I have a business card of his."

"*Bueno*. You bury in dirt, name up." The *curandera's* gap-toothed smile creased her wrinkles as Ofilia held out a hand, palm-up. "Okay, *Padre*. Herb tea, candle, advice. Now you ask the *santo* for help. *Por favor*, fifteen dollar."

The Ghosts of Glorieta

25 la fonda / june 14

Fr. Jake followed the old *curandera*'s advice and searched a field behind his house for flowers still wet with morning dew. In a soft June breeze, he found only dandelions—flat yellow blossoms stunted by a climate so dry that most greenery would not revive until the monsoon rains arrived in a month or so. He brought the yellow heads inside the kitchen and used trash bag ties to hold the blossoms together in a necklace shape. It was a delicate task he had not attempted before: in Michigan, parish women came to decorate altars for Sundays and feast days. The most flowers were displayed on May first, a month dedicated to the Virgin Mary, and with the lush pots of December poinsettias arranged around altars at Christmastime.

Decorating a wooden statue is one thing, but believing that it can help us is a matter of faith. Even Saint Augustine quoted the paralytic boy's father in Mark's gospel who told Jesus, 'Lord, I believe. Help my disbelief'."

In Church tradition, saints were petitioned for their intercession in various causes—the restoration of health, finding lost articles, good fortune in love, obtaining employment, and so on. San Isidro might have been involved when Duane Fortgang injured his hand on that splinter and unwitting supplied his blood for DNA testing. Who could be sure? Still, here he was, building a "little altar," as Ofilia called it, to a long-dead Spanish holy person, yet he had left the archbishop's gift of the *Virgen of Guadalupe* to gather dust, not even gluing the detached shells back on.

After a short prayer to San Isidro for success in finding Duane Fortgang, Fr. Jake stepped back from his decorated *altarcito*. "Isidore," he confided

247

Albert Noyer

to the saint, "Elder J. and his Pentecostals would disapprove, but I'm sure that you and I understand each other. I'll read my breviary for today. On occasion, the readings seem to be prophetic."

The First Reading from the second letter of Paul to the Corinthians was hopeful. "'For God says: at the favorable time I have listened to you; on the day of salvation I came to your help.' Well," the priest murmured to the saint, "now is the favorable time; this is the day of salvation."

○

Monday, June 14, was Flag Day, and about ten weeks since Fr. Jake had taken a good look at himself in a mirror. "When you last saw yourself on your birthday, Father Jake," he told his uneven bathroom reflection, "little did you know where you would be ten weeks later." He scratched light dandruff from his scalp. "Hair probably a little grayer and you look tired, Father." The priest pinched light flab around his belt line. "Weight is somewhat less, which is good, but you're not getting enough exercise. After breakfast, jog over to that abandoned building across the highway and see what name is on it. Well, okay, at least walk to it. Take your mind off of what happened last night."

After brushing his teeth, for no particular reason he put on khaki slacks and his short-sleeved blue summer shirt with an attached Roman collar. During his usual raisin bran-and-banana breakfast, a bugle assembly call sounded from the reenactors' camp. It was the last day of training before the men and women broke up their encampment and left Providencia. Captain Schiller had told him he planned a public farewell parade on the field for 10:00 A.M.

Fr. Jake rinsed out his dish and coffee cup, then plugged his cell phone into an outlet to recharge the battery. He found his sketchbook, tucked the vinyl pencil case in a back pocket, and locked the front door. Outside, he crossed the Calle and walked past the church, noting the three bullet holes still marring the stucco. He picked his way through greening brambles in the field toward the captain's tent.

Schiller looked up from polishing his cavalry boots and extended a hand.

"Mornin', Father. Say, did you hear all that shooting up in the forest early last evening or see all those law enforcement vehicles that went up there? I even heard an ambulance."

"I did, Captain."

The Ghosts of Glorieta

The officer picked a newspaper off his cot. "Here's the *Valencia County Herald*. Check out that headline."

Drug Corridor Raid Succeeds

Survivalist Compound Breached.

Leader Killed, Followers Arrested.

"So the news is already out," Fr. Jake said. "One of the sheriff's deputies must be a friend of a *Herald* reporter and gave him that information." He read the brief article aloud, "'In an early evening raid, an Albuquerque Drug Enforcement Agency SWAT Team and Socorro County sheriff's deputies were able to breach entry into an anti-government survivalist camp near Providencia on Highway 310. A DEA official, speaking on condition of anonymity, said that information about the raid was scarce at present because multiple felony charges and an investigation of alleged narcotics activity in the camp are ongoing'."

Schiller asked, "Isn't that where Colonel Scurry lives?"

"Lived," Fr. Jake corrected. "Scurry is the survivalist leader that was killed."

"Involved in drug running, was he? Guess I'm not too surprised. I was leery of the man from square one."

"So you told me." Fr. Jake put the newspaper down. "Captain, Scurry wasn't a colonel and isn't related to that Confederate officer you mentioned. In fact, he received a Bad Conduct Discharge from the Army."

"Imagine that. Well, he fooled me at first. One never knows..." The captain gave his left boot a final brushing. "You staying for our parade, Father?"

"Probably not, Captain. I'm going to take a look at an empty building across the highway, then pick up a couple of things at Carlotta's grocery."

"Then you should come out to Las Golandrinas for our Fourth of July reenactment of the Battle of Glorieta Pass."

"I'd like that. Perhaps I could go with Cynthia and Armando."

Schiller grinned and tipped his forage cap. "A pleasure meeting you, Father, and don't forget that chaplaincy I offered."

"I won't." Fr. Jake gave the captain a passable salute. "Good luck, Sir."

The white building on the west side of Highway 310 was almost directly across from San Isidro church. Twin ruts in a weed-overgrown driveway indicated that automobiles once had come to the site. The building's wall stucco and terracotta roof tiles looked relatively new, probably not much more than a year old. Four large windows in rooms on either end of a central

249

Albert Noyer

entrance were boarded up, but one side of a double entry door lay open. A sign above read:

PROVIDENCIA COMMUNITY CENTER.

Fr. Jake walked up four steps into a lobby reception area. A large multi-purpose room with kitchen facilities was on the left. It flanked a hallway on the opposite side that had restroom facilities and class or meeting rooms. Out in back, against a background of cultivated fields and the Rio Grande *bosque*, colorful playground equipment sat dusty and unused. Inside vandalism was light—mostly paper trash and plastic grocery bags that littered the floors. No La Raza or other graffiti defaced the facility, probably because spray can wielders could be seen: Big-Valu Hardware, the Providencia Grocery, and Armando's auto repair shop all fronted the highway immediately east of the center.

What a waste. I'll have to ask Armando why this facility isn't being utilized. He went back out to the front, made a quick sketch of the building, then cut across the field toward the mechanic's garage.

Fr. Jake found Armando bent over the engine compartment of a PT Cruiser. The young man looked up and briskly wiped his hands on a rag to greet the priest.

"*Buenos dias*, Father. How are ya?"

"Keep working, Armando. I'm just out getting a little exercise." He pointed back to the empty building. "Why isn't anyone using that new community center?"

"Y' know, Father, some county commissioner wanted to be re-elected and built it for us. We didn't ask for it, didn't want it, an' when he lost the election, no money ever came to start it runnin'."

"A pity, it's very promising facility that would help unite this community. You could hold various classes and after-school activities for children. The playground equipment could easily be fixed up."

He voiced doubt. "Ain't' gonna be, Father. Hey, you seen today's paper? The front page is all about that shooting I heard up in the woods last night."

"I did see it, Armando."

"I thought those Civil War guys were havin' a night battle or somethin'. It sounded like it was near Mister Fortgang's house, so I wonder if he knows about it yet? He just got here from Mexico to leave more *santos* with Carlotta."

250

The Ghosts of Glorieta

"What?" Astonished, Fr. Jake was unsure of having heard correctly. "You say that Duane Fortgang is here at the grocery?"

"Yeah, Father, out front. Man, is his van ever dirty. He sure don't... doesn't... take the freeway to get here from Santa Teresa."

A stroke of real luck! Fr. Jake hurried around the building. At the front, he saw Fortgang glancing around as he folded a copy of the *Herald*. The accountant had on a rumpled white summer suit. A week's worth of beard darkened his cheeks. Hatless, his bald scalp shone in the sun as he strode rapidly toward his van.

"Hold on, Duane," Fr. Jake called out to him. "I need to talk with you."

Surprised, Fortgang peered back at the priest through his glasses, then ran and jumped into the driver's side of his delivery van. Without securing a seat belt, he gunned the engine, screeched the tires onto the highway, and sped south in the direction of La Fonda.

"Armando, get your Camaro!" Fr. Jake shouted to the mechanic, who watched from a few steps behind. "We have to stop Fortgang."

"Aw, he ain't...*isn't*...goin' too far. The highway dead-ends at La Fonda."

"Nevertheless..." He pushed the young man toward his parked car.

By the time that Armando found his keys and drove the Camaro onto the roadway, Fortgang's delivery van was out of sight.

"Do you have a cell phone to call 911?" Fr. Jake asked. "I left mine at home charging the battery and we need to notify the police."

Armando shook his head. "Mine's in the shop, Father. That's where I take calls. What's the big hurry about getting to the guy?"

"I'll tell you later. Right now concentrate on catching up with him."

Southbound traffic was light; as Armando had pointed out, the highway ended at La Fonda and not many residents went in that direction at this hour.

"So, Armando," Fr. Jake asked, "what happens at the dead end you mentioned?"

"A main street goes right and left through the village. On the right, it passes Immaculate Conception church, then stops. Left, it crosses train tracks and ends there."

"So...where will Duane go?"

"Father, he's gotta stop at the church or the tracks."

251

Albert Noyer

"I never thought I'd say this, Armando, but…ah…drive a bit recklessly. Maybe someone will notice and call 911. A sheriff's deputy might stop us and I could tell him about Fortgang."

"Jeez, Father Hakub…" Armando crossed himself and touched his rosary dangling from the rear view mirror. He accelerated enough to pass two older model cars with weather-faded paint, probably senior citizens without cell phones. A quarter mile on, he was forced to slow down behind a green, rust-speckled John Deere tractor. The sputtering engine pulled a flatbed trailer of alfalfa bales at what seemed less than a snail's pace.

Fr. Jake felt his blood pressure pound in his temples and the emptiness in his stomach ached. After Armando tried to pass the John Deere three times, by swinging his Camaro into the opposite lane, then swerving back in from oncoming traffic, the priest shouted, "Pass that idiot on the right!"

Gravel rattled the Chevy's undercarriage as the young man complied. Up ahead, Fortgang was not yet in sight. Armando desperately sounded his horn to warn a motorist in a side street, who attempted to turn left onto the highway. He careened into the north-bound lane to avoid him. "Son of a bitch," he muttered. "Father Hakub, you suppose Fortgang turned his van into one of these side streets along the road?"

It was a possibility he had not considered. "Unless we see him on one, Armando, keep straight ahead."

Houses already far apart became even scarcer in the flat countryside. Ahead, in the distance, the Magdalena Mountains still hosted delicate brushstrokes of white snow in northern hollows. The range blocked a flat horizon of sandy wastes, scrub sage, and cholla cactus. To the right, the jagged Ladrones rose purple, briefly chewed at the sky, then flowed down to meld into the landscape.

The highway became more hilly. Dangerous blind corners behind limestone outcroppings blocked the view of sharp turns on the twisting road. A series of S-curves, winding downhill, further slowed the car in trying to catch Fortgang.

"La Fonda isn't far…" Armando swung the steering wheel to the right, around a near 90-degree turn. "Jeez, with these curves we might see the guy's van upside-down anytime."

"I don't wish Duane harm." Fr. Jake said. "Detective Mora only wants to ask him some questions."

Near the bottom of a final 35 m.p.h. hill, a brown Scenic Historic Marker gave a synopsis of La Fonda's Pueblo Indian and Spanish history, and its

The Ghosts of Glorieta

once-important location on the Spanish Camino Real caravan route into Mexico.

A half mile beyond, twin, graffiti-sprayed red stop signs, warning chevrons, and black directional arrows on a yellow background marked the highway's end.

Armando skidded the Chevy to a stop ten feet in front of the signs. A green street marker read, Calle Centro de La Fonda. He breathed hard, gripped the steering wheel, and glanced sideways at the priest. "Which way, Father?"

San Isidro? On impulse Fr. Jake blurted, "Go left!"

Armando turned sharply onto a narrow asphalt road that soon merged with gravel-topped dirt. The Camaro bounced past crumbling adobe open barns, a few surviving homesteads, and a boarded-up post office. About two hundred yards further along, an **X** railroad crossing warning appeared. Twenty feet beyond the tracks, the road disappeared into encroaching sand hills without a warning sign.

Armando stopped and looked down the railway line to his left. In the near distance, a cloud of tan dust billowed out behind a fast-moving vehicle. "Father," he said, "I bet that's Fortgang driving crazy on the railroad service road."

"That would explain the dust," the priest agreed. "Follow him!"

A choking, gritty powder obscured both the van and shallow drainage ditches on either side of the narrow track. Bouncing along the ruts, Armando complained, "This gritty stuff ain't good for my carburetor. Besides, in a coupla miles, Fortgang'll be in another county."

"Keep going..." Fr. Jake felt a rare sense of complete helplessness. *Duane takes this route to avoid border checkpoints and Armando is worried that his Camaro's engine will fail. Fortgang will be out of our jurisdiction and we have no way of notifying police.*

Up ahead, the van's brake lights abruptly flashed red. The vehicle's front wheels hit a protruding edge on the concrete slab of a bridge that spanned an arroyo. The clumsy delivery van soared upright through the air and landed hard on the road in a puff of dust. The vehicle very gradually slowed before swerving to a stop against a telephone pole. At the impact, the van's two front compartment airbags deployed.

Armando's Camaro bounced over the cement slab. He braked the car a few feet behind the disabled van, then got out to wrench open the driver's door. Partially engulfed by his wooden saints, Duane Fortgang lay unconscious, his head resting against the seat back. Blood from his mouth

253

Albert Noyer

and nose glistened in the week-old beard. He had not clicked on a safety belt at Carlotta's, but a deflated air bag that saved him from serious injury hung from the steering wheel like a shriveled palm tree leaf.

Fr. Jake ran up to look inside. The furniture in back had shifted forward, and a rack just behind the front seats, which held the wooden statues, was nearly empty.

"Fortgang left the grocery in such a hurry, that he didn't take time to re-tighten the restraining straps," he said to Armando. "All his statues were jarred loose when he hit that pavement. Then, for some reason he slowed down so rapidly that all of them began to spill forward. When he lost control and hit that pole, most of them bounced into the front compartment."

Puzzled, Armando pushed back his cap. "What I can't figure out is why *did* the guy slow down? Like I said, he woulda been across the county line in another minute or two."

"And out of this jurisdiction."

"Right…" The mechanic bent to rummage between the accountant's limp feet for a moment, then straightened up. "Hey, Father Hakub, you won't believe this." Armando grinned and held up a *santo* in one hand. "I found a San Isidro wedged under the accelerator pedal. Fortgang couldn't go no faster."

A flash of insight streaked through Fr. Jake's mind as he reached for the wooden carving. "Armand, I do believe it. The saint came through for us in the very best way he could."

26

Fr. Jake stood the statue up on the dashboard, then took Sonia Mora's card from his wallet and handed it to Armando. "We need to get help. Find a sheriff in the village and have him notify Detective Mora. Also, ask about the nearest EMT station."

"Right." The mechanic looked anxious. "You'll be okay, Father?"

"I'll be fine." The priest held Fortgang's head steady to mop blood from his mouth with a handkerchief. "Do you have bottled water in your car?"

"Got some left in a six-pack." Armando returned with two plastic 16 oz. bottles and unscrewed one. "Here, Father. I'll be back with help fast as I can."

"Thanks." As Armando pulled his car around toward the village, Fr. Jake wet the handkerchief and cleaned Fortgang's beard. In a few minutes, the accountant moaned and tried to ease himself upright. "Easy, Duane," the priest warned, "you were in an accident and shouldn't move. Help is coming."

Wincing from pain, Fortgang turned his head to look toward the voice. "Father Jake? Where...? He closed his eyes and sagged back against the seat. "Oh, I remember now."

"Just take it easy, Duane. EMT paramedics will be here shortly." Fr. Jake held the water bottle to the man's lips. "Can you have a drink?"

Fortgang sat up a bit to take a sip, then lifted his right hand to make a feeble sign of the cross. "'Bless me, Father, for I have sinned.'" he mumbled in a weak voice.

255

Albert Noyer

His penitential words surprised Fr. Jake. "You want to make a confession? Duane, I don't think you're in any danger of dying."

"Want to confess," he insisted. 'O my God, I…I am heartily sorry for having offended thee and detest all my sins, especially…. especially—"

Duane…" Fr. Jake wiped fresh blood from his nose. "Duane, wait till we get back. Besides, I don't have my stole with me."

"Doesn't matter…it's confessing…to a priest." Fortgang breathed in gasps from the exertion of speaking. Barely audible, he managed to whisper, "Father…I… killed Aimée Parker, Father Mora, and…and Raylene Maldonado. 'I firmly resolve with the help of thy grace to sin no more'…" He gave a reflexive shudder before asking, "Now, Father Jake, assign a penance and absolve me."

"Duane, absolution doesn't quite work that way. I must…" Fortgang's head fell to one side and his breathing became shallow. *Unconscious again.*

Still stunned by the injured man's unexpected admissions, Fr. Jake mopped Fortgang's face with water, while trying to make sense of what he had said. *Duane admitted to three murders. He obviously became involved with Aimée when she came to Fr. Mora for advice. We've speculated that she might have blackmailed the father of her child…of Caleb…for escape money, and that's surely the case. Raylene helped Duane suppress announcements of the tax delinquencies. Lord knows what he might have promised her to do that. She may have wanted to tell me about it, but was murdered before she could. Father Mora was killed because he wouldn't sell the church to Tex? Yet the Seal of Confession makes all of these disclosures privileged.*

○

In less than an hour, an undulating crescendo of sirens and the insistent flashing red and blue lights of emergency vehicles appeared at the north end of the service road. Tan dust clouds obscured a volunteer fire department ambulance and the black and white squad car of a La Fonda sheriff's deputy. Armando's Camaro, brought up the rear, eating their dust.

After introductions, two EMT paramedics began to treat Fortgang, while the deputy inspected the van's contents. A short time later, the deafening overhead clatter of a helicopter engine shattered the quiet. A hundred yards to the east, the black, predatory shape of a Socorro County Sheriff's Department helicopter, settled on the ground in yet more curtains of choking dust. Fr. Jake and Armando turned away, shut their eyes, and

The Ghosts of Glorieta

cupped their hands over mouths and noses. When the racket ceased, they turned to look back at the chopper.

Sonia Mora stepped out of an OH58 single engine helicopter from the Socorro police unit. She held a hand over her baseball cap to keep it from flying off in a dusty wind kicked up by the rotor's blades. Instead of her usual dark uniform, the detective wore casual jeans and a Madras-patterned summer shirt.

Bent low against rotor blade wind, Deputy Griego followed her, holding onto his service hat.

When she reached the priest, Sonia held up a hand. "Before you ask, Father, I gave Carlotta Ulibarri my card the day I went in to look over her *santos*. When Fortgang left in such a hurry, and she saw you chasing him in Armando's car, she gave me a call—"

"—And," Fr. Jake finished for her, "you alerted the helicopter unit for a ride."

"Exactly. A La Fonda sheriff's deputy gave me your location. I had stayed home today to write my report on last night's raid with Deputy Griego. Also try to piece together related elements of the case." She glanced over at the wrecked van. "Is Fortgang all right?"

"Bruised and quite well shaken up, but he'll recover."

"I'll take a look at him." As Sonia reached the van, she smoothed a hand over the dusty side panel. "Well, well, what have we here? It seems that the metal 'Mexican Woodcrafts' sign slipped down at the impact."

"It was attached to the van by magnets?"

"Right, Father. See what's underneath?"

He read, "'Burlington National & Santa Fe Service Vehicle.'"

Sonia continued, "I'll bet we'll find a fake card in his wallet, IDing him as a BN & SF track inspector. Fortgang obviously drives back to Providencia along this service road. Where he accesses it is YTBD. Let me see how he's doing."

The paramedics had revived the accountant. He slumped with his head against the seat back.

Detective Mora flashed her identification at a woman EMT applying antibiotic salve to bruises on his mouth and face. "Can Mister Fortgang be moved without being in an ambulance?"

"Yes," she said, "but the gentleman should be checked out at a hospital. He wasn't wearing a seat belt, so the air bag didn't fully protect him. He might have internal injuries."

257

Albert Noyer

"Thanks. We'll drive Mister Fortgang back in the Camaro and hold him over-night for observation at Presbyterian in Belén."

The paramedics finished paperwork, then packed up their medical kits and returned to the ambulance.

Sonia waved off the helicopter and turned to Griego. "Deputy, help Mister Fortgang out of his van and book him for reckless driving and vandalizing railroad property, i.e. that telephone pole. Cuff him." She turned to the priest. "Father, you ready, to go back?"

"Wait until I get my San Isidro off the dashboard."

"What? Why is it even up there?"

"I'll tell you later, Sonia, but I'm definitely going to buy this saint right now." Fr. Jake turned the statue over to look at the price sticker. "Eighty-five dollars!" he exclaimed, in economic shock. "The San Isidro I have and all the other *santos* were forty-five. What's going on?"

"Let me see that…" Sonia checked the bottom, then went to look at bases on other fallen statues. "Forty–five dollars. Forty-Five. Another forty-five. Ah, here's an eighty-five-dollar one. Let me have yours, Father, while you go pay the man."

"I…I don't have that much cash on me."

"How much do you have?"

Fr. Jake fingered through his wallet. "Thirty-two and some change."

Sonia looked toward the two men. "Griego? Armando?"

Both grumbled, but between them came up with the balance of fifty-three dollars.

"Guys, you'll get paid back. This is probably going to be evidence." She folded the bills, tucked them into the pocket of Fortgang's suit coat, and then peeled the sticker off Fr. Jake's San Isidro. After easing out the cork, she pulled a plastic tube of white powder from the hollow center. "I'm bettin' this ain't bakin' soda," she quipped, mimicking an accent. "So this is the way Fortgang's supplier in Mexico identifies the *santos* that contain cocaine or heroin for him. We've already determined that the citronella smell would probably throw drug-sniffing dogs off scent. And if a statue with drugs was accidentally left for sale, a tourist would question the high price and buy a different one of the same saint. Deputy, get our perp in the car."

Griego sat Fortgang in the rear seat, between Sonia and the priest, then took the front passenger seat. Fr. Jake held his sketchbook and the San Isidro on his lap.

The Ghosts of Glorieta

As Armando drove back slowly to avoid stirring up dust, Sonia poked the deputy's shoulder. "Griego. Did you read Mister Fortgang his Miranda?"

"Yeah, detective, I done that."

"He's a lawyer, so he'll take the Fifth if we question him now, and even in court."

"Damn right," a sullen Fortgang muttered.

Sonia ignored him. "Sure, aside from the drugs, all of our evidence may be circumstantial, yet I think we'll come up with a tight case." She flipped open her note pad. "Father, I made little diagrams, trying to find a connection between everyone involved with the three deaths."

"So did I, detective." He opened his sketchbook to show her the page.

She compared the two diagrams. "Hey, that's not bad sleuthing, Father. Maybe you should have gone into law enforcement."

"Maybe in a sense I did."

"Yeah?" she asked. "How so?"

"Well, as priest I try to enforce the Ten Commandments."

Everyone except Fortgang laughed. Griego kept chuckling, "That's pretty good, Father."

"The way I see it," Sonia continued, "we know from DNA evidence that Mister Fortgang is Caleb's father. I figure he met Aimée when she came to talk with Father Mora. Being quite a stud and the girl vulnerable…or maybe promiscuous…our accountant fornicated with her. Yet, Aimée wasn't quite that innocent a gal."

Fr. Jake said, "Detective, do you think that about four years later on she may have tried to blackmail him for enough money to get away from the commune?"

"It's possible, Father. That's when she was killed and her body buried. I think our perp here stole that communion host for her, got Father Mora drunk, and took him up to the Elder's Black Mass. Tattooed his feet as proof he'd been there, and blamed him for both Aimée's pregnancy and stealing a host."

"I also came up that theory while waiting for help," Fr. Jake said, closing his sketchbook.

"That's all it is," Fortgang muttered. "A ridiculous theory."

"So our perp held that over the priest's head for years and made him believe he was the boy's father," Sonia added. "He probably kept reminding Father Mora that he sinned badly in committing adultery and giving away a host for that satanic ritual."

259

"The unforgivable transgression your uncle almost told me about."

"Correct, Father, then our perp got mixed up with Tex Houston. Recall that he worked for Pentacle in Austin."

"Right, Sonia."

"When Father Mora refused to sell his church to Tex…remember, it didn't belong to the archdiocese, only to the Mora family…my uncle probably checked and found out about the quitclaim deeds. Only thing the perp could do was murder him and try to blame his death on one of the dancers with the broken wand. Oh," she recalled, "I didn't have time to tell you. We obtained a limited warrant to search the perp's garage while he was gone. We found fifty-pound sacks of sand with a Chihuahua supplier's name on them. That's how the *santos* were refilled and sold after he removed the drug tubes. Those statues that he didn't refill with sand, because the cocaine might have leaked and contaminated the opening, were burned in a trash incinerator. Remember the day we saw smoke coming out his chimney?"

"I do, detective."

"'Course, with Donny as Raylene's abusive husband, it was easy for the perp to take the woman as a lover and persuade her to 'forget' to mail tax notices to my uncle. But she was a smarter cookie than he thought. Raylene kept the unmailed letters as insurance. I'm pretty sure he promised to take her away from Donny and resettle in some Mexican love nest, like, say, Acapulco or Puerto Vallarta. Me, I personally don't think he would have done it. Too many Latinos down there. When Raylene realized he was stalling …well… blackmail is such an ugly word. Maybe she tried once too often to 'persuade' him to come through with his promise."

Fr. Jake said, "If she released the un-mailed letters, that would not have been good for Tex Houston's plan to take over Providencia."

"No, indeed, Father."

Fortgang became increasingly agitated as his body twitched between the detective and priest. With both hands manacled together, resting on his lap, he consciously clenched and unclenched stubby fingers.

"And those guys we arrested in the raid on Billy Ray's compound are 'survivalists' in more than name. As soon as the D.A. offers those Scurry boys dual plea bargains, they'll sing about their druggie connections like nervous canaries—"

"Or like parrots," Griego quipped. 'Polly want crack'."

As the deputy laughed at his joke, Fortgang abruptly brought his hands up and swung them to the left, at Sonia's head. The edge of a metal handcuff

The Ghosts of Glorieta

bloodied her lip. Griego heard the commotion and half-turned; constrained by his seat belt, he could do nothing. Fr. Jake grasped the accountant's hands, brought them down, and held them in his lap with a force he never realized he possessed.

Sonia touched her lip with the back of a hand, saw blood, and licked the wound. "Sir," she told Fortgang calmly, "we'll just add assault on a peace officer to our charges."

"Go to hell, detective!" he exclaimed under his breath. "And some Catholics want to make you women deacons and even priests." He looked at Fr. Jake. "You can let go and add assault to my confession."

"Confession?" Sonia's raised eyebrows emphasized a question. "What's he talking about, Father?"

Fortgang turned to her with a smirk. "Detective, a priest can't possibly tell you about what I might have confessed to him."

Sonia did not pursue the matter and licked a lip that was swelling up a bit.

They drove the rest of the way back in silence. When Armando reached the south end of Providencia, he slowed the Camaro to the 35 m.p.h. speed limit. At Mamacita's, a few villagers watched two sheriff's deputies stringing yellow crime tape over the entrance. A CLOSED sign was taped to the front window.

Sonia explained, "We suspect that Mister Fortgang laundered drug money through his restaurant. We'll impound all his *santos* both here and at Carlotta's."

Armando pulled over at the Calle San Isidro. "Father, you want me to drop you off here?"

"Sure," Sonia answered for him. "Griego and I can take Fortgang to the hospital with those deputies. We'll drive back to Socorro with them." She reached over to shake the mechanic's hand. "Thanks, Armando, you were a great help." After Griego maneuvered Fortgang out of the car, she told the priest, "Father, we'll have to talk about any confession the perp made to you."

"Good bye, detective...deputy Griego," he only replied to her proposal.

After Armando let everyone out and was ready to go back to his garage, Fr. Jake poked his head in the car's open front window. "On Saturday, I'd like to start a five o'clock Mass at the church. Can you and Cynthia get the word around?"

261

Albert Noyer

"Sure thing, Father. Leave it to us."

"Would you have music ready? Cynthia told me you've been practicing."

"Oh, I ain't so sure of that, Father," he hedged. "You know…some of the guys. Well, it takes time."

Disappointed, the priest stood back. "I understand, Armando, but please give it a try."

○

On the following afternoon, Fr. Jake looked up from raking dry weeds on his small patch of Indian grass in front of the adobe. Sonia Mora's red Plymouth had stopped at the curb. He braced himself for what was sure to be questions about Fortgang's time with him before she arrived, and to what he may have confessed.

He went open her car door. "Come inside, detective. Can I get you anything?"

"I'm good, Father. Just want to bring you up to speed."

"Isn't 'speed' the nickname of an amphetamine?"

"Funny." Unsmiling, she held up a manila folder. "However, I am here to question you about both the raid and G. Duane Fortgang."

Sonia had dressed in her detective clothes: Black hair tucked under a Baker-Boy cap, nylon jacket, neatly creased dark slacks, and small-size men's black work shoes. Light lipstick. She settled in the living room armchair without being asked, took off her cap, and clicked open a ballpoint pen. Fr. Jake waited for her to begin.

"Deputy Griego and I finished our report about the raid on the survivalist compound. I just need a few details about how you got up there."

"Glad to help," he said, settling back on the couch.

Sonia opened the folder and read for a moment. "You said that Jon Scurry came down around sunset to drive you up to Fort Liberty."

"Correct, at gunpoint. I thought they had learned about the raid and wanted me as a hostage. Up there, Billy Ray told me they were planning a 'sovereign citizen's' demonstration against Tex Houston destroying people's homes in Providencia. It was to be a statement by his survivalists to curry favor with the villagers. Scurry was afraid that I'd influence everyone against taking any violent actions."

262

The Ghosts of Glorieta

Sonia pointed out, "Scurry and his followers were taking a chance by coming down into the village."

"I warned him that all he might accomplish was their arrest."

Sonia wrote in her notebook, then continued, "Agent Herrero thinks that publicity about the action as reported on anti-government networks might encourage others to similar, but better planned demonstrations."

Fr. Jake added, "Scurry also wanted to take over empty houses in Upland Heights with phony deeds in the name of his common law sovereign republic."

"Thus tying up local courts with frivolous lawsuits..." Sonia glanced toward the kitchen. "Father, I will have coffee if you have any. Black."

"Sure, it'll only take a few minutes." *Sonia is bracing herself with a little caffeine before questioning me about Fortgang.* He stayed in the kitchen as the coffee brewed, watching the detective leaf through her folder. She seemed uncharacteristically nervous.

He came back with two steaming mugs and placed one on her armchair's side table. "Almost as good as at Mamacita's."

"Thanks. I wanted to tell you about the latest on Fortgang."

Here it comes.

She took a cautious sip of hot coffee and held onto the mug handle. "We're booking him on a reckless driving charge, so I was able to get a warrant yesterday afternoon to search his entire domicile, not just the garage. We found zamia plants in his sunroom."

"Cynthia said they were a decorative house plant that many people buy."

"Exactly, Father. His computer had a file with the 'Hecho in Mexico' stickers, but we didn't find a broken *matachine* wand."

"If he had one, it's been burned."

"Yes, Fortgang only needed that small fragment to throw suspicion onto one of the masked dancers. We also found a gasoline can, so, what we have are those bags of sand, house plants, and a truck full of statues, a few of which... seven to be exact... contained cocaine. All are circumstantial evidence that a Law 101 student could argue Fortgang used for other purposes, or else didn't know anything about."

"What of his delivery van?" Fr. Jake asked. "His attempt to escape along the railroad service road?"

263

Albert Noyer

She shook her head and put down the mug. "Father, I need solid evidence. Did… did he confess to you about what I speculated upon in the car yesterday?"

Fr. Jake took a sip of his coffee and looked directly at her. "Sonia, you know I can't tell you that."

"You'd rather let a drug dealer and three-time murderer go free? Jeez, he wasn't even in church at the time."

"I've heard the last confessions of accident victims on Michigan freeways. Chaplains in Iraq and Afghanistan routinely hear them under horrendous conditions."

"So you won't help me nail the bastard who murdered my uncle?"

"Detective, I'd have to testify and that actually would work against you."

Her eyes widened as she questioned, "How so?"

"Consider that probably half the jury would be Catholic, maybe more in Socorro. To hear a priest break his seal of confession would scandalize them. They would find Fortgang 'not guilty' just to teach me and all other priests a lesson. I mean, confessions are way down as it is. The Church would lose every Catholic on that jury, plus every relative and friend they told." When Sonia did not react, Fr. Jake continued, "The best friend I had at my parish in Michigan was Al Franzek, an attorney. We used to sit around in my yard with a glass of wine, while he discussed his cases with me. Between listening to him and watching *Law and Order* on TV, I'm convinced that Fortgang would be acquitted if I testified. Sonia, I understand that you want justice for your uncle, and Aimée, and Raylene. Duane is a despicable hypocrite, hiding under one of the Church's ancient rules, but you're going to have to convict him some other way. Tex Houston must know a lot more about Duane Fortgang than he's told you so far. Talk to him."

"I guess I am pretty close to the case. It's just that…" She stood up and turned away to wipe a tear. "Thanks, Father. I'll leave now." She looked at his table shrine to San Isidro. "Oh, and I'd like to take that statue you bought from Fortgang."

"I'm glad, Sonia. San Isidro has been helpful to me."

"You misunderstand. I need it as evidence. You were present when I pulled out the cocaine sausage. Father, you *would* testify to that?"

"Of course." He went to get the *santo* from his bedroom and handed it to her. "Sonia, this week I'm going to start a five o'clock Saturday Mass. You're invited to the first one, if you'd like to attend."

264

The Ghosts of Glorieta

Sonia was noncommittal as she tugged on her cap. "I'll think about it. Be in touch. Goodbye."

○

Detective Mora did not contact Fr. Jake again that week. UPS trucks delivered the new missalettes he had ordered and the booklets that Cynthia Plow wanted to start her children's Faith Formation classes. He found the address of a Belén print shop in the phone book and drove there to arrange for the publication of weekly Mass bulletins. The first would be a single page: a front side with the name of the liturgical Sunday; a parish Mass schedule; his phone number, and the day and time of confessions. He would write a commentary on the back about the three Sunday Mass readings as a basis for a mini-sermon that applied them to the parishioners' daily lives.

The most difficult to write would be a summary of his ten weeks at San Isidro and his genuine admiration for the people of Providencia. That might encourage more Mass attendance. If he turned in written copy for the bulletin by Thursday, the printer promised to have one hundred copies ready on Friday afternoon.

Reporters from Socorro and Belén newspapers—even the *Albuquerque Journal*— had caught wind of the priest's involvement in the raid on the survivalist compound and the arrest of Duane Fortgang. Details from law enforcement agencies were scarce, but when reporters came to interview him, Fr. Jake referred them to Sonia Mora.

○

A little before 3:00 o'clock on Saturday, Fr. Jake finished the last editing of his sermon for the afternoon Mass. The opening phrase of the First Reading from Jeremiah 20: 10-13, was disconcerting: the prophet lamented the vicious disparagement of his countrymen. "Terror from every Side! Denounce him! Let us denounce him! All those who used to be my friends watched for my downfall. We will master him and take our revenge." Yet the passage ended with the prophet expecting God's vengeance and hope of deliverance.

The Responsorial Psalm continued with the hope that justice would overshadow the taunts of evil men. Matthew's opening gospel verses seemed to have been written for that day:

Albert Noyer

"Do not be afraid. For everything that is now covered will be uncovered, and everything now hidden will be made clear."

A knock on the door startled Fr. Jake out of musing on the timeliness of the Scripture readings.

Armando greeted him. "Hi, Father Hakub. Hope I'm not disturbin'?"

"No, I finished writing my sermon. Come in. What can I do for you?"

Armando pointed to the priest's car parked in the driveway. "I got to thinkin' that you need a oil change on Nissy out there."

"Thanks, that's very thoughtful of you. I'll bring it in on Monday."

"Nooo, Father. I finished workin' on my other stuff for today. Bring it in now."

Fr. Jake glanced at his watch. "Armando, it's after three o' clock and I have Mass at five."

"Oh, I'll have it done on time. You get yourself a coffee at Carlotta's, on me." The mechanic pulled him outside by the elbow. "Got your key?"

"In my pocket."

"Then follow me to my shop."

Armando had washed the dust off his Camaro; in the afternoon sun, the black finish gleamed like obsidian. The mechanic led Fr. Jake inside the grocery store at the front of his garage.

"Carlotta," he said, winking at the woman, "coffee an' anythin' else Father Hakub wants, on me. I'm changing Nissy's oil, might be awhile."

She laughed and pointed to the back. "*Padre*, you heard the man. You know where the coffee machine is, so go help yourself. I got slices of nice homemade cheesecake in the fridge."

"Thanks, Carlotta, just coffee for now."

"Then take a slice back with you."

Fr. Jake carried his Styrofoam cup clockwise around the aisles to look for anything new in the store. He arrived back at the rack that held the *santos*. It was empty.

Carlotta noticed and came alongside. "Shame about Mister Fortgang. I was glad to get that little bit of extra cash from selling his statues. What finally happened?"

"The detective isn't sure yet." To keep from answering more questions, he checked his watch. "I think I'll go out and see how Armando is doing."

266

The Ghosts of Glorieta

The Nissan was up on a hydraulic lift, dark amber liquid dripping from the oil pan into the funnel of a scrap oil container. Armando stood to one side, inspecting a round metal fitting. He saw the priest and held it up.

"Father Hakub, these oil plug threads are pretty near stripped. I probably got another one 'round somewhere. An' as long as I got Nissy up there, I'll check out some other stuff. Could take just a bit longer."

Fr. Jake looked at a wall clock that advertised Pennzoil. "Armando, it's a quarter to four."

"I'll get ya back on time, Father, just don't worry. Go sit in my office an' look at car magazines. C'mon I'll show you."

The single chrome kitchen chair next to a stained desk cluttered with paperwork and auto parts catalogs had a tattered plastic seat. Automotive magazines were stacked on a rickety table alongside—*Motor Trend, Car and Driver, Road and Track.*

Fr. Jake noted the framed photographs of a middle-aged couple draped in black crepe and hung on a wall opposite the desk. "Armando, are those your parents?"

"Yeah. They were killed by a drunk *pendejo* goin' the wrong way on I-25. They were almost home from a wedding."

"Cynthia told me. I'm so sorry."

He nodded grim acceptance. "Big problem in this state, Father. I pretty much quit drinkin' after that." Armando went to straighten out a side of the crepe. "Dad didn't wanna work in the fields an' he could fix anything. Myself, I started workin' with him here after school. Well, I better get back and finish up."

"Thanks, Armando." Fr. Jake sat down to flip through the pages of a magazine titled *Dirt Road. All about environmentally incorrect off-street driving. Automobilia is a subculture certainly understood in Michigan, yet obviously also of interest here in New Mexico.*

Armando's magazines were not all up to date, but a February *Motor Trend* already pictured several of next year's models. The magazine's Car Reviews and Road Test information covered Audi, and Citroen DS3 models. Fr. Jake's mind was locked on Duane Fortgang, yet he briefly dozed off reading about a new model Jaguar XJ, a car he would never buy nor particularly want to own. He was startled awake when Armando brought the Nissan down to his garage floor with a soft thump. The Pennzoil clock hands were on 4:42.

"All set, Father." Armando grinned as he wiped his hands on a dirty blue shop rag. "I'll write up your bill now."

267

Albert Noyer

"Can I pay you after Mass? I really must get over to the church and vest."

"Oh, sure, Father, an' I better be on time, too. Wait a sec 'til I wash my hands."

Armando went into a less-than-spotless restroom and came out a minute later, drying his hands on a paper towel that he crumpled and tossed into an overflowing waste basket. "Father, hop in my Camaro. No sense losin' time with your car."

Only three automobiles were in the church parking lot, many less than the priest had hoped to see for the inaugural Saturday Mass. One was Cynthia's Tucson. No parishioners stood outside the church.

Armando parked at the curb nearest the entrance. "See, we made it on time."

Disappointed, Fr. Jake remarked, "Doesn't seem like anyone else did, or even were interested."

Armando walked up to the door with Fr. Jake and pulled on the handle. It failed to open. "Uh, oh…" He frowned, looking at the priest. "Father Hakub, I think you're locked out again."

"What?" Let me…" He tugged at the door. "It is locked. Wh…what's going on here?"

The young man sucked breath through his teeth and glanced at the ground. "I'm real sorry Father, but I warned you the first time we met. Remember, I said that people here were not gonna like you?"

After an achingly long pause, Fr. Jake nodded acceptance. "Fine, Armando. I'll just leave them alone and walk over to your garage and bring back my car."

The Ghosts of Glorieta

27 / san isidro church / june 19

Fr. Jake started to walk across the weed-grown field that was a shortcut through the parking lot in reaching the highway. He went about fifty feet, then paused to shade his eyes against glare. The late summer afternoon sun shone high and warm on the priest's face and a west wind ruffled his hair. He normally kept it short, but he had not gotten a haircut since the morning before leaving Michigan. He rubbed at wiry stubble on his cheeks. He had planned to shave before the service, but Armando had interrupted that. Now it was not necessary.

The breeze brought scents of the Rio Grande *bosque* and the warm earth of cultivated fields between the river and highway. An apple tree, possibly planted by Fr. Mora, and leafless when Fr. Jake arrived in April, was now speckled with small green bulbs. *New Mexico is beautiful in its way and I was starting to feel comfortable here.* Ahead he glimpsed the abandoned community center building that he hoped would hold promise for uniting the residents in working together on its completion. *No point in pushing for that now.* The Providenceños *don't really care. The Biblical Jeremiah was a better prophet than he thought when he wrote, "Denounce him. We will master him and take our revenge—"*

An abrupt tolling of *Fidelidad*, San Isidro's broken bronze bell, intruded on his thoughts. Along with the metallic clanging, guitars playing the music of a festive melody drifted toward him from the direction of the church. Fr. Jake had heard it in Michigan immigrant workers' camps:

Que linda está la mañana en que vengo a saludarte,

269

Albert Noyer

Venimos todos con gusto y placer a felicitarte.

"That's a *Mañanita*," he recalled. "'How lovely is the morning in which I come to greet you. We all came with joy and pleasure to congratulate you'." He turned to look back at the church.

On the front steps, Armando put down his guitar and called out, "Hey, Father Hakub, c'mon back! We got somethin' to say to you."

Cynthia Plow, wearing a low cut summer dress with a blue and white mosaic pattern, ran forward to pull him toward the building. "Father, I didn't want them to surprise you this way. It's kind of a dirty trick."

"Yet look at you!" he marveled. "That new hairdo and coloring are very becoming. And you're not wearing glasses—"

"New contacts." She flushed at his compliment on her short cut, bangs, and the maroon tint of her hair. "But this is about you, Father, not me. Come inside the church."

Armando and his four musicians grinned as they stepped aside to let the priest enter. San Isidro was crowded with applauding parishioners, some of whom he recognized, yet had not met. Ofilia Herrera beamed at him from their pew. In back, Elder Jeremiah sat silently between Caleb and Rodrigo in "the house of idols." A banner made by Cynthia's 5th grade students stretched across the nave's center.

¡Bienvenidos. Fr. Jakub! Muchas Gracias!

A profusion of summer flowers decorated the base of the altar and statue niches displaying the Sacred Heart and San Isidro. On the adobe ledge to the right, small vases of blossoms stood between each statue. Several of Ofilia's sage bundles smoldered with a pleasant scent that resembled incense.

Sonia Mora, wearing a light green blouse, jeweled at the neckline, white slacks and sandals, stood next to agent Juan Herrero on the top altar step. Both smiled as they applauded. Deputy Griego, in uniform, stood in the second pew with a restraining hand on the arm of a handcuffed Tex Houston. When Cynthia and Fr. Jake reached the front of the aisle, Sonia beckoned him up the steps. The priest awkwardly wiped wet eyes and stood next to her. After she motioned several times for everyone to sit down, the applause gradually died away to a few scattered handclaps.

Sonia walked over to the pulpit, and turned toward the priest. "Father Hakub, I'm sure you felt betrayed for a few agonizing moments, but Armando insisted on surprising you this way. He told us of warning that villagers might resent you, and so this would be kind of a dramatic redemption for Providencia. I'm not sure what he meant by that, only that you persisted where a lesser priest…a lesser man… might have packed up and left.

The Ghosts of Glorieta

"Yes," she repeated, "a priest is above all a man, although consecrated to serving God's people. I'm not going to get into theology here, but my uncle, Father Mora, served his parishioner's physical needs by allowing them to live in houses that his family owned. Yet, unfortunately, he became obsessed with his personal salvation and neglected this congregation's spiritual wellbeing. That should have been his first priority. I'll let Mister Houston address the housing situation in a moment, but first—" She gestured toward Juan Herrero.

The DEA agent, wearing a tan summer suit and paisley tie, waved Fr. Jake forward with one hand and held up an engraved plaque in the other, for everyone to see. "Reverend Casimir Jakubowski, I'm pleased to present you with this Drug Enforcement Agency 'Distinguished Public Service Award' for your role in aiding law enforcement officers in neutralizing a significant drug corridor operating in this part of New Mexico."

Herrero stepped forward to shake the priest's hand. After applause diminished, Sonia walked down the steps and stood next to Tex. "Mister Houston is in custody pending an arraignment hearing, but acknowledges that he owes all of you at least two apologies. One is for thinking he could buy up on the cheap property that has been yours for generations. Another is for wanting to turn Providencia into some kind of horror movie set." She gestured toward the filmmaker with a hand. "That right, sir? Stand up, please."

Tex eased himself upright, both hands cuffed together. A bronze tan that might soon fade away in prison screened any flush of embarrassment he might feel. "Y'all do deserve my apologies, folks," he said in an uncharacteristically sheepish voice. "I am sorry, but I'll go a step further. Now, I really did help nail them anti-government crazies up at their fort with my virtual reality total immersion show. That ought to be worth something, correct, agent?" He glanced back at Herrero, who responded with a slight nod. "All right… two things. I'm building my movie set about a mile north of here, where I got my mobile home and the crew trailers. It's near that empty schoolhouse, so I'll have me a haunted school and then—"

Sonia sighed in exasperation. "Sir, get to the point."

"All right, detective. Folks, I'll be hiring construction people from the village, and I'm letting everyone here keep their houses, but"—he chuckled—"I'd advise y'all to pay your county taxes on time."

Light applause accompanied a few laughs at his attempted humor. Fr. Jake surmised that the Texan had won some sort of plea bargain agreement

Albert Noyer

that would reimburse the county for any other back taxes in exchange for his cooperation during the raid.

"Thank you, sir," Sonia said. "You may sit down."

"Wait, detective…" Tex shook his shackled hands at her. "How about mentioning my other offer? Roberto will be back in a half hour."

She explained, "When I told Mister Houston that San Isidro parishioners decided to make this a sort of Father Hakub Day, he offered to have his Belén food caterers bring everyone supper after Mass…" After clapping interrupted her, Sonia continued, "Sir, everyone here thanks you. Now, we should hear a few words from our… well…from our surprised guest of honor. Father Jake?"

"Wait!" Armando sprang up, waving a hand. "Can I say somethin' first?"

Sonia looked toward the priest, who grinned agreement. "Go ahead, son."

Armando fussed a moment with his brass Camaro belt buckle. "Don't forget…I was the guy found Father Hakub. Cynthia, she headed for the airport, but got a flat tire near Los Lunas. I was the backup and waited at the Belén train station. When that cabbie dumped Father off around midnight and I found him, I said that Belén means 'Bethlehem' like in the *Natividad* story. I thought of the Wise Men findin' baby Jesus, sort of like I found Father Hakub." Some parishioners nodded understanding at what they considered more than a coincidence. Armando took a deep breath and continued, "We know that poor Father Mora woulda been murdered even if Father Hakub wasn't here, but he helped uncover the fact that Mister Fortgang did the murder of him and two other ladies." He looked toward the priest. "Like you was sent here, right, Father?"

"Well, Armando, I don't really claim supernatural connections. In the Bible, God ordered Abraham to go from Ur to Haran. When I asked to continue my Michigan ministry, an archbishop sent me to Providencia."

"Yeah, but Father, ain't"—he glanced at Cynthia and corrected himself— "*isn't* that like heaven was involved? How do you explain San Isidro stoppin' Fortgang's van?"

Ofilia sprang up and glanced around to boast, "I told *Padre* Hakub to fix an *altarcito* for the saint!"

Everyone clapped support for the old *curandera*. Sonia checked her watch. "Thanks, Armando. I noticed a few sheets of paper in Father's hand, so I think he planned to say something to us at Mass."

272

The Ghosts of Glorieta

"I did, Sonia."

"*Padre*," a parishioner Fr. Jake knew called out, "what about Mister Fortgang? Sure, he kept to himself, but he was holy. Always sayin' his rosary during Mass and all."

"Javier, I can tell you that Duane Fortgang misunderstood a lot of things, including when to pray the rosary. He betrayed our trust in him, yet because some of you might be on the jury if he goes on trial, I'll only say that the district attorney's office is examining charges against him. When the time comes, that jury will hear what they are, and decide if he's guilty or not."

Sonia asked, "Father, what was it you wanted to say to us?"

He held up the pages she already had mentioned. "Now, it isn't this speech."

As he went to the pulpit, agent Juan Herrero came down the steps to sit with Sonia in the first pew. After they both sat, he reached over to clasp her hand in his. Fr. Jake noticed and winked at her. She half-smiled and winked back at him.

He leaned the plaque against the pulpit's base, folded his prepared statement in two, and tucked it onto a shelf at the back of the stand. "Friends, *amigos*, I'll put away the remarks I wrote before knowing about this…this unexpected 'tribute,' if you will. Yet honoring your '*Norteño padre*' honors everyone here. Many of you had an important role in how these tragic events were resolved in the end.

"As you may know, a priest has a daily lesson in the breviary he must read every day. I try to find some clue of what Armando mentioned, some 'connection' between that reading and what might happen that day. Today, Saint Paul wrote to the Corinthians about being content with the insults, hardships, and persecutions that he endured for the sake of Christ. I don't for a moment compare myself to the Apostle, yet as I walked away from this locked church I thought of that reading."

A few people stirred in their seats and glanced at each other: would the priest be critical of their deception.

"But," he continued, "the Psalm following was, 'Come children and hear me, that I may teach you the fear of the Lord.' Now, don't misunderstand. 'Fear' doesn't mean to be afraid. Rather, it means to have reverence for God in the same way that you honor your parents…grandparents…and should have respect for each other. Let's all of us work on doing that. With that said, and sincere thanks to all of my dear *Provideñcenos,* I will go and vest now to begin Mass." Fr. Jake held up a hand to limit applause and looked

273

Albert Noyer

toward the Pentecostal leader sitting in back. "Jeremiah, you are cordially invited to stay for the service."

The Elder stood, nodded his thanks, then tried to squeeze past Caleb and leave.

"Dad, please stay," the young man pleaded, grasping his arm. "Please, dad…" Jeremiah paused, tousled Caleb's hair, and settled down again in the pew.

Fr. Jake paused on the platform's bottom stair. "Friends, you'll find new English / Spanish missalettes in the pews. A church bulletin in the vestibule has announcements, which include a Faith Formation class that Cynthia Plow will begin in the fall. There's a call for boy and girl altar servers. Armando, while I'm vesting, why don't you and your musicians play number eight in the *canto* section, '*Este es el dia que hizo el Señor.*' I'm sure you know it."

He grinned. "*Bueno*, Father…Jay-ke."

"Hakub is fine." The priest laughed and spread his hand toward the congregation. "Everyone please join in to sing the verses."

Cynthia stood. "Everyone…'This is the day the Lord has made. I will rejoice and celebrate.'" She hesitated a moment before venturing, "Father, are you staying at San Isidro?"

Others nodded at a question none had dared ask.

As he started for the vestibule, Fr. Jake opened his hands in a gesture of uncertainty. "Archbishop Benisek told me that I'd still be assigned here awhile, Cynthia, but we'll have to wait and see what my Michigan prelate decides. Meanwhile, I shall rejoice and celebrate this day among *mi buenos amigos*…my good New Mexican friends."

About the Author

Born in Switzerland but raised in Detroit, Albert Noyer pursued an interest in art at the city's Wayne State University. He subsequently worked as a commercial artist before entering a Detroit Public Schools career teaching art at the high school technical/vocational level. He also was part-time art history instructor at a Catholic college. Noyer, after retiring to New Mexico with his wife, Jennifer, exhibited watercolor paintings and woodcut prints in numerous regional exhibitions. The March 1994 New Mexico Magazine and December 2006 Mature Life in New Mexico supplement of the Sunday Journal featured his work. In New Mexico, he began writing published A.D. fifth century historical mystery novels in the Getorius and Arcadia Mystery series, and a yet-unpublished retelling of Julius Caesar's conquest of Gaul, but seen from the viewpoint of a Celtic youth caught up in the Romanization of the country.

Noyer is a member of SouthWest Writers, Sisters in Crime, Croak & Dagger, the New Mexico Watercolor Society and New Mexico Veteran's Art. The Ghosts of Glorieta / A Fr. Jake Mystery is his initial contemporary mystery novel, published by Plain View Press.

CPSIA information can be obtained at www.ICGtesting.com
226008LV00002B/13/P